# SHADOWS
## and
# LACE

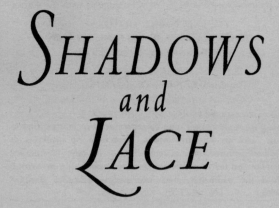

# TERESA MEDEIROS

BANTAM BOOKS

This edition contains the complete text of the
original hardcover edition.
NOT ONE WORD HAS BEEN OMITTED.

Shadows and Lace

A Bantam Book/Published by arrangement with the author

PUBLISHING HISTORY
Berkley edition published September 1990
Bantam edition/November 1996

ISBN-0-553-57623-2

Published simultaneously in the United States and Canada

Bantam Books are published by Bantam Books, a division
of Bantam Doubleday Dell Publishing Group, Inc. Its
trademark, consisting of the words "Bantam Books" and
the portrayal of a rooster, is Registered in U.S. Patent and
Trademark Office and in other countries. Marca Reg-
istrada. Bantam Books, 1540 Broadway, New York, New
York 10036.

PRINTED IN THE UNITED STATES OF AMERICA

OPM    10  9  8  7  6  5  4  3  2  1

# A DANGEROUS TEMPTATION

*She met Gareth's gaze* across the teeming hall. A shock as warm and brilliant as lightning passed between them. Warmth flooded her body. The word she had sought for the change in him rose unbidden to her mind.

*Possession.*

It was written in his eyes, every elegant line of his being. For some unknown reason, Sir Gareth of Caerleon had chosen to play lord of the manor this night.

He sat at the end of the hall with one foot propped in a massive carved chair Rowena had never noticed before. The thronelike seat would have dwarfed a lesser man, but its graceful curves only enhanced the edge of dangerous masculinity held in check by Gareth. He was garbed all in black threaded with silver. The king of the underworld himself could not have looked more regal and striking than Gareth at that moment. When he cocked his head at her, she floated to him as if she were his Persephone, bound by an invisible chain.

"My sweet," he murmured . . . and Rowena sank down, fearing him for a new reason. Her pounding heart confirmed that she would never have the strength to resist a genuine attempt at seduction. . . .

*Bantam Books by Teresa Medeiros*

BREATH OF MAGIC

FAIREST OF THEM ALL

A WHISPER OF ROSES

ONCE AN ANGEL

HEATHER AND VELVET

THIEF OF HEARTS

*To Kim-Poo,*
*who writes her own happy endings,*
*and to Michael, my hero*

# SHADOWS
## and
# LACE

# Prologue

### 1279 England

The boy slipped into the bower without a sound. His steps faltered as the ethereal scent of rosemary raked like tender claws down his spine. He closed his eyes briefly, letting the scent envelop him as it had the night before when his stepmother had curtsied to him in the dance. Her raven curls had brushed his cheek, unmanning him with their softness as she taught him each step of the carol with the sweetest of patience. He opened his eyes; dark lashes fringed their bleak depths.

He should not have come here. Writing music could be learned at his father's desk. Courtesy, in the great hall. What knightly skill might he learn in his stepmother's chamber? His father would be home from battle within the fortnight. He only wanted to see her— to offer his thanks for her kindness and attention in his father's absence.

Lances clashed outside the open window, followed by a roar of laughter. The courtyard below where the squires played at tilting seemed a world away. Before

him, sunlight bathed the empty chamber. Disappointment and relief gripped him as he slipped forward with
a grace beyond his fourteen years.

Damask curtains the same deep, rich blue of her eyes
were drawn back from the rumpled bed. He ducked
under the carved canopy, his hand shaking as he
touched the hollowed cave in the feather pillow where
her head had rested.

A tiny sound came from the alcove behind him. He
rapped his head on the canopy and swung around,
wide-eyed with guilt. His smooth brow furrowed with
annoyance.

He had forgotten the babe. His stepsister stood in
the oaken cradle, the tangled remnants of her swaddling
hanging from her tiny paws like a shroud. Sunlight
kissed the halo of golden curls poking out of her silken
coif. Her lower lip trembled and her round, blue eyes
welled with tears, but she did not cry. Her forbearance
seemed to be such that she would have stood there forever, waiting for someone to happen by and pick her
up. He supposed he should see to her before she
tumbled out of the cradle and cracked her silly head.

As he approached the cradle, she held out her
chubby, little arms and smiled through her tears. What
if her napkins were wet? He looked around to make
sure no one was watching before gingerly lifting her. She
was solid, as heavy as a baby piglet in his arms. 'Twas
impossible to imagine his stepmother's lithe, dark grace
giving birth to such a clumsy creature. He held her awkwardly over one arm as if she might bite him. What
should he do with her now?

She knew what to do with him. Cooing softly, she
laid her head against his breast. Her fist curled around a
strand of his dark hair, tugging as if to remind him of
her presence.

Without warning, tears stung his eyes. He had not
cried for as long as he could remember, not even when
his mother died. He buried his face in the child's sweet-
smelling curls as the knot in his throat choked him. She
was so fresh and untainted, so free of the guilty stain of

his feelings for her mother. It made him feel twisted and ugly to hold such innocence in his arms.

The door swung open. His stepmother swept in, her eyes darkening unaccountably at the sight of the golden head next to the dark one.

She snatched the child from his arms. "Is the silly babe troubling you? Forgive me. I don't know how she manages to wiggle out of her swaddling."

He watched, his arms empty, as she stuffed the plump limbs back into the binding linen. The child's lips trembled, but she did not cry. Her eyes were not on her mother. They were on him. "Is she not old enough to toddle about?" he said faintly.

"Toddle into mischief! What do lads know of babes? The swaddling will help her limbs grow straight and strong." His stepmother flashed a vivacious dimple. "And contribute to the sweet demeanor that every man prizes in a wife." She took his hand, her soft, ivory-colored fingers playing over his knuckles. "Come. Forget the bratling. You've much to learn before your father returns. I've yet to see you make a proper kneel."

She drew him away from the cradle. "Now, pretend I am your queen."

He was not pretending as he cleared his throat awkwardly and dropped to one knee. He reached for her outstretched hand. Her middle finger bore the rubies and emeralds of his father's betrothal ring. His head dropped. He could not touch her. His hands clenched into fists at his sides. He hardly dared breathe as she touched him, her fingernails gently tracing the shapes of his ears beneath his thick, dark hair.

"My man," she crooned. "My sweet, young man. I've so much to teach you."

He closed his eyes as she drew his face into the rose-mary-scented velvet of her bosom. But as he buried his face in her softness, 'twas not darkness he saw but the reproach in round, blue eyes the color of the spring sky.

# PART ONE

Take thou this rose, O rose
Since love's own flower it is
And by that rose
Thy lover captive is

—ANONYMOUS

# Chapter 1

**1298 England**

The hare's nostrils quivered an inch from hers. If anyone had been as near to Rowena as the hare was at that moment, they would have sworn her lightly freckled nose also quivered. She lay in the sweet-smelling grass of the moor, her chin nuzzled in the crook of her arm. Her cap slipped over her blue eyes, and the slight movement startled the hare into flight. Rowena swore softly and climbed to her knees, adjusting the cap with a jerk. With stinging fingers she plucked thistles from her overtunic. She had lain motionless in the tall grass for hours to gain the trust of the hare bouncing cheerfully toward the rosy pocket of the western sky.

She shook her fist at the animal, then laughed ruefully. Sheathing the long knife that hung forgotten in her hand, she trudged toward Revelwood where eight hungry boys were doomed to be hungrier.

As the only girl in a family of seven brothers, one male cousin, and a father given to long disappearances,

it had taken Rowena both time and ingenuity to convince the family she was indifferent to the cobwebs fes-
tooning the grim remnants of Revelwood. She had
learned at a tender age that her only escape from a life
of perpetual drudgery lay in becoming a terrible cook
and a clever huntress. She tackled both tasks with
enthusiasm, leaving her brothers to till the stony ground
and freeing herself to roam the wild moor.

Rowena spread her arms, emphasizing their empti-
ness as she leaped from stone to stone across a
sparkling stream. Little Freddie would even now be
preparing the spit for the game she did not bear. Her
youngest brother had rescued the doomed family from
a life of raw cabbage when his first tottering steps had
led him to the dusty kettle on the hearth where he
promptly fell in. His hollow cries had echoed through
the castle until Rowena's oldest brother, Big Freddie,
fished him out.

Dead drunk on the occasion that marked the birth of
his youngest son and the death of Rowena's mother,
Althea, Papa had promptly christened the red, squalling
infant Frederick, just as he had christened his firstborn
Frederick. In the years to come, Papa would fondly brag
that he had named the babe Roderick in honor of his
oldest son—the first fruit of his loins whom he cherished
beyond all measure. With a gentle poke, Rowena would
whisper in his ear that the name was Frederick. Papa
would shrug and smile and turn up his goblet again.

The dry grass crackled beneath Rowena's heels. The
late summer twilight descended around her in a
lavender haze—a gentle reproof for the long hours she
had spent running through the meadows, whistling at
the larks and tracking a wide-eyed doe at the edge of
the forest. To come home empty-handed would be to
admit the folly of her day and succumb to a supper of
boiled turnips for the third time in a week.

Setting her jaw in determination, she unsheathed the
knife and turned to the forest. The sour, cracked note of
a badly blown trumpet shattered the quiet like a golden
fanfare.

*Papa!* Papa was home! Rowena sprinted toward the decrepit castle she called home and the charming braggart she called Papa.

Eight months had passed since he had left without a word to pursue his fortune. In the past those same pursuits had brought him home with a leather pouch of golden coins which he had scattered among his children like a jolly harbinger of happier times. Rowena would laughingly scramble for the coins, knowing all the while that the gold would be regathered in time for Papa's next expedition. She dreaded the times he returned with nothing but a massive headache and a kick for the cur that skulked around the hearth. He never dared raise a hand to any of his children; even Rowena outmeasured him by two inches.

However hapless his journey, he never returned without some scrap of a present for his only daughter. The tattings of lace and velvet bows had been tucked away, forgotten, to be replaced by soft-beaten leather and a curved dagger. Rowena expressed her needs with a candor not inherited from her father.

With a hint of the ingenuity they did share, she thought with glee that Papa's return would draw attention from her empty hands, especially if he packed the carcass of a deer on his aged gelding as he was wont to do when his wagers had been successful.

The weatherbeaten stones of Revelwood came into view as she topped the hill. She paused to grasp her side and rub away the stitch that had stolen her breath away. Her mother's ancestral home crouched on the edge of the moor, the battered walls no longer a defense against the wind that roared through the widening cracks in the mortar. But in the rapidly dying light of the summer sun, the ancient castle gleamed in a poignant reflection of its former glory.

Rowena's joy overflowed in a whoop as she skipped down the hill. But her throat went dry when she saw Papa's slopebacked gelding tethered to a post, an empty pouch draped over its heaving flanks. She ran her hand over the horse's withers, then wiped the slimy film of sweat on her braies with a grimace. The horse gave a gurgling snort, its head buried in a wooden bucket. Shaking off a shiver of foreboding, Rowena bounded up the splintered planks that served as a bridge over the dank moat.

Arrow slits set deep in the masonry held the twilight at bay. Rowena blinked away blindness as her eyes adjusted to the gloom of the cavernous hall. A fire dwarfed by the immense hearth strove to add cheer to the vaulted room but succeeded in casting more shadows than light. The corners of her mouth tilted upward at the sight of Little Freddie stirring the contents of an iron kettle. The pungent odor of turnips floated to her nose.

She leaped out of the doorway, warned by the clatter of large feet on the planks. Her brothers burst into the hall bearing an array of hoes and rakes.

"Where is Papa?" bellowed Big Freddie.

He led five men who could have been smaller, paler twins of himself with their lank hair and hunched shoulders. He tossed his scythe to the flagstones. The others exchanged doubtful glances, then dumped their tools with equal carelessness.

Rowena's cousin Irwin stepped out from the stairs. His plump face held an oddly glum look; he twirled a rusty trumpet between his fingers.

"Your father is abovestairs," he announced. "He wanted you gathered. Said there wasn't much time."

Even as he spoke, a deafening crash sounded from the upper reaches of the castle followed by a bellow and a flurry of imaginative curses. They all stared upward as if an explanation for Irwin's cryptic speech would float down with the dust motes loosened from the beams.

Big Freddie knuckled his eyes. "Is Papa in foul spirits, Irwin?"

Irwin scratched his head with the trumpet. "I don't believe he is in spirits at all. I believe he is sober."

Rowena's brothers nodded to each other, accepting the news with puzzled solemnity.

Rowena snorted. "Nonsense. Have you ever seen him sober, Irwin?"

Her cousin turned to her, unable to stop blind adoration from conquering his calflike eyes. "Nay. But I've never seen him like this before, either."

Rowena tweaked Irwin's nose with fond contempt. "If you say he is sober, then I say you've been dipping into the ale with your own greedy paw."

Irwin choked out a meager chuckle. The others laughed aloud at the thought of their pasty-faced cousin swilling a goblet of brew.

"Papa is probably just hungry," Rowena pronounced with conviction.

The look Little Freddie gave her was so devoid of reproach that she ducked her head in shame, regretting her thoughtless fling with the summer day. The mention of food started all their stomachs rumbling. The black bread crusts dipped in lard they had broken their fast with that morn were a fond but distant memory. Rowena started for the wall that housed the old bow and arrow. Little Freddie's words stopped her.

"Apples, Ro. We can spare a few. I can cook them on the coals the way Papa fancies them."

With a grateful smile she took the sack he held out. Little Freddie seemed to have inherited intelligence equal to all that was divided so sparingly between her older brothers. Pulling her cap over her ears, she ducked into the deepening night.

The door had hardly closed behind her when Papa came stumbling down the stairs.

My God, thought Little Freddie. Irwin was right. Papa never stumbles when he's drunk.

Gone was the strutting gait, the bleary, sated gaze. In their place were feet that took each step as if mired in molten lead and eyes that shone with the weight of unshed tears. Lindsey Fordyce, Baron of Revelwood, stood at the foot of the stairs and surveyed his sullen sons as if seeing them for the first time.

"Sweet Christ. I didn't know there was such a

godawful lot of you." He rubbed his eyes as if to make some of them disappear.

"There are nine of us, Uncle Lindsey, counting Rowena," said Irwin, ever eager to please.

He peered around the hall again. "Where is Ro? I do not see her."

Little Freddie stepped away from the hearth. "Gone to fetch apples, Papa."

" 'Tis just as well." Papa dragged his right leg as he crossed the hall, his faint limp painfully pronounced. He sat heavily in an ancient chair. The wood creaked beneath his weight. "Water, Freddie," he croaked.

Papa leaned back and closed his eyes, missing the struggle that ensued as Big Freddie and Little Freddie tugged at the stoneware flagon, sloshing tepid water over their bare feet. With a choked mutter, Big Freddie jerked the flagon out of his brother's hands and poured the water into a rusty goblet. He allowed Little Freddie the honor of presenting it to their father with a flourish.

Papa's hands shook as he took the goblet. He drained it as if it contained something far more tasty than dirty water and an errant gnat.

"Gather around, sons. I have glad tidings," he announced.

Spreading his arms wide as if to embrace them to his bosom, he grinned. His sons took a hesitant step forward, and Irwin took a step backward.

"Join us, Irwin. I would not choose to cheat you of a chance for adventure simply because you had the misfortune to spring from another man's loins."

Irwin blushed and sidled closer. "Adventure, Uncle Lindsey?"

The boys exchanged blank glances, unable to comprehend the idea of any existence or experience beyond their own. Surely farming turnips in rocky fields that were never meant to be farmed was adventure enough.

Papa leaned forward with a conspirator's wink. "You see, my boys, I truly found my elusive fortune in the course of this expedition. I was on my way home to share the prosperity with my precious offspring." He clucked sadly. "But my purse was weighted down by so many gold coins that the old gelding could hardly bear it."

Little Freddie crossed his arms, his eyes narrowing in blatant skepticism.

"So I stopped for a night's rest at the castle of a friend."

Irwin wondered what it was like to have a friend. He had never met anyone he was not related to.

"And they had a jolly game of hazard going at the castle, did they not, Papa?" Little Freddie interrupted.

Papa rumpled his son's silver-blond hair. "Roddy, you never cease to amaze me."

"It's Freddie." Ducking away, Freddie returned to the hearth, busying himself once again with the kettle.

"So," Papa continued briskly, "seeking to rid myself of some of this cumbersome load—for the dear gelding's sake, of course—I entered into a game of hazard with an old acquaintance of mine, the son of an earl whose fief I held long ago. The lad once bore me a great fondness and is now grown into a great and noble knight."

Something about the way Papa spoke the last two words sent a chill down Little Freddie's spine. He straightened, the turnips forgotten.

"First I wagered what I had. Then I wagered what I didn't have. Mayhaps I had imbibed a tad too much ale." He held his thumb and finger apart in illustration.

Little Freddie's arms spread as wide as they could go, adjusting the inaccurate measure. Irwin smothered a giggle behind his plump hand. Little Freddie pretended to stretch as his father's gaze fell upon him.

Papa shrugged. "So I lost my fortune. When my old friend discovered my penniless straits, I fear he lost his temper. With the unfortunate memory of a winner, he recalled my boasts of the eight strapping lads who tended my castle while I sought my fortune. So the gist of the matter is that one of you lucky lads is going to serve an earl for the period of one year." He beamed at them, his bright pig-eyes awaiting their congratulations.

Only silence greeted him.

"You wagered one of your children?" Little Freddie pushed through the forest of shoulders to face his father.

Lindsey Fordyce's smile faded. He rubbed his head, peeling back the hair to reveal the bald spot he usually struggled to hide.

"Not precisely. The choice was not mine to make." He surveyed them glumly, dropping all pretense of happiness. "He said he would journey to Revelwood to choose one of my lads for service, or he would journey to Revelwood bearing my head on a pikestaff."

"Oh, Uncle," breathed Irwin, paling to an unpleasant shade of green.

" 'Tis your good fortune he was not your enemy. Does this virtuous knight have a name?" Little Freddie's eyes narrowed to slits.

Fordyce mopped his brow with his sleeve, the heat from the small fire suddenly oppressive. He froze as the thunder of hooves echoed in the courtyard. Silence followed. Then the door flew open with a mighty crash that nearly shook it from its hinges.

Rowena came bursting in like a ray of sunshine cutting through the stale layer of smoke that hung over the hall. The wild, sweet scent of the moor clung to her hair, her skin, the handwoven tunic she wore. Her cheeks were touched with the flushed rose of exertion; her eyes were alight with exuberance.

She ran straight to her father, her words tumbling out faster than the apples dumped from the sack she clutched upside down.

"Oh, Papa, I am ever so happy you've come home! Where did you have the stallion hidden? He is the most beautiful animal I ever saw. Did you truly find your elusive fortune this journey?"

Falling to her knees beside his chair, she pulled a crumpled bunch of heather from her pocket and dumped it in his lap without giving him time to reply.

"I brought your favorite flowers and Little Freddie

has promised to cook apples on the coals. They will be hot and sweet and juicy, just as you like them. 'Twill be a hundred times better than any nasty old roasted hare. Oh, Papa, you're home! We thought you were never coming back."

She threw her arms around his waist. The uninhibited gesture knocked the cap from her head to unleash a cascade of wheaten curls.

Fordyce's arms did not move to encircle her. He sat stiffly in her embrace. She lifted her face, aware of a silence broken only by the thump of a log shifting on the fire. Her father did not meet her eyes, and for one disturbing moment, she thought she saw his lower lip tremble.

She followed his gaze. Her brothers stood lined up before the hearth in the most ordered manner she had ever seen them. Irwin beamed from the middle of the row.

Bathed in the light of the flickering fire, the stranger stepped out of the shadows. Rowena raised her eyes. From where she knelt, it was as if she was peering up from the bottom of a deep well to meet the eyes of the man who towered over her. His level gaze sent a bolt of raw fear through her, riveting her to the floor as if she stared into the face of death itself. A long moment passed before she could pull her eyes away.

"Papa?" she breathed, patting his cool, trembling hand.

He stroked her hair, his eyes distant. "Rowena, I believe 'twould be fitting for you to step outside till we have concluded our dealings."

"You made no mention of a daughter, Fordyce." The stranger's gaze traveled between father and child.

Papa's arm curved around Rowena's shoulders like a shield. The stranger's mocking laughter echoed through the hall. Only Rowena heard Papa's muttered curse as he realized what he had betrayed.

"Your interest is in my sons," Papa hissed, a tiny vein in his temple beginning to throb.

"But *your* interest is not. That much is apparent."

The man advanced and Rowena rose, knowing instinctively that she did not want to be on her knees at this stranger's feet. She stood without flinching to face the wrought links of the silver chain mail that crossed the man's chest. From broad shoulders to booted feet, his garments were as black as the eyes that regarded her with frank scrutiny. She returned his perusal with arms crossed in front of her.

A closer look revealed his eyes were not black, but a deep, velvety brown. Their opacity rendered them inscrutable, but alive with intelligence. Heavy, arched brows added a mocking humor that gave Rowena the impression she was being laughed at, although his expression did not waver. His sable hair was neatly cut, but an errant waviness warned of easy rebellion. His well-formed features were saved from prettiness by an edge of rugged masculinity enhanced by his sheer size. The thought flitted through Rowena's mind that he might be handsome if his face was not set in such ruthless lines.

He reached down and lifted a strand of her hair as if hypnotized by its brightness. The velvety tendril curled around his fingers at the caress.

Rowena's hand slipped underneath her tunic, but before she could bring the knife up to strike, her wrist was twisted in a fearful grip that sent the blade clattering to the stones. She bit her lip to keep from crying out. The man loosed her.

"She has more fire than the rest of you combined." The stranger strode back to the hearth. "I'll take her."

The hall exploded in enraged protest. Papa sank back in the chair, his hand over his eyes.

"You cannot have my sister!" Little Freddie's childish tenor cut through his brothers' cries.

Smirking, the man leaned against the hearth. "Take heart, lad. 'Tis not forever. She is only to serve me for a year."

Rowena looked at Papa. His lips moved, but made no sound. Her brothers spewed forth dire and violent threats, although they remained in place as if rooted to the stone. She wondered if they had all taken leave of their senses. The stranger's sparkling eyes offered no comfort. They watched her as if delighting in the chaos he had provoked. The tiny lines around them crinkled as he gave her a wink made all the more threatening by its implied intimacy. A primitive thrill of fear shot through her, freezing her questions before they could leave her lips.

Papa's whine carried just far enough to reach the man's ears. "We said sons, did we not?"

The man's booming voice silenced them all. "Nay, Fordyce. We said children. I was to have the use of one of your children for a year."

Rowena's knees went as slack as her jaw. Only the sheer effort of her will kept her standing.

"You cannot take a man's only daughter," said Papa, unable to keep the pleading note from his voice. "Show me some mercy, won't you?"

The knight snorted. "Mercy? What have you ever known of mercy, Fordyce? I've come to teach you of justice."

Papa mustered his courage and banged with force on the arm of the chair. "I will not allow it."

The stranger's hand went to the hilt of the massive sword sheathed at his waist. The muscles in his arms rippled with the slight gesture. "You choose to fight?" he asked softly.

Lindsey Fordyce hesitated the merest moment. "Rowena, you must accompany this nice man."

Rowena blinked stupidly, thrown off guard by her father's abrupt surrender.

Little Freddie charged forward, an iron pot wielded over his head like a bludgeon. The knight turned with sword drawn. Rowena lunged for his arm, but Papa sailed past both of them and knocked the boy to the ground with a brutal uppercut. Freddie glared at his father, blood trickling from his mouth and nose.

"Don't be an idiot," Papa spat. "He will only kill you, and then he will kill me."

Still wielding his sword, the stranger faced the row

of grumbling boys. "If anyone cares to challenge my right to their sister, I would be more than happy to defend it."

The broad blade gleamed in the firelight. Big Freddie returned the man's stare for a long moment, his callused hands clenched into fists before turning away to rest his forehead against the warm stones of the hearth.

The stranger's eyes widened as Irwin stepped forward, trumpet still clutched in hand. Papa took one step toward Irwin, who then plopped his ample bottom on the hearth and studied the trumpet as if seeing it for the first time. The knight sheathed his sword.

"A wager is a wager." Papa ran his thumbs along the worn gilt of his tattered surcoat. "As you well know, I am a baron myself—an honorable man."

He sighed as if the burden of his honor was too much for him to bear. The short laugh uttered by the knight was not a pleasant sound.

Papa gently took Rowena's face between his moist palms. "Go with him, Rowena." He swallowed with difficulty. "He will not harm you."

The stranger watched the exchange in cryptic silence, his arms crossed over his chest.

Rowena searched her father's face, blindly hoping for a burst of laughter to explain away the knight's intrusion as a cruel jest. The hope that flickered within her sputtered and died, smothered by the bleakness in the cornflower-blue eyes that were a pale, rheumy echo of her own.

"I shall go with him, Papa, if you say I should."

The man moved forward, unlooping the rope at his waist. Papa stepped back to keep a healthy sword's distance away from the imposing figure.

Rowena shoved her hands behind her back. "There is no need to bind me."

The man retrieved her hands. Rowena tried not to flinch as he bound her wrists in front of her none too gently.

Her soft tone belied her anger. "If Papa says I am to go with you, then I will go."

The dark head remained bowed as he tightened the knot with a stiff jerk. Coiling the free end of the rope around his wrist, he led her to the door without a word. She slowed to scoop up her cap. Feeling the sudden tautness in the rope, the man tugged. Rowena dug her heels into the flagstones, resisting his pull. Their eyes met in a silent battle of wills. Without warning, he yanked the rope, causing Rowena to stumble. She straightened, her eyes shining with angry tears for an instant. Then their blue depths cleared and she purposefully followed him through the door, cap clutched in bound hands.

The boys shuffled after them like the undead in a grim processional. Papa meandered behind. Little Freddie was gripped between two of his brothers, a fierce scowl darkening his fair brow.

Night had fallen. A full moon cast its beams through the scant trees, suffusing the muted landscape with the eerie glow of a bogus daylight. Big Freddie gave a low, admiring whistle as a white stallion seemed to rise from the thin shroud of mist that cloaked the ground. The creature pranced nervously at the sound of approaching footsteps.

Rowena's eyes were drawn to the golden bridle crowning the massive animal. Jewels of every hue encrusted its length. Why would a man of such wealth come all the way to Revelwood to steal a poor man's child? The knight's forbidding shoulders invited no questions as he mounted the horse and slipped Rowena's tether over the leather pommel. The horse's iron-shod hooves twitched, making her wonder how close she could follow without being pounded to a pulp.

Irwin stepped in front of the horse as if accustomed to placing his bulk in the path of a steed mounted by a fully armed nobleman. The knight leaned back in the saddle with a sigh.

"Kind sir?" Irwin's voice was a mere squeak, so he cleared his throat and tried again. "Kind sir, I hasten to remind you that you are stealing away our only ray of light in a life of darkness. You pluck the single bloom in our garden of grim desolation. I speak for all of us."

Irwin's cousins looked at one another and scratched their heads. Rowena wished faintly that the knight would run him through and end her embarrassment.

"You make an eloquent plea, lad," the knight replied, surprising them all. "Mayhaps you should plead with her father to make his wagers with more care in the future."

From behind Big Freddie, Papa dared to shoot the man a look of pure hatred.

"You will not relent?" asked Irwin.

"I will not."

"Then I pray the burden of chivalry rests heavily on your shoulders. I pray you will honor my sweet cousin with the same consideration you would grant to the rest of the fair and weaker sex."

Rowena itched to box his ears, remembering the uncountable times she had wrestled him to the ground and pinched him until he squealed for mercy.

The stranger again uttered that short, unpleasant laugh. "Do not fear, lad. I will grant her the same consideration that I would grant to any wench as comely as she. Now stand aside or be trampled."

Irwin tripped to the left as the knight kicked the stallion into a trot. Rowena broke into a lope to avoid being jerked off her feet. She dared break her concentration only long enough for one last hungry look at her family. She heard the soft thud of fist pummeling flesh and a familiar cry as Little Freddie tackled Irwin in blind rage and frustration.

Then they were gone. She focused all of her attention on the rocky turf beneath her feet as her world narrowed to the task of putting one foot in front of the other without falling nose first into the drumming hooves.

# Chapter 2

❧❦

The ground blurred beneath Rowena's pounding feet, slipping out from under her with alarming frequency. The tangled grasses of the moor were left behind as they entered a forest. A thick net of branches diffused the brilliant moonbeams into a treacherous web of shadow and light. A dead branch she did not see slammed into her knees even as she stumbled over a rock that was only a reflection in the slick leaves. Surely her whole life had been spent following the flowing tail of this monster steed and the forbidding back of its demon rider. The aching rhythm of her heels faltered, and she stayed on her feet only by entwining her fingers around the strand of rope that bound her wrists. Her cap was now crushed, but she refused to drop it.

"Pardon me," she gasped.

The broad shoulders did not turn.

"Excuse me . . . sir?"

Nothing. Rowena could think of only one way to get his attention. She sat down, throwing her legs around the rope to keep from being pulled to her stomach. She had counted on the nests of pine needles to cushion her.

She had not counted on the knight continuing for several feet until her bottom was dragged into a shallow stream with a defeated splash.

He halted and pivoted the prancing mount to face her. Rowena was not sure who she hated more—the smug stallion or the knight who raised one inquisitive eyebrow at her. She collapsed against the bank and closed her eyes. The rope relaxed as he dismounted. She sighed at the sheer luxury of stretching her bound wrists over her head and slowly opened her eyes. The man knelt a few feet away, filling a leather canteen from the stream. His dark eyes never left her.

Water filled her braies. The annoying sensation fanned her flames of indignation. "Would you drown me like an unwanted kitten, milord, or is there that much compassion in you?"

"Why did you not ask me to halt?"

"Would you have listened?" Rowena fought to steady her breathing.

"Aye."

Rowena rolled her eyes and turned her face away to hide her obvious skepticism.

"How did your little rooster of a father manage to raise such a spiritless brood?" he demanded, rising to his feet and tucking the canteen into his belt.

"We are not spiritless," she protested. "You've no right to call us that."

He crossed the stream with one stride and squatted in front of her. "Your father was once a knight. Has he no skill with a sword?"

Rowena's eyes sparkled with pride. "Papa had to lay down his arms through no fault of his own. He was lamed in a fierce battle with the Welsh devils."

Gareth snorted. "Devils, indeed. What of the six grown men besides your papa? They let me dance out of there with you as if it was naught. You do not call that spiritless?"

"You could have slain every one of them, could you not?"

He shrugged. "Perhaps."

"Then they were not without courage. They were intelligent."

The knight's face dissolved into hearty laughter, dispelling its menace and softening its lines to boyishness for an elusive instant.

"I fear the only quality more lacking than courage was intelligence. Who was the plump boy? I feared he was going to trumpet me to death."

" 'Twas Irwin. And he is not a boy. He is as old as I."

"I suppose that makes him a man?"

Rowena searched her mind for some weapon to wipe the smirk from his haughty lips but knew the moment she spoke that she had chosen poorly.

"Irwin is my betrothed."

She sniffed with injured pride as the man burst into new peals of laughter.

She spoke quickly. "He is my cousin. Papa took him in as my betrothed when he was but a lad. Knowing he could provide no dowry, Papa sought to make me an early match and save me embarrassment."

"I sense you are still embarrassed."

Rowena sighed, missing the absurdity of sitting in a stream and discussing matters of the heart with this stern stranger.

"Do you love this Irwin?"

"I feel a sort of affection for him. He has always been around."

"Like a faithful hound?" he offered.

Nodding briskly, she admitted, "I'd sooner love a toad."

"I found his display of affection rather touching. Did it not melt your heart?"

She shook her head. "You don't know Irwin. He has probably been waiting his whole life for a chance to wax poetic before a peer of the realm."

A smile touched the man's lips. He tilted her face with one finger, studying its softened planes in the moonlight. Rowena, suddenly wary, blinked back at him.

"I'd have fought to the death to keep my betrothed

from falling into the hands of a man like me," he murmured. His finger traveled upward to trace the curve of
her lower lip.

Rowena's heart slipped into a thunderous rhythm
she did not recognize. She tried to smile, less than comforted by his words. He stared down at her, his dark
eyes succumbing to the shadows of the forest. The last
traces of laughter vanished from his face. Rowena
shifted, painfully aware of her vulnerability as she lay
half in and half out of the stream with her hands bound
and this enigmatic stranger crouching over her. The wet
braies clung to her thighs; her skin glistened with the
water's mist.

He pried the crumpled cap from her hands. Placing it
on her head, he tucked each strand of flaxen hair
beneath with great care. "If you must go about
sprawling in streams like a wanton nymph, pray do
wear your cap to discourage would-be assailants."

He hauled her to her feet and unbound her wrists.
Water dripped steadily from the seat of her braies as he
mounted the horse without a word.

She smiled hopefully. "I daresay Papa has learned his
lesson by now. I believe I can find my way home from
here."

"Will you mount with me or shall I bind you again?"
The knight stared down at her, his dark eyes hooded.

She approached the massive steed, dwarfed by the
man who sat with such ease upon its back.

She swallowed. "You wish for me to ride with you?"

She was suddenly astride the horse as he lifted her
with one powerful arm and placed her on the saddle
in front of him. Her wet braies tangled beneath her
but she barely had time to focus on that discomfort
before he kicked the horse into a canter. She realized
how much time her pride had cost them since leaving
Revelwood.

The horse flew down the path, the thunder of its
hooves muffled by the luxuriant carpet of pine needles.
Rowena leaned forward to place a safe distance
between her back and the broad chest of her captor,

only to find herself jerked against him by a muscular arm wrapped around her waist.

"Be still. You'll spook the horse," he commanded.

Rowena surrendered to his iron grip as the horse careened off the path and darted among the trees as if following some esoteric equine map. The knight's chest became a haven that protected her from being crushed as tree trunks lurched into their path with frightening regularity.

When she realized the arm locked beneath her breasts would not allow her to sail off the horse, she settled back, lulled by the novel sense of security the warm chest afforded. She slipped into sleep with uncommon ease.

Rowena awoke in time to keep from falling to her knees as the knight lowered her unceremoniously to the ground. She yawned and rubbed her eyes. Halos of torchlight shone through the trees. The sounds of clumsily plucked lutestrings and voices blended in drunken laughter floated into the night. She blinked up at the forbidding knight.

"Trot behind me like a good squire," he commanded. "Keep your hair up. Perhaps 'tis late enough and they are drunk enough to believe you a lad."

"This is not your home?"

"Nay. But 'twill do to pass the night."

He urged the horse into a walk. Rowena fell into an awkward swagger behind him, at a loss as to how the squire of such a man would act.

The knight spoke without turning. "You will be left to your own devices when I retire. If you have any thoughts of escape, think again. If you run, I shall return to your home and slay your entire family. When I find you, as I most certainly will, you will wish you had been among the ones slain."

Rowena forced her feet to keep moving. His words sent the skin at the nape of her neck crawling. She pictured Little Freddie, lifeless, a gaping sword wound where his heart should be. Anger flared in her eyes only to be quenched by common sense as the man turned in the saddle and fixed his dark eyes on her. She nodded, eyes wide and without guile.

The merriment within the castle courtyard came spilling out with the light as couples stumbled down a drawbridge that spanned a twenty-foot moat. One of the men faltered in front of the knight's horse.

"Welcome all. The feast is just beginning," he announced, his words slurred. His eyes rolled back in his head as he fell straight into the dirt, arms still spread wide in greeting.

The woman on his arm flounced back into the castle as the other couples dissipated like giggling phantoms in the night.

The knight guided the horse around the prostrate form without so much as a flick of an eyebrow. Rowena followed, cutting a wide swath around the fallen man.

Gareth dismounted, handing his reins to a pock-marked lad who materialized out of the shadows. Before they could take three steps, the same woman reappeared on the arm of another stumbling man. Rowena dodged them as they passed within inches of her. The woman's brittle laughter rent the air. Rowena gaped as the man's hamlike hands caught the woman's hips and bore her backward. Her grimy toes curled into an embrace at the small of his back. With a grunt and a grind of his hips, he pinioned her to the wall.

Rowena had forgotten the knight until she felt his firm grasp on her forearm as he tugged her away from the lurid scene. She was so intent on peering over her shoulder at the mingled pain and ecstacy on the woman's florid face that she did not see the man who leaped in front of them until she slammed into his hauberk with a force that set her ears to ringing.

"Who goes there? Gareth, my man, could that really be you?" came the urgent voice.

"Nay," she replied without thought. " 'Tis Ro—"

The knight clapped his hand over her mouth.

"Aye, Blaine. 'Tis Gareth. I do believe you've knocked my squire insensible. Clumsy lad, Ro is. I shall have to beat that out of him." The knight loosed his grip on her mouth and gently boxed her ears.

This was followed by a hearty slap on the back from the slender gentleman. He peered drunkenly into her face, and a smile quirked the corners of his thin lips. Rowena gasped, unable to remember a time when she had been knocked about with such relish.

"Who would be foolish enough to trust their young whelp into your blackhearted hands?" Although he addressed her captor, Blaine's gaze traveled from her face to her felt-clad feet with insinuating slowness.

"Need I remind you how many times these black-hearted hands have unseated you in a tourney?" Gareth replied.

Blaine ignored him and circled Rowena. "Small, is he not?"

"You were small yourself once, Blaine." Gareth slapped a muscled arm around Blaine's shoulders and guided his stumbling steps away from Rowena and toward the drawbridge. "Have you forgotten the time I pitched you out the window with one hand when we were but lads?"

"How could I? I landed in a bramble bush and spent the rest of the night soaking my finer parts in a barrel." Blaine shielded his eyes from the torchlight and hooked one arm around Gareth's neck. "Yet still I welcome you to Ardendonne. What a fool I am! I should feed you to the man-eating fish in my moat."

Gareth rolled his eyes. "After the camels ran away, I thought you'd give up on exotic animals."

"When the Prince of Wales took to bragging about his pet lion, I had to find some way to best him." Blaine shook his head sadly. "I lose two or three guests every feast day. One splash and they are no more. Nothing left but bones to be fished out when the sun rises. Ah, well."

Gareth jerked him back as he swayed toward the side of the drawbridge. Rowena hugged herself and edged closer to the center of the bridge, refusing to raise her eyes for fear of finding bleached bones floating in the bubbling water.

She followed the men through the bailey and into the vaulted hall, her eyes locked on Gareth's back as he steered Sir Blaine away. She read a thousand warnings in the glance he threw over his shoulder as they disappeared into the milling crowd.

She halted, her captor's desertion making her feel oddly at a loss. Thrusting her hands deep in her sleeves, she whistled, pretending to be unaffected by the strangers reeling about her in various states of drunkenness and dishabille. As her gaze traveled the room, it lit on a sight that made her mouth water and the rest of the hall fade to invisibility.

She shouldered her way through the galloping dancers and halted as close as she dared.

A man in a red velvet mantle grinned and nudged her. "Make haste, lad. 'Tis been picked to bare bones, but you might yet find a few choice morsels."

Rowena started to laugh and cry at the same time. The man sidled away, believing her daft or drunk or both. On a table that stretched twenty feet along the wall lay the remnants of Ardendonne's feast. Revelwood would not see this much food in a year.

Rowena's stomach rumbled a warning. She placed her feet farther apart to keep from swaying. A half-eaten boar's head stared her down with glassy eyes from the center of the table. Stealing a hasty glance around her, she plucked the apple from its mouth and shoved it up her sleeve. Her trembling hand dipped into a silver bowl and came out with a mound as golden as the sun that floated over the moor on a spring day. She dared to lick it. Sweetly seasoned apples coated her tongue. She closed her eyes in rapture.

With the hunger of a lifetime unleashed, Rowena darted up and down the table, dipping a hand into each bowl and snatching at each platter, pausing long enough to stare at what could have only been the remains of a whole cow sprawled at the end of the table. A mean-eyed yellow hound stood on the table with his hind legs in the gravy. Rowena wrestled a turkey leg from him and washed it down with a half-full tankard of ale she found abandoned in the honeyed plums.

With a huge sigh, she plopped down on the stale-smelling floor rushes, lulled by her sated belly. The hall spun around her. The silken veils of the dancing women swirled in violent splashes of purple and peach against the bright red and blue of the men's surcoats. She swiped at her moist brow, wondering what sort of peculiar people would waste a roaring fire on a summer night.

"See how he charms," came the hissed whisper above her.

Rowena's gaze followed the stained satin bliaut of the woman beside the table up to a round face wreathed in a malevolent smile.

"I daresay Alise will lift her skirts before morning is nigh," murmured the tall, bony woman beside the other. "Sir Gareth garners few refusals."

Rowena's eyes widened as she followed their gazes to her captor. The unadorned black of his garments was unrelenting against the backdrop of bobbing reds and greens. He stood with one foot propped on a stool, his dark head inclined toward a laughing woman. The woman's hand slipped farther up his thigh with each of her whispered words. A tight smile curved his lips in a mocking travesty of the smile he had given Rowena at the stream. His hand lightly caressed the woman's slender neck even as his gaze pulled away and traveled the hall. Rowena leaned deeper into the shadows under the table, not wanting to be found by those dark eyes.

"Charmed the king himself into knighting him, he did, at the tender age of seventeen."

"Oh, go on! If you'd have stepped between a Welsh sword and old Longshanks on a battlefield running with England's blood, I daresay he would have knighted you, too." The plump woman plucked something off the table and tossed it in her mouth with a sat-isfied smack. "Dare I pop a fly in Alise's pudding?"

"If you refrain, the dark lord will pop more than a fly in her pudding tonight," the thin woman replied.

"Alise can handle de Crecy. She has outlived two husbands, has she not?"

"I'll wager she wouldn't outlive that one." Both women cackled.

"See how Mortimer watches with jealous eyes. I believe he fancies Gareth himself. Let us determine if he is drunk enough to be stupid."

"Or stupid enough to be murdered." The thin woman giggled. She stumbled away from the table, treading on her friend's embroidered train until the woman snatched it up and threw it over her arm, slapping several dancers more insensible than they were.

The women descended on a pasty-faced minstrel. His long, delicate fingers continued to pluck his lute as the women flanked him, leaning forward to capture both ears with sly, sidelong glances at Gareth and his lady. He shook his head, but the plump woman only leaned closer, smothering him with her ample bosom. He shrugged and nodded. The women backed away, whispering behind their hands. Rowena tugged a strand of her hair from her cap and tucked it into her mouth.

The jolly tune halted abruptly, to the groans of the dancers. A man near Rowena continued to dance, slinging invisible partners to and fro with a regal air. The minstrel pulled a flask from his vest and took a long swig. Most of the wine missed his mouth and dribbled down his chin.

A stumbling knight cried out, "Play now, Mortimer. Quench your infernal thirst later."

"Play and I shall send my squire to your chambers after the revelry to quench it for you," called Sir Blaine.

At the hoots and catcalls of the crowd, Mortimer wiggled his fingers at Sir Blaine in an effeminate salute of thanks. Blaine made the sign of a cross as if to ward him away. The crowd rocked with laughter. Rowena smiled without understanding. Sir Gareth still leaned over the canary-garbed woman on the stool, oblivious to the musical entertainment or lack of it. As Rowena watched, his hand slid beneath the woman's wimple. His lips brushed her swanlike throat. How could such a pale, delicate neck support a brocade wimple, much less a head? Rowena wondered. She touched her own throat, comforted by its sturdy familiarity. No matter how much her head was spinning at the moment, she knew it would not fall off.

Mortimer's fingers gently teased the lutestrings. The crowd fell silent as he drew bittersweet chords out of the instrument with a skill they had forgotten he possessed.

"You see, my dear lords and ladies, I have a new tune, a new song," he said softly.

Tears started in Rowena's eyes at the haunting melody. Longing for home, she wiped them away with the same strand of hair she had been chewing on. The crowd crept nearer to Mortimer, starved even in their drunken stupor for fresh words and melodies. His lank hair fell across his face. They leaned forward to hear his muted words.

" 'Tis a tune I first heard a fortnight ago at a castle across the channel in Touraine."

Sir Gareth straightened with a frown. A chill of apprehension shot through Rowena as his brow darkened. But he was not seeking her; he was staring at the minstrel.

Mortimer began to sing, his voice deep and pleasant.

> *The fair Elayne*
> *Unfairly slain*
> *Her faithless hand*
> *Stilled by a name.*

With a nervous murmur and clearing of throats, the crowd took a step backward.

> *The fair Elayne*
> *Hath fled the pain—*
> *With fearful flight*
> *From one dark knight.*

> *The fair Elayne—*

Rowena was humming brokenly along when Mortimer's words choked to a halt. The lute crashed against the stones as the minstrel fell to the floor with Gareth's boot on his throat and the chiseled tip of a sword at his breast. The crowd cleared a healthy circle around the two of them. Rowena saw the two women who had accosted the minstrel duck out the door. She came to her feet, tucking her hair into her cap.

Gareth's eyes glittered like black diamonds. His broad chest rose and fell in uneven rhythm. "If you care to sing another day, canary, tell me who wrote that song," he growled. Mortimer's pale hands fluttered upward in a mute plea. Gareth lifted his shiny boot half an inch, but his sword pressed deeper into the man's tunic. "Speak now or forever hold your tongue."

Mortimer coughed weakly. "I told you. I learned it in Touraine. At a castle."

"What castle? And from whom?"

"I cannot remember."

"You lie." Gareth's boot came down on his throat again.

The crowd parted to let Sir Blaine through. The master of the castle cast a careless arm around Gareth's shoulder. Gareth whirled around, and, for a breathless moment, Rowena thought he would lop off his friend's head.

"Come now, my brother-in-arms. Skillful minstrels are hard to find. I will be hard-pressed to find another if you skewer this one. Pardon his insolence this once. Perhaps 'twas an honest mistake." Blaine's smile was a shade too bright.

Gareth stared down at his friend, his face as drawn and expressionless as a mask. He looked down at the minstrel. Mortimer grimaced hopefully. Gareth sheathed his sword with a snarl of contempt, but kept his boot on Mortimer's throat.

He leaned forward, his whisper audible throughout the hall. "If those words ever leave your throat again, they will be your last."

The crowd fell back as Gareth crossed the hall in long strides. Rowena started after him, uncertain if she should follow, but stopped when he reached the doe-eyed woman on the stool. Without a word he caught the woman's hand in his. She rose and followed him up the stairs, casting a look back at the crowd that was both demure and triumphant. Gareth stopped on the landing. His eyes searched the hall and found Rowena standing in the middle of the floor, feet poised for movement if he should beckon.

He nodded, but she had no way of knowing if it was a nod of approval or warning. Then he disappeared with the lady into the shadows at the top of the stairs.

A giggling squire emerged from the crowd and pulled Mortimer to his feet, brushing him off with a suggestive leer. The crowd cut a wide swath around the splintered lute. Without the music, the dance and the revelry died. Those who could walk paired off and stumbled up the stairs or out into the night. Those who could not wrapped their cloaks around them and stretched out on the tables and floor. A short blond boy cleared a corner of the table with a single swipe and rolled onto it with a gurgling snore. Rowena watched him sleep for a moment, wondering with longing what Little Freddie was doing at the moment. Her stomach ached. She sighed and curled up in the corner, bunching a grimy handful of rushes into a pillow.

A vision of the man and woman she had seen outside the castle drifted through her weary mind. The thought of the lady Alise's delicate face screwed up into such an expression made her smile. She found it even more difficult to imagine Gareth's strong form caught in such a graceless act as skewering a woman like a trapped bug against a wall. Even the hogs at Revelwood, when they still had hogs, had possessed more finesse in their mating. A wave of homesickness faded her smile. When the yellow cur sank down beside her and lapped at her nose, she threw an arm over him and drifted into a restless sleep.

As Gareth climbed the steps, the weight of Alise's hand in his felt cold and insubstantial. The melody of Mortimer's song echoed in the back of his skull, taunting him with its eerie refrain. Curiosity shone in Alise's hazel eyes. Perhaps she could hear it, too. He snatched his hand out of the web of her fine-boned fingers without explanation. There was no time for her gentle reproof. The door of a chamber lay before them.

A baby-faced squire and blushing maidservant pushed past them with knowing glances as they entered. Their giggles floated back as they fled down the stairs. Gareth slammed the door and jerked the tousled counterpane off the mattress. At the violence of the gesture, a tingle of fright shuddered down Alise's spine, deepening the sparkle of anticipation in her eyes. Gareth felt sickened.

She glided toward him, twirling like a leaf in the wind when he caught her arm and drew her into his embrace. Her lips spread hungrily, drawing him into a lake of fire. Even as his body responded in all the right ways, his mind wondered how many women bedded him out of curiosity, seeking the razor-edge thrill of danger, and hoping what others said about him was true.

Alise backed away, her eyes darkening pools of invitation. Her fingers caught like claws at his leather gauntlets, peeling them from his forearms like a second layer of skin.

A chord of memory chimed within him. He remembered the nightmares that had beset him after he had buried Elayne. He dreamed her moldering corpse would come dragging up the hall. Her skeletal claws would paw his bolted door until he would awaken, screaming and drenched in the scent of his own fear.

He pulled Alise to him, burying his face in her smooth throat to vanquish the memory. His broad fingers splayed over the ridges of her ribs through the heavy brocade.

His eyes opened of their own volition as he remembered without warning the warmth of something more solid against him—the girl sleeping in his arms on the journey to the castle. Her body, vulnerable and warm, nestled against him. Her head had fallen to the side, and her gentle breath had passed through his chain mail like a spring wind. She was so young, and he suddenly felt very old trapped in the sharp embrace of a woman he hardly knew. He could see the girl standing in the center of the hall, her golden mass of hair caught in the shapeless confines of her cap, looking more self-possessed than any of those who stumbled around her. Only her eyes had lacked certainty. They had locked on him as if his will could determine the very direction of her thoughts. The vision made him uneasy. Would she flee, or would she heed his warnings? Stumbling across her father had been a stroke of fate. He had searched for her too long to lose her now.

Alise moaned against his lips as her teasing fingertips glided over his hip and downward with practiced skill. Groaning his surrender, he dragged the wimple from her head. Her hair came spilling out in a pale cloud around their faces.

Rowena awoke with a firm hand clamped over her mouth. She struggled for consciousness through a groggy haze and reached for her knife. Her hand came up empty. A rough hand plunged inside her overtunic.

"If you are a lad, sweet squire, then I am a vestal virgin," came a hoarse whisper against her ear.

The fire had died to embers, leaving her attacker's face in shadow. His wandering hand slid downward outside the coarse braies and clamped between her legs. Panic sliced through the last vestiges of sleep, and Rowena struck out in earnest. The man's cry of triumph was cut short as her fist connected smartly with his smooth chin.

He caught her wrist and wrenched it. "Damn you, wench. You may fight like a lad, but I swear I'll make you glad you're not one before this night is done."

A heated breath of ale filled her nostrils. Wet, greedy lips closed on hers. Rowena drove her knee toward his groin but found only air as a shadow fell over them and the man's weight vanished. She sat up, struggling to catch her breath. Her cap fell off, freeing her golden hair to tumble over her face. She tossed it back from her eyes to find her host, Sir Blaine, slammed against the wall with Gareth's misericord pressed to his throat.

Blaine shrugged as well as he could in his awkward position. "What did you expect, my friend? Did you think me so drunk as to believe her a lad? That mouth may have been fashioned by heaven to service a knight, but not as a squire."

Rowena touched her lips. They felt hot and swollen. Gareth's gauntlets were gone. The muscles of his forearm knotted beneath dark curling hairs. "The lady is not to be troubled." The small dagger in his hand did not waver.

Blaine's eyes narrowed. "If you cannot offer this . . . *lady* any more protection than leaving her unattended in my hall, how can you dare reproach me for offering her my protection?"

"You were offering her more than your protection. If you find my care lacking, old friend, mayhaps you would care to challenge me to a joust."

Blaine looked away from Gareth's steady gaze. A muscle in his cheek twitched.

Gareth's smile held little humor. "I thought not." He loosed Blaine and sheathed the dagger. "Now be a good drunken boy and find your bed. I fear I had to disappoint Alise. Perhaps she will consent to soothe your wounded pride."

Blaine forced a rueful smile and rubbed his chin. "I suggest you armor yourself ere you take this chit abovestairs. She tosses a nasty punch."

"I know. I saw."

Gareth pulled Rowena to her feet. She had no choice but to follow him. She glanced back to find Blaine staring after them, his smile gone and his eyes smoldering with an emotion far deeper than annoyance.

# Chapter 3

∼❧∼

The climb up the stairs was far too brief. Before she knew it, Rowena found herself in the middle of a modest bedchamber, twisting her cap in her hands as a heavy door slammed behind her. Would this night never end? She tried not to tremble as Gareth's knuckles trailed gently over her cheek.

"Did he hurt you?"

She shook her head, exhaustion making her honest. "Have you brought me here to paw me yourself?"

He turned away with a disparaging laugh. "God forbid. I've no taste for dirty little moor urchins."

Rowena opened her mouth to protest that she had been swimming in her clothes only that afternoon, then snapped it shut. If the sweet, pure dirt of the moor would protect her from the attentions of *honorable* knights like Sir Gareth and his friends, she would give up bathing altogether.

Gareth turned his back to her and drew his tunic over his head. A web of pale scars crisscrossed his broad shoulders. Rowena wondered which scar should have belonged to the king.

" 'Tis no wonder," she murmured. "You've chal-
lenged everyone but me to a tournament this eve."

Gareth turned on her, his eyes bright. Dark, curling
hair furred his chest. His lips quirked upward in what
might have seemed amusement in a less guarded man.
Rowena realized she had spoken her thoughts aloud.
She sank down on the woven rug beside the bed and
nervously began to braid her hair.

The feather mattress shifted as he lay his solid weight
on it. His dark head appeared over the edge of the bed.
"No one accepted my challenge, did they?"

"Are you that good?"

He threw his weight back on the bed. She took his
grunt to be one of assent. Realizing that she was tying
her hair in knots, she abandoned the braids, longing for
Little Freddie's competent hands. She lay back and
hugged her overtunic around her, missing the musty
warmth of the hound in the hall. Overwhelmed by the
weight of the day, her tired eyes fluttered shut. She
sensed a shadow fall over her.

Gareth loomed above, and Rowena's breath caught
in her throat. She waited for his strong hand to cover
her mouth, his smooth lips to clamp down on hers in
demand. Instead, a coverlet fell on her chest. His misericord thumped to a halt on top of it.

"If anyone else attempts you tonight—including
me—gut him."

Her unblinking blue eyes met his dark gaze. The bed
creaked again. She waited in silence for the sound of
steady breathing that would tell her he slept. It did not
come. She curled up on her side, her hand clenched
around the hilt of the tiny dagger.

Rowena awoke to a sun-warmed and empty chamber.
She uncurled her stiff back and stood, rubbing her eyes.
The goose-down coverlet slid around her ankles. The
rumpled tick on the deserted bed was its only sign of
recent occupancy. She glanced around guiltily, then
threw herself on the feather mattress with a sigh. The
bed frames at Revelwood had been sold long ago,

leaving only moldy heaps of straw in the hall for all to share. She rolled over, burrowing her face in the luxuriant softness. Her body fit neatly into the larger imprint of the man who had slept there. She breathed in a scent of leather, deeper and more evocative than the smell of old feathers. She flopped to her back and bounced up and down, giggling with delight. The timber frame creaked a shrill complaint, but Rowena was still gleefully bouncing when the door flew open.

Gareth stood in the doorway, a pair of dripping chausses draped over one arm. Rowena froze, though the bed kept reverberating for an excruciating minute. Gareth's face revealed nothing, yet for the first time in her life, Rowena wondered what she looked like. The hand she raised to her hair found it half braided and half matted around her face.

She grinned weakly. "Good morn, sir. I was awaiting your pleasure."

He lifted an eyebrow and Rowena bit her tongue. He shut the door.

"As your squire, I meant, kind sir." She casually sidled off the bed. "I was awaiting your pleasure as your squire this morn to learn how I might best serve you." Rowena winced and pondered taking a vow of silence. She started for the coverlet, but his tall form blocked her path.

"My dagger, please." He held out a broad palm.

"I was just going to fetch it."

" 'Tis what I feared."

He stepped back a few scant inches, forcing her hip to brush against his thighs as she bent and scavenged through the blanket folds for the dagger. She slapped the hilt into his palm and stepped back. He tucked the jeweled weapon into his boot and bent to gather his scant belongings.

"You will find a tub in the chamber at the end of the corridor. The water remains from yestereve, but you're welcome to it if you desire."

Rowena shook her head with maddening complacency. "Nay, sir. There is no need. I bathed only last month."

Gareth's head jerked up. She struggled not to squirm under his frank scrutiny. Had it been only yesterday she had plunged beneath the chill, tumbling water of a stream and lain in the warmth of the noonday sun until her clothes dried crisp and hot against her skin? This tyrant would not learn of it.

He mumbled something unintelligible and laced up his leather gauntlets with swift, sure motions before holding out his arms expectantly. Rowena took another step backward, which brought the back of her legs in uncomfortable proximity to the bed frame.

Gareth cleared his throat. Leather thongs dangled from the burnished gloves. "Would you mind?" he asked, the very picture of pained patience.

Rowena crept nearer. A proper squire would help him dress, would he not? And that is what she was meant to be, was it not? Her tongue slipped out of the corner of her mouth at the effort of working the slick thongs into a proper knot. Twice she included her thumb in the tidy parcel.

On the third try, after she had tangled not only her little finger but a large strand of her hair in the endeavor, he snatched his hand back with a growl. "Unless I care to nip your fingers off or snatch you bald, I'd best find another to assist me."

Rowena shoved her hands behind her back, lacing her fingers together in a protective knot.

He slipped the woven chain mail on over his head. "Tarry here. I will seek out Blaine and thank him for his hospitality ere we take our leave."

Rowena remembered a heavy hand clamped between her legs and thought of several ways she would like to thank Blaine for his hospitality—most of them involving the blunt end of a cudgel. She hid her thoughts behind the hand that tucked her tangled hair back into her cap. Gareth left her sitting dutifully on the edge of the bed, hands folded.

A tiny spark in the pit of her stomach ignited a

burning hole. After her sating last night, Rowena recognized the sting as hunger. She had lived with the ache so long it had taken on a certain normalcy.

She crossed her legs, uncrossed them, and rose to pace the chamber. She drank a bit of water, sloshed the remains out the window, and sat down again. The pit in her gut swelled, threatening to suck her in and swallow her completely.

She opened the door and peered both ways before creeping out. The hour must be earlier than she thought. Bodies still littered the stairs in various positions of sleep and stupor. She picked her way down the stairs and across the great hall. A man reached for her ankle, but she nimbly skirted his fingers, eliciting a strangled murmur before he curled back into his cloak.

The table loomed before her, no less beautiful in the harsh light of morning than in the romantic hue of torchlight.

Rowena whirled around when Gareth came plunging down the steps several moments later. He caught hold of the wall to steady himself. She knew from his expression that he had been to the empty chamber. As she imagined his confusion at her absence, a sparkle of satisfied malice touched her eyes, but it was gone before he could cross the sea of bodies. Rowena took advantage of his concentration on that task by running her palms beneath the table, then rubbing her cheeks, leaving powdery smudges of dirt wherever she touched.

Gareth opened his mouth to speak, then closed it. His eyes traveled over her from head to foot, narrowing in suspicion as if wondering if the faeries had come in the night and left this pudgy, dirty changeling in place of his lithe captive.

Rowena smiled brightly. "I grew weary of waiting, milord. I trust I did not anger you."

"Of course not."

Rowena knew from his clenched jaw that he was lying. Her smile grew broader. She wished she had gained the time to black out one of her pearly teeth with soot.

"I would prefer in the future that you obey me," he

said. "Unless you would prefer to fall into the hands of another Sir Blaine."

His barb stung. Rowena hid it behind flowery words that mocked his precise French without meaning to. "Where is our fair host? Has he no words of farewell to offer at our leavetaking?"

Something like a grin touched Gareth's lips. "I fear Sir Blaine finds himself indisposed this morn. He bids us a safe journey with special good wishes for my new squire. He has even instructed his stableman to gift you with a horse for our journey to Caerleon."

Rowena took the hand he proffered to guide her across the hall, wondering what fits of joy and jealousy it would give Mortimer to see Sir Gareth holding hands with his squire. She had always thought her blunt fingers ungraceful, but they were dwarfed in the cup of Gareth's palm. She heard a snuffling noise at her leg and looked down to find the yellow hound. She scratched him absently on the head, considering it a fitting farewell for a faithful friend.

Horse was a kind word for the swayback nag Sir Blaine had provided her. The inverted hump between withers and rump was deep enough to hold three Rowenas. If the early morning silence had not been broken by a halfhearted stamp of one hoof at their approach, Rowena would have thought him dead. She heard a snort behind her far more lively than any she could expect from the horse. When she turned, Gareth's face was curiously stern.

"Blaine's judgment of women has always exceeded his judgment of horseflesh," he said.

A more experienced woman might have read a compliment in Gareth's words, but they sailed over Rowena's head. A warm muzzle poked at her hand. The yellow hound was still following her. He had been joined by a grizzled mutt and an oversized mastiff who stood as high as her waist.

The mastiff jammed his nose into the sleeve of her tunic. "Begone, please," she hissed.

Gareth frowned at her. His stallion pranced nearby,

unnerved by the yelps and whines of the milling dogs. Rowena swatted at the hound. The mastiff tugged at her sleeve. Three tiny dogs came yipping down the drawbridge, their jeweled collars flashing in the morning sun. They made a straight path for Rowena. She decided this might be an opportune moment to ignore Sir Blaine's diabolical sense of humor and throw herself on the nag's back. She lifted one leg only to have the mastiff catch the cuff of her braies between his powerful jaws. She gritted her teeth and pulled, caught in an all-out battle of strength with the slavering beast.

Rowena's waist slid nicely into the groove of the nag's back, leaving the foot not encompassed in the mastiff's jaws dangling helplessly. Gareth stroked his short beard, his stance one of complete relaxation.

"Pardon me," she grunted. "I would be ever so appreciative if you would help me mount. I seem to be having some difficulty."

He scattered the dogs with a masterful bellow. The yellow hound crept away, shooting Rowena a reproachful look. Gareth's arms circled her waist. He paused. Then sniffed.

The ground beneath her feet was a more welcome sensation than Gareth's hand on her elbow as he spun her around. "I am not given to rudeness, but I must insist you bathe. When the dogs start following your scent, 'tis a hearty indication . . ."

He trailed off. His nose quivered. His gaze slid downward, caught by the spectacle of half a roasted hen hanging out of her torn sleeve. He gingerly plucked it from her and cast it in the midst of the widening circle of dogs gathered in the courtyard. They attacked it with snarls of satisfaction.

Gareth glowered at her. Rowena lifted her arms in mute surrender. He delved beneath the overtunic, fishing out a handful of bread crusts, two pork loins, a wad of stewed raisins and prunes, three whole onions and the rotting apple she had stolen from the boar's mouth. When he had removed the pudginess she had acquired so abruptly, he held out his hand. Rowena slipped out of her overtunic and laid it in his hands. The tattered garment followed the food to the dogs.

She could not hide her crestfallen expression as she watched her succulent treasures disappear into their yawning maws. How Little Freddie would have savored the cinnamon and honey flavoring the raisins! Rowena shivered in her thin shirte. This knight was more than cruel; he was a monster.

Gareth unlatched a woven basket from his bridle, and dropped it at Rowena's feet. He tilted her chin upward with one finger. Her eyes were dry, but her lips were set in a bitter line.

"Did you think I would starve you?"

Her silence was reply enough. A thin layer of dust coated his fingertip where he had touched her chin. He swept back the lid of the basket to reveal two loaves of steaming bread, a crock of creamy yellow butter and three swollen strings of fresh sausage. He heard the teasing growl of Rowena's stomach before she felt it.

She slammed the lid with her foot and sat down on top of the basket. She clutched his leg, her eyes as blue and earnest as the brightening sky.

"You won't give it to the dogs, will you? You mustn't. Say you won't."

Her reaction mystified Gareth. He squatted beside her, convinced if he dared toss the basket to the dogs, he would have to toss her, too. Her arms were smooth and fair, unmarred by the dirt streaking her cheeks.

He spoke slowly and patiently. "I packed the food for our morning repast. I thought it might be more pleasant to partake of it away from the stench of yestereve's merriment."

She stood as abruptly as she had sat down. She handed the basket to Gareth, marveling anew at its weight. "Of course. A grand idea. To break the fast of the night. Some days at Revelwood we do not break the fast until nightfall. We are simply too busy and the delay heightens our anticipation and whets our appetites." Rowena was chattering because she knew if her appetite was whetted any more, she might gobble up Gareth where he stood, basket and all.

He hefted the basket to its rope. "Are you hungry?"

She poked the dirt with her toe and shrugged. From beneath downcast lashes, she watched him open the basket and tear off a hunk of bread so fresh that butter still dripped from it. Hardly daring to breathe, she waited for him to eat the bread and throw her the crust. Her hands almost didn't react when he tossed the entire hunk to her.

Gareth mounted the stallion without a word. Clutching the miracle of flour and yeast between her fingers, Rowena dragged herself astride the nag and followed him over an arched bridge into the pocket of cool air hanging over the misty lake.

As Gareth had promised, they picnicked in a sunny meadow at midmorning. He ate little, seemingly content to recline in the grass a few feet away and watch Rowena polish off both strings of sausage and a creamy hunk of cheese. Sir Blaine's keep of Ardendonne crowned a distant hill, giving Rowena a shining view of the grandeur she had only guessed at in the night. Sunlight spilled over the tiled roof of the donjon, casting shadows behind the rounded tower. Rowena sighed at its beauty and gently sucked the sausage grease from each of her fingers with dreamy satisfaction.

She glanced up to find Gareth staring at her lips with hypnotic intensity. His gaze flicked guiltily to her eyes. He sprang to his feet, barking a command that she mount.

They left the meadows for a tangled forest thick with the bracken of late summer. The pit in Rowena's stomach had been soothed to a warm glow. Lulled by her sated senses and the melancholy rhythm of the nag's laggard pace, she began to hum absently. The words of Mortimer's ballad rose from her throat in a sweet, off-key alto before she even realized she remembered them:

*The fair Elayne,*
*Unfairly slain—*

Gareth moved with such speed that the nag was still walking when he snatched Rowena down by the scruff of her sleeveless shirte. He drove her backward until she felt the rough bark of a tree slam into her shoulders. Without wanting to, she remembered again the man pinning the woman against the castle wall.

Gareth's nostrils flared. "Do not sing that song. Not now. Not ever."

A darkness deeper than color loomed behind his eyes. Even when he released her, all she could do was nod, rendered mute by the oddly tender brush of his gauntlet against her cheek.

He stalked back to the stallion, never hearing her faint, "As you wish, milord."

Her knees shook. Gareth threw himself on the stallion's back and spurred the horse forward. Had he forgotten her? She was already wondering if she dared return to Ardendonne to ask directions to Revelwood when Gareth spun the mount around. The stallion pranced sideways, its satiny coat rippling in shimmering contrast to the black-clad knight on its back. Gareth and the stallion could have been one creature, so sharp and precise were their movements. They stopped, poised and waiting. Only the velvety lift of the wind through the stallion's mane assured Rowena they were real and not the product of a starved imagination fed on the paltry dreams of Revelwood.

She mounted the nag without a word, lacing her hands in the wispy mane to hide their trembling.

By late afternoon the sun had disappeared behind a solid bank of gray clouds. Day faded painlessly into dusk as they slipped off the old Roman road and entered a forest of tall and ancient trees. Rowena stared upward. Through the creaking boughs, the wind whispered of rain. The trees were so huge, her arms could not have circled a single trunk. When she began to see faces etched in the gnarled bark, she fixed her eyes straight ahead and edged her mount closer to Gareth.

His broad shoulders lost their menace and became as much a comfort as the rhythmic jingle of the bridle in his steady hands. A wolf howled in the distance, sending pinpricks of fear down Rowena's spine. Gareth glanced back at her, his eyes shadowed by the forest.

He might have been a wolf himself with his shaggy hair and gleaming white teeth. Irwin had told them all of a werebeast from hell, half-man and half-wolf who lured innocent damsels into the forest to feast upon their tender flesh. Rowena's cheerful whistle held a hollow ring. She slowed her mount, putting a more healthy distance between herself and Gareth.

With an earsplitting screech, a silvery bat came swooping out of the trees to crash into Gareth. The impact unseated him with a clang that echoed through the still forest. The nag responded with his first indication of life in the long day by rearing with a half-paw at the air, dumping Rowena on the damp ground. Her hair spilled out of her cap, rendering her blind. She could hear nothing but Gareth's muffled curses.

When she untangled her hair from her eyes, Gareth lay flat on his back. An armored figure straddled his shoulders. His steady stream of curses brought a blush to Rowena's cheeks. She leaped to her feet in a frenzy of indecision.

"Surrender!" bellowed the helmed creature, bouncing up and down on Gareth's chest.

Rowena hopped from one foot to the other, pondering what to do. Why did Gareth not simply throw his assailant off? Perhaps he had been injured in the fall, though he certainly had enough wits and breath left to curse.

Deciding a known evil was preferable to an unknown evil, Rowena snatched up a stick and whacked the helmed figure on the head.

Groaning, the creature fell off Gareth. Gareth rolled to his side and pounded the ground with his fist. Rowena took a step backward when she realized he was laughing. Her brow furrowed. She could find nothing amusing in his being rescued by someone who by all rights should have hit him on the head.

The armored stranger sat up with a moan. Rowena lifted her stick, prepared to dispatch them both if Gareth's hysteria persisted. Still weak with laughter, he reached out a restraining arm.

His attacker reached for the helm. From under the tarnished silver came a straight dark fall of hair. The one dark eye that glared at Rowena from beneath the stray locks was unmistakably familiar. Rowena glanced between Gareth and the stranger, wondering if she or they had lost their senses.

Gareth gasped for breath. "Allow me to introduce my sister Marlys."

Marlys rubbed her head, her glare undiminished. "Your new whore packs a powerful wallop."

"And a well-deserved one, I might add." Gareth sat up, flexing his long legs. He tucked a twig between his teeth, addressing Rowena although he was looking at his sister. "Marlys delights in ambushing me upon my return to Caerleon. She believes it keeps me on my toes. How long have you been hanging in that tree, dear? Two days? Three? A week?"

Marlys climbed to her feet, her rusty knee mail clanking. "As if I would waste so much time on you, brother. You've been letting your women swell your opinion of yourself again."

Rowena was too disturbed by Marlys's uncorrected impression of her to notice when the girl came to stand in front of her. Marlys rested her hands on her hips. Rowena squinted, trying to determine if the face was as formidable as the hair. Instead of pushing back the dark mop, Marlys shook it forward, making it impossible for Rowena to determine her age.

When Marlys reached out a hand to capture a wheaten strand of Rowena's hair, Rowena had to resist the urge to jerk it back. The golden strand curled around a fingernail tipped with a crescent of dirt. Marlys stared at it for a moment, then drew it across the tip of Rowena's nose in a gentle caress. Rowena swallowed the urge to sneeze.

"Pretty," Marlys pronounced, her lip curling in a sneer.

Gareth rose to stand behind Rowena. "Hands off, little sister. She belongs to me. Not you." He did not touch Rowena. He did not have to.

"Where did you come by such a find?"

"I won her with a throw of the dice in a game of hazard."

Marlys lifted the one eyebrow visible beneath her hair. "Original. Tell me—does she always dress like a boy, or have you acquired some new tastes on your journey?"

"I don't have to answer that question. Especially not for you."

Marlys circled them both. "Does it talk, or only hit?"

Rowena was beginning to feel like a Christian caught between two lions. "I talk," she said, a shade too loud.

Marlys ignored her. "Does it have a name?"

A pride she'd long forgotten infused Rowena's clipped words. "Its name is Lady Rowena Fordyce."

A current so deep and swift that Rowena might have imagined it passed between Marlys and Gareth. The tiny hairs at the nape of her neck stood erect.

Marlys snorted, granting her the courtesy of addressing her directly. "You look like no lady I've ever seen."

"She might say the same for you," Gareth retorted smoothly.

Marlys screwed up her face in a childish gesture of defiance. She stuffed two fingers in her mouth and whistled shrilly. A piebald mare trotted into view, as shaggy and heavy-footed as its mistress. Marlys settled herself on the horse's back with a tremendous clinking.

She tossed her head at the nag. "Did you win that, too, or was he a penalty forced on you for losing?"

Gareth mounted. "The jade was Blaine's twisted idea of a jest. We had to travel slowly to keep from killing the poor beast." His disparaging glance seemed to take in Rowena as well.

"Pity you didn't." Marlys kicked her mare forward.

A kindred sympathy for the nag welled up in Rowena. She stroked the beast's nose before mounting to follow them into the deepening dark.

As they reached Caerleon, the rain began, pelting them like fists from the sky. Rowena had a dim impression of a sloping drawbridge, a shadowy courtyard, black and towering stone. Strong arms circled her waist. Gareth pulled her off the nag and bustled her through a yawning door.

She stood breathless and dripping inside a vast well of darkness. She gazed upward but could find no roof to mark an end to the barren blackness. Only when her breathing steadied did she realize the darkness was only darkness because of tiny pinpoints of light trailing down each wall. Tapers. Tapers in a hall that demanded torchlight for any vision at all. A chill touched her damp clothes as Gareth moved away.

A sharp clang and a hearty volley of curses marked Marlys's progress through the hall. "Dunnla!" she bellowed.

A splash of light wavered into the hall. At first Rowena thought the torch had walked out of the wall itself, but a harder glance showed her an old woman with a crooked back entering the hall from a narrow corridor. The torch she carried almost brushed the floor. That would have been disastrous, for in the wake of the light she cast, Rowena discovered the stones were covered not by floor rushes, but by opulent Oriental rugs, embroidered edge to edge in a never ending sea of luxury.

The woman bobbed out of the darkness with a toothless smile and crooked a finger at Rowena. Rowena bent forward. The stale smell of boiled sage brushed her nostrils as the woman touched her lips to Rowena's ear.

"Welcome!" she roared.

Rowena leaped backward, striking her shin on some immovable object. Gareth had to bend double to kiss the old woman's papery cheek. She beamed up at him.

"Dunnla is mostly deaf," he explained. "She thinks we all are."

"Aren't we, though, after being bellowed at since we were babes?"

Marlys's voice thundered back to them on the heels of an echo. There had to be a roof above them somewhere. Rowena was forced to stagger back as Dunnla swung around, nearly igniting Rowena's braies with a sweep of the torch.

Gareth caught the corner of Dunnla's shawl, making a tiny leap himself to keep from being torched. Rowena started to giggle but stopped when Gareth pointed at her.

She cocked her head to the side, watching Gareth's hands dart through a foreign dance. Dunnla bobbed up and down sending shadows billowing over Gareth's face. From somewhere in the darkness, Rowena could hear the harsh sound of Marlys's breathing. With a final curtsy, Dunnla gave Gareth a shove. He cast Rowena an unreadable look before making his way through the invisible chaos of the hall without a single pause or bump.

Rowena was still staring after him when she felt a tug on the leg of her braies. Dunnla started toward the corridor with Rowena's leg in tow, oblivious to the fact that the rest of her was still rooted to the floor.

"What does she want?" Rowena whispered. "What did he tell her?"

Marlys's voice boomed out of the darkness. "He told her to feed you well and bring you to his chambers."

Rowena felt herself drawn irresistibly toward the corridor. The worn homespun of her braies groaned a protest as Dunnla tugged harder.

A deep ripple of laughter underscored Marlys's words. "He also told her to ensure you had a bath."

Rowena lurched forward to keep from falling. She threw a look over her shoulder, but saw only gleaming white teeth bared in a hungry smile. Somewhere in her mind she heard once again the cry of the wolf in the forest.

# Chapter 4

∂≈∂

Even a tray of cold mutton, so fresh the grease beaded on it like drops of nectar, failed to cheer Rowena. The name Marlys had called her set up echoes that grew louder each moment against Gareth's pointed lack of denial. The scene played itself over and over with a different outcome each time.

"Whore?" Gareth would answer in a booming bass. "Nonsense. I thought she might help us plant barley this spring" or "Silly girl! Does she look like my whore? I've won her to help Dunnla in the kitchen" or best of all, "Bite your tongue, sister. This fair child is a lady. How dare you insult her by branding her with false names?" These imagined replies were always followed by the dissipating of Marlys's bravado and a heartfelt apology with Gareth, preferably on bended knee, kissing her palm.

The image of her forceful captor on his knees at her feet brought her back to reality with a jolt. She was still picking at the meat with her knife when Dunnla entered the kitchen, dragging a round wooden tub twice her size. Rowena watched glumly as heated water was poured into the splintery vessel. As Dunnla stripped her and cheerfully tossed her clothes in the fire, Rowena prayed Gareth would not wander in for his supper. A puff of black smoke and her garments were gone up the chimney like her life at Revelwood.

She sank into the steaming water up to her chin and her hair floated to the surface in a tangled skein. The warm water loosened the lump in her throat. If Gareth had truly intended to use her for his pleasure this long year, why had he left her untouched last night? He had even gone so far as to give her his dagger to protect herself. Had it been only her supposed dirtiness he feared? Now he wanted her clean. And in his chambers. As Dunnla scrubbed her face with a melting ball of soap, the hot, greedy feel of Sir Blaine's lips on hers seared her memory. Marlys's accusation darted in a vicious circle between her ears.

When Dunnla raised the bucket to rinse her hair and screeched, "More?," Rowena thought she said "whore" and burst into tears. The night blurred as Dunnla extracted her from the tub with a sympathetic cluck, dried her, and dropped a clean white bliaut over her head. The tunic was long and shapeless, with no waist to speak of. Its fine linen brushed like feathers against her skin.

Before she realized what was happening, Rowena was standing barefoot outside a massive oak door banded with iron. Her damp hair fell around her shoulders. As Dunnla waddled away, Rowena touched the door, then drew her hand back. She could run now, but where would she run to? The castle with its dark mazes held as many terrors as the encroaching forest.

A low voice shot out of the darkness, giving Rowena no less of a start than if Marlys had jumped on her fully armored from the rafters. "Why do you hesitate? Are you afraid?"

She peered into the shadows. Marlys sat with her back against the wall, her knees drawn up in a casual sprawl.

An uncharacteristic streak of stubbornness prompted Rowena to reply, "Nay. I am not."

Marlys took a long swig from a grubby wineskin before drawing the back of her hand across her mouth. "He gobbles up little country girls like you just to whet his appetite." Rowena smoothed the unfamiliar skirt to hide the trembling of her hands. Marlys corked the wineskin and laid it aside. "He has not touched you, has he?"

Rowena searched her memory. "He threw me up against a tree because I sang a song that displeased him."

Marlys rose and swaggered toward her. Before she could even gasp, Rowena found herself pushed against the door. Bullying must be a family trait, she thought dryly.

"What was the song? Tell me the words," Marlys rasped.

Struggling not to shiver, Rowena repeated the words she could remember. Marlys's mouth tightened in a grim smile.

She pushed her face closer to Rowena's "Go to him. Hide your fear well. He hasn't murdered any of his women—not lately, anyway." She threw back her head in a burst of wild laughter, reached past Rowena, and threw open the door. Rowena was thrust backward into the chamber. The door slammed in her face.

For a long moment she stood with her forehead pressed to the hard wood, afraid to move. Exhaling a deep breath, she finally turned. At first glance, the chamber appeared empty. A cheerful fire crackled on the long hearth, easing the dampness of the rain pounding against the shutters. Candles flickered in iron sconces, dripping wax down the stone walls in melting cascades. A bed frame sat against one wall, devoid of ornamentation, yet, ostentatious with its fine mahogany canopy and massive size. Rowena tiptoed toward the bed.

Gareth lay on his back, one leg thrown outward in surrender to exhaustion. His dark lashes rested on his cheeks. Rowena crept forward, biting her lower lip without realizing it.

Sleep did nothing to diminish his size and strength.

The hand flung out beside his bearded cheek could have crushed her as if she were no more than a gnat. His mouth was closed as if even in sleep there were thoughts to guard and secrets to keep. Dark hair furred the muscular expanse of his chest, trailing into a single line that flowed toward his hips and the thin sheet draped there. Unlike his back, his chest was unmarred by nicks or scars. The men who had bested Sir Gareth of Caerleon had bested him from behind. He stirred and Rowena took an involuntary step backward, fearful the camlet sheet might fall away and reveal more of his slumbering form than she cared to see.

Her feet were cushioned in unearthly softness. She glanced down to discover a pile of furs heaped beside the bed. Gareth must have kicked them away when the warmth of the fire reached the bed. He stirred again, moaning hoarsely, then was still. Rowena looked at the bed, then back at the floor. Her thigh muscles ached from the long hours of clinging to the slippery nag. With a small sigh, she sank to her knees and curled up in the nest of furs.

Rowena had been asleep for a long time when Gareth rolled out of the bed and sank his heavy frame into a carved chair in front of the hearth. He rested his chin in his hand and studied the girl slumbering at his feet. Hair that had grown limp during their dusty journey now shimmered as thick and ripe as wheat around her face. The kiss of fire gave her skin a rosy flush. Her fist was curled against her parted lips like a child's.

Gareth stirred restlessly at the thought. Lindsey Fordyce's hair had once been as thick as this girl's, his eyes as blue. Only days after Gareth's father had brought home his vivacious new bride, Fordyce had followed, swearing his fealty and skimming like the golden-haired tail of the sultry-eyed comet who would sweep their lives clean, leaving desolation in her path. The years had not been kind to him. At Revelwood his hands had trembled as if palsied. Dissipation had spun its web into the bags of flesh beneath his eyes. 'Twas no wonder the man had eluded him all these years. Gareth had been searching for a powerful baron with a fortified stronghold, not a strutting wastrel burdened with a crumbling castle. Within Fordyce's pudgy frame, Gareth had not found even a hint of the dapper, jovial knight who had taught Gareth how to dice and bragged ceaselessly each time he journeyed to his castle in the north to tuck another babe in his wife's belly.

Of its own volition Gareth's gaze followed the smooth planes of Rowena's bliaut down to her flat stomach. What would she do if she awoke to find his lips pressed to hers? he wondered. A faint smile curved his lips. Like Blaine, he would probably taste the bite of her fist against his jaw. That would not be a hindrance. It would not have been a hindrance for Blaine if he had not intervened. He could subdue her with one hand, leaving his other hand free to plunder the ill-gotten gain of his wager with Lindsey Fordyce, Baron of Revelwood.

He remained in the chair by the fire. There was nothing to do but wait and see if he had baited his trap well enough to awaken some sleeping vestige of honor in Fordyce. Surely even the most indifferent of fathers would not sacrifice a rose like Rowena into his vengeful hands. When the last flame died to a glowing ember, he still sat, watching his captive sleep and wondering if he had made a terrible mistake.

# Chapter 5

The familiar fingers of dawn coaxed Rowena from sleep. She snuggled deeper into the furs. Grinning hares bounced across the backs of her closed eyelids. She twitched, believing for a moment that she must strap on her knife and take to the moors to hunt. A shutter creaked. She opened her eyes. Hazy light filtered through the open window, haloing Gareth's dark hair in silver. Rowena sat up, clutching the furs to her chest, forgetting for a moment the modest garment she wore.

Gareth turned at the movement. To her relief, he wore loose fitting chausses, though his chest was still bare. "You may sleep longer if you like," he said. "You were not abed as early as I last night."

"You were resting well when I came to the chamber. I did not see fit to awaken you."

"How thoughtful." His even tone implied the opposite.

Rowena looked away to escape his mocking gaze. Tapestries ringed the walls, their rich burgundies and russets granting an illusion of coziness to the chamber. Directly above her head in a delicately painted mural, the bright, dark eyes of a serpent beguiled a naked and demure Eve.

A loud crunch made her jump. Gareth stood a hand's breadth from her, cradling a half-eaten apple in his palm.

"Fruit?" he asked cheerfully.

Never one to refuse food, Rowena took the apple and snapped a hearty bite out of it. As her eyes glided between Gareth and the serpent, she handed the apple back. He smiled and took another bite before holding out his other hand to her. "Come."

Rowena paled. Had she escaped his attentions in the night only to earn them now? She touched her hair, praying that sleep had left her rumpled and dirty. If Gareth's sparkling eyes were any indication, she was not rumpled enough. She slipped her hand into his, then held her breath as he brought it to his lips. He paused, studying the thin line of calluses marring her palm. His brow furrowed and Rowena feared she had somehow angered him. She knew he must be accustomed to the downy softness of a lady's hand. She would not need dirt or untidy hair to repulse him. She tried to draw back her hand, feeling unaccountably ashamed, but he gently tucked it into the crook of his arm and led her to the window. She followed, intensely aware of the warmth his touch had ignited.

He leaned an elbow on the stone ledge. The apple core fell from his fingers to disappear into the mist below. "Welcome to Caerleon. The grandfather of my grandfather christened it after Uther Pendragon's Caerleon. He was a romantic soul. Quite touched in the head. He adored the Pendragon legend."

"Irwin told me stories of the Pendragon and his court. Your Caerleon must be as lovely as his."

The castle sprawled below was not fashioned of black obsidian as Rowena had fancied in the pouring rain, but of deep gray stone kissed with the wearing of rain and wind. Mist drenched the battlements. Outside the castle walls, the early morning sun slanted through the fog, burning it away in patches to reveal a forest so thick it glistened black instead of green. In the distance, cut off from its hill by a shimmering platter of mist, stood another castle with pennons flying a red and yellow welcome in the ethereal light.

"Ardendonne," Gareth said when he saw her lips part. "I expect to see Blaine's banner come flying over the hill at any moment. His curiosity is insatiable, especially when it involves a comely damsel who scorns his advances."

His gaze strayed from her lips to her eyes. Rowena propped her hip on the ledge and began to braid her hair. The clean strands slipped through her fingers like corn silk.

"Allow me," Gareth said, plucking the coil from her hand. "I thought to provide you no maidservant."

Rowena hardly dared to breathe as his broad fingers intertwined the sections of hair with a deftness that implied an intimacy with womanly grooming she did not care to examine. Such lazy grace in a man of his size was jarring. Rowena stared at the top of his head. His hair was still tousled from sleep.

"Irwin said I was too lazy to tend to my own hair."

"But not too lazy to be up at dawn to hunt the game to stuff his plump face."

Rowena started to nod, then stopped, squirming under a pinprick of disloyalty. "Little Freddie helped me with my braids."

"Hmmm," he said noncommittally. "Would Little Freddie be the gray-eyed gallant who sought to bash me over the head with the cooking kettle?"

Rowena's jaw tightened at the memory. "He would."

Gareth finished one braid and started on the other without a pause. "Tell me, Rowena—has your dearest betrothed ever touched you in an untoward manner?"

Rowena snatched her braid out of his hand. "Indeed not! I'd have cracked his skull if he had."

Gareth bared his white teeth in a smile. "Pray do not crack my skull for asking. You are of an age to marry. 'Twas an honest enough question." He pried the braid from her hand and began to gently undo the damage she had done.

Rowena sniffed, disowning her braid as if it belonged to someone else. " 'Twas an honest enough question coming from you. Perhaps my kin have the moral fortitude your friends lack."

"Trust me, my dear. Moral fortitude does not run rampant in your family."

"I suppose it does in yours? Along with dicing, leaping out of trees at people, and abduction." She glared at the forest, waiting for him to cuff her out the window for her insolence. Fortified by indignation, she drew in a deep breath and announced, "I am experiencing some confusion as to my purpose at Caerleon."

Gareth finished the braid and let it swing against her throat. His teasing tone mocked her anger. "We cannot stand for that, can we? I assume everyone had a purpose at Revelwood."

"Of course," she replied, as if the thought of anyone not having a purpose was ludicrous to her. "I hunt. Little Freddie cooks and weaves. Big Freddie and the boys tend the crops. And Papa . . ." She fell silent with a puzzled frown.

Gareth's smile was bitter. "Papa squanders away his only daughter to a lecherous nobleman."

"Which returns us to the subject of my purpose here." Her bright blue eyes studied his face. "Am I to be your whore, milord?"

Gareth cleared his throat. He was a man accustomed to wasting a thousand words to arrive at one lucid point in his banter with women. Rowena's forthrightness disarmed him.

He crossed to the leather gauntlets on the table and began to work a leather thong from its lacings.

She stumbled on, " 'Tis just that I know more of hunting than whoring. I fear I should be a great disappointment to you."

Gareth bit his tongue as he snapped the thong in two with his teeth. He returned to wrap the ends of

Rowena's braids, all laziness banished from his precise motions.

"It might amaze you, my dear, to realize there are an abundance of purposeless ladies—and noblemen—in this world."

It was a feeble comfort and not the answer she deserved, but it was all he could give her. Rowena lowered her eyes before he could read the doubt in them. His fingers tightened for an instant on a silky wisp of her hair.

He was still holding her braid when the door crashed open and Marlys burst into the chamber. "I heard no grunts, moans, or screams so I assumed it was safe to enter." Gareth dropped the braid. Marlys took in the motion with a bitter smile. "How sweet! Is he dressing you? As his squire, I thought 'twas your duty to dress him. Or does he prefer you to undress him?"

"A good morn to you, Marlys." Gareth rose from the window.

Marlys was unarmored and unarmed except for a dirk crammed in her belt. Her black tunic and breeches hung in disheveled folds as if she had slept in them. From the awkward patching, Rowena realized the garments must have once belonged to Gareth. Cracked leather gauntlets covered her arms to the elbows, incongruous against the radiant sunlight breaking through the fog to stream over the windowsill. Her hair hung in ratty hanks over her face.

She prowled the chamber like a hungry bear. She picked up Gareth's dagger, feinted twice at the air, then threw it down. Her foot scattered the furs beside the bed. "A bed for your new puppy, brother? A warm pelt and some scraps from your table and I'll wager she'll be at your feet like a bitch in heat, just begging to lap your—"

"Marlys," Gareth warned.

Marlys stepped up to Rowena. The corner of a naughty grin peeped out from behind her hair. "May we pat its pretty little head?"

Before Marlys could move, Rowena's hand shot out

and grasped her wrist. A glimmer of doubt touched
Marlys's eye. Rowena pulled Marlys's hand down
between them before loosing it.

Marlys massaged her wrist under the gauntlet with a
wounded pout. "Beware, brother. Your puppy has
fangs."

Gareth lifted one eyebrow. "I thought you well
warned of that after she knocked you over the head last
night."

"Mayhaps the blow dislodged my memory."

"Not overmuch, I hope. I have a task for you, and
your memory will serve you well." He threw open a
chest and drew a plain black tunic over his head. He
scrounged deeper in the chest and came up wielding a
tiny silver flute. "What are your interests, Rowena?
Music? Embroidery? Dancing?"

Rowena looked puzzled. She knew of no interests
except the gallant pursuit of food for their table. Gareth
waved a scrap of linen embroidered with dancing
pheasants beneath her nose.

"Pheasant stew," she said suddenly. "That holds my
interest."

The scrap of fabric went limp. Gareth's eyebrows
drew together in a forbidding line. He returned to the
chest. "You mentioned Irwin telling you tales. Are you
fond of the chansons, the romances?"

She raised her palms in a shrug. She adored tales of
monsters and heroes, but did not realize that was what
he had asked her. Gareth gave an exasperated snort.
"Are you fond of anything you cannot eat?"

Marlys muttered something under her breath, which
earned her a searing glance from her brother. He pulled
forth a creamy sheet of parchment, a cow horn, and a
feathered quill. "You may put your impertinence to
good use, sister. You will teach Rowena to write."

Marlys gagged. "I detest writing. And I detest
catering to your doxies. If you must consort with un-
educated villeins, could you not hire a priest to under-
take their education? I would have thought she'd
already know everything necessary for the tasks you

have in mind. Some things do come naturally, you know. If she can lay on her back and spread her legs, then she ought to be able to—"

"The lady Rowena is not a peasant. She is the daughter of a baron," Gareth interrupted, watching Rowena turn from pale white to pink to a mild shade of purple. " 'Tis no fault of her own that her education has been neglected."

Marlys crossed her arms over her chest. "Command the village priest to come teach her. He has been idle too long."

"You know 'tis impossible." Gareth slipped behind her and put his mouth next to where an ear should be. His soft words were audible throughout the chamber. "I suggest you follow my wishes. The next time you ambush me, I might forget you are my beloved baby sister and regrettably skewer you."

Marlys's fingers flexed in her gauntlets as Gareth buckled on a silver belt. He started for the door, whistling a jaunty tune. "If you are entertaining notions of his goodness," Marlys snapped at Rowena, "then beware. He may kill you with kindness."

Gareth stopped for a moment, his broad shoulders filling the doorframe. Then he continued on, and Marlys's low laughter flooded the chamber.

Rowena sidled around Marlys, trying to steal a glimpse of the deformity the young girl must be hiding—a twisted lip or perhaps a milky white cataract.

Marlys inclined her head. Her hair fell like a curtain over her anger. "You'd best break your fast," she muttered, "before Dunnla throws your porridge to the hogs."

The memory of snarling dogs tearing at the remains of Ardendonne's feast sent Rowena rushing for the door, Marlys's face forgotten. She hesitated.

Marlys anticipated her question. "Left, right, down, north, left and east. Take care not to get lost. We still haven't found the bones of the last chit who lost her way."

Rowena's eyes widened. She stepped out the door and turned to the right. Marlys's laughter rang after her.

Rowena wandered for an interminable time, trapped in a maze of corridors. She trotted along, out of breath, but refusing to sit down and rest lest they discover her bones months from now, crouched in defeat in some deserted corridor. She found herself at the door of Gareth's chamber twice before stumbling onto the wide stone steps that curled downward into the heart of the castle.

Last night's impression of vast space was only reinforced by the beams of sunlight pouring through the arrow slits: The great hall of Caerleon stood at the base of a square tower three times as large as all of Revelwood. A vaulted ceiling loomed high above. A faint draft stirred a crested banner suspended from the oaken beams.

Swallows darted like shadows between the massive beams. Ardendonne's hall seemed a cottage dwelling compared to this, and Revelwood fit only for swine and dogs. Sunlight drifted through the open door. Carved chairs and tables littered the floor with no apparent pattern to their arrangement.

Rowena picked her way along the wall, dodging table legs and chair backs. Her foot caught in the foreign fabric of an Oriental rug. By the time she reached the kitchen, Marlys was cheerfully polishing off the last of the porridge.

"Too late, love," she said at Rowena's crestfallen expression. "Dreadfully sorry." A smile gleamed between her matted strands of hair.

Rowena slid onto a bench and folded her hands on the empty table. A wizened man close to seven feet tall ducked through the kitchen door with an armload of wood. Rowena scooted backward as he dumped the wood on the table in front of her.

"Gridmore," Marlys grunted. "Dunnla's husband. He is as blind as she is deaf. If I were you, I should move. He thinks you are the fire. You've probably been stoked well enough after a night with Gareth."

Gridmore turned on Rowena, poker in hand. Rowena ducked and slid down the bench. He jabbed at the air a few times before the poker found the hearth.

Marlys lapped at the inside of her wooden bowl. "My mind reels at the vision of their antics in the marriage bed. Mayhaps she folds him up and slips him in the cupboard each night."

Marlys jumped guiltily as Dunnla shuffled up behind her and bellowed, "Eating again, Lady Marlys. I see you've finished yesterday's porridge. Sir Gareth ordered some fresh made for Lady Rowena."

Dunnla clunked a bowl on the table in front of Rowena. Marlys's visible eye glared at her as Rowena dipped a spoon into the steaming goodness, not caring if she burned her tongue. She swallowed the creamy mush and licked her lips, refusing to bite back a grin. Marlys slammed her spoon on the table, sending bits of barley flying.

Throughout the next few days, Rowena came to regret every spoonful of that porridge. Marlys proved to have a long memory.

Her writing lessons consisted of Marlys pacing beside the table while Rowena struggled to form the letters of her name on scraps of parchment. Marlys would pause only long enough to tweak Rowena's ear or poke her with the tip of the quill when she thought Rowena stupid. Rowena fancied herself terribly stupid. Her arms remained dotted with ink and her ears bright red all the day long. Trying to peep beneath Marlys's hair earned her an especially vicious jab. Rowena always jumped when Marlys jerked out her dagger to scrape another blunder from the page. Suppose the churlish creature confused quill and blade and stabbed her?

One afternoon after Rowena had spelled her own name *Wenrona* for the third time, Marlys boxed her ears and drove all the parchments into the floor with a sweep of a gauntleted hand. "I'm weary of teaching a lackwit to write. The time has come for you to learn something useful."

Afraid to even speculate on what Marlys might consider useful, Rowena tripped after her charging path down the stairs and into the beckoning sunlight of the list. Marlys's hunched shoulders disappeared in a crude wooden chest set against the bailey wall. She rummaged through the chest, humming a melody of grunted curses. Rowena ducked as a rusty helm went sailing past her head. She picked it up, running her fingers over the crusted visor.

Marlys reappeared, wielding two long poles, their ends blunted by a conflict long forgotten. "These would never do for a proper joust, but they'll do for you. We'd best abandon the list for the forest. If Gareth finds me tilting instead of teaching, there will be a beating in it for both of us." She leered at Rowena through a matted cloud of hair.

"I've yet to see him lift a finger to you."

Marlys hooked a finger in the neck of Rowena's kirtle and shoved her face at her. "I suppose you think 'twould benefit me if he did?"

Rowena cleared her throat awkwardly. " 'Tis late in your life for Gareth to chasten you. Mayhaps your papa should have done it when you were but a babe."

"My father never had the time to beat me. He was too busy fawning over his precious son." Marlys slung her toward the barbican. "Onward, insolent puppy. We shall rout the Saladin's armies and spill the heathens' blood before this day is done."

Caught in the spirit of Marlys's playacting, Rowena marched forward, giving the sharpened wooden sticks implanted around the castle a wide berth.

The rain that had ushered Rowena to Caerleon marked the dying breath of summer. The nip of autumn sweetened the air. Leaves were beginning to crisp at the edges in flagrant hues of orange and yellow. Marlys led them to a fern-filled glade rich with the scent of damp earth and summer's decay.

Rowena gathered her kirtle between her legs and tied it around her waist. Marlys slammed the ancient helm over Rowena's head. She was lost in the salty tang of metal and old sweat. Before she could reach for the visor, a mighty buffet set her head to ringing with the hellish echo of bells. She sat down abruptly.

She jerked the helm off, her hands trembling. Marlys stood a few feet away, the lance turned across her body like a shield.

Her laugh was the low ripple of a deep flowing stream. "Did I truly look so stupid when you bested me from behind?"

Rowena rubbed her ears, glaring at Marlys through narrowed eyes. "Infinitely stupider."

Snorting with laughter, Marlys pulled on her own helm. The lance in her hands came shooting at Rowena. Rowena caught it in one fist. She banged the helm on the ground, loosening the visor before she donned it. She barely had time to raise the lance as a shield before Marlys charged her, knocking her flat. She rolled to a crouch and Marlys roared past again. The side of her lance caught the side of Marlys's, deflecting the blow. Marlys was on her again before she could drag in a heated breath.

The afternoon wore on with Rowena doing little more than dodging and falling. Triumph sang through her blood each time her lance slowed Marlys's charge for the barest instant. At Marlys's command, she jerked down the visor and peered through the narrow slits at a world divided into the dappled shadows of the forest and the dark figure of Marlys hurtling toward her. She was staggering to her feet once again, every muscle aching, when she saw Marlys freeze. The tilt of her head locked on the forest behind Rowena.

Marlys jerked off her helm. "Good day, brother dear. We thought you'd gone pillaging the peasants."

Rowena spun around and curtsied to the nearest tree.

Gareth's voice came from somewhere to the left. "I was forced to subdue my love of rapine and mayhem when I heard the clash of two mighty dragons in the forest. You've been up to mischief. I don't suppose 'tis Dunnla you've got under there?"

Gareth plucked off Rowena's helm, sending her golden hair spilling around her face. She bobbed another curtsy. "Good day, Sir Gareth. I pray we have not displeased you."

"God forbid," Marlys muttered.

Gareth tucked a strand of Rowena's hair behind her ear. His eyes sparkled beneath his dark brows. "Are you harmed?"

Rowena shook her head.

"Then you have not displeased me."

Marlys groaned into her helm.

Gareth's fingertips slid beneath the sleeve of Rowena's kirtle to probe a purpling bruise. A frown darkened his brow. He pointed a finger at Marlys. "You, on the other hand, have displeased me greatly."

Marlys sank into a mock swoon. "Pray do forgive me, milord. I tremble at the mere thought of your displeasure."

Rowena's giggle deepened into a cough as Gareth turned his frown on her. "You both ought to be sent to bed without supper for your dangerous play."

Rowena's face fell.

Marlys swaggered up to Gareth. "Don't you think I'm a bit old to be sent to bed without my broth? If you send Rowena to bed, she will at least have you to nibble on." She patted his beard with her cracked nails. "Why do you flush, brother dear? Do you resent your honeyed scabbard learning to pierce you back?"

Gareth caught her wrist in his hand. Her fingers curled into claws, then went limp. He dropped her hand.

"Damn you to hell, Gareth." Marlys's low mutter sent a shiver down Rowena's spine. "The devil take both of you." She scooped up her lance with a vicious jab at the air and loped into the forest.

Rowena shook her head. "I fear your sister bears no fondness for me."

Gareth snorted. "Marlys has never been fond of anyone but me." At Rowena's quizzical look, he added, "Is her tender regard for me not obvious?"

They both laughed. Tension seeped from Rowena's spine.

Gareth's laughter faded to a rueful smile. "Marlys loves and hates me with equal passion. On the sixth anniversary of her birth, she cut off all her hair so as to look more like me. My father took no notice. He only patted her on the head and ordered her a new kirtle. She cut it into a kite and flew it from the highest tower." He shook away the memory. "Come. I shall walk you back to Caerleon. With that helm under your arm, you might be mistaken for a robber baron and carried to the lord of the castle for justice."

Rowena started down the path, unable to hide the half-skip the autumn day put in her step. "And is the lord of the castle a merciful man?"

"On the contrary!" Gareth exclaimed. "I hear he is a dreadful wolf of a man who would as soon roast a robber baron as hang him."

"And if that robber were a baroness?"

Gareth's voice lowered to a husky growl. "Why he'd gobble her up in a single bite!"

"Why 'tis just what Marlys said—" She spun around to witness the guilty slide of Gareth's gaze from her legs to her face. She had forgotten the immodest slant of the kirtle tied between her thighs.

Her cheeks burned as her fingers stabbed at the knotted skirt in what she hoped was a subtle effort to free it.

"Be still." Gareth's hand closed over hers. She stumbled to a halt. He knelt on one knee before her, his deft fingers tugging at the knot. "We shall have you garbed as a proper lady in no time."

If his open smile was an attempt to calm her, its effect was the opposite. Her muscles contracted as his knuckles brushed her stomach, heightening the flames in her cheeks. She stared at the top of his head, counting two gray hairs amidst the shaggy black.

"How many years are you?" she asked softly.

"How many years do you think I am?" He leaned back, resting an elbow on his knee.

"I do believe you are older than Big Freddie."

Gareth's grin deepened the tiny crinkles around his eyes. "How old is Big Freddie?"

Rowena's blush disappeared in a frown of concentration. Gareth crouched patiently at her feet while she counted on her fingers. Finally she said, "Older than all of us. So how many years does that make you?"

With one finger, Gareth dislodged the knot. The skirts of the kirtle came tumbling around his hands. "Too old, I fear. Thirty-three."

Rowena flitted forward on the path. Gareth cupped his chin in his hand, watching her. Sunlight burst through the uneven branches of an ancient oak, gilding her hair into waves of coarse gold. She skipped from one side of the path to the other. Her hands darted out to caress the rough bark of a walnut tree. She crumpled a thinly veined leaf between her fingers, then spun around, smoothing her skirt in a fit of demureness.

Her question came to him on the wings of a cooling wind. "Thirty-three years, Sir Gareth. Is that dreadfully old?"

He lowered his eyes before she could read the expression within them. "Sometimes, Rowena, it feels it."

She waited for him to rise, then danced on, her exuberant flight defying the deepening shadows as determinedly as the last fall of sunlight warmed the top of Gareth's head.

In the days following the jousting lesson, neither Marlys nor Gareth sought her company. Rowena threw herself into a life of leisure. Despite boundless enthusiasm, she did not excel at it. She would start out for a gentle meander in the forest and return mud-stained but grinning. Dunnla would look the other way as she thumped a skinned hare on the hearth, grinning sheepishly. Gareth would lift an eyebrow at the freshness of the meat on days he did not hunt and murmur something about the "prevalence of poachers in his woods." Dunnla would only smile and nod, feigning blindness as well as deafness, while the serving girls exchanged knowing giggles. Rowena took to tagging after Gridmore, who was too blind or too polite to chasten her.

She knew little of noble life. Papa had squandered away her mama's fortune long before she was born. But she could sense the unnatural isolation of Caerleon. There should have been knights and squires and pages and servants enough to meet all of Gareth's needs. Instead, he dressed himself, armored himself, and made do with a few scores of servants in a castle that should have had a thousand.

As her loneliness deepened, her thoughts turned again and again to Revelwood. She sat by the fire in the solar one night, hugging her knees and thinking how Little Freddie would have enjoyed the steaming blancmange Dunnla had served for supper. A fraction of the rice and milk Gareth had left unfinished on his manchet would have filled the boy's stomach for a week. Angry tears stung her eyes. She was nothing at Caerleon but another mouth to feed. As little attention as any of its inhabitants paid her, she might run away and not be missed for days.

She lifted her chin, forgetting to dim the rebellious glitter in her eyes. Sir Gareth stood in the doorway, his long frame propped casually against the timbers. His eyes assessed her coolly, giving Rowena the maddening sensation that he could read her mind. He had just returned from his fields. His immaculate surcoat was thrown carelessly over one shoulder. He was stripped down to tunic and chausses, dusted with chaff and dripping sweat like a peasant. The happy glow of exhaustion bathed him. His eyes sparkled in the firelight. Rowena inclined her head, struggling to reconcile the vision of the knight who had threatened to slay her family with the laughing man who only last night had tossed honeyed raisins in the air for her to catch on her tongue. She supposed to him she was only a pet, and according to Marlys, not a very clever one.

She wanted to shake him, demand answers to questions she'd never dared to ask, claw away the mask that hid the man.

But the answers might be worse than the questions, and the man more dangerous than the mask. She rose and brushed past him without a word, answering his murmured good night with a stilted nod. She had promised Papa she would stay for a year, and stay she would. Gareth's dark eyes bored into her back as she climbed the winding stairs.

As fall waned, daylight grew shorter, each hour bringing Rowena nearer to nightfall when she would curl into the bed of furs on the floor at the foot of Gareth's bed. She knew now that the furs had not been careless cast-offs from Gareth's bed, but had been artfully arranged for her comfort from the first night. She waited for him to suggest she move into Marlys's chamber or sleep huddled in the great hall, but he never did. The pattern of the first night was not repeated. She was always snug and dreaming before Gareth came to bed. Some nights he did not come at all. Once an entire week went by without his presence at Caerleon or in his bedchamber.

Rowena started awake one night, her heart heavy with nameless longing. She rubbed her cheek against the soft fur, but did not find the comfort she sought.

She tossed back the furs and padded to the window. The shutter creaked open at the touch of her fingertips, and pallid moonlight streamed into the chamber. A cool breeze poured over her. She shivered, knowing the wind blowing cool at Caerleon would soon blow cruel at Revelwood. The silver glaze of the moon burnished the cobblestones to the color of Little Freddie's hair. She lay her cheek against the shutter with a sigh.

Gareth's voice came out of the dark, as warm and intimate as a touch. "Are you saddened, Rowena?"

Rowena lifted her head. "I knew not that you were here, milord."

"Why do you sigh? You are well fed and warm and no longer have to toil from dawn to dusk."

"But I have no Irwin to tell me tales and no Little Freddie to comb my hair." The words came out more bitter than she intended. Gareth would think her an ungrateful wretch, but tonight she did not care.

Gareth rose from the bed, slipping his chausses over his naked form. Rowena turned her face to the night outside the window. He reached for the comb on the table, then paused. His callused fingers crept upward. He stared at his scarred nails. They seemed suddenly broad and common, unworthy of touching the silky mass at his fingertips. But he buried his fingers in the coarse softness of her hair anyway, drawing them downward in a gentle motion.

"You've grown wan and pale in the past fortnight. Do you pine for your betrothed?" His teasing tone masked the huskiness in his voice. He reached around and touched what he knew to be a cheek newly flushed with good health. Wetness bathed the back of his fingers.

He froze. Before he could command any semblance of restraint, his arms had slipped around Rowena's waist and pulled her against him.

Rowena stood barely breathing in Gareth's embrace. The cool wind flooding the chamber fled before the warmth of his hips pressed to her back. His head bent to hers. His lips touched her throat.

"You don't have to be lonely, Rowena," he whispered. Rowena melted against him, letting his warmth envelop her in a cocoon of safety. His lips brushed her ear. She shuddered, his invitation a more compelling temptation than if he had made the choice for her.

*See how he charms.*

The words came from nowhere, an ugly whisper fraught with accusation. Rowena stared down at the arms circling her waist. The dark hair that furred them stood out stark and foreign against the whiteness of her bliaut.

A bitter knot tightened in her chest. She stiffened. She was no Lady Alise to warm a nobleman's bed for a night.

Her voice was an octave lower than normal. "And what price your company, milord?"

Gareth's arms dropped. He took a step backward and the wind blew very cold indeed.

Rowena bowed her head. "Could you not send me home?"

"I could. But I won't."

Rowena spun around. "Then send word to my papa that I am well. Not starved or"—she briefly dropped her gaze—"sorely abused. You have it within your power to ease my family's torment. Surely you could grant me such a small boon."

Gareth turned away from her, able to face anything but her pleas. 'Twould be far easier to deny her if she stamped her foot with petulant demand like the pampered bratling he had hoped to find. Little did she know his whole life these long weeks had been consumed with sending word to her father. Through malicious gossip spread among the villeins, an offhand remark to a neighboring lord, a casual leer in the village. Word of Rowena's captivity and brutality at his hands was spreading like wildfire through all of England. He was likely to bring down the wrath of King Edward himself before Lindsey Fordyce mustered enough courage to confront him. A part of him blanched before the stories he had spread, but another part of him recognized them for what they were—the product of his own dark fantasies.

Rowena touched his bare arm. "I beg you, milord . . ."

He recoiled as if she had wounded him. His fist came down on the table, shattering the shell comb. "Nay! If your father wants word of you, then let him come to me."

Words of anger died in Rowena's throat when she saw the fire that smoldered in Gareth's dark eyes, not yet banked. She could not hold his gaze, and her lashes swept down to veil her eyes. The door slammed with a mighty crash, and she was alone.

Gareth's shin slammed into an immovable wooden object. He bit off a curse that reverberated from the rafters.

"My, my," came Marlys's voice, low and taunting in the darkness. "Such curses in the presence of a lady."

Gareth's eyes adjusted to the dim light of a dying fire. Marlys had draped her stomach across a wooden lounge next to the door. Her feet swayed in childish rhythm.

"Show me a lady and I will beg forgiveness," he snarled, jerking on his gauntlets as he walked.

Since the door was the obvious goal of his ragged path, Marlys jumped up and sat down, pressing her shoulders to it. "Does your whore displease you so?"

Gareth halted before her. His brows drew together in a glare that would have sent most men cowering in fear. "Stand aside."

Marlys studied her ragged fingernails. "I think she does not displease you at all. But she does not please you, either."

Gareth caught Marlys's tunic in his hand. He lifted her until her nose touched his. "You may not know as much as you think you do, little sister." He dropped her as if she were a sack of apples and flung open the door.

"I know if that sweet morsel in your chamber was warming your bed, you would not be storming out of Caerleon at midnight."

Gareth stopped.

Marlys's tone lost its mocking edge, leaving it flat in the echoes of the hall. "Why, Gareth? She is only a pawn in your game. Surely her papa has had word of the golden-haired angel imprisoned in your bedchamber. Even the peasants whisper of it. Is that not what you wanted? Why not finish it and send her home?"

Gareth turned on his heel, his eyes darker than the midnight sky. "If I send her home raped and with child, what have I gained?"

"Revenge."

"Revenge on whom? Her? Me? Nay, Marlys. I want the truth more than I want revenge. And I am willing to wait for it."

Marlys reached for his hand, but he was gone, his shoulders hunched against the bitter wind.

Rosy dawn crept through the shutters. Rowena flung herself over and tossed away the furs. She lay still for a moment, feeling hot and vexed, then jerked the furs back up until only her nose protruded. She rolled to her side with a disgusted grunt and glared at the dust balls under Gareth's bed. She threw herself over again, slamming her eyes shut as the door to the chamber glided open.

Gareth's steps were heavy and stumbling. Rowena heard the solid thwack of a foot striking wood, followed by a slurred curse. Silence followed. She did not dare open her eyes. The smell of him wafted down to her—sweat and ale and the ridiculous scent of lilacs overlayed by an earthy tang she did not recognize. His footsteps moved away.

He fell to the bed without bothering to disrobe. Only when his even breathing filled the chamber did Rowena open her burning eyes. She dressed in silence and slipped out of the chamber.

Marlys was leaning against the post at the bottom of the stairs. Dark eyes gleamed from somewhere beneath her mop of hair. Without a word, she scooped up a helm and lance and tossed them to Rowena. Rowena caught them. They started into the chill dawn, pausing in the list to divide the steaming barley bread Marlys had stuffed in her pockets.

# Chapter 6

Marlys charged through the open door of Gareth's chamber. Her roar nearly sent Rowena tumbling out of her chair.

"He comes! He comes at last! I saw his flags from the north tower. May I ambush him? Please, say I can. Gareth, I beg you. Do let me give his pride a damnable whack!"

To demonstrate the whack she would give, Marlys slammed her mace on the table. The parchment Rowena had been studying split and rolled into two halves. Rowena reached for the torn parchment, only to have the precious paper flutter into the air and out the window on the chill draft Gareth invited when he pushed open the shutters.

Gareth swore under his breath.

Marlys joined him at the window. "By God, there he comes! Do let me ambush him. I know just the tree."

"He left us in peace longer than I thought he would," Gareth said. "The torture of his curiosity must have bested him."

Rowena stood on tiptoe behind them but could see

nothing but the broad expanse of their shoulders. She elbowed her way under Marlys's arm only to have her cheek smashed against the shutter when Marlys turned.

"Why, look at his retinue! He must have brought half of England with him."

Gareth sighed. "The scoundrel is determined to see us civilized. He has never forgiven me for dismissing Father's knights. He makes no secret of his contempt for our country life."

Rowena dropped to her knees. Gareth glanced down at her with a lift of one eyebrow as she wiggled between his legs and knelt at his feet. She absently leaned her cheek against his hand, all of her attention captured by the spectacle rolling over the hills toward Caerleon.

The festive party flowed away from Ardendonne, dotting the barren landscape with splashes of purple and crimson. Chariots and hand-carried litters brightened the gray day with their gaiety. Prancing horses followed, decked in hangings of yellow and emerald satin tasseled in gold. Rowena breathed a sigh of awe, hearing in her mind the steady flapping of the pennons affixed to the litters, the snort of the magnificent steeds blowing clouds of fog into the chill air, the heady laughter of the ladies being coiffed in the litters.

"One good thump," Marlys pleaded. " 'Tis all I want to give him."

"Nay," Gareth replied.

"I shall free him after one whimper. I swear it."

"Nay," Gareth repeated.

Marlys's lip protruded through a tangle of hair.

Gareth wagged a finger at her. "I forbid it. Blaine hasn't the fondness for you that I have. He would welcome any excuse to poke his lance through your black little heart."

Marlys sniffed. "Blaine has been striving to poke his lance in me in one fashion or another ever since I disdained his suit."

"He might have forgiven you for disdaining his suit. 'Twas knocking him off his horse in front of his father that gained his disfavor. Sir Bryan had finally knighted him. He was a proud lad."

"A foolish lad to lay his lips on me."

Rowena shivered in excitement. Gareth glanced down at the golden head resting on his hand. Her eyes were misty, her lips parted in dreamy perusal of the color-splashed meadows. Gareth's hand tightened on the windowsill as he wondered what effect it would have on him if she ever looked at him that way.

Rowena felt the almost imperceptible movement. The wiry coil of hairs on the back of Gareth's hand pricked her smooth cheek. She shifted, suddenly conscious of the gentle pressure of his thighs against her shoulders. She lifted her gaze past the clinging folds of his hose, past the silver threads embroidered in the hem of his tunic, to meet his dark eyes. In the guise of a casual gesture, his fingertips stroked her cheek. A shiver that had nothing to do with Blaine's retinue lifted the tiny hairs on the back of her neck. Confusion flooded her in a wave of heat.

Marlys smirked as she watched the exchange. Gareth stiffened and gave Rowena's cheek a fatherly pat. "I'm off to the village for more servants. If we are to sup tonight, we will sup in style or not at all. If I know Blaine, he hopes to be trapped by the winter snows and forced to spend the winter feasting on our beef and ale."

"And our maidservants," Marlys added as Gareth left them. Her speculative gaze dropped to Rowena's head.

Moments later, Rowena cupped her chin in her hands, the resplendence of Blaine's procession forgotten as Gareth mounted Folio in the list below. Folio pranced as Gareth gave their window a jaunty salute before squaring his shoulders and sending the horse cantering through the castle gate.

"You don't hate him nearly as much as you'd like to, do you?"

At Marlys's gentle question, Rowena swung around. Marlys swiped a strand of hair out of her mouth. A smile of terrifying sweetness appeared. She extended a grimy palm to Rowena.

"Come, Lady Precious. If I am to be denied my ambush, I've time to find you some garments for the feast. If you go down wearing that silly rag, you'll quite fade in the presence of so many ladies. 'Twould not be your desire, would it?"

Rowena reluctantly took the hand Marlys proffered, half preferring a cuffing to this unexpected kindness.

The door creaked open on iron hinges. Rowena clutched Marlys's hand and peered around the taller girl's shoulder. Marlys moved forward into the shadows of the chamber, her normally exuberant footsteps muffled.

The chamber was not in total darkness. The afternoon sun touched the sheets of velvet spiked over the windows, casting a pall of blue gloom over the shrouded furniture. A delicate mingling of rosemary and mildew wafted to Rowena's nose, making it itch. Marlys's hand slipped from hers. Rowena pinched back a sneeze.

"Everything's the same," Marlys whispered.

Cobwebs draped the candle sconces in elaborate falls of gray and white. A canopied bed frame even larger than Gareth's sat in the center of the chamber, covered by a single linen sheet. Rowena half-expected the shapeless mound beneath to rise and float toward them.

Marlys shook her head as if to clear it and crossed to an oaken cupboard in the corner. "I daresay we'll find a kirtle for you here."

Her matter-of-fact words were both comforting and irreverent. Rowena started as the door of the cupboard crashed into the wall. While Marlys dug through the cupboard, Rowena sidled toward the bed. She reached out a tentative finger and poked at the lump in its center. The straw tick erupted in a frenzy of squeaking and skittering, and she snatched her hand back.

"Mice," Marlys pronounced without turning around. "There would be, you know. The cats don't come here. Keep an eye out for rats, won't you?"

Rowena peered around, unnerved by the sheer size of the chamber. She sat down on the corner of the bed frame. Her toe explored the dark stain spilling over the stone floor beside the bed.

From beneath the bed came the faint skitter of claws on stone. Rowena jerked her feet up. Marlys paid her no heed; she had crawled into the cupboard. Only the soles of her boots were visible. Her voice was muffled. "Used to hide in here when I was little. Goes clear through the wall. Big enough for a family of ten."

Rowena leaned over the side of the bed and gingerly lifted the sheet. In the eerie light, she could barely make out the faint outlines of a cradle. She ran her hand along the beautifully carved surface. Her finger came back furred with dust.

She dropped the sheet guiltily as Marlys rose from the chest with a hiss of satisfaction, unfurling a mound of peacock blue trimmed in ermine. In the eerie blue light, the crushed velvet seemed to hover above the floor with a life of its own.

Marlys lifted one trailing belled sleeve of the matching undertunic. "What do you think? Perfect for you, is it not? Blue to match your eyes."

The rich blue was not near to the color of Rowena's eyes, but she did not say so. " 'Tis a lovely kirtle. But I dare not wear another's garments without their leave."

Marlys snorted. "The lady who would mind is long gone. My stepmother has been dead for nigh on twenty years. You have *my* leave. 'Tis all you need."

She piled the dress in Rowena's arms, then dove back into the cupboard to pull out a wimple and girdle. Marlys muttered to herself, "Stand up straight, Marlys. Comb your hair, Marlys. Don't slouch like an ape, Marlys. Silly bitch thought she'd make a lady of me."

"Silly, indeed," Rowena said softly. A veil came sailing over to land on her head. Rowena swept the gauzy softness from her eyes. "Was she pretty?"

Marlys threw back her head in a bay of assent.

"God, she was beautiful! With raven black curls that tumbled to her waist and flashing blue eyes."

Rowena touched the cradle with her toe. "Did she and your papa have a babe?"

"She brought her bratling with her when she came. Never had time for it though. Kept it swaddled all the time. I used to hide in the cupboard and sneak out to untie the fat little thing when she left it unattended. Used to drive her batty. She never could figure out how the creature wiggled its way out. She was blessed with beauty but no brains." Marlys slapped a comb in her hands. "Much like yourself."

Marlys crossed the chamber, her strides quick and sure. She swept back the linen covering a table, carelessly knocking a pine box to the floor. Rowena bent to retrieve it. Her finger traced the sloping wing of a bird carved into the pale wood, and she started to open it.

Marlys snatched the box from her hand. "Gareth spent days carving this for her when Father sent word he was bringing home a new mother for us."

"How did she die?"

Marlys lifted her gaze from the box. Her lips quirked in a strange smile. "She had a bad heart."

Rowena flinched as Marlys flung the box behind her. "Don't stand there gaping at me, Ro. We've work to do."

Rowena gave a secret smile, thinking how pleasant it was to be called Ro instead of Puppy and wondering what Marlys hoped to gain with her kindness.

Sir Blaine of Ardendonne conquered Caerleon without drawing a single sword. By nightfall, the castle was ablaze with light and laughter. Music rang from the rafters. The swallows darted into the night, seeking any surcease from the raucous merriment. Burly villeins with sleeves pushed up over hairy forearms dragged the furniture along the wall to make room for dancing. Dunnla shuffled in and out from the kitchens, bellowing commands that sent more than one lady into a genteel faint. Gridmore followed her commands by putting plates of cold partridge on the hearth and loads of firewood in ladies' laps. Blaine supervised the chaos with hands on hips and a proprietary smile. He single-handedly rescued a squealing midget from the oven where Gridmore had tossed him after mistaking him for the roast boar.

In a deserted chamber at the top of the keep, Rowena heard the faint piping of bells and a heated squealing as if a herd of pigs had laid siege to the feast below. She stared into a mirror of hammered silver. A stranger blinked back at her. Her chest rose and fell in shallow rhythm. She touched her cheek with two fingers. Her skin was as cold and foreign as the polished surface of the mirror.

Two brilliant slashes of crimson stained her cheeks, matching the lavish red of her lips. A thick line of kohl rimmed her eyes. With each blink, her eyelids clung, and she feared they would be stuck forever closed. Darkened with ashes and stiffened with oil, her lashes swept upward like rebellious spiders to meet the darkened arch of her brow. A golden crespine net confined her hair. A blue wimple flowed from it, hiding her sturdy neck in folds of plush velvet.

*Count to one hundred. Then come down and join the feast.*

Rowena began counting aloud as Marlys's words returned to her. She got as far as eight before forgetting the next number Marlys had taught her and being forced to start again. Her hands fumbled nervously with the exotic jars of ashes and berries spilling from the teak box to the table. "Fourteen," she mumbled. "Sixteen, forty-four, sixty-eight, twelve, one hundred."

She leaped out of the chair, tripping over the sleeves of the undertunic. By holding her arms at stiff angles in front of her, she maneuvered the door open. The golden girdle resting on her hips caught on the iron handle as she tried to slip through. She tugged herself free with a curse learned from Gareth and perfected by Marlys. If things proceeded in this alarming manner, Gareth would not fail to notice her. She would be the only lady in the hall laying flat on her face.

A sweet tenor drifted to Rowena's ears, followed by a nasal bray of laughter. Her steps slowed as she entered the open gallery leading to the stairs. Entranced by the flood of colors and lights sweeping through the hall below, she sank to her knees, clutching the balusters in her sweaty palms.

The candles had been replaced by a blaze of torches. A fire roared along the length of the wide fireplace, banishing the drafts to the deserted corners. A line of ladies clasped hands and wound among the men, leading their perfumed sleeves and wimples in a seductive dance of shimmering silk. Gareth was nowhere in sight.

A handful of dice clattered on the stones in the center of a kneeling circle of squires. Their hearty shouts rose above the din. Rowena was not surprised to find Marlys among them, her only concession to the celebration a shiny black pair of gauntlets newly pilfered from Gareth's chamber. Her rusty scabbard clanked on the hearth as she swaggered to the other side of the group.

Her dark eyes lifted to the gallery. Rowena ducked behind a wooden column.

"You do seem to turn up in the most remarkable places."

Rowena looked up as the smooth voice poured over her.

Sir Blaine leaned against the opposite wall, arms crossed. The corner of his mouth curved in a smile. "Sleeping in my hall. Crouching behind pillars. You are a lady of mysterious pursuits. I've been asking Gareth where you were all evening. He simply replied, 'About' in the most infuriating manner. His habit of babbling all the time is one of his more endearing traits." He extended his hand to Rowena.

She took it, her eyes narrowed. He gently pulled her to her feet. "Ah, you have not forgotten me, either." This with a sheepish grin that must have gotten him far with his nurses. "I swear to you I have no intention of ravishing you here in the gallery. I mistook you for a different sort of lady at Ardendonne. There now. Do stop yelling at me. I can see you've acquired Gareth's loquaciousness in your stay at Caerleon."

Rowena opened her mouth and closed it. She had not said one word.

"That will be quite enough," he went on. "I will not tolerate that sort of talk from such a charming damsel. You should be ashamed."

Rowena found her tongue. " 'Tis you, sir, who should be ashamed. Regardless of the sort of lady you mistook me for, you had no right to force your attentions on me. Knights are supposed to stand for something noble and good. Would you not give even a lady of low birth a choice? Have you no respect for chivalry?"

Blaine applauded. "How your eyes sparkle when you chasten! More, more! Don't stop now."

"I should think—" Rowena paused, realizing she had been baited into berating him. Her glower collapsed into a reluctant smile at the mischievous sparkle in his brown eyes.

"You see, my fair lady, I was not only besotted with your beauty on that night, I was besotted with ale. I awoke the next morn with pounding head, aching chin, and cringing with mortification at my ill-mannered treatment of you. I humbly beg for the boon of your forgiveness."

Before she could answer, he had taken her arm and led her to the rail of the gallery.

Directly below them, the minstrel Mortimer bent over his lute, his mop of blond hair hiding his face. A lady clad in scarlet from wimple to slippers plopped down on his lap. He pushed her away with a sour note from his strings. A laughing squire took her place and Mortimer's music took wing. The hall rocked with laughter.

"Gareth has always told me Caerleon was my home as well as his," Blaine said.

"You take his words to heart, do you not?"

"Not as I take yours to heart. What does the merriment put you in mind of, dear lady?"

Rowena rested her chin in her hand to relieve the weight of the wimple. "An undignified siege."

"A charming thought! A siege not of blood and battle, but of music and laughter, wit and pleasure. Does it not make your blood sing?"

Rowena shrugged, ignoring the husky note which edged his voice. He rested his elbows on the rail, leaning nearer as if they had been friends for years.

"What would you do if it were a real siege disguised beneath the cloak of hospitality? Mayhaps I've only hastened abovestairs to carry away the lady of the castle while the master is distracted."

"Marlys is the lady of Caerleon."

Blaine's smile tightened. "Marlys is no lady."

Rowena edged away from him. Her gaze darted over the hall. "Where might the master be?"

"Probably in the bailey discussing some of the duller aspects of knighthood like tournaments and horses."

"Those are not the aspects you prefer?"

"I prefer ladies to mares, if that is your meaning."

"Ladies who throw themselves at your feet, no doubt, to beg for your attentions."

"I prefer ladies who throw themselves at my chin. And quite effectively, I might add." He rubbed his smooth chin as if the memory still stung.

Rowena bit back a smile. His winsome grin was hard to resist. "I shan't beg forgiveness if that is what you await."

"I would wait an eternity for one plea from you."

He would have to wait, for at that moment Gareth entered the hall from the bailey. He came not with the laughing group of knights Rowena had expected, but alone. He stood head and shoulders over most of the men in the hall. His demeanor was not that of the jovial host but of a stranger, his stiffened shoulders defensive to the point of arrogance. Was it Rowena's imagination or did the laughter grow shriller and the silences more pointed? The strumming of Mortimer's fingers against the lutestrings took on new violence, as if to fill the void with music. Gareth took the goblet offered from a lady's hand and raised it in a mocking toast to the minstrel.

After he drank, Gareth lifted the lady's hand to his lips. She curtsied as he kissed her palm. Pale blond strands of hair escaped her silver wimple and Rowena recognized Lady Alise.

Gareth's dark head blurred before her eyes. A knot of unfamiliar hunger tightened her belly. This hunger was subtle and piercing, twisting like a thousand tiny daggers in her gut. Blaine watched her face, his caramel-colored eyes dispassionate.

Gareth lifted his head and glanced up at the gallery. Rowena threw herself behind the column, pushing her back to it as if she might sink into the wood and disappear. She squeezed her eyes shut, thinking she must be mad. How could she have let Marlys dress her like some mummer's dummy to gain Gareth's attention? Gareth's attention was the last thing she needed.

She gathered her skirts to flee, but before she could, Blaine's hand caught her wrist. "Shall we dance, milady squire?" He lifted one eyebrow in a challenge, his lips warm against the racing pulse in her wrist.

Rowena snatched her hand back, and for a gratifying instant thought Blaine was going to duck. Instead, he turned his dip into a mocking bow, the sweep of his hand motioning her toward the stairs.

The ballad swept Mortimer's voice high enough to escape its nasal tones. A lady in the corner wept prettily at the bittersweet tale of a peasant girl taken and forsaken by a philandering knight. The roast mutton and boar spread on the table against the wall were increasingly ignored for the casks of warm ale tapped on the hearth. A pall of fashionable sadness held the crowd rapt as Mortimer's voice soared in a triumph that would be lost to stupor by morning.

Gareth gently dried Alise's tears with the hem of her train. As the last notes echoed through the sniffs and applause, Rowena glided down the stairs, her sleeves flowing behind her like a separate entity. Blaine held her arm with a carefully crafted expression of delight and guilt.

A curious murmur filled the silence. Marlys took two steps toward them, then stopped, her long arms hanging loosely at her sides. At the foot of the steps, Blaine faced Rowena with a sweeping bow. She sank to a curtsy at his feet.

When Gareth drew away from Alise, the sight that greeted him was a regal figure kneeling in a billowing cloud of velvet at Blaine's feet. The peacock blue of her dress stained his vision. His goblet clanked to the stones, spattering burgundy wine over the lavender train of Alise's gown. He rose as if drugged, not realizing every eye in the hall was locked on him.

His hand closed on Rowena's ermine-trimmed sleeve, finding the arm within. His fingers dug like steel into her warm flesh. Gentle blue eyes smothered in a sultry outline of kohl blinked up at him.

"What in the name of God are you doing?" he demanded, his voice harsh in the sudden silence.

Caught in his grasp, Rowena bit her lower lip to control its trembling. "Milord, I came to the feast. You did not forbid me to attend."

He shook her. "Where did you find these things?"

"I—we—" Rowena's gaze found Marlys against the wall. She was staring at her boots. The bile of betrayal rose in Rowena's throat. She stared into Gareth's eyes, choosing silence as her only plea.

Gareth released her arm. Blaine's hand supported her back as her knees betrayed her.

Gareth's face was suffused with red. "You look ridiculous." He snatched the wimple and coif from her head and hurled it to the floor.

Rowena paled as if he had struck her. Her hair fell to her shoulders, lank and dull from the weight of the wimple. She looked around her, taking in at a glance the ashen brows and unadorned eyes of the ladies. The back of her hand lifted to her cheek. Crimson smudged her knuckles like a bruise of blood. Into the silence fell a nervous titter of laughter. Then another.

With spine straight, Rowena lowered her eyes and curtsied to Gareth. "Forgive me, milord. I have lived too long outside the realm of current fashion. I will not trouble you again."

Her skirts felt trimmed in lead as she gathered them in her hands. The crowd parted to let her through, their snickers dying, leaving Gareth to face Blaine's smirk. Blaine took a goblet from a servant's tray and pressed it into Gareth's hand.

"Drink, my friend. 'Tis your feast, after all."

The heat of the goblet warmed Gareth's hand. He swirled the amber liquid around the rim before draining it and reaching for another.

# Chapter 7

Rowena broke into a run, ignoring the curious glances of the stragglers in the bailey. As she fled across the drawbridge, Mortimer's lutestrings leaped into song, pounding out a rhythm for her flight to follow. Bursts of laughter chased her through the courtyard. Tears streaked her cheeks, staining the pristine blue of the dress with crimson rivulets. Her train caught on a stray stake, and she ripped it loose, taking perverse satisfaction in the shredding of the costly velvet.

"Rowena!" came a cry, hoarse and breathless behind her.

She paused at the outer wall, impaled by a slanting beam of moonlight. The cry came again, nearer this time. She flung herself forward, her feet caught in a lilting cadence that propelled her without a beat of hesitation through the blocks of shadow cast by the towers. She passed into the list. Three more strides, and the forest would be hers.

"Rowena!"

The note of unfamiliar pleading weighted her feet. She stumbled to a halt, resting her hands on her knees.

Moonlight bathed the deserted list. Footsteps crunched on the dead grass, the only sound except for the muted nickering of the horses in the nearby stable. Marlys stood just inside the gate. Her eyes were veiled by a web of hair as she took a step toward Rowena. Rowena inched toward the darkness of the forest as smoothly as a doe poised for flight.

Marlys raised one hand. "Please. Don't. I never intended—"

Rowena's voice cut like flint. "What did you intend?"

Marlys shook her head. "I don't know. Not that." She sank down on the chest against the wall, dragging a hand through her hair. " 'Twas a harmless bit of mischief—a prank."

"Your brother did not find your humor to his liking."

"Gareth has found little humor to his liking for a very long time." Marlys absently rolled her feet over the lances piled in the grass below the chest.

"Why did he look at me that way? Did he bear your stepmother no fondness?"

Marlys threw back her shaggy head to the moon with a harsh laugh. "He bore her all fondness."

Rowena crept nearer. "Then it pained him to be reminded of her?"

"When Gareth was twelve, my father brought our new mother to Caerleon. She was younger than Father—always laughing and gay. Like a vivacious angel sent to sweeten our lives."

Marlys gave the lances a vicious kick, scattering them in the grass. Rowena was too lost in Marlys's story to heed the painful thud of a lance against her ankle.

Marlys's voice lowered. "Her sweetness held only poison. Gareth was barely out of the first flush of boyhood, yet she was captivated by his smooth skin, his innocence. When my father was called away to help King Edward fight the Welsh, she begged him not to send Gareth to Blaine's father for fostering as was the custom. Instead, she had Blaine sent here. She undertook their training as pages herself." Marlys met Rowena's gaze with uncompromising candor. "She taught Blaine courtesy. She taught Gareth everything else."

Rowena held out a hand to stop the torrent of words that threatened to come spilling from Marlys's lips, but it was too late.

"So at the tender age of fourteen, my brother suffered the guilt of loving his father's wife. When Blaine's father brought word of my father's death from a poisoned arrow wound, Gareth went to her to tell her he had begged the priest for forgiveness for both of their souls. He found her in her bower in the embrace of one of my father's knights. My father still lay on a muddy Welsh battlefield, his flesh not yet cold." Marlys jerked up one of the lances and paced the list like a caged wolf.

Rowena sank down in the grass, fingering the comforting contours of the lance beside her. "What did Gareth do?" she asked softly.

Marlys spun around. The gleam of one eye shone eerily triumphant through a mat of hair. "There's the question. You see—no one knows. They found her the next morn with Gareth's sword through her heart. Elayne's fingers still lay in the pool of blood she had drawn from to trace Gareth's name on the bedclothes beside her."

The broken words of a haunting melody tore through Rowena's brain:

> *The fair Elayne*
> *Unfairly slain*
> *Her faithless hand*
> *Stilled by a name.*

*Elayne.* Rowena rested her forehead on her palm. Her brow felt cool and clammy. Her fingers plucked fretfully at the velvet skirt as she raised her head.

"You put me in her garments," she said calmly.

Marlys stood in a shaft of moonlight, leaning on the lance like a staff. "I did not intend—"

"You put me in her garments," Rowena repeated, louder this time. She stood in one fluid motion, the lance finding a place in her sweating palm.

"Ro, I would not have—"

"You made him look at me and see her. How he must hate me . . ."

The pain of Gareth's censure amazed her. Fury swept the dazed curtain from her eyes. Marlys barely had time to bring the lance across her body as a shield before Rowena charged her. The solid thwack of wood meeting wood echoed through the deserted list. Marlys stumbled backward, keeping her footing by the barest of chance. Rowena did not pause to question the source of this terrible anguish. With a roar of rage more animal than human, she lunged forward, hurtling all of her weight into the charge. Marlys's lance splintered beneath hers with a deafening crack. Marlys fell backward, her body trapped beneath Rowena's weight, her breath paralyzed by the pressure of the lance laid across her windpipe. The fall had flung back Marlys's hair, baring her face to the merciless moonlight.

Rowena had never stopped wondering why Marlys took such care to keep her face veiled. Her imagination had provided scores of romantic stories involving terrible burns or disfiguring scars. The truth was far worse.

Marlys was beautiful.

The rugged imperfections of Gareth's features had been smoothed and refined in his sister. Square of jaw and high of cheekbone, Marlys glared at Rowena, her dark eyes sparkling like chips of obsidian in the moonlight. Her full lips tightened to a proud line. The tangled fall of hair hid a woman that made the Lady Alise appear an insipid imitation of what God intended a woman to be. Rowena's eyes shifted to bewildered blue as the lance went limp in her hands.

"Why?" She whispered, unsure herself of the question she asked.

Marlys gave her a shove; and Rowena rolled to the side without protest. Marlys sat up, scooting around so

her back was to Rowena. Once again her hair hung in a
lank curtain over her face. By the time she could speak
without her voice cracking, Rowena was gone.

Rowena tore off the dead woman's kirtle as she ran,
shedding layer after layer of velvet sodden with the
stain of Marlys's betrayal. She clawed at the embroidered bodice until it ripped beneath her nails. A bush
shuddered beneath the weight of the camlet under-
gown. She flung aside the golden girdle as heedlessly as
the silken kerchief. Stripped to her thin linen chemise,
she flew through the forest, dodging the tree trunks
with a flawless grace born from the wings of freedom.
She was free. Free as she had been before Gareth had
come to Revelwood. Nothing could stop her now. Not
Gareth, and not even Papa. No threats. No promises.

Ignoring the twigs slapping her face, she fled deeper
into the forest, leaving behind the dying leaves for a
stand of pine. Cone-laden boughs admitted the moonlight in dappled patches. She stopped, feeling the chill
of the November air against her heated skin for the first
time. Gooseflesh prickled her arms at the eerie creak of
branch against branch. Caught in the whisper of the
wind, the thin trunks swayed to and fro in the ghostly
moonlight.

She jerked off the satin slippers and sprang forward.
Her bare feet crunched on the prickly needles. Only
when she came to the edge of the copse did she stop, her
arm flung around the rough bark of a pine. A rumble
deeper than the wind warned her. Rushing out of the
ground and into a pool silvered with moonlight flowed
a fresh spring.

Without hesitation, Rowena plunged down the hill
and into the chill water. She dove deep, then broke
through the surface, sending water shooting from her
hair in a sparkling spray, baptizing herself free of the
dark stain of Caerleon.

Marlys watched Gareth approach through a veil of hair
that colored the world dark. He sauntered through the

list, his grace so deliberate that she knew he had been drinking. She leaned back on one elbow and tucked a hollow tube of grass between her teeth. She blew softly. A haunting whistle drifted into the night. Gareth stopped in front of her, legs planted firmly apart.

"Have you seen her?" he asked. His diction was flawless.

Marlys blew a short blast on the reed. "She's gone off."

"Gone off to sulk?"

Marlys spit the grass at his feet. "She's not given to sulks, in case you haven't noticed."

"Then where is she? She is not in the kitchens. She is not in my chambers."

"You've hardly given her a reason to stay there, have you?"

Gareth stared blankly at Marlys. "Do you know where she is?"

"I told you. She's gone off."

Gareth squatted beside her. He crooked his thumb in her hair and gently lifted it from her face. For the second time that night, searing moonlight bathed the slanted planes of her cheeks.

"Gone off where?" he said softly.

Their dark eyes met. With a short jerk of her head, Marlys indicated the forest. "She's gone off for good. Why don't you leave her be? Can't you get it through your thick skull that her papa's not coming? Or do you even care anymore?"

Frowning, Gareth stood, leaving Marlys in darkness once more. "She is a stranger to the forest. She could be lost. She could be attacked by wolves or bears."

"And eaten?" Marlys volunteered, her smile a grimace.

Gareth's frown deepened. He spun on his heel and strode toward the stables. Sobered by purpose, he tightened his gauntlets with efficient jerks.

As she watched him, Marlys rested her cheek on her knee. Her eyes narrowed as Blaine slipped out of the shadows and caught Gareth's arm.

"Gareth, I heard. Give me leave and I will summon the knights and organize a search."

Gareth jerked his arm free. "Rowena is already helpless prey for one sort of boar. I'd rather not expose her to your kind as well."

He disappeared into the stables and reappeared leading Folio. As Gareth mounted, Blaine had to dance sideways to avoid the horse's flailing hooves.

"Gareth, you've made it clear you bear the girl no fondness. You won her in a wager. Let us wager together. Give me a chance at her."

Gareth wrapped the reins around his hands, bringing the prancing horse under his control. The corner of his mouth lifted in a cold smile. "What sort of contest would you prefer? Hazard? Chess? Tilting?"

Blaine took a step backward and raised his hands in surrender. Gareth pushed Folio past him. The thunder of hoofbeats rolled through the long courtyard, fading into the night.

Blaine glanced back at the list. Moonlight spilled over the empty grass where Marlys had been. A pebble rolled against stone on the wall above. As he glanced up, a helmed figure grasping a splintered lance came sailing over the roof of the stable. It crashed into his shoulder, screeching victoriously.

The castle with its lights and laughter seemed a world away as Gareth picked his way through the primeval hush of the forest. Night sounds came to him in crackling spurts: the flutter of unseen wings against a branch above; the indignant croak of a frog; the whisper of a leaf surrendering its embrace of a twig and drifting down to brush Gareth's cheek in the darkness. In places where the leaves still clung in dying bunches to hide the moonlight, he guided the horse forward more on instinct than sight, his eyes blank and shining like the eyes of a blind man free of the encumbrance of sunlight.

He was deep into the forest when he stopped and called her name. His voice rolled back to him on a hollow echo, jarring him with its hoarseness. Between his knees, Folio's sleek flesh quivered. The lonely cry of a nightjar spilled into the silence. He urged the horse forward through a tangle of vines. Folio balked and tossed his head as nettles pricked his fetlocks.

Gareth dismounted. Unsheathing his sword, he cut at the web of underbrush, clearing a path for Folio to follow. The horse nickered softly, blowing a musty breath against the back of his neck. He paused as his fingers closed around a scrap of velvet dangling from a low-hanging branch. He stared at it for a long moment, then touched it to his cheek, rubbing its softness against his beard. He lifted his eyes to the light that came streaming through the bushes ahead, then parted the branches. Moonlight bleached the pine needles in a wash of silver.

Sword hanging forgotten in his hand, he moved toward that alluring absence of color with a sleep-walker's gait. The shadows fell away as the crisp scent of evergreen filled his nostrils.

At the bottom of a treeless hill, a figure in white lay sprawled beside a spring. At first Gareth thought she was dead. Her limbs were so pale, her chest so still. But as his heavy steps drew him closer, he could see life coursing through her, coloring her cheeks with its rosy hues, parting her lips with its nourishing breath. She lay on her back, her legs parted in unconscious innocence.

The chemise, so shapeless when dry, clung to her damp skin. Gareth's gaze raked her, searching the teasing demarcations of shadow and light beneath the linen. His groin tightened and he swore softly, his oath more endearment than curse.

She must be cold. To lay so exposed to the cooling winds and not shiver seemed unnatural. Then Gareth remembered the grim keep of Revelwood and the winters she must have endured. The autumn wind must be no more than a passing breeze to her.

He was not cold. On the contrary, his skin prickled with heat as if he had taken a sudden fit of ague. He opened his mouth to awaken her, then closed it. He half turned away. Folio watched him curiously from the top of the hill.

She nestled her cheek into the damp tendrils of hair that pillowed her head. The sight made Gareth bite back a groan. She belonged to him. A wager was a debt paid in honor. She was his for a year. He could work her in his fields or his kitchens or his bedchamber if he so desired. No man could condemn him as a scoundrel for his actions. No man could stop him from kneeling at this moment between her parted thighs and making her his own. Rowena stirred. A wince furrowed her smooth brow.

He stood over her, barely breathing. A part of him still wanted to hate her, had longed to find her cosseted by an adoring father, bred for charm and deceit as Elayne had been. 'Twould have made it far easier to break her then, to punish Fordyce by sending her back, ravished and shamed, her pride torn, her conceit in shreds. But there was nothing of Elayne in this girl. Bred in the poverty Fordyce had sunk to since the night he'd fled Gareth's sword, she had a spirit devoid of conceit, as bright and shining as the sun. What right did he have to stain her with his darkness?

His possession of her did not have to be cruel. He could make her life pleasant enough in the year she spent at Caerleon. He could give her comforts and luxuries she had only dreamed of at Revelwood. And at the end of the year, he could find her a worthy husband or send her on her way with a weighty sum of gold and a future free of poverty and hunger.

*A future with men like Blaine waiting to snatch up your scraps.*

The voice in his head was Marlys's and he hated it. With a curse, he drove his sword into the damp earth. He unbuckled his scabbard with shaking hands. Rowena moaned softly as his shadow fell over her.

*The sun beat down like a hammer. A warm wind rippled the tall grasses into a swaying symphony of green and gold. A dot on the horizon grew larger as it hurtled toward her. Rowena's heart swelled with joy. The sun glinted silver on Little Freddie's hair as his childish sprint drove him toward her waiting arms. Her heart thudded in her ears. She lifted her knees higher, exalting in the clean, sweet beat of the run.*

*But her steps faltered as a dark shadow loomed behind her brother, closing the distance with the inevitability of a hawk swooping down on a mouse. Rowena screamed a warning, but Little Freddie continued toward her, oblivious to the menace sweeping down on him.*

*A knight armored all in black pounded across the moor, the silky white mane of his mount rippling in the wind. A gridded helm hid his face. The knight bore down on her brother, his outstretched lance aimed straight for the small of Little Freddie's back. The thunder of hoofbeats drowned out Rowena's scream, and she fell to her knees, clapping her hands over her ears. When she opened her eyes, the moor was empty and silent, except for the lonely whistle of the wind.*

*She was crouched in a sea of peacock blue, her hands spread in a plea in front of her. Gareth stood over her, his blade lifted. Tears trickled down her cheeks as her pleas filled the merciless silence. She had not meant to run. She had forgotten his threat, forgotten Papa's wager. Shame flooded her. Her gaze dropped to her gown, but she could not remember why she should be ashamed. Gareth's dark eyes flicked over her. His lip lifted in a sneer of contempt. Just as she clasped her hands to beg for his forgiveness, the blade descended in a flash of silver.*

Rowena turned her head and opened her eyes, tasting the salt of a single tear in her mouth. A blade silvered with moonlight filled her vision. She stared blankly at the sword, awaiting the horror of another nightmare.

Warm lips brushed her throat, saturating her senses with a spicy breath of ale. She lay without moving as a mouth glided up her throat. Sharp teeth caught her earlobe in a tingling embrace. She was being eaten by a wolf, she thought vaguely. A slow, enticing wolf with meticulous table manners. He nibbled the tender flesh of her shoulder. Only when his teeth gently dragged down the top of her chemise so his mouth could claim the swell of her breast did Rowena turn her face. The wolf lifted his shaggy head and she found herself gazing into eyes that were dark and dangerous and sleepy. Gareth's eyes.

Her gaze flicked to the sword, then back to him. The weight of his body was poised above her, impaling her to the ground more effectively than the sight of the sword driven into the soft earth. Yet except for his mouth, not an inch of him touched her. A pine needle pricked her thigh, assuring her that she was not dreaming. Her lips parted as the dreams came flooding back. She trembled inside, but not a muscle moved. She turned her face away, but it was too late. Gareth had already sensed her fear.

Gareth caught her chin between his finger and thumb, his grip none too gentle. Rowena forced herself to meet his steady gaze. She could still feel the imprint of his fingers when he rose and paced away. He stood with his back to her, hands on hips.

"Marlys told you," he said flatly.

Rowena sat up. "How did you know?"

"I've seen that look before in a woman's eyes. Fear. Doubt. Morbid curiosity."

Rowena bowed her head, hoping he'd misjudged her. "Were you brought to trial?"

Gareth spun on his heel. "What would have been the use? I was judge and juror after my father's death. They preferred to condemn me with their whispers and their looks. I would never have become a knight at all if Blaine's father had not fostered me."

"And if the king had not knighted you," Rowena murmured. She lifted her head. "Your villeins seem loyal enough."

His nod was untouched by mockery. "They are. I am their lord. I hold their fiefs. 'Twas they with their primi-tive sense of moral justice who were the first to whisper that the lady of the castle needed killing. That she got what she deserved. But the village priest still refuses to pander his prayers at Caerleon."

"You could force him to, could you not?"

"Why bother? Whether I am a murderer or not, I am an adulterer. Any of the nobility feasting in my hall as we speak would be overjoyed to proclaim me both."

"How do you silence their whispers, milord?"

He came and knelt beside her. He reached for a tangled strand of her hair, the caress as soft as his voice was hard. "I challenge the men. I bed the women."

Rowena dropped her gaze. The sight of Gareth's scabbard and gauntlets laid neatly on the ground hardened a knot of resentment in her stomach. " 'Tis most unsporting to fall upon an opponent while they are sleeping."

"I was not aware you were an opponent."

"I stand corrected. I am a possession—akin to your sword or your mount."

He twisted her hair into a curl around his finger. "You are."

"But far more trouble than a sword or a horse, I would wager. Dragging you away from your feast, leading you on a merry chase."

His hand slipped beneath her hair to cup her neck. "Swords must be learned. Horses must be broken." Before she could retort, his lips grazed hers with a teasing stroke of his tongue. He drew back and stared into her face, his arrogance bridled by curiosity.

"Shall you break me, milord?" she queried softly.

Gareth could find no trace of accusation in her eyes. He stood and whistled softly between two fingers. Folio came trotting down the hill to nuzzle Gareth's cheek. Gareth entwined his fingers in the horse's forelock and gently tugged. Folio ducked his head and sank to one knee in a pretty bow. Rowena applauded.

Gareth's teeth gleamed through his dark beard as he met Rowena's gaze over the stallion's head. "Before I could break Folio, I had to teach him to trust me."

Rowena picked at a patch of sap on her chemise to

hide the effect of a smile that held no mockery. Gareth gathered his belongings and sheathed his sword. He mounted. She stood awkwardly, wondering if she was to be left alone in the vast forest as punishment for her flight.

Folio pranced forward under the invisible rein of Gareth's control. Rowena held her feet steady, refusing to flinch.

"Gareth?"

She looked up at him, not realizing it was the first time she had said his name without prefacing it with "milord" or "sir." To Gareth, it held the ring of music.

His knees tightened. Folio tossed his head. "What is it?" Gareth said harshly to hide her effect on him.

"God does not fight on the side of the guilty. If you have won every challenge to your honor, does that not mean you are innocent?"

Gareth stared down at her, the well of silence deepening between them.

He held out his arm to her. Rowena clasped his forearm and found herself mounted on Folio, sitting sideways behind Gareth.

The nearness of his warmth lent a dangerous edge to his soft words. "Don't be so quick to exonerate me, Rowena. I've killed men who've done nothing but accuse me of being a murderer."

"And bedded their widows?"

He did not reply. He urged the horse up the uneven terrain of the hillside and did not betray himself with so much as a shiver when Rowena's arms crept around his waist.

Blaine was sitting in the bailey with his back to the wall when Folio came walking into the courtyard. The merriment within the castle had long ago died to broken snores. He lowered the damp rag from his split lip and squinted through the eye that was not swollen shut. Rowena's cheek rested against Gareth's back. Her eyes were closed. She murmured a sleepy refrain as Gareth slid off the horse with one arm held behind him to keep her from falling. Then his hands caught beneath her arms and drew her to her feet.

She opened her eyes. The untarnished emotion within their blue depths sent a thrill of pure lust shooting through Blaine. He climbed to his feet, the ache of his battered knee forgotten in the harder ache of his groin. Rowena's eyes drifted closed again, and she swayed in Gareth's embrace. Blaine started forward, but Gareth's furtive glance around the bailey stopped him in the shadows. Rowena never felt the brush of Gareth's lips against her temple. Blaine sank against the wall as Gareth scooped Rowena into his arms and carried her into the castle.

Blaine rolled his eyes skyward with a groan. A yellow stab of light flickered in the tower on the other side of the bailey. His eyes narrowed, fixing on the unshuttered window where a dark and shaggy head loomed behind the flame. With a crash, the shutter slammed, and Blaine threw back his head and laughed aloud until blood from his torn lip trickled down his chin.

# Chapter 8

The first snowflakes of winter came spinning out of a sky laden with gray. They darted and spun on an icy wind to be captured by the castle walls and sent drifting into the bailey. The doors of Caerleon were flung open. Knights and ladies bundled in wool and ermine spilled into the courtyard, their laughter ringing like bells in the crisp air as they turned their faces skyward. Brittle bits of snow tapped their flushed cheeks. They opened their mouths hungrily to catch the flakes on their tongues.

As the snow frosted the brown grass, then carpeted it in white, the men snuck up behind one another and shoved handfuls of snow down tunics. Someone found the chest of lances in the list and soon mock tournaments were being held with the men sliding on the slick grass beneath the snow.

Rowena slipped out of the castle behind the others. She pressed herself to the wall, wondering if the nobility were not tinged with madness. Snow had never meant joy to her. Snow had meant a winter trapped inside a dark castle with drifts piled so high against the doors that they could not be opened from December to March. Snow had meant one rag of a coverlet spread over nine people and nothing but raw turnips and Irwin's tales to nibble on through the short days and endless nights. Snow had meant bowls of soup flavored more with water than barley.

As Gareth had predicted, Blaine and his retinue settled themselves at Caerleon and proceeded to eat up the stores of years. Dunnla ordered about villeins summoned from the village, frightening them into fits with her bellowing. Gridmore led an alarming number of pages into stone walls and onto window ledges before they could be rescued. Blaine lounged around the castle, posturing like a satisfied cat, ever hungry for new entertainment.

Traveling troupes, quick to hear rumors of Blaine's largesse with gold coins, flocked to the castle. Mummers were followed by puppeteers, acrobats by rope dancers, and troubadours by a sword swallower.

The snow brought with it a fresh entertainment and infused the courtyard with joy. Rowena hugged herself, stifling a shiver. She wore no mantle, but only a shapeless cotte of white wool. She had learned well the value of simple garments on the night of the first feast. She had no desire to fuel the whispers spoken behind the sleeves of the ladies. They knew she shared Gareth's bedchamber. Whether she was his leman or a glorified maid kept to stir the fire, no one knew. Gareth treated her with nothing but distant courtesy in front of them. Or alone with her.

The only time Gareth showed any interest in her at all was when Sir Blaine approached. Then he would spring from the very walls to inquire about her writing lessons or ask if her porridge had suited her that morn. It confused her and infuriated Blaine, whose courtesy grew to terrifying proportions when he was angry. She would stammer a reply with all the grace of the village idiot and stumble over her own feet to escape them both.

The snow billowed down in a deepening curtain of

white, frosting beards and capping the turrets in a pearly blanket. Across the bailey a spray of snow shot into the air as Marlys tusseled with a chubby squire. His howls for mercy drew a smile from Rowena. Snow caught on her eyelashes and melted like tears down her cheeks. She had been watching Gareth for several minutes with growing disquiet.

Lady Alise knelt at his feet. She scooped a swath of snow into her satin gloves, her ferret-trimmed pelisse spread around her in rippling elegance. She lifted her face to Gareth, her delicate features aglow with laughter. He offered her his hand, and she took it. He ducked as she leaped to her feet, blowing snow like sparks of moondust in his face. Then she gathered her skirts and dodged behind a squealing lady as Gareth started after her with a growl. Across the bailey, his gaze met Rowena's.

He straightened and lifted a black-gloved hand in greeting. Rowena managed a wince of a smile before slipping back into the shadows of the keep. Her feet carried her to the kitchen, where she plopped down on the bench and rested her chin on her hands.

"Half frozen, are ya?" Dunnla wailed in her ear.

Rowena didn't even jump as Dunnla slammed a bowl of lentil stew on the table. Rowena stared into its bubbling depths, then pushed it away. She had seen Gareth's smile fade when he saw her. Why did he keep her around if he detested her so? She folded her arms on the table and rested her head on them. She did not see Gareth pause in the doorway or Dunnla shake a spoon at him. When she lifted her head, the doorway was empty and Dunnla was bellowing a tune about the gruesome end of a lusty knight.

Rowena huddled on the lowest stair in the hall, wrapped in a musty pelt. Icy gusts rattled the shutters against the stones. When the shutters resisted the battering siege, the wind went wailing around the ramparts in furious protest. The eerie wail rose to a howl, and Rowena signed the cross on her breast beneath the pelt.

At last the wind sated itself by shooting blasts of cold through the arrow slits. Even the richness of Gareth's keep could not halt the attack of England's winter.

A week ago the sky had begun to spill new snow. Rowena had gathered on the parapet walk with the others to marvel at the size and beauty of the snow-flakes. Within minutes every tower carried a frosting of white until the castle itself looked as if it had been fash-ioned of snow by a giant child with an artist's hand. The lash of the wind soon drove them inside. The men escorted the women down the winding stairs with forced jocularity, but beneath their smiles, Rowena saw the strain of frowns. The murmur of "blizzard" passed between them like some dreadful incantation.

By dawn of this, the seventh day, Rowena could see no more than a hand's length in front of her from any window in the castle. The world darkened to whirling white as the invisible sky dumped snow into the merci-less hands of the wind. Snow billowed around the ram-parts, rolling into ice-capped drifts at every wall. Gareth's guests wandered to the great hall without being summoned, trying to ignore the sharp gestures and raised voices of Gareth and Blaine at the hearth.

Finally Blaine lifted a finger for attention, his smile deadly sweet. "Our host has wracked his mind for a way to relieve our tedium and provide us an entertain-ment on this grim day. Every man in the castle is to join in a hunt to bring back meat for tonight's feast."

A halfhearted cheer went up from the men. The Lady Alise pressed a kerchief to her trembling lips. Gareth's face was set in grim lines.

Woolen greaves and fur vests were fetched by the armloads and tossed in a heap on the rugs. The men shifted from foot to foot like restless children as the women bundled them into cloaks and wound their capuchins into hoods. They tossed challenges and taunts across the hall to keep the silence from closing in. Shrill laughter rang out as the women pressed kisses of luck on clammy brows. A matronly woman patted her husband's rump as he turned to go. A freckled girl no older than Rowena pressed her kerchief into a knight's hand.

"Have you no favor for me, sweet Rowena?" Blaine whispered. He had crept up behind her as silently as a cat. A fur cap hung jauntily over one ear.

"What might these favors indicate?"

Blaine placed a hand over his heart and blinked winningly. " 'Tis a pledge of eternal love from a lady I adore."

Rowena glanced down. Her simple cotte was unadorned by girdle or kerchief. "I fear I have no such favor to give."

"I beg you. Mayhaps a kiss then, one memory of your soft lips. Pray do not send me to an icy grave with naught."

Rose stained Rowena's cheeks. She swayed backward as he leaned forward.

"Stand aside, Blaine, or I shall give you the favor of my lance against your brow." A bear with a muffled growl came clumping down the stairs between them.

Blaine leaped backward, giving the shaggy giant a wide berth. A woman screamed, and all eyes turned to the bottom of the stairs. Bound in ragged pelts from ankle to nose, Marlys stomped into the hall wearing what could only be kitchen trays strapped to her feet with leather thongs.

Gareth crossed the hall to meet her and a hissed but heated exchange followed. Marlys ended it by hurling her lance across the hall. A page ducked, his face ashen as the lance impaled the oaken beam he had been leaning against. Rowena flinched as Marlys proceeded to tell Gareth loudly and explicitly what he could do with his hunt. She grabbed a flagon of ale and stomped out of the hall, her curses ringing behind her.

Blaine shrugged his wiry shoulders into a vest. "What does he expect? He lets her run wild like a beast. A good thrashing might cure her ill temper."

A nearby squire chortled. "Or a good—"

Rowena cleared her throat. The squire met her level gaze and slunk away. Rowena had no idea why she should be defending Marlys, though she supposed Marlys and Gareth were the only family she had now.

At Gareth's signal, two men wrenched open the door. The silence everyone had feared fell over the hall.

A solid mound of white covered the doorway. The muffled scream of the wind behind it shielded the nervous beat of a hundred hearts. The men stood as if frozen themselves until Gareth's cry flung them into movement.

"Lances! Bring all the lances you can find."

Lances were brought amidst excited jabber. The women stood back with clasped hands as the men stabbed the snowy beast. The snow collapsed in a powdery avalanche. A cheer went up. A rush of arctic wind and blinding snow shot into the hall. Last embraces were exchanged. Then, with Gareth in the lead, the men climbed over the crumbling hill in the doorway and disappeared into the white.

Rowena turned and ran up the stairs. She flew down the long corridors, through a squat hall, and up a narrow spiral staircase she thought would never end. Her harsh breathing sent puffs of fog into the stale air.

She burst into the north tower and stumbled to her knees at the bottom of a narrow window. Her stiff fingers tugged at the shutter latch, but the latch held. Too cold to feel her knuckles tear against the rough wood, she rammed both fists against the shutter. With a crack of protest, it flew open.

The burst of cold air and the dizzying height of the tower knocked Rowena backward. Icy flecks of snow blinded her, melting to tears beneath her eyelids. She rubbed them away. Gripping the icy stone windowsill with both hands, she leaned into the blizzard. Her eyes narrowed against the wind, and her fingers went numb. Squinting, she could make out blurred shapes creeping down the drawbridge far below. The man at the head of the hunting party held all of her attention. The wind whipped from the north, hiding him from her view for an agonizing second, before the straggling line reappeared. Rowena leaned out farther, her hungry gaze following Gareth until her hair hardened to icy strands and the last dark shape disappeared into the crystalline forest.

Shivering, she pulled the shutter closed. It banged wildly as she left the tower, pulling the door shut behind her. Her slippers made no sound against the stones. She drifted to the bedchamber she shared with Gareth. The morning's fire had died to embers. She spread her palms over their glow to capture a hint of warmth. The snow trapped in her hair and kirtle melted and dripped into her kid shoes. She scooped a pelt from her nest of furs, then let it roll from her fingertips as her gaze locked on the bed frame that dominated the chamber.

She dragged one of Gareth's pelts from the bed and buried her face in it, closing her eyes as the sweet, musky scent of him filled her senses. Her lips moved wordlessly against the fur. Throwing the heavy pelt over her shoulders, she went to the stairs to wait with the rest of the women for their men to return.

As the afternoon waned to dusk, the chatter of the women sharpened, honed by the passing of minutes and the increasing frequency of their glances at the door. The snow had been swept outside by laughing maidservants, the door shoved closed against the wind. Only a dark puddle remained to mark its passing.

Hours passed. The silences grew longer and the laughter more scarce. The ladies bent their heads to their embroidery and pretended not to start at every sound. Dunnla shuffled between them, offering lark pasties and mead, but her platter remained untouched.

In a silence broken only by the howl of the wind, Mortimer hefted his lute and plucked gently at the strings. He was the only man left behind, except for a handful of smooth-chinned pages. Mortimer stroked the beginning notes of first one tune and then another, playing more to comfort himself than to amuse the women. Rowena's head flew up as she thought she heard the haunting notes of a ballad she had thought never to hear again. The lyrics circled unsummoned in her mind, then Mortimer's fingers shifted to the chorus of another tune. Rowena dipped her nose into Gareth's pelt, seeking some comfort to soften the sharp edge of her despair.

When she lifted her head, the Lady Alise's gaze rested on her, curious and cold. Rowena met her gaze unblinkingly until Alise bent her head to the cambric in her lap.

Marlys paced the hall like a caged wolf. The ladies drew in their feet each time she passed and tried not to flinch.

A plump woman encased like a sausage in ocher wool gave a bright, false smile. "Was it not clever of Sir Gareth and Sir Blaine to organize a hunt? Men do so hate to be confined."

Marlys spun around. Her deliberate swagger carried her back to the woman. She leaned forward, resting her hands on the arms of the lady's chair.

The caress of her voice could be heard in every corner of the hall. "You silly bitch. Believe it or not, freezing to death in a snowdrift is a worse confinement than being locked up with a ninny like you. Your fat little belly might crave meat ere this blizzard ends. My brother took your men out there so the villeins would not find a castle full of noble bones come the spring thaw."

The woman stared into her lap, lips quivering. Her needle stabbed the linen kerchief and sank into the tender pad beneath her thumbnail. She burst into tears. Marlys backed away, sneering her contempt.

An uneven melody rose from Mortimer's lute. It seemed there would be no more idle chatter to hold the fear at bay. Marlys strode to the stairs where Rowena huddled and sank down beside her, cracking knuckles stiff with cold. Rowena loosened the pelt beneath her and dropped it like a cape over Marlys's shoulders. It enveloped both of them easily.

Without a word, Marlys scooted against the warmth of Rowena's body. They sat wrapped together for a long time before Rowena's head nodded against Marlys's shoulder in a fitful doze.

Rowena awoke to a silence so profound she thought she was dreaming. She opened her eyes to meet Marlys's quizzical gaze. Not a murmur or a whisper of wool broke the quiet. This was more than silence. It was a terrible absence of sound, as if even the beat of their hearts had stilled. Marlys threw back the pelt and they peered upward. The shadows under the rafters surrendered no answers.

"The wind," came a choked whisper. "The wind has stopped."

"Has it?" The lady who spoke was the freckled girl who had pressed her kerchief into the young knight's hand. "Has it really stopped or are we just deaf to it?" Her voice rose with an edge of hysteria. "Perhaps we are buried alive and can hear nothing. Perhaps the men are behind the snow right outside that door, begging and pleading for us to let them in and we cannot hear them. Perhaps their bodies stiffen and die even as we sit and sew. Perhaps—"

"Stop it." Marlys crossed the space between them in two strides. Her slap rang out in the silence. The girl sank into the arms of a matronly woman.

The woman glared up at Marlys. "I told my husband we never should have come here. All of England knows your brother is a madman. Dismissing all his fiefs. Living like a hermit with no one but cripples and villeins to serve him. Letting you run wild like an animal instead of shutting you in a convent as he should. Caerleon is cursed. Damned by the dark deeds of its master."

A dull flush darkened the back of Marlys's neck. The Lady Alise kneaded her cambric between her thin fingers as Rowena stepped between Marlys and the woman. Those who had never heard her utter a word strained to hear her soft voice.

"You have no right to speak so."

The woman's virulent gaze shifted to Rowena.

"Who are you to defend him? We know where he keeps you at night. Chained to his bed. Forced to satisfy his darkest and most unnatural desires. You should wish his death with your every breath." The woman absently patted the hair of the sobbing girl in her lap.

Rowena fought an absurd desire to laugh, but the cruel words coupled with a jolting realization of her true feelings suddenly did not seem very funny.

Even to her own ears, her voice sounded faint and far away. "You will owe Sir Gareth an apology when he returns."

Marlys's voice was strangled with bitterness. "*If* he returns."

Her words were followed by a distant sound, as deep and rolling as the ocean. Frowning, Rowena cocked her head to the side. The Lady Alise came to her feet. Voices. Male voices, lifted in song, rumbling with vibrancy. And followed by each swelling chorus was an echoing slam, as if a gong sounded deep underwater.

The auburn-haired girl sat straight up. "Holy Mother of God preserve us. They are dead. We hear their angels."

Mortimer threw aside his lute. "If angels sing a song such as that, 'tis not in heaven they reside."

The ghostly chorus swelled:

> Me Jenny is a fiery lass
> Whose love is ne'er too cold
> With her sweet thighs to sheath my sword
> I ne'er shall grow too old.

Rowena's lips curved in a smile. The massive door shook in its frame as the battering ram broke through the ice and thundered to a halt against the sturdy wood.

"Do our fair ladies deny us entrance?" came a voice that was unmistakably Blaine's.

Mortimer's wiry arms knotted with effort as he swung open the door. "They might, but I never would."

He was nearly trampled as the ladies surged forward in a mass of squeals and tears. The men swept in to meet them. Ice and snow clung to every fiber and hair, rendering them crackling mountains of white. Suspended on poles between every two men hung wild boars with blood caked and frozen on their carcasses. Cheers rocked the hall.

Rowena stood alone amidst the furniture. Tears misted her eyes as Marlys flung herself on the neck of a snowy giant just inside the door. When he could disengage himself from her embrace, he lowered her, shaking snow from his dark hair. His cheeks glowed with good health. His teeth gleamed through his frosted beard in a smile that held no hint of bitterness as he accepted the embraces and salutes of both men and women. His dark eyes sparkled as he swept Lady Alise under his arm.

Rowena's stomach churned as her feelings for Gareth broke over her like a storm. Believing herself invisible in the joyful chaos, she crept up the stairs, dragging Gareth's pelt behind her.

Dunnla's knock came twice upon the door, then came again in another hour. Each time, Rowena answered the same way. "Go away. I am ill."

How could Dunnla have missed her in the revelry below? Snatches of music and cries of joy drifted up through the stone floor to Rowena's ears. She snuggled deeper into her pelts and stared into the deepening shadows. The snow had stopped but the wind still wailed against the latched shutter.

Rowena *was* ill. Self-contempt curled like a fist deep in her gut. How could she have been such a fool as to let herself be won over by a pair of somber dark eyes and a fine set of muscles? She was no better than Lady Alise. She drifted into sleep more than once, but always awoke with the restless shivering of one fevered and the wetness of tears on her cheeks. She would have a long time to nurse her shattered pride. Gareth would no doubt be celebrating far into the night, first in the great hall, then in the Lady Alise's bedchamber.

She did not even bother to roll over when the door creaked open.

"I beg you, Dunnla. Go away," she said crossly. "I am ill. I am not hungry."

" 'Tis no wonder you are ill with no fire on the grate. I can see my breath in here."

Rowena rolled over and sat up, her hair tumbling over the fur she'd drawn to her chin. Gareth leaned against the closed door.

He held out a white bundle. "I brought you some hot pastries. Apple. Your favorite."

Rowena sniffed. "Nay. I do not want them." She rolled away from him.

There was a moment of puzzled silence, then the gentle thump of logs being tossed on the grate. The rhythmic snap of a fire followed, making a pretty noise but doing little to warm the icy air. Rowena waited for the slam of the door. It did not come.

She peeked out of her nest. Gareth was pacing in front of the hearth, chafing his arms. "I cannot seem to get warm."

She watched in surprise as he pulled his tunic over his head. Howls of laughter and voices raised in song floated up from below.

" 'Tis poor manners for a host to abandon his own feast, is it not?"

Gareth shrugged. "I tire of their toasts. Fickle lot, are they not? Stuff them with roast boar and they drop their suspicious glances and lift their goblet to you. I came up here to seek a warm bed. I fear I've come to the wrong place."

His words were more ill chosen than he realized. Rowena's lips tightened as she jerked the pelt over her head. Gareth shoved two more logs on the fire, ate one of the pastries he had brought for Rowena, then dove into the center of the bed, and spread the pelts over him.

Even as the fire roared upward, the chill in the chamber deepened. The wind whistled with joy at the plunging temperature. The shutter trembled as stubborn drafts pushed themselves through the narrow slats. Soon Rowena could feel the cold emanating from the stones beneath the thick fur. A shudder wracked her. She wrapped her arms around her back but found little comfort in her own heat. A heap of pelts could not compare to the warmth of nine bodies curled under a single coverlet. She had no Little Freddie, snug and sweet-smelling, to throw her leg over.

She crawled toward the fire, dragging the pelts behind her. She arranged them at the base of the hearth and crawled inside, shivering in the scant warmth. The shadows dancing on the wall cast an illusion of warmth, all the more cruel for its cozy deception. Cold seeped into her bones. Her teeth began to chatter. She wrapped the pelts around her and climbed up to sit on the hearth itself, pressing her cheek to the warmth of the stones.

With a crash, the wind slammed the shutter open. Rowena started as cold wind poured into the chamber, sending the snow piled on the windowsill into a sparkling whirlwind. Gareth jumped up and forced the shutter closed with a curse. He turned, stomping his feet on the stones, to find Rowena huddled on the hearth. Only her eyes and a thatch of golden hair were visible over the dark fur.

He climbed back into the bed. "How am I to sleep with that infernal chattering?" he growled.

"I humbly beg your forgiveness, milord," Rowena choked out between clenched teeth. "You may banish me to Marlys's chamber if it displeases you. I am not accustomed to sleeping alone in the winter."

"I am. But not with half my pelts. This is absurd. There is no benefit in both of us freezing to death within five feet of each other." He threw back his covers in an unmistakable invitation.

Rowena's eyes widened. The tip of her reddened nose poked over the furs, but she only hugged the pelts tighter.

Gareth rolled his eyes. "Your hesitation is flattering, but I can assure you that any part of me amenable to molesting you is frozen solid at the moment."

Rowena looked at him sideways, still uncertain. He

puffed out a fog of breath in exasperation. She screwed her eyes shut and made a mad dash for the bed, bounding next to him with a leap that shook the bed frame. She snuggled deep into the feather tick, her back to him.

Gareth stared at the graceful curve of her back beneath the cotte and wondered if he had spoken in haste. He tucked the combined pelts around them both, then rolled to his side and closed his eyes.

A steady rustling seized the tick. Gareth opened his eyes and rolled over. Shivers wracked Rowena's slender spine.

"Good God, woman! If your teeth don't make a racket, your bones do."

Rowena erupted from the pelts in a flurry of gold and sable. "Pray do forgive me, milord." Her talent for mockery provided the precise words she sought. "Mayhaps you'd prefer to chain me to your bed and force me to satisfy your darkest and most unnatural desires."

Gareth rubbed his already tousled hair. The words she hurled at him were his own, whispered to a lecherous old earl from London whose lady could be counted on to spread the malicious gossip to the four corners of the known world.

His mind keened a warning, but his hands ignored it as they cupped Rowena's neck and pulled her forward until only her palms pressed to his bare chest kept them from colliding.

" 'Tis a tempting invitation, milady, but we both know there would be no need of chains between us."

Rowena quailed before the devilish light in his eyes, wondering what idiocy had prompted her to taunt him. He was twice her opponent out of bed and even more her master in it. His hateful Elayne had trained him well. She dropped her gaze. Her hands looked stubby and ungraceful against the sleek fur of his chest.

Gareth's fingers tightened on her neck. Her meek acceptance of his bullying angered him more than rebellion. To him it spoke of a lifetime of acceptance of whatever foolish excuses her papa had chosen to offer.

He wanted to shake her. To urge her to speak up for herself, or even to strike out at him. He wanted to stir the spark of spirit he'd glimpsed so briefly in her complacent gaze. His hands itched to lay her back among the furs and slowly and patiently stir another spark into roaring flame. His own desire threatened to consume him as he buried his lips in the ethereal softness of her hair.

His harsh words echoed against her skull. "A peaceable sleep is all I desire. Is that so unnatural? Do I have to chain you to get it?"

"Nay, milord."

"Then roll over."

Rowena rolled over as if she half expected to feel the sting of his palm against her rump. Groaning silently, he slipped his arms around her waist. She sank into the warmth of his embrace without further protest.

Long after Rowena's shivers had stilled, she lay curled like a statue against the hard length of his body, basking in his nearness but afraid to stir lest she betray herself with a caress or word of folly in her sleep. Exhaustion finally steadied her breathing to the gentle rhythm of slumber. Gareth stared at the shadows of leaping firelight against the wall, his chin resting on her silky head, fearful of moving lest she realize he was not as frozen as he had believed. If Lindsey Fordyce did not come soon, 'twould be he who would need to be rescued from the silken snare of her embrace.

# Chapter 9

⬥⬥⬥

Somewhere in its cold heart, winter found a trace of mercy and sent a reprieve. Beneath the melting snow, the land waited, silent and sleeping. Black branches stood naked and stark against the gray sky. Winter stripped of snow was an ugly creature, plain but habitable. Several of the guests at Caerleon took their polite leave, including the woman who had pronounced the castle cursed. Others followed Blaine's obstinate example and stayed on, filling their days with wagers over chess and draughts and their nights draining Gareth's generous supply of ale.

The first day the list was no longer a sea of mud found Rowena and Marlys tilting at a battered quintain. Marlys flung herself on the back of her piebald mare and charged the scarred shield nailed to the post.

Her lance grazed the wooden shield, sending the quintain spinning. Rowena jumped up and down, clapping her hands, as Marlys guided her mount around the post before it could swing back and strike her. From where he sat on the gate, Blaine applauded dryly, though his eyes were not on Marlys, but Rowena.

Rowena's blond hair spilled over the stark black of garments that had once been Marlys's after they had been Gareth's for a very long time. The tunic hung well past her knees. Uneven patches dangled from tangled threads. She should have looked ridiculous, but her slender figure endowed the garments with an awkward grace like that of a regal jester, funny and heart-catching at the same time. Each time she jumped up and down, Blaine caught a milky glimpse of one knee within the torn hose. He was forced to shift his weight and cross his legs.

Rowena grabbed the shaggy mane before Marlys could finish dismounting and dragged herself on the horse's back.

"Suit yourself, Lady Precious." Marlys gave Rowena's rump a hearty shove, then jerked her tunic down. "Beware creeping garments. Blaine's tongue has wrapped itself around the fencepost."

Her words were just loud enough to carry across the list. Blaine waited until Rowena was facing the quintain before giving Marlys a friendly smile and an unfriendly gesture. Marlys slapped a lance in Rowena's palm. Rowena lowered her head, frowning with concentration. Her booted feet dug into the mare's sides. The horse surged forward. The shield flew toward her as if she were standing still and the quintain moving. Her lance struck the red heart painted in the center of the shield with an enviable thud.

She raised the lance in a salute of triumph and cantered around the quintain. She was a hoofbeat away from being clear of the careening post when she saw the dark figure standing behind Blaine. Her knees tightened convulsively, bringing the mare to a dead halt. The quintain slammed into her back, neatly unseating her.

Blaine leaped off the fence, but it was Gareth who reached her first. His hand gently cupped her neck, feeling for lumps beneath her hair. She tried to draw in a breath but could not; her lungs had gone hollow and empty. She blinked up into Gareth's eyes, unable to speak or stir. Two other pairs of eyes joined his.

"Knocked the breath out of her," Marlys pronounced from somewhere above. "No need for the last rites yet. If the priest would come to Caerleon, that is. The vicious bastard's done it to me many a time."

It took Rowena a foggy moment to realize Marlys was referring to the quintain, not the priest. Marlys struck the shield a savage blow of revenge.

Blaine's eyes burned an indignant brown next to Gareth's. " 'Tis your fault for letting the child amuse herself with this hoyden."

"Safer for her to amuse herself with Marlys than with you," Gareth retorted.

He caught Rowena's arms and lifted her to her feet. By that time she had gathered enough breath to speak and enough humiliation to wish she hadn't any breath at all.

"I am all right," she rasped. Her head ached and her mouth tasted like old blood, but she would not have confessed it for the world. She jerked out of Gareth's grip and brushed herself off with jerky motions.

Gareth frowned. Blaine hid a smile behind his hand. "I came to inform you all that I've planned a feast for the morrow," Gareth said gruffly.

Blaine snorted. "*You've* planned a feast?"

"Aye, my gallant friend. Since certain guests whose names will remain unmentioned show no sign of taking their leave from my castle, I've decided to invite some civilized folk of my own. I will expect to see each of you in the great hall tomorrow night."

Gareth's sweeping gaze ended its sweep on Rowena. For a moment, she thought he would speak, but he did not. She stroked the horse's quivering withers, hiding her blush. Gareth turned on his heel without another word and strode out of the list. Rowena led the mare into the stables, murmuring soft words into her mane.

Marlys squinted into the sunless sky. "Those two creep off to bed earlier than anyone else at Caerleon.

How is it that they awake with such foul tempers and dark circles under their eyes?"

Blaine growled at her under his breath. Marlys ducked his slap with a laugh that was almost girlish.

When a rap sounded on her door that evening, Rowena dropped the braid she was tidying. A vision of the hand on the other side of the door quickened her breathing. Powerful knuckles, laced with pale scars and dusted with dark hair. The knock sounded again.

"Enter," she said.

She rose as Gareth's dark presence filled the doorway. Their eyes met, and Rowena's cheeks flooded with a heat she despised. There was a difference to his gaze tonight. The cool distance was gone, replaced by something assessing and almost predatory. His smile did not reassure her.

He hefted an object of shimmering gold in one hand. "I brought you an adornment for your kirtle."

Rowena stood mesmerized by his bright, dark gaze as he slipped behind her. His strange excitement was almost palpable. Her lashes swept downward as his arms moved around her waist without touching her. She caught her breath at the sight of emeralds and amethysts sparkling up at her from a girdle of the finest gold. As he prepared to lower it to her hips, she caught his wrists in her hands.

"I've no need for such finery, milord. I have none of my own and would prefer not to wear someone else's."

Gareth paused. His lips brushed the nape of her neck in a gesture as unconscious as the emotion that prompted it. Rowena shivered.

"This girdle has belonged to no one but you." Ignoring her protest, he lowered the gilded weight to her hips. His deft fingers brushed the small of her back as he hooked the clasp. Rowena wondered if he was lying.

His warm hands grasped her shoulders, turning her to face him. She stared up into the shadows of his face, finding an uneasy heat in his tightened jaw, his arched brows. Without a word, he untied the thongs binding her braids and dragged his fingers through each plait until her hair lay in a shining curtain around her shoulders.

"Wear your hair loose tonight." His words were soft, his tone of command unmistakable.

He turned at the door with a frown, then closed the door behind him. Was it a shadow of regret she had seen in his eyes? Rowena wondered.

Rowena tripped over a silver chain stretched taut across the lowest stair. She followed it to its source and clapped a hand over her mouth, stifling a shriek. A toothless bear sat beside the stairs, his furry legs spread on the stones like a child playing ball. A veiled wimple sat atop his shaggy head. At second glance, the bear did not look nearly so fierce—only mangy and somewhat embarrassed. A dwarf cavorted on the other side of the stairs. He held the chain up so a line of ladies could pass beneath its links, then dove under one of their skirts. They scattered, squealing with delight. Mortimer's steady strumming drowned out all but the most determined shouts of laughter.

As Rowena passed a trestle table laden with food, she plucked a dripping honeycomb from a bowl and tossed it to the bear, remembering what it felt like to be alone and hungry at such a feast. He caught it between his clumsy paws and sat happily sucking the honey from its combs.

Rowena tucked her fingers in her mouth and lapped at the lingering sweetness. She met Gareth's gaze across the teeming hall. A shock as warm and brilliant as lightning passed between them. Warmth flooded her body. The word she had sought for the change in him rose unbidden to her mind.

*Possession.*

It was written in his eyes, in every elegant line of his being. For some unknown reason, Sir Gareth of Caerleon had chosen to play lord of the manor that night.

He sat at the end of the hall with one foot propped

in a massive carved chair Rowena had never noticed before. The thronelike seat would have dwarfed a lesser man, but its graceful curves only enhanced the edge of dangerous masculinity held in check by Gareth. He was garbed all in black threaded with silver. The king of the underworld himself could not have looked more regal and striking than Gareth at that moment. When he cocked his head at her, she floated to him as if she were his Persephone, bound by an invisible chain.

Rowena felt other eyes on her as she picked her way through the dancers. She curtsied before Gareth and felt the shimmering weight of her hair on her shoulders. He brought her hand to his lips. Instead of kissing her palm, his tongue curled between her fingers as he licked away the last trace of honey.

"My sweet," he murmured. Rowena pulled her hand back, as shocked as if he had bitten her. Most nights went by without one word of acknowledgment from him.

A cushion spread with furs lay at Gareth's feet. He indicated it with a mocking nod and Rowena sank down, fearing him for a new reason. Her pounding heart confirmed that she would never have the strength to resist a genuine attempt at seduction.

Afraid to turn and meet his gaze, Rowena studied the faces she did not recognize. Two very familiar faces danced to a halt in front of them. Blaine bowed. The Lady Alise gripped his arm as if he might somehow slide out of her grasp.

"You have outdone yourself, Gareth," Blaine said with an admiring glance around the hall.

"Nonsense. I've outdone you. 'Tis what truly vexes you," Gareth replied.

Blaine lifted a hand in a masculine salute. "Look. There by the door. Sir Martain, the Earl of Gloucester giggling with Marlys. And there is Baron Medford prowling around the pudding. I half expect the door to fly open and the king to stroll in."

"Edward is in France. He sent his regrets." Gareth plucked a goblet off a passing tray. "However, you will find the Prince of Wales in the midst of the hot cockles game."

Blaine paled with envy as his gaze followed Gareth's to a willowy young man with his head resting on a lady's lap. Nothing was visible beneath his blindfold but a mass of frizzy blond curls. Black and white squares checkered his surcoat, making Rowena dizzy to look at him.

"The lad resembles a chessboard," Alise said. "Pray tell, is he your mysterious guest of honor?" Her nose was tilted so high in the air Rowena could see little but her flared nostrils.

Gareth shrugged. "Perhaps Bartholemew the Bear will take the seat of honor."

"Bartholemew is a fine fellow, is he not?" Rowena chimed in. "When I first came down the stairs, I thought he was Marlys, but his melancholy eyes made me realize I was mistaken. My heart goes out to him. A fine fellow like he must be mortified to be wearing that ridiculous wimple." She giggled. "I would cower under the stairs myself if I had to wear such a silly structure on my head."

There was a beat of silence. Too late Rowena realized the flowing tower perched on Alise's head was identical to the one Bartholemew wore. Alise's nostrils flared large enough to swallow her. Blaine cleared his throat.

Gareth lifted a strand of Rowena's hair. It flowed through his fingers like liquid gold. "Very observant of you, dear. Bartholemew is a fine fellow. He eats far fewer guests than Blaine's fish."

Rowena bowed her head, wishing the bear would trundle over and eat her. A florid man in a feathered cap paused to exchange pleasantries with Gareth. As the glib conversation went on above her, Rowena tired of studying Alise's slippers and began to arrange her own skirt in neat folds. She had the soft camlet laid out in a perfect fan when the door swept open and a line of colorless shapes slumped into the hall. Rowena's heart lurched into an uneven rhythm.

"What might this be?" Blaine murmured. "A peasant revolt?"

"Revolting indeed," Alise said.

The new guests slunk around the fringes of the hall as if their drab rags might allow them to fade into the stone. But at the end of their unobtrusive parade walked a slender figure whose straight shoulders and cap of silver-blond hair would not let him melt away like the others.

Rowena had half risen when Gareth's hand slipped beneath her hair and tightened on her neck. She shot him an agonized look. His face revealed nothing, but the subtle bite of his fingers forced her back down.

Lindsey Fordyce, Baron of Revelwood, strutted into the hall behind his seven sons and one nephew, his plum chausses and yellow tunic making him look like a garish peacock following a flock of sparrows. His eyes darted from side to side. His hands twisted one against another. When Mortimer broke into the violent chorus of a *chanson de geste*, he jumped straight into the air. Little Freddie's gray eyes searched the crowd. It was he who spotted Rowena sitting at Gareth's feet. His nudge went down the line, rocking his brothers like a wave until it exploded against Fordyce with a thump on the skull from Big Freddie.

Papa's eyes lit with benevolent welcome. Before she could raise her trembling hand, Gareth tilted her chin between thumb and forefinger, forcing a bewildered Rowena to stare up at him. He leaned over and touched his mouth to hers. His moustache tickled her nose as his lips brushed the corner of her mouth in a teasing caress. Too surprised to resist, her lips parted beneath his. He turned his head from side to side, drawing a feathery threat with his tongue until he felt the tiny, white ramparts of her teeth part to draw him into her moist, sweet mouth.

A shudder twisted Gareth's gut. He tried to pull away, but a powerful thread of longing held him fast. When he finally freed her, it was he who had to look away. Sinking back in the chair, he snatched a goblet off the tray Dunnla offered, drained it, then took another.

Rowena plucked the last goblet off the tray to occupy her shaking hands, splashing ale heedlessly on her skirt. Blaine led Alise away, his smile as fixed as her grimace. Papa stood frozen by the door. Rowena waited for him to cross the hall to her, to come and bid his only daughter a greeting. He glanced over his shoulder at the arrow slits set high on the walls as if expecting a feathered plume to embed itself in his back. Rowena watched in amazement as he shooed the boys toward the overflowing tables and bowed to a plump woman sitting along the wall. They joined the dance, the woman's cheeks pinkening at his flowery prattle.

Rowena's brothers cleared three tables of all but bones in a matter of minutes. Dunnla shuffled in, shook her head in exasperation and went back for more food. Gareth's dark eyes brooded over the hall. He stroked his beard with one hand, ever conscious of the blond head at his knee and the faded gold of her Papa's bobbing across his hall.

It took Papa two flagons of ale, six galloping turns at the dance, and a bawdy ditty to gather his courage and three of his kin and approach Gareth's chair.

Rowena watched Little Freddie as if his shining head were a beacon. She would have risen again had Gareth not chosen that moment to gently cup her cheek with one hand in a proprietary gesture that reminded her oddly of the way he handled Folio.

The crowd cleared before Papa's strut. The foot he dragged behind him only served to put more bounce in his step. The ladies murmured behind their sleeves at the hulking creature that followed him.

Behind Big Freddie trailed Irwin with a nervous chorus of, "Pardon me. Pardon me. Do pardon me. I beg your forgiveness, milady. 'Twas not my intention to trod upon your train. Do forgive me." He kept this up until he stumbled into Big Freddie's back and Little Freddie stomped his shin.

Fordyce honored Gareth with a sweeping bow. Irwin stared down at Rowena from a height she did not remember. From this angle, his legs looked less like sausages. But his rapt gaze held the familiar adoration that still turned her stomach.

Papa ignored her. "My dear Sir Gareth," he began, his voice cracking. He coughed, spat on the floor, and continued. "I cannot begin to express our delight at your kind invitation. We feared the snow would detain us, but God has been merciful and brought us unscathed to Caerleon."

"I always said He had a wicked sense of humor," Gareth replied. His fingers stroked Rowena's cheek with the expertise of a diabolical minstrel. Her heart skipped more beats than it hit.

Papa tittered and wiped spittle from his moist lips with the back of his hand. "Not as wicked as yours, kind sir."

By poking her foot out from under her skirt, Rowena was able to touch Little Freddie's ankle with her toe. Her kid shoe was as white as snow against the bound rags that served as his excuse for shoes. A quick, bright glance was his only betrayal of her touch.

"Do you still find Caerleon to your liking, Fordyce?" Gareth drained his goblet and let it fall to the stones with a thump.

Rowena's father peered around with the jaundiced eye of a potential buyer. "A bit large for my tastes. I prefer a more cozy abode for my lads. Keep 'em humble, I say."

Big Freddie shuffled his feet as if pondering the charms of humility.

"Do you find Caerleon as you remember it?" Gareth added.

Fordyce cleared his throat. " 'Twas many years ago I served your father. My memory fails me."

Rowena frowned quizzically. "You served Gareth's fath—"

Gareth's fingers tightened imperceptibly on her cheek. He turned his hand, and the back of it glided down her throat. Papa's gaze dropped for an instant to the provocative motion. Rowena stared into her lap. Little Freddie swallowed hard.

Gareth leaned forward, impaling Papa with his dark gaze. His other hand caressed the silver hilt of his sword. Irwin took an involuntary step backward.

"Mayhaps there is need I refresh your memory," Gareth said.

Papa looked wildly behind him, as if a horde of knights was going to rush out of the crowd and skewer him. Mortimer's lute fell silent for the first time that night. The minstrel pretended to tune it, watching Gareth through a curtain of hair.

Fordyce rubbed his head, fluffing his scant hair into tufts. "Before my unfortunate accident, I sold my services to many men. Your father was only one of them. I cannot be expected to remember everything, can I? Caerleon is but the shadow of a memory to me. What difference does it make? Did I mention our gift? We've brought you a gift to honor you." He clapped his hands together. "Gifts, Freddie, bring on the gifts!"

Big Freddie and Little Freddie struggled over a burlap sack. Papa boxed Irwin's ears for standing there with his mouth open and snatched the bag. He waved it with a flourish. The rusty goblet from the mantel at Revelwood rolled into the folds of Rowena's skirt. In her embarrassment, she forgot the havoc Gareth was wreaking with her heartbeat. She reached to throw a corner of her kirtle over the goblet, but Gareth's boot came down neatly beside her fingers.

"Charming," he said dryly, nudging the relic with his foot. "But not nearly as charming as the other gift you provided me.

Before Rowena could do more than gasp, Gareth's hand slid into the bodice of her kirtle. She reeled beneath the shock of his warm hand cupping her bare breast, his fingers fondling her with crass familiarity. Papa's eyes widened. Irwin's face went as plum as

Papa's chausses. But worst of all was the steady motion of Little Freddie's fists clenching and unclenching.

Rowena flushed scarlet as her hand came up in an instinctive gesture of outrage. She intended to strike Gareth but had forgotten the goblet in her hand. As it passed in front of her eyes, she hurled its contents straight into his face. He blinked stupidly at her, ale dripping from his brow to his chin. Then his lips tightened and he snatched her up by the hair, dragging her between his knees until all she could see were eyes darkened to jet by burning rage. Her jaw was set in an anger as deep as his own.

Someone coughed. The sound echoed clearly in the silence of drawn-and-held breaths. Gareth tore his gaze from Rowena's to find a hall of eyes filled with sly satisfaction. They had waited for this moment for almost twenty years. Waited for his iron control to snap. Waited for a glimpse of the man who had murdered Elayne of Touraine in her bed. And Rowena had given it to them.

His hand slowly relaxed its grip on her hair.

"Begone," he said between clenched teeth. "To your chamber."

She held herself rigidly against his knees to keep from falling. For a moment, he thought she would defy him, then she bowed her head and said softly, "As you wish, milord."

Every neck in the hall craned to follow her path through the crowd and up the stairs. Her head was modestly bent, but her back was painfully straight.

It was Marlys who broke the silence with a round of mocking applause. "Now, Mortimer. Can you give us any entertainment as grand as that?"

"I think not. Perhaps you'd best turn to Bartholemew the Bear. He is a better man than I."

"Marlys is a better man than you," someone called out to the delighted hoots of the crowd.

No one dared look at Gareth as he wiped away the last traces of ale with his sleeve. Lindsey Fordyce backed into the crowd, dragging Irwin and Little

Freddie by their hoods. As the dwarf led Bartholemew into the center of the floor, Gareth took the goblet Blaine offered him and drained it. He knew he should be following Fordyce's blundering path through the hall, but instead found his burning gaze drawn to the top of the stairs.

# Chapter 10

❧❧

Gareth stumbled past the door of the chamber he had occupied since he was a boy, then backed up. He groped for the handle. His head rapped the door frame as he ducked through the door. Groaning, he kicked the door shut then stood with head down like an ox ready to charge. The ale he had consumed to blunt his anger might as well have been water. His fury churned anew at the sight before him.

Rowena did not pace before the fire wringing her hands. Nor did she cower at the window, her brow darkened with distress. Instead she lay sleeping, nestled in the center of the vast bed like an angel in a cloud of fur. Her golden hair roamed untrammeled across his pillow. Her brow was smooth and sweet, untroubled by even the hint of fretful dreams. The sheer audacity of it dragged a growl from deep in Gareth's throat.

With one hand, he grasped the edge of the furs beneath her and jerked. Rowena rolled rudely onto the floor.

"Ha!" Gareth hoisted the pelts like a flag of triumph.

Rowena sat up, blinking and rubbing her elbow. The

sight of Gareth would have quelled his staunchest adversary. He stood with feet slightly apart, his usually impeccable garments rumpled and stained. His hair stood out in wild tufts, untamed by fingers or comb. The scent of danger rolled off him with the scent of ale.

"*My* bed," he snarled through bared teeth.

He drew his surcoat and tunic over his head before tossing the pelts back toward the bed. Without removing his hose, he threw himself after them. The bed rocked with his weight.

Rowena sat in wide-eyed silence for a moment, pondering his timely disappearance. She shrugged and curled up on the stones with no pelts to cushion or cover her. Shivering, she rolled to her back. She had never realized how many sharp edges the stones possessed. A solid lump poked at the base of her spine. Despite her discomfort, a perverse calm claimed her.

"You had no right," she said softly.

She was hardly aware she had spoken aloud until Gareth's incredulous face appeared over the edge of the bed. "What did you say?"

She met his gaze with perfect serenity. "I said you had no right. To touch me that way in front of my papa."

"No right? *No right?*" Gareth climbed off the bed knee over knee. Rowena scrambled backward, but his hands caught in the wool of her bliaut. Her feet left the floor as he picked her up and slammed her to the feather tick. "I had no right? Let me inform you of a few facts about my rights, sweet Lady Rowena Fordyce."

His eyes were very close to hers. Only his elbows resting on either side of her head kept his weight from crushing her.

"I won you in an honorable game of chance. Your bastard of a father wagered you as any decent man would a cow or a parcel of land. You belong to me. I have the right to do whatever I please with you, and I've had that right from the first day I laid eyes on you. If I care to drag you down those stairs and spread your legs at your precious papa's feet, 'tis my right. Not a man in the hall would dare condemn me for it."

Her aching pride made Rowena careless. "They condemn you for other things, do they not?"

Gareth's eyes narrowed into the eyes of a stranger. Rowena tried to turn her face away, but he caught her chin in one hand. "Watch your tongue, girl. I've quaffed enough ale tonight to ravish five maidens before dawn without a qualm of conscience."

"If you've quaffed that much ale, you're probably not able," she retorted.

"Try me."

He lowered his lean warrior's body with a deliberate motion, and Rowena felt an unfamiliar hardness graze her abdomen. Her eyes widened. It was a cruel thing to do, but Gareth never went into battle without showing his weapons. Her skin shrank from the crude caress. The wool and linen between them was suddenly like so much parchment.

Rowena bit her lip and blinked back tears. "Do you seek to make me what you would have Papa believe I am?"

Her tears were as sobering as a dash of cold water. Gareth buried his face in her hair to hide their effect on him. "I know what you are. I've known your kind before. All soft and sweet and as deadly as poisoned honey. If your father only knew what restraint I've used . . ." His heated lips brushed her temple.

"Do not mock me," she choked out. "The only thing you've used is me. You invited my papa here so you could humiliate the both of us in your little game. You dragged my family here in the dead of winter, half-starved and freezing, knowing they could be trapped by a snowstorm at any time."

"Why do you defend your papa?" he murmured against her hair.

"Why do you despise him?"

Gareth made no reply. His mouth glided over the tiny hairs at her temple and down to the corner of her mouth.

"Have you lodged my family in the next chamber?" She was desperate to stop him before she tasted the ale on his tongue. "The better to hear my pleas and screams? Nay, Gareth, if you will make a whore out of me, you shall do it in silence, for I swear not one whimper will escape my lips."

He caught her hands in his and held them captive on each side of her head. "If you think I could not make you cry out, you are wrong." His eyes warned her that it was not pain he threatened.

Rowena caught half a breath before his lips descended on hers. She steeled herself against his kiss, preparing herself to be punished and hurt. But she had not prepared herself for the tenderness of his assault. As his mouth met hers, the violence left his body with a wracking shudder, to be replaced by a gentleness as disarming as it was potent. His tongue tasted her lips, then dipped inward in a leisurely exploration of the sweetness within. When his fingers laced around hers, Rowena held on, clinging to the one thing of substance that kept her from drowning in a luxuriant sea of fur and sensation.

He lowered his body against hers, thigh to thigh, belly to belly, balancing his weight perfectly to keep from crushing her. His dark head glided downward, pushing her bliaut away until his mouth tenderly grazed the peak of her breast in a caress that bore no relation to his crass pawing in the great hall. Her nipple shivered and contracted beneath his tongue. She moaned softly as pleasure and shame quickened within her.

The low sound brought Gareth's head up. Rowena's eyes were clenched shut. He freed her hands and cupped her chin, coaxing her to open them. Not even a cloud of tears could dim their brilliance. The trust with which she had welcomed his kiss in the great hall still shone within, battered and bruised, but unsurrendered. He had seen that look once before in blue eyes welling with tears. Her trust was a formidable enemy. It had conquered poverty and betrayal with a dignity he could barely understand. Now it would conquer him. If he had been a man who begged, he might have pleaded with Rowena then and there to open herself and let him slake his bitterness in her healing warmth.

She snuffled softly.

He rolled off of her without a word and sat on the edge of the bed.

A terrible coldness pricked Rowena where his body had been. She hugged her bliaut to her neck and sat up, biting a lip that felt tender and swollen.

Her fingertips touched one of the rigid scars on his back. "Gareth, please . . ."

He flinched as if her touch had scorched him. For her to beg now was more than he could bear. "Go away, won't you? Leave me be."

If Gareth could have guessed what Rowena's plea was going to be, his response might have been very different. She had opened her mouth to beg for any kindness, for a hint of his smile, for the courteous attention he had waved before her like sugar before a starving child. She was willing to pay any price to stop him from turning his back on her. At his words her hand fell away from him like a dying flower.

Silence followed, then the soft pad of her feet against the stone. The door creaked open.

Gareth did not have to turn to sense the straightness of her spine, the hurt pride in her voice. "I may not be able to spell my own name, but I am not so foolish as to be blind to the truth. There is only one man in all England you would hate so well. The knight you caught with your precious Elayne."

Gareth wanted to turn and shout the truth at her. To cross the chamber and shake her until she opened her eyes and saw her father for what he was. Instead, he stared at the back of his hands.

"Despite your feelings for Papa, you've treated me with nothing but kindness since bringing me to Caerleon. Why you would have him believe otherwise, I do not know. I cannot fathom what I've done to make you hate me so." The door closed with a final thump.

"I don't hate you," Gareth said to the empty chamber. The words that followed were only a whisper in his mind as he buried his aching head in his palms.

Rowena wandered the endless corridors, deaf to all but the sputter of the ebbing torches. The snores and moans that drifted out from behind the closed doors held the cadence of unreality in the darkest morning hours, like echoes from a time long past. The shadowy corridors grew longer and longer.

"Holy Mother of God," she swore as Marlys erupted from a darkened doorway. The oath coming from Rowena's lips stopped Marlys in her tracks. "Spare me your offended glare, Marlys. Did it never occur to you that I am sick to death of you stalking me like the grim reaper? I weary of it."

Marlys stepped in front of her, but Rowena shoved past her easily. "Leave me be." She echoed Gareth's words without realizing it.

"Wait." Marlys caught her arm. "There is someone you must see."

Rowena glanced over Marlys's shoulder where a heavy door stood ajar. She shrugged Marlys's grip away. "Another of your twisted jests? Have you Blaine lurking inside to ravish me? Or mayhaps the ghost of Lady Elayne cowering on the bed with a sword through her breast?"

Beneath her dark strands of hair, Marlys paled. "Rowena, please."

Begging did not suit Marlys. Rowena slid her hand under Marlys's hair and flipped it back. Marlys flinched. Rowena could find no trace of laughter or mockery in her face. Surprised by her own cruelty, she freed the hair, then gave a curt nod. Marlys gripped her arm and drew her forward.

Rowena's nose twitched at the odor of stale rosemary. The blue pall of daylight was gone from Elayne's chamber. In its place were the flickering shadows cast from a tallow candle shuttered by translucent slices of horn. Rowena strained her eyes to see. The door slammed. The cupboard door creaked open, and hot, wet lips sucked at her cheek. For an instant, she believed once again that Marlys had betrayed her. But even Blaine at his crudest could not compare to the lack of finesse in this kiss.

Her hand curled into a fist and crashed into the head attached to her cheek.

"Aaaargh!" Irwin reeled backward, clutching his ear. "Gads, Rowena, no need to deafen me, you know. I had hoped you had abandoned your violent ways for a gentler demeanor."

"That scene in the great hall should have warned you differently," came a boy's voice rippling with laughter. "If she'd toss ale in de Crecy's face, I shudder to think what she'd do to you."

Rowena glanced wildly around the chamber. The pale sheen she had been searching for glided into view. Little Freddie found his way into her arms.

"There now," he said, patting her back awkwardly. "No need for tears. We've come to make it all better."

Rowena's tears soaked his shoulder. She knew the time when things could have been cured by optimism had long passed. Irwin stole a pat but jerked his hand away when she turned her watery glare on him. Big Freddie shuffled forward, cobwebs draping his ducked head.

Rowena sat on the edge of the musty counterpane, smothering the last of her sniffles in a rag torn from Big Freddie's sleeve. Marlys stood leaning against the door with arms crossed.

"This familial display of devotion is touching," she drawled, "but I must remind you that haste is of the essence. Gareth's stupors are short and his temper fierce when he awakens."

Rowena was hard pressed to imagine his temper being any more fierce than it had been moments ago. Irwin knelt on one knee at her feet. He *had* grown taller since she had seen him last. The beginnings of a moustache fuzzed his lip.

He beamed up at her. "We have come to rescue you."

"You mean Papa regrets his wager? He has come to carry me home?"

Irwin cleared his throat. Big Freddie glared at his feet as if he found them offensive.

Little Freddie stepped forward, loving her too much to lie. "Papa is tucked under a table in the great hall, snoring soundly. He wants no part of our plan."

"But surely if you told him—" Rowena started.

"We did," Little Freddie said flatly.

"I see." Rowena tried to withdraw her hand, but Irwin held it fast with a strength that surprised her.

His eyes devoured her face. "I'm not sure that you do. I am still your betrothed, Rowena. We have been betrothed since we were but children. I hold fast to that oath. I care not what that beastly wretch has done to you. I am willing to overlook any defilement, any breach of innocence you bring to our marriage bed."

Marlys's cough sounded more like a shout of laughter. In that moment Rowena almost hated her. She resisted the urge to plant her foot in Irwin's chest. Her gaze dropped. He was kneeling in the center of the dark stain that spread from the bed to the stones—the last trace of the life that had dripped away on that night so long ago.

"How kind," she said faintly.

She rose, slipping out of his grasp like a wraith, and brushed past Big Freddie. More by instinct than sight, her hands found the heavy velvet folds draped over the windows. She drew them back and slipped into their shelter. Her hands fumbled with the shutters. Fresh, cold wind poured past her and into the chamber, sending the drapes into a lashing dance. Before the voice could sound low and pervasive in her ear, she knew who it would belong to.

"Did he whisper sweet endearments to you? Murmur of marriage? Plight his troth?"

That picture was so far from the truth of their encounter that Rowena had to close her eyes.

The voice went on. "He will use you if you stay. The winter nights are long and cold. Even a monk would be sorely pressed to resist a chit as convenient as you. He might even be kind to you. When he tired of you, he would send you on your way with a few trinkets, a family brooch, a brotherly kiss."

Marlys's diatribe died on a hiss. Her voice softened. "I shield my face because I have no desire to be a man's chattel. Every time my father looked at me, he saw nothing more than a future alliance with Blaine's father. Be it whore or wife in merry old England, a woman is still a man's property—his toy. Is that what you wish for your life, Lady Precious?"

Rowena opened her eyes. Every line of the courtyard below was drawn with painful clarity. Beneath the empty boughs of an oak, four horses milled on their tethers. All she wished for was yesterday when the tenuous thread between she and Gareth had not been laced with revenge.

Marlys's gaze dropped to Rowena's stomach. "What if he should get you with babe? Gareth does not fancy children. He despised Elayne's brat."

The courtyard blurred. Rowena brought a strand of hair to her lips. She kept her tone light, refusing to betray the cost of a question that had been niggling at the back of her mind for weeks. "What became of the child when Elayne died?"

Marlys gently pulled the hairs from Rowena's lips. "No one knows. The child disappeared on the night Elayne was murdered. Some say Gareth strangled her and buried her in the orchard."

Rowena's fingernails dug into the stone. The chestnut mare in the courtyard tossed its head, nickering softly. Rowena gripped Marlys's hand. "Will you help us?"

Marlys nodded.

"Papa . . ." Rowena began.

"I shall get him free of Caerleon before Gareth can kill him. He deserves no more."

"And what of you?"

Her white teeth flashed in a carnivorous grin. "Gareth cannot kill me. He loves me."

Little Freddie was standing outside the curtains.

Rowena knew he had heard every word. He extended an arm to her. "Shall we go home?"

"Home," Rowena repeated. "To Revelwood."

"Keep off the main roads," Marlys commanded. "Stay away from Revelwood for at least a week. The bread will last if you are sparing. Eat only when you are hungry." This earned her a dubious glance from Irwin.

"Must we steal the mounts?" Rowena said from the back of the chestnut mare.

"Would you care to be run down by Folio?" Marlys arched one eyebrow. "Or hunted by Gareth's wolfhounds? Most of them are trained to kill, you know." Rowena did not know and wished she had not asked. "Anyway," Marlys added with a smirk, "I'd never allow you to steal our horses. These mounts belong to Blaine. Even if he catches you, a flutter of those eyelashes will probably save you from the hangman."

She jerked Rowena down by the neck of her woolen kirtle. Her eyes nervously scanned the horizon. Between the stark branches of the trees, the black sky was melting to gray. "Heed my words well. Don't let him find you. Gareth hates to lose anything that belongs to him."

Rowena straightened in the saddle. "Soften the blow, won't you? Tell him I never belonged to him at all."

Marlys nodded with an approving smile. Rowena had to grab the bridle with both hands as Marlys smacked the mare's rump with a hoarse cry. The mare bolted. The other horses followed, stretching their long legs in an exuberant canter toward freedom. The damp, chill air filled Rowena's lungs but failed to drive out the oppressive heaviness in her breast as she left behind the shadow of Caerleon and its master forever.

# Part Two

Western wind, when will thou blow,
The small rain down can rain?
Christ, if my love were in my arms
And I in my bed again!
—Anonymous

# Chapter 11

Marlys tumbled into bed with a groan. The flat, pale sun had done little to warm her chamber. She thought of reaching to the end of the bed to drag the coverlet over her, but the contemplation of such motion after finally laying down her aching bones drew another groan from her throat. She threw herself on her face and burrowed deep into the feather tick.

"Marlys!"

The bellow warned her an instant before the thunderous rapping exploded on her door. With a last spurt of energy, she flopped over and dove headfirst into the counterpane bunched at the foot of the bed. As the door crashed open, she curled into a ball, knowing the inert lump she had become had little chance of fooling her brother. She was right. The flat side of his sword smacked into her rump with a twang that sent the blade vibrating into song.

She popped up with a growl. "Suppose you had inadvertently whacked the wrong end? You would have brained me."

"Methinks there are as much brains in one end as in

the other," Gareth shot back. He faced her like a savage twin, his hair tangled in a dark web around his face, his eyes red-rimmed and wild. "Where are they?"

"Who?" Marlys sank back on her knees and gathered the coverlets around her shoulders like a shawl.

"You know who. Fordyce and his damnable litter of pups."

"How should I know? I was abed as soon as Dunnla gave me my milk bath and coiffed my curls."

One eye fluttered prettily at him. Gareth plucked a twig from her matted hair. "A new fashion, I suppose?" His gaze dropped to the feet poking out from under the blanket. Their soles were as black as the grubby tunic she wore from yesterday. She jerked them back. He grabbed her big toe and twisted.

She howled.

"Where?" Gareth demanded.

She pounded on his shoulders with open palms until he freed her toe. "What do you care of Lindsey Fordyce's comings and goings? You could have tossed him in the dungeon last night if you were hoping for public confession. 'Twas you who chose to torture Rowena instead of him."

He had the good grace to color. " 'Twas Rowena's insolence that demanded my attention. Fordyce had enough ale in him to keep for a few hours. He was fair pickled 'ere I went abovestairs."

"As were you."

Gareth chose to ignore that. "If not for your cursed interference, the fool would've slept till I was ready to conclude our dealings."

"He has no dealings with you. You heard him. He barely recalls holding Father's fief."

"We both know he lies." His shaggy head bent over her as his voice lowered. "If you do not tell me where they are, I swear I shall see you married to Blaine yet. The priest may not come to Caerleon, but I shall have you dragged before him. 'Twould suit Blaine's sadistic streak to finally have a chance at taming you."

Marlys gave an injured sniff, but Gareth knew her

well enough to duck before her hand whistled past his jaw. He caught her fist in his. "Shall I have the joyful banns of your upcoming nuptials read in the village? Or would you prefer to tell me what you've done with Fordyce?"

Marlys glared up at him. "The bandy-legged little rooster has gone scampering for home."

Gareth loosed her and started for the door. Marlys buried her mouth against her knee, muffling her words. "Let the puppy go, Gareth."

Gareth stopped. "What did you say?"

Marlys lifted her head. A woolen fuzz clung to her tongue. Gareth turned, his face white. Marlys realized she had made a terrible mistake, but it was too late to bite back the words.

Pained bewilderment twisted Gareth's features. "You let him take Rowena?"

Her brother's vulnerability was more than Marlys could bear. She summoned a smirk to her lips with an effort he would never see. "She begged I give you a message. 'Soften the blow,' she said with that tinkling little laugh of hers. 'Tell him I never belonged to him anyway.' "

Gareth's breathing was suddenly the only sound audible in the chamber. With mingled relief and regret, Marlys watched a cold mask of fury slip over his features.

His hands balled into fists. "When I get my hands on her, I shall leave no doubt in her mind as to whom she belongs to."

Marlys stretched out her long limbs and rested her head on laced hands. "You should have thought of that before she fled from you. A dark-eyed bastard in her belly would have kept your memory fresh." She watched him through slitted eyes, expecting a curse, or maybe even a blow. The speculative gleam in his eyes frightened her. She rolled to her side, faking an indifferent yawn. "Tell Dunnla if she disturbs me before nightfall, I shall cut off her head."

"Aaaah, the sleep of the innocent. Free of any unsightly twinges of conscience."

"I told you long ago. I have no conscience."

"For once," Gareth said, "I must agree."

The door softly closed and Gareth was gone. Marlys jumped out of bed and stumbled to her knees before the window. A moment later, Gareth appeared far below, leading Folio out of the stables at a run. Without slowing, he flung a long leg over the stallion's back and drove him through the castle gates.

"Ride hard, little one," Marlys murmured. "Ride as if the devil himself were on your heels." She knelt there as if in prayer until her knees went numb, dashing away her tears before they could splash on the stones.

Lindsey Fordyce swore under his breath as he slid off the nag for the third time. His bad leg throbbed. He lay on the frozen dirt like an amiable cherub swaddled in scarves from toe to brow. The illusion was shattered when he opened his mouth and a new string of curses spewed forth. His sons loped to his rescue, tugging him to his feet and dusting him off with hamlike hands. Two of the boys rewound a scarf over his pink-tipped nose and across his eyes.

He clawed at the scarf. "God's nightgown, why don't the lot of you just throw me on the ground and smother me? Are you in that much haste to gain your inheritance?"

The boys looked at each other blankly, then broke into grins. Fordyce shook his head. "Scold you and you grin. If I thrash you, will you laugh?" He shook his fist at the shuffling circle of giants, then thought better of it.

He satisfied himself with kicking the nag. The beast rolled its eyes but did not flinch. "I cannot fathom where that chit found such a creature. 'Tis not fit to feed the vultures. More carrion than horse, I say. But the chit was more man than woman if you ask me. Wouldn't surprise me if she were hiding a healthy moustache beneath all that hair. She was a beastly little girl, too, always tagging after that arrogant brother of hers. You there—William. Nay, Phillip. Whatever the hell your name is, hasten over here and help me mount."

The hulking lad he pointed to got down on hands and knees. Fordyce trundled up on his back, heedless of the dig of his heels into his son's ribs. He laid across the horse with a solid "oomph." His rounded gut fit neatly into the hollow of the horse's spine. The other four boys pushed him into place as their brother lay gasping for air.

The ribbon of road unfolded through the massive trunks of trees scarred with winter's grayness. The ancient forest had lost none of its menace with its leaves. An aura of stillness and decay hung over it like the pall of the sun pasted in the gray sky. Fordyce rubbed his dripping nose on his scarf, his temper unimproved by the memory of the warm hall he had been forced to desert as dawn had claimed the skies.

He might still be languishing there now if that hairy creature had not thrust his tunic into his hand, hissing of danger and flight. His regret sharpened with the chill in the air. He had so hoped to deepen his acquaintance with that ample widow he had danced with the night before. Images of pleasant days spent living off de Crecy's food, ale, and hospitality rolled before his eyes to be obliterated by the narrow road leading back to Revelwood. He considered sending the boys on and braving a return to Caerleon. His body followed the direction of his thoughts, pivoting on the horse so he could peruse the ancient Roman road they had traveled from Caerleon.

Rowena had done well enough for herself there. She had sat like a princess on a throne of furs at Sir Gareth's feet. Why should her father be responsible if she had thrown a tantrum and ran off to sulk? Surely a man as reasonable as Sir Gareth would not blame him for the folly of a woman. Rowena had probably trotted back to the castle at first hint of dawn and was even now cuddled in the knight's arms, begging prettily for his forgiveness.

If he returned to Caerleon, he and Gareth would

raise a mug around the fire and toast the stubbornness of women. A smile played around his lips. 'Twould not be the first time they could ruminate one with another over the fickle heart of a woman.

He was still lost in his pleasant reverie when a nightmare garbed in black rounded the bend and hurtled down the long stretch straight for him.

Ignoring the open-mouthed mutters of his sons, he slammed his heels into the nag's flanks. The horse did not budge. A frantic glance over his shoulder showed the dark shape looming larger, riding as one with a white beast whose hooves skimmed the earth as if winged.

Fordyce bounced up and down to jog the horse into motion. The nag shuddered and leaned backward. For one terrible moment, Fordyce feared it would sit down, dumping him onto the packed earth for the fourth time. The nag swayed but held firm. He wrested a rusty dagger from his waistband and drew the blade neatly across the nag's hide. With a bray of pain, the horse lurched forward in an uneven canter Fordyce would have thought impossible seconds before.

He heard the cries of his sons and dared a look back to see them trotting after him, arms upraised. Almost upon them was the thundering shadow. Chuckling with glee, he humped over, his heels beating a sharp staccato against the nag's ribs. His next look back showed the boys staring after him, limp-handed and open-mouthed. He twisted around, gripping wisps of mane to hold his seat. The stretch of road between them was empty. The dark rider had vanished.

A flash of pure black out of the corner of his eye warned him. His pursuer was no longer behind him. He wheeled around with a choked squeal as a muscled arm shot out and curved around his windpipe. The nag galloped on without him, finding a grace it had forgotten in the freedom from his bulk. The sun went purple before Fordyce's eyes. For a moment, he thought he would simply hang there, finished by that merciless arm with no noose, no gallows, no noble speeches of farewell. When Sir Gareth launched himself off his stallion without losing his grip, he knew he would not be so fortunate.

They hit the ground with an impact that had to hurt Gareth as much as it hurt him. The thought gave Fordyce satisfaction even as his lungs sucked in on themselves. Their momentum sent them rolling off the road into the dead underbrush of a ditch. A twig dug a shallow trench in his forearm, but the pain was a welcome reprieve from the numbness in his chest.

Gareth straddled him. Fordyce dragged in a breath as the arm at his windpipe was replaced by the icy tip of a misericord. "What have you done with her?" Gareth rasped. Blood trickled from a corner of his lip.

Fordyce started to say "Who?" but wisely refrained. He satisfied himself with blinking owlishly until he could summon enough breath to answer. He made a decision he would not make often in his life. He told the truth. "How many lads do you see?"

Gareth looked at him askance, wary of a trick. Neither the misericord nor the hand that held it wavered as he raised his head. "Five. And if they are lads, they are overgrown indeed."

Fordyce gave a fraction of a nod as if that settled the matter. "Five. Then mayhaps you should pursue the other three and ask them what *they* have done with her."

The five shaggy men crept nearer, hands shoved deep in flaps that were once sleeves. A frown of consternation touched Gareth's brow. Fordyce bit back a smile.

Gareth settled back on his heels. Dirt smudged his cheek, making him appear as sinister as if he had been driven from hell itself, trailing sparks and ashes. "The silver-haired boy has her. And Irwin—the one who tells the stories. They are the ones who carried her off? Where might they be?"

Fordyce shrugged. "How should I know? They came to me last night, blathering about some preposterous plan to rescue Ro." He embellished the tale with typical dramatic flair. "Irwin told me how she came to him on

her knees, weeping piteously and begging her rightful
betrothed to free her from your monstrous bondage."

Gareth opened his mouth, then closed it. The hand
holding the misericord went limp. "And you refused to
help her?"

Fordyce sniffed. "I made a wager. I am an honorable
man." He nudged aside Gareth's blade with one finger
and sat up, plucking dead leaves from his scarf.

Gareth's gaze traveled frantically from Fordyce to
the road. His brow furrowed, the weight of decision
obviously paining him. His words were more for himself than Fordyce. "There is no telling what those fools
will lead her into."

He stood, towering over Fordyce. The baron climbed
to his feet to find himself glaring at Gareth's hauberk.
When had the lad grown to such monstrous stature? He
threw the ends of his scarf over his shoulders and
started up the ditch bank. "To be so accosted! There
are laws to protect innocent travelers. England is a civilized land. Why, if the king had any inkling—"

His words died on a gurgle as Gareth caught the
ends of Fordyce's scarf and wound them around his fist.
He was jerked against a body as hard as iron.

Gareth's breath was hot in his ear. "You haven't
seen the last of me yet, Fordyce. I'll be back for you.
And if I find her with you—if I find out you lied—
neither law, nor Edward, nor God Himself will stop me
from killing you. Do you understand?"

Fordyce managed a cough that Gareth blessedly took
for assent. The knight freed him. He scrambled out of
the ditch, heedless of the dirt and leaves he scattered on
Gareth's head. The nag was nowhere to be seen, and
Fordyce eyed Gareth's stallion wistfully. The beast
rolled its eyes and pawed the dirt. Mustering the remnants of his dignity, he limped down the narrowing
road, his eyes darting from side to side in search of his
own dismal excuse for a mount. The boys followed in a
bedraggled parade.

He was well out of arm's reach and almost out of
earshot when he called back in the tones of a benevolent

papa, "Don't fret about the girl, Sir Gareth. She is in good hands. Little Roddy is a responsible lad."

"His name is Little Freddie, you idiot!" Gareth's cry was filled with such virulence that Fordyce began to march in double time and the lads had to lope to keep up with him.

Rowena should have grown accustomed to the cold. But as her numb fingers uncurled from the reins, the prick of it stung her anew. The fingerless gloves swathing her palms hung in tatters. The air was different today—lighter somehow, and sparkling with an airy iridescence that rendered its raw chill all the more cruel. Rowena felt giddy, as if the air burning her lungs lacked substance. The sun hung like a flat yellow disk in the sky, mocking them with its illusion of warmth.

A harmless ribbon of gray clouds unfurled themselves on the horizon. She glanced at Little Freddie. After a week of huddling in the forests, nibbling on what berries or acorns they could scrounge, his cheeks had taken on the sunken look she hated. Sensing her somber gaze, he swiveled on his pony and gave her a heartening smile.

They sat on the hill overlooking Revelwood. An unbroken stretch of gray swelled behind the castle, resembling more a vast sea than the moor it was.

Without wanting to, Rowena saw another castle transposed over the crumbling ramparts of Revelwood. She blinked to dispel the image, knowing she might as well imagine her hands cupped around a steaming bowl of barley stew or her hair untangled by hands that mocked her with their tenderness. Below them, nothing stirred but the wind. Irwin's bay snorted nervously.

"No reason to dawdle now." Irwin chafed his palms. "Home awaits us."

But none of them moved until Rowena clucked softly to her mare to lead them down the hill. They dismounted clumsily, their limbs stiff with cold. Big Freddie took a step toward the frozen moat.

"Wait!" She caught his arm.

They all looked at her, then at the moat. The splintered planks that had served as a drawbridge were gone. Between them and the iron-banded door lay a ditch fifteen feet wide, ten feet deep, and mottled with water frozen to a grimy dun.

Big Freddie dropped to hands and knees to peer into the abyss he had almost walked into. Little Freddie paced along the moat, his gaze trained to the ground. His smooth forehead puckered in a frown.

Irwin hugged himself and stamped his feet. "Hullo," he called out.

The cry echoed, then went drifting over the moors. A rising wind whipped tears into Rowena's eyes. The impassive stone walls blurred before her watery gaze. She shivered with a chill that had nothing to do with the cold as she remembered Gareth's long-ago threat. Perhaps even now the bodies of her papa and brothers littered the great hall, their eyes frozen in sightless horror, a single line of crimson staining their throats.

Irwin blew into the cup of his hands. "How we reached Revelwood before they did I do not know. This beastly week has gone on forever. Did Uncle remove the planks when we left? I cannot recall it, but he must have."

"He did not." Little Freddie straightened, his lips compressed to a thin line. "Do you see any planks? The ground was soft from the melting snow when we started out. Do you see any ridges or marks where the planks might have been dragged away?"

Irwin gave the ground a halfhearted sweep. "Well, nay, I suppose not . . ."

"Of course you don't," Little Freddie said. "Because the planks were not dragged away. They were—"

Rowena finished the sentence with him. "—dragged inside."

They lifted their gazes to the weather-beaten stones; seeing their home as an impenetrable fortress for the first time. The empty eyes of the arrow slits stared back at them.

Big Freddie ambled to his feet, scratching his head.

"The ice is solid enough. I could climb down and cross it."

"How would you reach the door? Spread your arms and fly?" Little Freddie shook his head. "Nay. 'Twon't be necessary." His voice cracked as it rose to a roar. "Whoever locked us out can bloody well open the door and let us in!"

Something in Rowena snapped to see her brother's even features contorted with rage. Her voice joined his in a mindless cry of anger. Irwin bellowed. Big Freddie scooped up a handful of stones and pelted the castle door. Their cacophony should have woken any dead Gareth might have left.

Rowena's cry died on a hacking cough as icy air paralyzed her raw throat. One by one, the others lapsed into silence. The air itself seemed to be waiting. A muted click from the door echoed with the resonance of a bell. Rowena held her breath as an iron panel slid open, driven by the chubby fingers curled around its edge.

"Begone," came a petulant voice. "There is no one home."

The panel slammed shut.

# Chapter 12

Rowena slumped against Little Freddie as bittersweet relief drained the remnants of her strength.

Irwin was the first to master his voice and his senses. "Uncle," he called. "Uncle, dear, 'tis your nephew and children come home. Do let us in, won't you, sir?" He mumbled in an aside to the rest of them, "Must not know 'tis us," then bellowed cheerfully, "hullo! 'Tis Irwin, sir. We are not beggars or robbers come to loot your castle. We are your kinfolk. Open up and let us warm ourselves at your fire."

Big Freddie stared at Irwin, his mouth hanging open.

"Mayhaps Papa does not realize . . ." Rowena said faintly.

"He realizes." A cold gray light burned in Little Freddie's eyes. "You try, Ro."

Rowena's first cry came out in a croak. She swallowed and tried again. "Papa, 'tis Rowena. We need your help. We have been hiding in the forests for over a week. But now we are home and ever so hungry and cold. I've fled Caerleon. I've come home, Papa. To Revelwood and to you. I beg you . . ." Her voice trailed into silence. Little Freddie's hand slipped into hers. Anger deepened the edge of her voice as she drew herself up straight and shouted, "Papa, open the door. We are exhausted and chilled to the bone. How long must we stand out here and beg for entrance to our own home? You must open the door. You must—"

Little Freddie tugged her hand. The icy wind bit at the tears wetting her cheeks.

With a click, the panel slid open. Papa's face appeared like a bright moon in a square sky. "Foolish child."

His words were all the more jarring for being spoken so softly. Rowena knew instinctively that he was referring to her. Her eyes widened. Papa had never once rebuked her.

Irwin started toward the moat, a grin curving his full lips. "My dearest Uncle, we've rescued Rowena from a ghastly fate and brought her home. Are you not pleased?"

"Get back!" Papa's spat words erased Irwin's grin. "Foolish children, all of you. Begone. Go as far away from Revelwood as you dare. We do not want you here. None of you."

Little Freddie's features hardened to a mask. "Tell me, Papa, was it a well-worn sack of gold that won your loyalty to the dark knight? Or mayhaps thirty pieces of silver?"

Papa sniffed. "You wound me, lad. Do you truly think no better of me than that?"

Little Freddie's sneer was answer enough.

"Twasn't gold or silver, was it, Papa?" Rowena cried. The wind sent her hair streaming across her face. Papa's face blurred and crumpled like a pudding in the rain.

"Not gold. Nor silver. But murder, Rowena. Murder in his eyes when he attacked me like the madman he is. He swore if he found you here, there would be no hope for any of us." Papa continued in more chiding tones. "By fleeing him, you have dishonored my good name."

Little Freddie muttered a word that would have done Marlys proud.

Papa's voice sank to a whine. "I beseech you, child. Save yourself and your kinfolk. Return to Sir Gareth on your knees. Beg for his mercy and forgiveness. Surely you can use your feminine wiles to win your way back into his heart and bed. Your papa cannot allow you to return to Revelwood in disgrace."

Rowena lifted her head. "I understand. If I go on alone, will you open your door to the boys?"

Irwin and Little Freddie broke into protest, but it was Big Freddie's baritone that silenced them all. "Nonsense. You'll go nowhere alone. I'll not be having it." Rowena stared at him and he ducked his head, his shy smile revealing a row of broken teeth.

When she turned back to the door, the panel had closed. All was silent within the castle. The gatekeeper was gone.

Rowena fought to keep the note of pleading from her voice. "Papa, we are starving. Can you not spare us some food to ease our journey?"

The panel slid open. Rowena ducked as four dark bulbs came sailing across the moat. A bruised turnip rolled past her feet and bounced into the moat. Irwin dove to his hands and knees, trying to save the other turnips from meeting a similar fate. The panel slammed shut.

Rowena sat down with legs crossed and chin propped in her hands. Out of the pale sunshine and borne on the airy wind came tiny flakes of ice that cut like daggers against her skin. She tilted her face upward and licked a snowflake from her cheek.

"Wonderful. Papa has forsaken me. I could be hanged for horse thievery. A madman is pursuing me. And now God sends us snow to brighten our journey."

Little Freddie knelt in front of her. "Papa forsook each one of us with his cry of pleasure when our seed left his loins."

She studied his face. Tiny cracks spread along the borders of his lips. His gray eyes were huge and eerie above the shadows etched in his fair skin.

"Perhaps Papa is right," she said. "Perhaps I should return to him. Throw myself on his mercy."

"From what I've heard of him, he has no mercy. Do you believe otherwise?"

Rowena's eyes darkened as she felt again the tender stroke of Gareth's fingers against her cheek. She had been a heartbeat away from surrendering herself to those hands when his cold words had stopped her. *Leave me be.* Could those same hands have used their diabolical expertise to end a child's life? She shivered at the memory of his caress. If Gareth ran her through, her pain would be over. His mercy might prolong it indefinitely.

" 'Tis what frightens me the most. I do not know."

"Then we go on." He offered her his hand and they rose in one motion.

"Where shall we go on to?" Irwin asked. Rowena flinched as his teeth crunched through the skin of a turnip.

Without wanting to, she remembered Dunnla's stew, steaming thick with beef and barley. The world wavered before her eyes as if seen through a haze of smoke. When Irwin offered her the turnip, she snapped a large bite out of it. Its bitterness was somehow heartening.

She tossed the turnip to Big Freddie.

"I've never had my own horse before," he said.

She lacked the heart to protest as he held the turnip in front of the horse's nose without even taking a bite of it. The sorrel swallowed it whole. Irwin's face fell. His hand darted to his sleeve to massage his other treasures.

"Horses are nice," Rowena said gently. "But we cannot eat them." She cuffed Irwin as he gave Big Freddie's horse a speculative look.

It was beginning to snow in earnest. Feathery flakes settled in Rowena's hair. Above them, the sun dissolved behind a veil of low-hanging clouds.

Rowena mustered a smile as she mounted her mare. "We shall go wherever we choose. The world is ours and we shall make our way in it as any travelers would do. What is hunger compared to the thrill of adventuring?"

"Damned inconvenient, I say." Irwin rolled onto his horse. "Pardon me, Ro. Shouldn't have sworn in front of you. Though I daresay you've heard worse living in that nest of noble vipers."

Rowena started to protest, then remembered she had heard much worse from Marlys's lips. She inclined her head in a regal nod. "I shall grant my forgiveness this time, Irwin."

"Frightfully benevolent of you," Little Freddie whispered with a smirk.

She nudged his pony with her foot. Of one accord, they circled the castle and started across the cold, gray expanse of the moor. Dead bracken crackled beneath the horses' hooves. The wind, unbroken by even the bones of trees, whipped flecks of snow into their faces. Rowena huddled deeper into her mantle, taking a perverse comfort in the bleakness of the landscape. There were no ancient trees waiting to spill a dark shadow armed with a silvery sword onto their heads. There were no dark blots of doubt on a barrenness that was a vast shadow in itself. In the most wintry, desolate season, the moor had once again become her friend.

Her optimism lasted until a nightfall which found them huddled behind a moldy hillock. They lay in the same heap they had slept in for years. Little Freddie's back fit to her stomach like a spoon. Rowena's leg was thrown over his waist. Little Freddie pillowed his head on Irwin's bulk and Big Freddie curled around their feet like a faithful hound.

The snow had stopped after laying a feeble blanket on the ground. The sky had cleared. The stars winked like cruel diamonds against a pelt of sable as impenetrable as Gareth's eyes.

"What ever shall become of us?" Rowena said to no one in particular.

Irwin burrowed into the dirt like a groundhog. "If we freeze to death, we shan't have to worry about it."

Little Freddie shrugged. " 'Tisn't much colder than Revelwood. 'Tis Rowena that frets me. She has grown accustomed to a warmer bed."

Irwin sniffed. "I daresay she has."

Rowena was too addled from hunger to retort. "We could become a traveling troupe of entertainers," she mused. "Wealthy wastrels like Sir Blaine tumble over one another to hurl them pouches of gold and silver. We could sing for our supper."

Little Freddie poked Irwin. "Can you sing?"

"Well . . . nay. I can play the trumpet and hum a little."

"How about you? Can you sing?"

Big Freddie shook his shaggy head.

He lifted an eyebrow at Rowena. "You?"

"I fear not, but perhaps I could learn to rope dance. And you could tumble. And Irwin . . ." her smooth brow furrowed, "Irwin could juggle. Aye, 'tis a fine thought. Refrain from eating the turnips, Irwin. You can juggle them."

"Can you juggle two turnips?" Little Freddie rolled to his back and cushioned his head on Irwin's belly. "The nobility are looking for oddities to amuse them. They tire of their own company."

"Nothing odd about us," Irwin mumbled.

Rowena giggled. "Shall we strap a bundle on your back, Little Freddie, and bill you as a hump-backed dwarf?"

Irwin flung himself on his side. "Can the two of you not freeze to death in silence and let a man sleep? Cease your musing. We have no coin, talent, or gross deformities to make such a venture worthwhile. If a dancing bear should happen by, you may awaken me."

Rowena looked at Little Freddie. They propped themselves up on their elbows.

Little Freddie's finger stabbed beneath Irwin's ribs, and Irwin lifted his head with a groan to find them grinning like idiots. He followed their gazes to their feet where Big Freddie had thrown out his limbs in a shambling stretch. His mouth fell open in a snore deeper than a growl.

Irwin frowned thoughtfully. "Can he dance?"

"As well as you can juggle, methinks," Rowena replied.

Rowena bent low over the mare's neck. A stone slammed into her shoulder. She cried out at the throb of pain and dug her heels into the horse's flanks. The ground unrolled beneath the mare's pounding hooves. The others were a blur of shadows racing beside her. Some distance from the village the shower of stones lessened, then ceased. Relieved, Rowena drew up the reins and the mare shuddered to a halt. She collapsed into its tangled mane, her breathing as ragged from fear as if she had outrun the bellowing mob on foot. A paroxysm of coughing wracked her chest.

Little Freddie gently drew her hair back and peered into her face. "Are you ill?"

She shook her head, summoning a feeble smile. "Winded."

Irwin's horse pranced in a circle, spurred by the restless bouncing of its rider. Irwin's cheeks were flushed an indignant red. "You would think we were murderers or child-stealers. 'Tis the third village we've been run out of in as many days. I had no inkling that people took their entertainment so seriously."

"Mayhaps the humbler art of begging would be a more profitable pursuit." Little Freddie put out a hand to stop Irwin's horse from trodding on his pony.

"Nonsense," Irwin snapped. "Not with our talents. I found it quite amusing when Rowena fell off the rope we had strung between the church and the stable."

Rowena looked at him askance. " 'Twas not supposed to be amusing. 'Twas supposed to be rope dancing. Even the village idiot knew that."

"But the way you hung there by your knees with your kirtle over your head . . ." Irwin chuckled at the memory. Rowena gave him a look that would have cut a diamond only to have its effect ruined by another fit of coughing.

Little Freddie slipped off his pony and unstrapped the bundle of rags from his back. He straightened with a moan. "Quarreling amongst ourselves won't put bread in our stomachs. We are as poor and hungry today as we were a month ago. We've had to beg or steal every crumb we've laid in our bellies. Not one ha'penny did we gain from that village today."

"Them folks had no coins. They were poor like us."

They all turned to look at Big Freddie. He scratched the top of his mangy head, forgetting he had two of them. A stuffed bear's head had been shoved back from his own lank hair. The stolen pelts trailing from it were bald in spots, thickly matted in others. Dark, sightless eyes stared back from the bear's head. Rowena blinked, forgetting for a moment which face belonged to her brother.

Little Freddie sighed. "Out of the mouths of bears . . ."

"He makes his point well." Irwin twirled the drooping ends of his moustache, an annoying habit he had adopted since they had grown long enough to droop. "The nobility seem to be eluding us. Where do all the rich folk go in the winter?"

"Winter is yet another pleasure for them." Bitterness laced Rowena's voice. "They proclaim it charming and pretty till it wets their woolen gloves. Then they weary of it and creep inside to languish before their fires and gobble their Christmas puddings."

Little Freddie ran his hands down the bony flank of his pony and gave her a curious glance beneath half-lowered lashes. Her callused hands kneaded the mare's mane.

"If the nobility will not come to us, then we shall go to it." Irwin smiled as if he had said something profound.

Rowena lifted an eyebrow. "Shall we ride to Londontown itself and demand an audience before the king?"

"We must stop spurning the castles. Let us play before those who would appreciate our talents," said Irwin.

Little Freddie mounted. "Barring you, that leaves only the blind and deaf. Castles are dangerous for Rowena. We have discussed this before."

Irwin sniffed. "She is being selfish. If she would accept my generous offer and allow the next village priest to marry us, she would no longer find herself in danger. Surely even this grim knight would hesitate to abduct a woman married before God and king."

"God and king mean nothing to him. Nor would you, if you stood in his way." With those words, Rowena nudged her mount past his and into the shelter of the woods. Big Freddie shrugged the bear head over his own and followed.

Irwin shook his head. "When did she become such a shrewish creature?"

"Don't be a pudding," Little Freddie said. "If she cared naught for you, she would wed you and let Sir Gareth whack off your head."

The boy stared back into the forest, wondering if Rowena had caught a glimpse of the man who had cantered into the village just as the mob began pelting them with stones. A mantle of the blackest fur had veiled his features. He shook away a shiver and urged his pony forward as the first snowflakes slipped from the sky.

By nightfall, their horses waded through the dim forest in a sea of white. Fat flakes drifted downward to mesh in a seamless pillow that muffled all but the gentle click of flake hitting snow. The wind blew deceptively gentle. Rowena's cough ceased as the beast in her empty belly curled tightly into her lungs and began to scratch. As a heated flush followed a tooth-chattering chill, she wanted nothing more than to sink into the seductive blanket of snow and sleep forever.

The snow masked all traces of a path. They wandered silently and without purpose over the dreamlike terrain. When a castle came looming out of the darkness, Rowena was too numb to be startled.

They halted their mounts at the edge of the wood.

" 'Tis smaller than Revelwood," Irwin said, subdued for once.

"Like an abandoned toy," Little Freddie mused.

"Not a toy. And not abandoned." Rowena pointed. The orangy glow of a torch threaded its light through a shuttered window.

"Not abandoned indeed." Irwin's horse quivered as his knees went taut.

His gaze had found another structure harbored against the outer wall of the castle. It was a makeshift stable, open on one wall, with smoke pots scattered along its length to cast warmth and feeble light on its occupants. A dozen horses shared the stable.

"Pretty," Big Freddie murmured.

It took no connoisseur of horseflesh to recognize the magnificence of the beasts. They were all stallions or destriers. Even in the smoky light the emeralds and rubies encrusted on their bridles sparkled brighter than the snow impaled in the glow from the castle window.

Rowena shivered. "We should not tarry here."

"Hold your tongue, Ro," Irwin said sharply. " 'Tis a godsend. A castle of bored knights and ladies trapped in a snowstorm. Why they'll be tripping over one another to surrender their gold for a bit of entertainment."

Rowena bit her raw lip. The sharp retort Little Freddie expected did not come. " 'Tis too charming," she said softly. "Like one of those enchanted castles you told us of. Suppose we enter and can never leave?"

"Pshaw! You are too fanciful. If I recall, most of those enchantments involved excesses of food and drink and a beautiful maiden or two. Would you rather we all freeze to death to humor your womanly foreboding?"

Rowena gave him a dark look. There was no court-yard, no moat and no drawbridge between them and the castle door. There was only a deep blanket of snow, unruffled by human or animal prints. Her eyes searched the stable. None of the stallions was pure white.

"Rowena, Irwin may be right this time. I don't know how we can go on in this snow. If we try to sleep, I fear we will . . ." Little Freddie's voice trailed off as he rubbed his raw knuckles over his dripping nose.

Irwin did not wait for Rowena's approval. He dismounted and trundled toward the door. The others followed with Rowena hanging behind Big Freddie's mangy pelts. As Irwin pounded on the door, Little Freddie slipped in front of him. They were engaged in a polite shoving match when the door slipped open.

Rowena's fears were greatly relieved at the sight of the face appearing in the halo of light. No ogre or goblin this, but a man's face, smooth of chin and pleasant of expression. It was a face Rowena would have considered the height of handsomeness prior to meeting Sir Gareth. He could not have been much older than she, but a trim blond moustache and a gleaming pair of golden spurs marked him as a knight. A burst of hearty male laughter rolled out from the hall behind him.

"I say," he said, "did someone knock?"

Little Freddie stopped squirming in Irwin's grasp. "We did, sir. We are humble beggars in need of charity. Can we offer you some tricks and songs for a bowl of porridge?"

Irwin hefted Little Freddie into the snow by the seat of his braies. He bowed deeply and twirled his moustache. "Our tumbler speaks in haste. We are a troupe of international fame fresh from the province of Anjou."

The knight's eyebrows swooped upward. Rowena groaned silently.

Irwin swept out his arm. "Allow me to present Petit Frederick, tumbler extraordinaire." He jerked Rowena out from behind Big Freddie. "And the charming Mignon, whose array of tricks will astound you." Rowena hissed at Irwin from the corner of her mouth and curtsied sweetly to the knight. "Most amazing of all—Freddie the dancing bear."

Big Freddie peered stupidly at him. Irwin jerked the bear's head down and slammed his fist on it. The knight glanced politely at Big Freddie's perfunctory shuffle, but Rowena bore the brunt of his smile. She smiled back, warmed by its welcome and the scent of roast pheasant wafting out the door. Her hunger returned with a ravenous growl.

The knight leaned against the doorframe and stroked his chin, his slender hips and broad shoulders silhouetted against the light. "How fortunate. My companions and I were weary from boredom. It seems the fates have favored us with rescue."

"All we ask," Irwin said, "is a chamber to prepare in, a little meat, a little gold—"

"And a little feed for our horses," the bear growled.

The knight made a gesture behind his back, and a squire scraped past them. Rowena watched their mounts being led toward the stable with a tiny thrill of trepidation. But she dismissed her fears as the knight threw a friendly arm around Irwin's shoulders and ushered them into a hall where warmth hung in the air as palpable as an embrace.

Handsome young knights ringed them, their curiosity held in check by good manners. After a month spent fleeing one peasant mob after another, Rowena found one quality most entrancing. The knights were clean. There was none of the stench of unwashed flesh so lethal to an empty stomach. A kettle bubbled cheerfully on the hearth. The scent of cinnamon wafted through the cozy hall to mingle with the crisp cleanliness of breath flavored with spiced ale. A sudden fit of horror washed over Rowena. Had it been today she had washed or yesterday? She slipped her nose into her kirtle in the guise of scratching it. Friendly young faces bowed to plant genteel kisses on her palms.

The knights clustered around as the blond knight introduced his new guests one by one. When he bowed to Rowena with a special mention of her "array of tricks," the men's smiles broadened. Several of them clapped the knight on the back with a general murmur of, "Jolly good, Percival" and "Array of tricks, eh? Simply grand."

Rowena barely had time to give the half-eaten slab of meat on the table a longing glance before they

were whisked into a tiny cell to prepare for their performance.

She slipped out of her ragged boots and smeared
rouge on her cheeks. After smoothing her tattered kirtle
as best she could, she raked her fingers through Big
Freddie's pelts.

Little Freddie mumbled something to himself as he
pulled on a hole-ridden pair of blue hose. He was
frowning thoughtfully, but before she could question him
the door thumped open and they were swept into the hall.
The knights had propped themselves up on benches and
tables in various states of repose. Most of them were
closer in age to boys than men. Rowena's mouth watered
at the sight of a turkey leg dangling carelessly from aristo-
cratic fingers. She inched toward the fire.

Percival led the knights in a round of applause as
Irwin stepped into the center of the hall. He pivoted on
his heel and threw kisses all around. Rowena grimaced.

"Welcome to our grand exhibition. For our first
entertainment of the evening, I should like to introduce
Freddie, the dancing bear."

Big Freddie shambled out, overturning a chair and
sweeping a goblet from a knight's hand in his blindness.
He had barely made two graceless turns and a clumsy
kick before the hall erupted into thunderous applause.

"Marvelous!"

"Bloody brilliant!"

"What a dance. Give us something else now."

Irwin frowned, bewildered, and gave Big Freddie a
shove toward the wall. One of the knights caught him
before he fell into a table.

Irwin shrugged. "If it pleases you, I call forth Petit
Frederick, master of the tumble and fall."

Little Freddie danced forward, a smile pasted on his
lips. His act was more fall than tumble, and after the
first genuine flip, Percival caught him in midair and
neatly set him aside.

The hall rocked with cries of admiration and more
applause. Rowena was baffled. She had never seen an
audience so easily satisfied. She blinked and shook her

head. The heat from the fire was making her giddy. Percival kept a friendly grip on Little Freddie's shoulders.

Irwin coughed and sputtered. The gleam of a trumpet hanging over the hearth returned his composure. "May I?" he asked.

Percival nodded shortly. His smile seemed less open now. There was an unpleasant twist to his lips that reminded Rowena of a sneer.

Irwin climbed on a stool and took down the trumpet, but before he could blow, the trumpet was snatched from his mouth by a genteel hand. The arm that had taken it remained fixed around his neck in a jovial embrace.

Rowena's sense of foreboding came flooding back too late. Faces that had been boyish and friendly hardened as they turned toward her. Chins tilted at arrogant angles. Tongues darted out to moisten lips. The barest shift of a stance or posture and she was at the center of a ring of men who had been born to privilege and denied too little in their short lives. She backed toward the hearth, but the heat was no longer welcoming. Sweat trickled between her breasts.

"Any one of you that touches her is a dead man!"

The cry was Little Freddie's. Its shrill, broken note only deepened the cold smiles. He struggled in Percival's embrace. Percival ruffled the boy's hair and passed him to a red-haired knight who pinned his thin arms behind him.

Firelight cast gold lights in Percival's cap of hair as he swaggered toward Rowena. "Stifle your whining, wee one. We only wish to see what we were promised—the charming Mignon's array of tricks. There will be gold enough in it for all of you."

Rowena saw Irwin's face go pink and then white. A moment later Percival blocked her view as the back of his hand gently brushed her cheek. His thumb cut a teasing path across her lips.

"Do not tremble, sweet Mignon. We only wish you to perform for us. We shall make it well worth your time."

Rowena made a pretty moue and rubbed the floor with one bare toe. Percival's breath quickened. His other hand lifted to her hair. He yelped as she jumped, planting both of her feet on one of his. His sword was half out of its scabbard in her grip when the side of his hand came down in a chop that deadened her wrist and flooded her eyes with tears. From the corner of her eye, she saw Big Freddie go down under a glancing blow.

Percival spun her around and twisted her arm behind her. "Foolish wench," he bit off. "You shall not tease us with promises of entertainment and then try to cut our throats."

"You misunderstand," she said as he shoved her toward the table. "Those were not the kind of tricks he meant. I am not a whore."

"You're not the Holy Virgin, either, or you wouldn't be traveling with this motley troupe. How else could they earn their living but from the sale of your sweet flesh?"

Rowena was fighting in earnest now, but Percival's smooth limbs were like steel. She glanced frantically around the hall. "I beg you. I am innocent. Is there no decency here? You are knights. Is there no chivalry amongst you?"

Hard, young faces stared back at her. One man unbuckled his scabbard with a deliberate motion and let it fall to the floor. Percival jerked her back to thrust her on the table. A dark-haired man stepped in front of them. When Rowena stared up at him he grinned at her, winking one green eye. Hope stirred in her breast.

His voice rang in the sudden silence. "If she speaks the truth, then the stakes are much higher."

A thoughtful murmur rose. Percival's fingers dug convulsively into her wrist as a rumble of thunder rolled through the hall. Rowena thought she was going mad, then she realized it was not thunder but the pounding of a dozen fists on wood as the knights chanted in one demanding chord, "Wager! Wager! Wager!"

Percival flung her from him in disgust. Rowena caught the edge of the table to keep from falling.

The voices throbbed to silence. Percival sneered. "If you care to put your faith in the word of a barefoot light-skirt, bring on the dice. The winner can take her upstairs and find out what a fool he has been."

Bone dice clattered on the stones in front of the hearth. Irwin, Big Freddie, and Little Freddie were bound and tossed in a heap in the corner. The knights clamored with excitement as they knelt around the game. Those in the back craned their flushed faces to watch. They seemed to have forgotten Rowena altogether in the thrill of the wager.

She backed away, not daring to breathe, but flight was stopped by an unyielding chest. She had not been left unguarded after all. Green eyes flashed a greeting as she looked back over her shoulder.

The knight's silky smooth voice poured into her ear like honey. "I could not bear to see you pinned on that table like a lamb for the slaughter."

Rowena stared straight ahead. "You would help me, sir?" she said with no change of expression.

"I would." His arms slipped around her waist. "Come away with me while they play. I swear to be gentle with you. When I am done, I shall help you escape before they can take their turns on you."

Rowena closed her eyes. Why did the kindest words she had heard that night also have to be the cruelest? "The others? The rest of my troupe? Will you see they escape with their lives?"

"For you, little one—anything." One of his hands glided beneath the worn linen of her kirtle to cup her thigh. His lips nuzzled her throat.

Rowena's mind raced. What would Marlys do with this lecherous man-child offering to politely ravish her?

She would take him upstairs and kill him.

The answer came with such haste that Rowena gave a pained yelp of laughter. Green Eyes groaned softly, taking her start as one of pleasure. His hand drifted between her thighs.

In the center of the circle, Percival's long fingers danced on the dice. Perhaps he was even winning.

Rowena made an awkward hop to avoid the probing fingers and turned in the knight's embrace to keep both of his hands in view. Green Eyes took it as a gesture of assent.

Before she could protest, he had laid his lips across hers. Oddly enough, his was the kiss of a whore, not hers. Teasing and practiced, with an undertone of passion held leisurely at bay by the exploration of his tongue. With another man, Rowena might have wondered what came after such a kiss. But Green Eyes was a stranger. How would Marlys kill him? Would she bash him on the head? Run him through with his own sword? Marlys would surely appreciate the irony of that. His roaming hand dipped into the neck of her kirtle, and Rowena squeezed her eyes shut in resignation. Unbeknownst to him, he was a dead man, anyway.

Lost in the throes of plotting the knight's imminent demise, Rowena heard the crash of the door as if it were a mere echo of her heartbeat. Icy wind poured over her. A beat of silence lasted too long, and the knight pulled away. Rowena raised her head. The faces at the hearth were all fixed on the door, frozen in expressions of boyish guilt Rowena should have found amusing.

Too late, she turned.

A snowy giant stood in the doorway. Snow whipped around his broad shoulders and into the hall, lingering for an elusive instant before being sucked into the void of warm air. The wind whistled an eerie refrain. Rowena clung to the knight's forearms to keep from swaying as black eyes darker than night and colder than ice froze the blood in her veins.

# Chapter 13

Gareth stood in the doorway like a snow-covered Thor fresh from besting the frost giants. So riveting was his dark gaze that Rowena could not have ducked if a lightning bolt had come hurtling from his fingers to fry her where she stood. Snow frosted his dark hair. Tiny icicles clung to a beard that had lost its neatly trimmed edges. He was shrouded in a mantle of fur so black and lush it could have been hours old instead of years. For one terrible moment, Rowena fancied the dark drops falling to the stone were not melting snow, but beads of blood from a fresh kill. Her hands uncurled their clawlike grip on the knight's arm. An awkward cough broke the silence.

Gareth swaggered forward, shedding snow with each step.

Percival rose from his kneeling position to meet him. "Sir Gareth! What a surprise! What brings you to Midgard?"

"Snow." Gareth reached down and tweaked the younger man's nose. "Does your father know you're here, Percival?"

Percival grimaced. "Nay, but I fear he will."

How could Rowena have thought Percival handsome? His classical features faded to pallid prettiness in Gareth's rugged shadow. His walk was little more than a strutting imitation of a man's.

Gareth's gaze swept the hall, taking in the kneeling figures at the hearth, the heap of bound and gagged bodies against the wall. His eyes passed over Rowena with the merest flick of an eyebrow. She stepped away from Green Eyes, putting her hands behind her back like a naughty child.

Gareth jerked his head toward the squirming heap. "They alive?"

"Hardly fit to be," Percival sneered. "But they are."

Gareth dropped an arm over Percival's shoulder and steered him toward the fire. "Then they're no concern of mine. Have you no warm ale to offer on such a treacherous eve?"

The knights leaped up, falling over one another in their haste to polish a goblet and pass a flagon down their ranks until it reached Gareth's hand. He bared his teeth in a growl of thanks. The knights ducked their heads, throwing covert glances at the massive broadsword hanging at his waist. The tip of his scabbard scraped the floor as he moved into their circle.

A foot moved to kick the dice under the table, but Gareth's boot came down in its path. He scooped the dice up, weighing them in his gauntleted palm like chips of gold.

"Wagering your father's castle again, Percival?"

"Nay, sir. I learned my lesson last time."

"Well you should have. You almost lost an ear to Marlys that night if my memory serves me well."

"Aye, sir. 'Twas fortunate you came home when you did."

Gareth leaned against the table and tossed first one die and then the other into the air. "What might you be wagering tonight?"

Percival shuffled his feet and fumbled for words. "Nothing of any import, sir. Just a whore." Gareth's gaze passed over Rowena with polite interest. Percival pointed. "Those fellows over there—the ones wiggling about—tried to sell her to us, promising us she was well versed in an 'array of tricks.'" Gareth cupped a hand over Percival's ear and whispered. In response, Percival shouted with laughter. "That, too, I'll wager. She has got the mouth for it." Fresh heat flooded Rowena's cheeks. Percival shrugged as if explaining away a boyish prank. "She claims to be an innocent. So we thought a toss of the dice might decide who would be the first to take her abovestairs and prove her a liar."

Gareth rubbed his beard and sidled off the table. Green Eyes melted back into the crowd of knights, leaving Rowena alone. She placed her feet in a wider stance but still swayed when Gareth's shadow fell over her. Her jaw clenched, she stared at the silver links of the hauberk beneath his mantle. When he did not budge, she was forced to lift her eyes to his face. His scathing gaze assessed her from head to toe, taking in her bare, dirty feet, her shredded kirtle, her tangled hair.

"Is she worth your gold?" he called over his shoulder.

Rowena's eyes narrowed in a look of genuine dislike. Murmurs of assent came from the hearth.

With a smile as sweet as any of Marlys's, Gareth shrugged. "So be it. On with it then. Don't let my presence hinder your game."

He turned away. Trembling with disbelief, Rowena tangled her fingers in the chain links of the hauberk and jerked him back. Her action was shielded from the others by the folds of his mantle.

"Gareth, please," she hissed, a more coherent plea deserting her.

His fingers gently untangled hers, and he pushed her hand away as if it had dirtied him. He stared down at her, his eyes narrowed and his smile compressed to a hard line. If Rowena had been versed in the art of begging, she would have let her round, blue eyes fill prettily with tears. Since she did not know the effectiveness of this trick, she blinked hard to smother the tears and sniffed twice with her reddening nose.

With a sweep of his mantle, Gareth turned away. "Mayhaps the chit would prefer to take a man above-stairs instead of a boy. The night is cold. I, too, might wish for a soft, young body to warm my bed. Throw my wager in with the rest."

A distinct bleating sound floated out from Rowena's pile of kinfolk. The knights exchanged nervous glances.

Percival cocked an eyebrow. "I had not heard such sports were to your taste, Sir Gareth."

Gareth loomed over Percival. "But you've heard other things about me, haven't you, Percival?"

Percival studied his immaculate fingernails. "Your wager is as good as the next man's, of course." He exchanged an uncomfortable glance with the others. "But do not misunderstand our intent. The man who takes her upstairs will only be the *first* man to do so."

Gareth's hand brushed the hilt of his sword in a loving caress. "If I win, I will be the first. And the last." His sweeping gaze dared any man in the hall to contradict him. None did.

" 'Tis because he is going to strangle me when he is done," Rowena murmured. No one glanced at her but Gareth. If looks could kill, he would have been spared the inconvenience of strangling her. She sank into a chair.

With chin propped in hands, she watched Gareth kneel in the circle of men. He received their thumps on the back and good-natured jests as if they were long-lost brothers. Not once did he glance at her.

Her eyes devoured him with all the fatal curiosity of a doomed man pondering his gallows. He shrugged away the mantle with his first toss of the dice. His hair had grown long and shaggy. Ebony tendrils curled over his broad shoulders. Rowena watched, barely breathing, as he scattered the dice into the folds of his mantle. He retrieved them with a smirk of apology for his clumsiness. The dice flew once, twice, and a third time in a graceful arc that wrung groans of disappointment and leering well-wishes from the other men.

She was still sitting with chin in hands when he thrust his gauntleted hand in her face. She ignored it.

"Come abovestairs with me, sweet Mignon. I am eager to sample your array of tricks," he said heartily.

She gave him a withering glance. The knights laughed.

Percival doused his goblet with a consoling dose of ale. "Shall we help you get her up? We've rope if she's quarrelsome. We'd be delighted to hold her down for you if that suits your tastes."

"I do hope that won't be necessary." Gareth knelt in front of her. His words were forced out between teeth clenched in a frozen smile. "Shall you accompany me, or shall I leave you here to be ripped apart by these arrogant whelps?"

"Are those my choices?"

"They are."

He held out his hand again. Her world narrowed to the soft beaten leather crowning his knuckles. "Bully," she said, taking his hand.

"Your opinion matters not to me." Gareth pulled her to her feet.

"Has it ever?"

She gave him no resistance until they passed the bundle of tangled arms and legs. Little Freddie's eyes stared bleakly up at her over an egg-stained gag. She stopped, and Gareth's hand tightened in a crushing grip around her fingers. She refused to look at him.

He stared at her bent head, then jerked a commanding thumb at the pile of bodies. "Feed them. But keep them out of my way."

The warning in his voice was palpable. The knights galloped around in a flurry of haste to do his bidding. This time when he squeezed her fingers, Rowena followed him meekly up the stairs.

Gareth dragged her into the first chamber with glowing embers on the grate. Without freeing her hand, he splintered a stool against the hearth and fed its spindly legs to the gasping fire. Rowena hung back, half-expecting him to heave her into the fire with his next motion. He puffed into the embers like a dragon. Sparks flew. The fire sputtered, igniting the dry wood into a snapping flame that filled the chamber with the heady scent of woodsmoke.

She stumbled after him as he threw open the door of the heavily carved ambry, kicked a chest until the latch broke, and popped the shutters open with his elbow. Snow swirled into the chamber. He leaned out, peering below the window at the unmarked quilt of snow. He was forced to free her to latch the shutters.

Then he turned on her, and she backed away as each word shot at her on a sharp puff of fog. "If so much as one brother, one uncle, or one twice-removed third cousin pops out at me, brandishing hoe, sword, or trumpet, I swear I shall cut off his head first and ask questions later. Do you understand?"

She nodded. The back of her knees came up against something solid, and she sat down. Gareth strode to the door and slammed down the slat of wood that served as a bolt.

Leaning against the door, he jerked off his gauntlets finger by finger. "Spare me the crestfallen look. I beg pardon if I am not the knight of your choice."

Rowena's eyes drifted away from his mocking gaze. The stone walls of the chamber were gently rounded to mark the interior of a miniature tower. A bed smaller than Gareth's sat in the center of the floor. On the wooden ceiling above it, fixed in entwined hands of gold, hung a mirror of hammered silver. Rowena frowned, pondering the disastrous effects if it should fall on the occupants of the bed. Her fingers absently toyed with the silken ribbons dangling from the arm of her chair.

"Do you know what sort of place this is?" Gareth's features were set in a stony mask.

Rowena squinted at the dim images in the tapestries that draped the walls. She had a fleeting impression of creamy flesh, contorted faces. "A castle," she said faintly. "Mayhaps a hunting lodge of some sort."

Gareth crossed the space between them. He leaned forward, imprisoning her with a hand on either arm of the chair. "Aye, Rowena," he said softly. "A castle. A lodge. Have you ever seen a mirror such as that?"

In a corner of the mirror Rowena caught a watery reflection of the burnished gold of her hair against the dark of his. She shook her head.

"A chair like this?" He trailed his fingernails over the plush red velvet of the chair arms. Rowena's arms prickled as if the caress had been made against her skin. She shook her head again. "This chair, my dear, was pilfered from an Arabian harem, probably by some devout Christian knight who brought it back for his mistress. 'Tis very costly and very rare. You see, these ribbons were fashioned to slide around your wrist." She sat paralyzed as a scarlet streamer was looped gently over her hand. "And these ribbons can be brought around like this." His broad fingers circled her slim ankle, parting it from her other ankle and pressing it toward the chair leg.

Her leg jerked convulsively. She realized too late that he had not secured any of the ribbons. Her foot slammed into his thigh and he caught it in an iron grip.

"Aye, Rowena. A castle. A hunting lodge. A dozen bored young knights. And their quarry? A lusty young widow mayhaps. Or an innocent peasant girl abducted from a village. If you will study the tapestries, you will get some idea of what sort of place this is."

He caught her chin and forced her gaze to the wall. Even a blur of tears could not disguise the arch of a swanlike neck as a maiden was forced to her knees at the feet of an armored warrior.

Rowena sniffed hard. Her voice was barely audible. "But they are knights . . . chivalry . . ."

Gareth knelt between her knees. "Welcome to the real world, Lady Precious. 'Tis no romantic tale of Irwin's. I hate to be the first to tell you, but the Pendragon and the Lionheart died long ago. Chivalry belongs to those wealthy enough to afford it."

Her eyes narrowed to suspicious blue slits. "How did *you* know of this place?"

"Blaine brought me here once when we weren't much older than those belowstairs. Did you think it was a place I would frequent?"

Rowena shrugged.

"How depraved do you think I am?"

She stared into her lap without answering.

Gareth caught her cheeks in his hands with a curse that gave new weight to her opinion. When he freed her, two bright circles of plum stained his palms.

"Sweet Jesu," he murmured.

His hands claimed her face again, chafing mercilessly until the pallor of her skin shone through the carelessly applied berry ash. Flesh that had once been rosy with health lay against her bones like melted wax. Her eyes glittered with unspilled tears.

She ducked out of his grasp with a yelp. He shoved her back into the chair and squatted in front of her. Rowena waited for the wrench of one knee away from another, the bite of a ribbon around her ankle.

"When was the last time you ate?" he demanded. Her face went blank. He shook her. "When did you eat last, Rowena?"

Her lips moved as she counted. She held up four fingers. "Three days."

Gareth's expletive was short and descriptive. He strode to the door. Throwing back the bolt, he leaned out and bellowed, "Bring me food. Make haste."

A chorus of "Aye, sir" floated up the stairs, followed by a symphony of banging and clashing. Gareth slammed the door and resumed his position at it, glowering at her. Rowena was spared the niceties of conversation by the crash of a knight against the door. Unaware that Gareth's bulk was on the other side, he had slammed into it at full tilt. Gareth jerked the door open, and the knight reeled into the chamber, balancing a full tray on one hand. He shot a quizzical glance at the fully clothed Rowena sitting with her hands folded demurely in her lap. Gareth snatched the tray and sent him stumbling out. Gareth dropped the tray on a small table. Rowena gasped as he lifted her, chair and all, and dropped her in front of the table.

He straddled the chair across from her, glaring at her over his folded arms.

Beneath his piercing stare, the beast of hunger in her stomach rolled over with a whimper and quietly died.

She stared glumly at hunks of salted boar meat smothered in brown dollops of gravy. "I should eat."

"You should."

"I shall need all my strength tonight."

"Well thought, milady."

A shiver that had little to do with cold ran through her. She speared a bean with her knife and began to eat. The food lay like ashes in her mouth, but she ate every bite of it. When her lips closed around the last bite, Gareth snatched away the tray, leaving only a flagon of sweet wine and a goblet on the table. He disposed of the rest by throwing it out the door. The tray clattered to a halt against the wall. The door slammed. The bolt dropped home.

Rowena jerked her head up as one of his boots struck the wall. He sat on the edge of the bed, drawing off the other one.

"Proceed," he said. "Let the entertainment begin. I want to see your tricks."

"Tricks," Rowena repeated stupidly.

Gareth tugged his hauberk over his head. Crisp hairs erupted from the neckline of his rumpled tunic. "Tricks. The ones Irwin sold so freely. Is he the one who taught them to you?"

"Some of them."

The hauberk clinked to the floor with more violence than was necessary. Gareth's smile was strained. "Then show me. As you well know, I am not a patient man."

Rowena mumbled something unintelligible, then stood with a curtsy. "As you wish."

Gareth's eyes darkened as he leaned back on his elbows, watching the play of the firelight through her threadbare kirtle. Her painful slenderness was broken only by the gentle swell of her breasts. She dropped to her hands and knees. Gareth sat up straight, his eyes widening. She rested the top of her head on the floor and balanced her knees on her elbows. Her shapely legs flailed wildly at the air. She held that pose, heedless of the fall of her skirts, for nearly a minute before toppling to the side with a grunt of exertion. She sprang to her feet with a graceful bow. Gareth stared at her as if she'd gone mad.

Her hopeful smile faded. "You did not fancy that trick? I have others." Her gaze darted around the room. "If you would call for some rope, I could string it from the mantel to—"

"Rowena."

"Sir?"

"Those were not the tricks I had in mind."

She met his gaze evenly. "They are the only ones I know, milord."

Gareth rose in one smooth motion. Rowena took a step backward. "I had something more in mind of the tricks you were showing that green-eyed whelp when I walked in."

He sauntered toward her. Her shins hit the Arabian chair and she leaped sideways as if scorched. What use would it be to explain that Green Eyes was as good as dead when she had kissed him? Her gaze swept the chamber, finding Gareth's sword propped against the hearth. She would be hard-pressed to murder Gareth with his own sword. Even Marlys might take a dim view of that. Her search for something to bash him over the head with proved just as futile. She realized too late that he had backed her into a circle. Her trembling legs were fast approaching the bed.

His voice lowered to a husky whisper. "I had thought to sample some of your tricks, and then show you a few tricks of my own."

Rowena smiled brightly. "Do you juggle, milord?" When her words failed to slow his advance, her smile faded. The backs of her knees locked against the mahogany bedstead. She put out one hand as if its fragile weight could stop him.

"Gareth, if you believe my family has taken to selling me and I to whoring to earn our bread, now would be a good time to admit you are sorely mistaken."

He gave her a long look from beneath his smoky lashes. "Mayhaps morning would be a more apt time to admit it. When I can kiss away your wounded tears and beg sweetly for your forgiveness."

She tilted her face to his, determined to reward his honesty with her own. "Such ploys might work on Lady Alise. They will not work on me. I will not forgive you."

"It might be worth it." He bowed his head. His fingers found a loose strand of her tangled hair and brought it to his lips. "Why did you flee Caerleon?"

The truth was too dangerous for Rowena to admit, even to herself. "Because you asked me to leave you be."

His snort might have been one of laughter. "If I had asked you to stay with me that night, you would have done my bidding?"

"I would."

His head flew up. The strand of hair slipped from his fingers and fell across her face in a silky web. She blew softly and it drifted upward. His hand slipped beneath her hair to cup her neck, his fingers warm against her skin.

"If I bid you to lay with me tonight, would you?"

"The choice is yours, is it not? Yours is the strength, the will. There is no one to answer my cries for help. Percival and his cohorts would only delight in them."

Gareth's thumb toyed with the feathery softness of her earlobe. " 'Tis not rape I speak of, Rowena."

"The knight speaks of little else, be it rape of the man less fortunate than he, or rape of the woman he chooses to subject in the guise of chivalry."

His fingers tightened. Her pulse began to race. His voice held an edge of bitterness. "Well spoken, milady. Marlys would applaud your newly found politics. You've become quite the learned woman beneath my tutelage."

"If you have your way, I fear I shall become more learned before this year is done."

His powerful fingers spread into her hair, cupping her skull with taut restraint. "I have lost a month of that year chasing you all over England in the bitter cold, one step ahead of a mob that wants to stretch your pretty little neck on the gallows. I could have better spent the time curled in my warm, cozy bed at Caerleon."

"With the lady Alise?"

His voice deepened. "With you."

Rowena dropped her gaze, longing to nuzzle her face into the soft folds of his tunic. The sating of her stomach had left her exhausted and terribly vulnerable to this dark-garbed man. His fingers lost themselves in her hair, stroking her scalp with hypnotic rhythm. She was so weary of taking care of others. To be taken care of by a man as strong and capable as Sir Gareth of Caerleon was a formidable temptation. To sway forward into his arms, to be carried to the ermine-trimmed bed and tucked beneath the warmth of his body. She knew instinctively that surrender would be as painless as he could make it.

*Surrender*.

Her head shot up at the glint of firelight off steel. Between Gareth's raised arm and rib cage, she had a perfect view of the window. Inching upward between the latch and shutter was the thin blade of a hunting knife.

"God's blood!" Rowena screeched as the latch went clattering up and the shutters flew open.

"Whatever is the matter?" Gareth's brows drew together in a puzzled line as she flew around him like a woman possessed.

"Whatever is the matter?" she parroted. "Whatever is the matter? Can you not even latch a shutter properly? I've spent the past month clambering around in the ice and snow. I should hardly have to put up with it in my bedchamber, should I?"

She grasped the edge of the shutters. A desperate glance out the window showed her a pair of eyes as silvery-gray as the blade held between clenched teeth. Little Freddie stood on Irwin's shoulders, his foot in Irwin's ear. Irwin teetered on Big Freddie's back. As Little Freddie caught the shutters and tugged, Rowena tugged back, steeling herself against his pleading gaze. Gareth's vow to kill first and ask questions later echoed through her mind. It was only when she heard his curious footfalls behind her that she found the strength to slam the shutters on her brother's fingers.

She whirled around, clapping her hands together to muffle the yelp of pain and solid "Oomph" that came from below the window. "There now. Where were we?"

Gareth came toward her, his steps slow and measured as if he was afraid she might bolt out the window. "I understand that you are afraid, Rowena. But there is no need for hysterics. I am not a brute. I can be kind."

She flashed him a brilliant smile. "Of course, you can." A timid scratching came on the shutter behind her as if they were being besieged by an obstinate rat. She shot forward and grasped Gareth's forearms with a strength that surprised even her. She propelled him backward into the arms of the Arabian chair. "Are you comfortable, sir?" She peered into his face with tender solicitude.

A flush of color had risen to her cheeks. Tangled curls tumbled over her brow. She could not know what an enchanting sight she made leaning over him in that manner.

"I should be more comfortable in the bed," he growled.

Rowena's tongue darted over her lips. She was at a genuine loss for words. The scratching against the shutter deepened to a persistent rattle.

Gareth peered around her shoulder. "The wind has risen most fiercely since we arrived."

Rowena's heart hammered. Her gaze danced around the chamber, seeking any diversion that might draw his attention away from the window. Her gaze lit on one of the provocative images embroidered in the tapestry.

She smoothed her skirts as if they were the finest satin, then sat gently on Gareth's lap. His legs went rigid like cords of iron. Before Rowena could lose her nerve, she cupped the satiny roughness of his bearded cheeks between her hands and pressed her lips to his.

His lips parted beneath hers as his tongue succumbed to the temptation of a mouth opened like a rosebud to the nourishing rays of the sun. His arm slipped around her waist, crushing her against him with a hunger that put her own to shame.

His roughened knuckles slid beneath the kirtle to graze the fluttering pulse behind one knee. Rowena shifted her weight only to realize she was trapped like a butterfly against his lap. Gareth's hand glided up her thigh until the worn linen of her undergarment was the only thing that separated his greedy fingers from the soft warmth of her. Beneath her palms, his throat vibrated with a deep groan. His hand cupped her, pressing her down until she feared not even the sheath of their garments would stop him from satisfying the appetite she had so heedlessly whet.

Drunk with the taste of Gareth's tongue against her own, mad with the rough caress of his beard against her throat, Rowena forgot her reason for provoking his tender onslaught. She thought the hammering of angry young fists against wood was only the slam of her heart against her rib cage until the shutters gave way in a shower of splintered wood and a silver-haired sprite came spilling into the tower.

# Chapter 14

Gareth slammed Rowena to the safety of the floor as an instinct bred deeper in him than bone or blood sent him diving for the hearth and his scabbard. He unsheathed the broadsword with both hands and crossed the tower in three strides. He drew the sword over his head, prepared to plunge it into the heart of the assassin who had burst through the window. The blade quivered, then froze in its downward motion.

Steel gray eyes glared up at him. Little Freddie lay on his back, knees akimbo, his weight propped on his elbows. A scarred hunting knife spun on the floor a few feet away. He regarded Gareth's blade without a hint of a plea in his silvery orbs.

"You," Gareth breathed.

The plea absent from Little Freddie's drawn features came tumbling into view as Rowena tripped over her brother's foot and sprawled across his thin body.

She tossed her head back. Her gaze traveled from Gareth's straddled legs to his poised blade to his features, which hardened as if someone had set them in stone.

Her voice was low and urgent. "Gareth, please. Don't chop his head off. I beg you. Don't hurt him. I shall do anything you ask."

A dull red flush suffused Gareth's face as he realized the reason for her sweet subterfuge of passion. His eyes raked her in a wordless insult, taking in the mop of tangled gold falling over her face, the slender curve of her hip where her skirt had ridden up, her parted lips.

"Anything?" he heard himself reply coldly. A mercenary song strummed to life in his groin.

"Anything," she repeated. Her eyes met his boldly even as she clenched her jaw to stop it from quivering.

"Rowena!" Little Freddie squirmed beneath her with an agonized croak. "Make no bargains with the devil." His foot shoved at the small of her back.

"Be still, boy!" Gareth brought the sword down with a roar. The blade sank nine inches into the wooden floor between Rowena's knees.

"I would have driven it through your hearts," he hissed, "if I thought either of you possessed one."

Two pairs of wide eyes blinked at the vibrating blade. Rowena swallowed audibly.

Gareth strode across the room and splashed wine into a goblet. "Mummers, indeed. If you could have extracted such a winsome performance from your sister at any one of those villages, you would be choking on gold by now."

Pink stained Rowena's cheeks. She and Freddie jumped as Gareth slammed the goblet down and paced back to them. He rocked lightly on the balls of his feet, locking his hands behind him. An unpleasant light glowed in his eyes.

"Let me insure that I understand you, Lady Fordyce. To spare the head of this brash stripling, you offer me anything I desire from you."

Rowena met his eyes over the sword hilt. She nodded, ignoring the vicious pinch Little Freddie gave her.

Gareth crossed his arms. "No remorse. No rebuke. No mewling tears of recrimination on the morrow."

"None," Rowena said softly.

"You heartless bastard!" Little Freddie flung himself at Gareth, but Rowena caught his neck neatly between her elbow and ribs, squeezing until his string of protests faded to garbled grunts. Her gaze never left Gareth's.

A cold smile flickered across his face. "All I must do is leave your brother's head attached to his shoulders."

She nodded solemnly, then hesitated. A thoughtful look crossed her features.

Gareth started to turn away. "Your offer is accepted."

"Nay," she said suddenly.

Beneath her arm, Little Freddie collapsed in relief. Gareth pivoted on his heel, arching one eyebrow. "Nay?"

"Nay. Little Freddie's life is not enough. I want more. You must promise him your protection. Even after my year is done and you've banished me from your company, you must find him a place in your household or in another. As a squire. When he comes of age, you will help him win his spurs."

Little Freddie's squirming began anew, intensifying with each word. His foot inched toward the hunting knife. Rowena drove a merciless elbow into his stomach, and he doubled over with a grunt.

Gareth's gaping mouth snapped shut. "Rowena Fordyce, as I breathe and speak! I thought your greed only extended to your charming little gut. You are a gem with many facets, indeed, milady."

Rowena refused to flinch at his mocking tone. Gareth's cynicism warred with amusement in the face of her stony reserve. A muscle twitched in his cheek. He turned his face to the fire, trusting the leaping flames to hide his expression.

"Your price grows steeper with each passing second. I should make haste to acquiesce before I am forced to foster your entire family and make your papa my page. What makes you think I wish to be saddled with this stubborn whelp for all eternity? He has proved himself painfully imprudent with a hunger for martyrdom that makes even myself skittish."

"He is bright," Rowena said quickly. Little Freddie's fingers curled toward the knife. She caught his hair and gently rapped his head on the floor until his eyes fluttered shut in groggy surrender. She cradled his head in her lap and stroked his brow. "He is brighter than all the rest of us."

Gareth stroked his beard. "I'll grant you that."

"He would have had his chance to be a knight if Papa hadn't been lamed. 'Tis his birthright, you know. 'Twas not his doing that robbed him of it."

"That it was not. But 'twould be your doing that restores it. How noble." Gareth's tone implied the opposite. "Mayhaps he is too young to be a squire."

"Mayhaps I am too young to be your leman."

His lips quirked to acknowledge her hit. He ran one finger lovingly over the hilt of the sword embedded in the floor. "Are you worth it, Rowena?"

Rowena tossed her hair back boldly. "You will have to be the judge of that, won't you, sir?"

Gareth felt his groin tighten as his eyes followed the arch of her throat down to the gentle swell of her breasts. "Very well. This devil accepts your bargain."

Rowena stood to face him in one smooth motion. Little Freddie groaned as his head was dumped from the cushion of her lap.

"Swear it."

Gareth stared at her. "My word is not generally suspect."

"Swear it."

"By God, you push me. As you wish. I give you my oath as a knight of—"

"On your knees."

With a growl, Gareth dropped to his knees at her feet, straddling the blade. His eyes burned up at her like live coals. For the first time, Rowena was glad to have the cold steel between them. He gritted out a guttural oath between clenched teeth, promising Little Freddie his protection as long as he should live. The boy moaned, but Rowena nodded, satisfied.

Gareth's hand shot out to encircle her wrist like a

band of iron. His words were clipped. "You may make your oath to me in private, milady. On your knees."

"As you wish, milord." Her eyes held a steely light Gareth did not recognize.

He climbed to his feet and plucked Little Freddie off the floor by the scruff of his tunic.

Rowena caught his sleeve. "You swore you would do him no harm."

Gareth shook her away as if she were no more than a bothersome flea. "I am doing him no harm. I am showing him out." He strode purposefully toward the window, stepping over shards of splintered shutter. Little Freddie's eyes popped open. "He can damn well leave the same way he came in."

Rowena flung herself on Gareth's back, wrapping one slender arm around his throat. "You mustn't. You shall kill him. You promised."

Gareth straightened with a sigh. Rowena's feet dangled a foot off the floor. "Woman, you try my patience."

Without bothering to unhook her, he leaned out the window. Two dark shapes milled nervously below.

"Who goes there? Irwin, is that you?" he called.

There was a moment of silence broken by nothing but the murmur of the falling snow, then a faint, "Aye, sir."

"I've something for you. Hold your arms out."

Rowena slid off Gareth's back, covering her eyes with her fingers as he dropped Little Freddie out the window. She waited for an agonized scream, but heard only a muffled grunt, followed by a timid, "Thank you ever so much, sir."

"My pleasure." Gareth leaned farther out the window, glaring down at the pale, worried circle of Irwin's face.

Irwin cleared his throat. "We must be going, sir."

"No farther than the stable, please."

"Of course not, sir."

Gareth dug his fingers into the snow crusted on the windowsill as the two dark shapes shuffled away, bearing their awkward burden between them. Rowena crossed herself, mumbling a prayer of thanks that Little Freddie had not been killed or maimed.

She watched as Gareth pried his sword from the floor and used its hilt to pound a tapestry over the yawning window. A cozy orb of color wreathed them. Rowena's eyes shied away from the sly winks and knowing leers of the faces frozen in the tapestries. Gareth knelt before the hearth and fed the planks of the hapless shutters to the waning fire.

Without turning around, he said, "Tell me, Rowena. How many men have you offered yourself to in order to save your hapless kinfolk?"

"One. Only you."

He gave the flames a vicious poke with the last plank. "If you're lying, I am about to find out."

Rowena picked at her cracked fingernails and studied his broad back beneath lowered lashes. He went to the table and poured himself another goblet of wine, his motions painfully deliberate. When he came for her with his hands so cold, Rowena wondered how she would stop herself from pleading. But she had sworn not to. She had sold herself as basely as any whore, forfeiting any tenderness he might have offered.

He sank into the Arabian chair. The goblet dangled from his fingertips. "Where were we? Shall I set the stage? I was here, and you were sitting in my lap, seducing me very prettily. Pray do continue."

Rowena's heart sank. She crossed the chamber and slid onto his lap. He stared straight ahead, his features as impenetrable and pale as marble.

Drawing in a short, jerky breath, she pressed her lips to his. Her kiss was inexpert, amateur, and she knew it. She drew back. His lips had not parted beneath her caress, but his gaze had shifted to her face. He was studying her through narrowed eyes. This emboldened her to kiss him again. She cupped his neck in her palms. Gareth remained unmoved by her softness, as unrelenting as a statue in her embrace.

She drew away. Heat flooded her cheeks, and she

hated herself for it. "You mock my inexperience, sir. I am not versed in the arts of love as you are."

The goblet rolled to the floor with a heavy clunk. Gareth caught her wrists in his hands. " 'Tis you who mock me. I know nothing of love. Nor do I care to learn."

Buried in Gareth's eyes, Rowena found a fear even deeper than her own. She felt the warning prick of his words like a dagger at her throat. But she would gladly impale herself on such a weapon to storm the wall he'd built so well around himself. Her hands laced around his own, disarming him with their surrender. She leaned forward and drew her small tongue gently along the seam of his lips, feeling them part beneath the coaxing motion. His smoky lashes veiled his eyes as he returned her kiss, his mouth spreading beneath hers, his tongue sweeping out to possess hers. His broad thumb probed the center of her palm, sending a rush of blood to her belly. She moaned softly against his lips.

He threw back his head with a laughing shudder. His knuckles rubbed the curve of her spine. "Do you seek to shame me with your surrender?"

"I swore not to beg or mewl, did I not?"

"And you are a lady of honor." Gareth's words held a strange note, as if it were himself he mocked. He gently pried her face out of his beard and cupped it between his hands. He looked down into her eyes. "If I gave you leave to beg, what would you beg for?"

"That if revenge on my papa was all you sought from me this night, you would throw me to Percival or one of the others." Her gaze did not waver.

Bewilderment touched his eyes. "Sweet Christ, I think you mean it. Do you hate me so well?"

Rowena lowered her gaze. "I could bear their cruelty better than your own."

He drew her against his chest and rested his chin on top of her head. "Fickle child. Whose touch would you prefer to mine? Mayhaps that green-eyed fellow you kissed with an enthusiasm denied me in the simplest greeting? Or your dearly betrothed?" His hand rode the curve of her rib cage around to gently cup her breast. His thumb circled, caressing its ripening peak beneath the coarse linen. "Is it Irwin's fumbling hands you would have touch you this way?"

Rowena's mouth opened in a soundless gasp as heat spread from Gareth's fingertips to her flesh. She nuzzled against him, pushing his tunic down with her nose until she could bury her face in the crisp fur of his chest.

"Irwin offers me an honorable union blessed by God." Even to her own ears, her pious words rang with lack of conviction.

Gareth tilted her face, studying her features in the gentle glow of the firelight. He punctuated each word with the brush of his lips down the purest curve of her cheekbone. "What do I offer you? A slow ride to hell?"

His lips came to rest against the thundering pulse in her throat. Bewitched by the lingering heat of his mouth, Rowena's head fell back in languorous surrender as if her neck had grown too lazy to support the weight of her hair. Spurred on by the ceding of her ivory throat to his dominion, Gareth dared to slip his hand into the neck of her kirtle. Her breast fit neatly into the cup of his hand. With a tenderness he had forgotten he possessed, his fingertips stroked and teased the hardened bud pressed to his callused palm until a shudder wracked her slender frame.

Rowena's head was thrown back, her sandy lashes pressed to flushed cheeks. With her legs parted slightly so her skirt fell into the valley between, she looked ripe for his taking. Gareth was not prepared for the trembling that seized his hands. His other hand cupped her cheek, coaxing her to open her eyes. They gleamed like stars in a sky that had known night for too long.

"I've been so cold and hungry without you, Gareth." Her fingers traced his lips as if memorizing their contours.

His lips parted as he bestowed a tender kiss upon each fingertip. The hand that had cupped her breast slid downward to tease the smooth, flat plane of her belly. Her blue gaze held him fast.

It seemed his whole life had brought him to this moment. He held the power in his hands to release her from a bargain made in wounded pride. But the time when Gareth could have stopped his hand's descent had passed. It slipped between her skin and the rough folds of her undergarment, finally coming to rest in the exquisite softness of the curls between her legs. Gareth lowered his head, partly to earn him time to steady his breathing, partly to hide the flush that bathed his cheeks like the flush of a youth in the first throes of manhood.

He pressed his lips to the delicate bell of her ear. "I am going to fill you, milady. I am going to fill you so you will never have to go hungry again." His husky words died on a groan as one of his fingers dipped into her, touching a warm, moist promise of ecstasy he had hardly allowed himself to dream of.

She slung an arm around his neck in a strangely fierce embrace as he slipped an arm under her knees and shoulders and carried her to the bed.

He laid her on the goose-down coverlet. Her nervous fingers plucked at the ermine trim. As the dancing flames threw Gareth's broad shoulders into silhouette, Rowena shivered, more from fear than cold.

Gareth knelt on the bed and gathered her in his arms like a child. "You'll not go cold again. If we are going to burn, then we shall burn together."

His fingers curled around the nape of her neck like a band of velvet. His mouth found the silky softness of her lips and parted them for a leisurely pleasuring. Rowena returned his kiss with a newfound ardor. She eagerly pressed her young body to his muscled frame until the suggestive rhythm of his tongue stroking the deepest corners of her mouth became impossible to ignore.

He broke away with a groan, tugging her kirtle off her shoulders as he went. Her hands caught in his shaggy hair as he lowered his head to her breast, gently teasing its coral peak with lingering strokes of his lips and tongue until an exquisite knot of longing tightened low in her belly. She stared with wonder at the coarse threads of silver woven through his dark hair. The feather tick rustled as he pushed her to her back. She lifted her hips obediently as he slid the kirtle down and followed it with the linen drawers.

A rosy blush crept over her breasts and throat as she lay exposed to the hungry heat of his gaze. But her eyes remained open and trusting, and it was she who caught his hand and brought it to her lips. Her teeth gently nipped his thumb.

"Come, milord," she said with a tremulous smile. "You promised me a respite for my hunger."

He drew his tunic over his head and bared his teeth in a wicked grin. "I misled you. 'Tis I who would feast on you."

Rowena was reminded once again of the wolf as he lowered his head to her throat. A playful caress from the roughened softness of his tongue was followed by the scrape of his teeth against her flesh. His mouth glided lower, following the valleys and hills of her smooth flesh with teasing determination. Rowena choked back a giggle.

Gareth lifted his head with a throaty growl. "You make sport of me, lady. I daresay a good tongue lashing would curb your impudence."

He proceeded to prove his point, devouring her with his mouth and hands until she tangled her fingers in his hair and begged for a mercy she did not want. His dark curls slipped like the silkiest pelt between her fingers. Pleasure spread through her body like an exotic net, trapping her in the web of her own need. His broad hands cupped her buttocks, then slid lower, coaxing her thighs apart with elaborate tenderness. She closed her eyes and turned her face to the coverlet with a breathless moan as his fingers and lips made melody on her until every muscle of her body arched into song.

She fell back to the bed, breathing as if she had been running for a very long time, her eyes huge and misty with wonder. Gareth met her gaze across the length of her body. She knew instinctively that the time for play had passed. His eyes were narrowed in dark slits of desire. A thrill of fear and anticipation shot down Rowena's spine.

Gareth's hands trembled as he climbed to his knees and began to unwork the points of his hose. Rowena pressed her fists to her eyes.

She kept her eyes clenched shut, even when he tugged one of her hands into his.

"Rowena?" he said softly.

"Hmmm?"

He drew her hand to him. Her fingers uncurled and she found herself touching something that had the resilience of steel sheathed in velvet. Her hand explored its length in curious wonder. A hoarse sound escaped Gareth's throat.

Rowena jerked her hand back. "I cannot," she moaned, ". . . you would surely slay me, milord . . ."

Gareth collapsed against her neck with a shaky laugh. "You flatter me, my dear." He raised himself on his elbows and stared deep into her eyes. " 'Tis passingly normal. I swear to you, I have not slain anyone with it yet."

The briefest of shadows passed over his features. Rowena could not bear to see it. She cupped his face in her hands and drew his lips to hers. His tongue gently penetrated her mouth, soothing and slaking as if to prepare her trembling body for a deeper invasion. She relinquished the fear that held her muscles rigid. Her knees fell apart and she felt Gareth's groan of pleasure like a purr against her palm.

At first the hardness of him was like an unrelenting blade driven with merciless slowness into her tenderest flesh. She muffled a whimper of pain against his lips. Gareth's heavy frame shuddered, and she realized his patience was costing him. He was a man accustomed to charging violently into every challenge life offered him. And now he was holding his own desperate need at bay to ease her pain.

Rowena tore herself away from his kiss and pressed her lips to his ear. "Fill me," she whispered. "Now."

She did not have to ask twice. Gareth drove the
length of his hardness into her, tearing away the last
fragile protest of her innocent body. He was still for a
long moment, basking in the miracle of her warmth.
Her breath came in short pants. He studied her face,
waiting for the abatement of tension that would tell
him she was ready to receive him fully.

She blinked quizzically up at him. "Is it over?" Her
crestfallen expression melted his heart.

"Nay, my sweet. 'Tis only beginning."

With those words, he began to move deep within
her. Her eyes fluttered closed. Her head turned from
side to side. Her moist, swollen lips caught threads of
gold on them. Gareth smoothed them away, deepening
and lengthening his strokes until Rowena learned there
was a deeper more insatiable hunger than that for food.
Her hands caught his shoulders, feeling the smooth play
of the muscles sheathed beneath rigid scars, urging him
on as he rode her to the edge of hell and back until she
swore she could see the exploding stars of heaven itself.

A gust of wind sent the tapestry billowing behind
Gareth like a cloak of darkness. A chunk of wood on
the fire breathed its dying gasp in a brilliant sputter of
light; the mirror above the bed gave up its secrets.
Rowena watched mesmerized as Gareth's back went
rigid. He arched his neck, his muscles cords of tension.
A guttural cry escaped his throat before he collapsed
against her, his weight no more a burden than her own.

She stared up into the mirror at the pale blond
stranger trapped beneath the sated body of the man she
loved. She watched the woman's fingers tenderly comb
through the man's sweat-tangled hair. Rowena closed
her eyes, a faint half-smile still on her lips.

# Chapter 15

❧❦❧

Gareth clattered down the steps two at a time, his thoughts centered on the sleeping angel he had left curled in the bed. He did not realize he was singing until he rounded the last step and his rich baritone burst into the dead silence like an unwanted gift.

Three glum faces surveyed him. For an instant, Gareth saw himself as they did—hair tousled, tunic rumpled, hose furred with dust where they had been tossed heedlessly on the floor. Irwin shoved away his trencher as if he had suddenly lost his appetite. Thrown over his shoulders was the fur mantle Gareth had discarded the night before. Big Freddie turned a sullen jaw to the fire while Little Freddie glared at Gareth, gouging a pit in the oak table with the blunt end of a knife.

Gareth's song subsided to a hum which ended on a faint questioning note as he surveyed the cozy hall.

"Confess, lads. Have you vanquished the knights of Midgard? Are they bound and gagged in the stables?" Gareth deliberately made his voice cheerful and booming.

Big Freddie snorted. "Knights indeed."

"The knights have fled." Little Freddie's words were laced with contempt. "Irwin blundered into telling them what Rowena was to you. They scurried like rats to their holes, fearful you might awaken in a cranky temper."

Gareth whistled as he hooked an iron pot over the fire. He stuck a finger in its contents and brought it to his lips. "Not much danger of that, now was there?"

"None at all. Treachery brings out the best in some men."

Gareth's fist descended on Little Freddie. The boy ducked, but Gareth only rumpled his hair. "Curb that tongue of yours and we'll make a knight of you yet, my lad."

Little Freddie's fair skin blushed a becoming pink. His hand reversed its grip on the knife, and Gareth knew he was one smirk away from getting it in his gullet. The knight's smile did not waver, and the boy was forced to satisfy himself with stabbing an errant roach that went scuttling across the table.

Irwin flinched and snuggled deeper into Gareth's mantle. He drew the wooden trencher close to his chest only to have it plucked out of his hands as Gareth paced behind him.

Gareth poked at the salted fish and cheese with interest. "Where did those cheeky bastards get fresh grapes this time of year? Is Rowena fond of grapes?"

Irwin opened his mouth to answer but it was Big Freddie who said, "Never had them. There were no grapes at Revelwood by the time Ro was old enough to taste them."

Gareth pursed his lips as if deep in thought. "What think you, Little Freddie? Would grapes make your sister happy?"

Little Freddie leaned back on the bench and crossed his arms. "Do you care?"

"Deeply."

Their eyes locked in silent battle.

"Water's boiling," grunted Big Freddie.

"So it is." Gareth bustled to the hearth. He wrapped

a rag around his hand and unhooked the pot, leaving it
to cool on the hearth. He plunked the trencher down on
Big Freddie's thighs.

"Watch those grapes, won't you?" he whispered
with a sidelong glance at Irwin. "I must see to my
mount."

"No need," Big Freddie replied. " 'Tis been done."

"Many thanks. Would you do something else for
me?" Gareth could almost see Irwin's ears perk up. He
leaned closer to Big Freddie's ear and whispered,
"Ready the mounts for the journey to Caerleon."

Big Freddie stared straight ahead. "Yours and
Rowena's?"

"*All* the mounts."

"Aye, sir."

Gareth tucked a small log under one arm, latched the
kettle over one finger, and held out his palm. Big
Freddie surrendered the trencher. Gareth gave Irwin an
infuriating wink as he started up the stairs, balancing
his treasures with elaborate care. It was not until he
rounded the first curve of the enclosed staircase that his
throat warbled into song.

Rowena hugged the pillow to her stomach, murmuring
Gareth's name into it. The pillow made no response. A
sound like ivory chittering against ivory brought her
tousled head up and her bleary eyes open. It was a long,
puzzled moment before she realized it was her teeth
chattering. She rolled over and sat up on her knees,
enduring the protest of her stiff muscles with a grimace.
She peeked beneath the coverlet, searching her body for
some cryptic sign of Gareth's possession.

His crest was not emblazoned upon her chest. His
brand upon her was an invisible chain binding her to
him by the faint tenderness between her legs, and the
quickening of her breath as scenes of the night flashed
through her mind in a dazzling procession. Her teeth
stopped chattering abruptly. She fell forward, burying
her face in the coverlet with a shriek of laughter.

A growl of hunger tugged her upright. The curve of

her hollow belly seemed to be touching her backbone. She drew the coverlet up around her shoulders, suddenly chilled to the bone. Had Gareth forgotten his pledges already? He had promised to banish both hunger and cold from her life. Had his oath only been pretty words designed to satisfy the lust that had driven him to take her again and again in the night, sometimes tenderly, sometimes savagely, until they had collapsed into each other's arms in stuporous slumber? What did he promise Lady Alise for a taste of her favors? she wondered. A bag of gold? A cluster of pearls? How he must be laughing at her! Poor Rowena Fordyce, won by little more than the promise of a basted ham and a stoked fire.

Despair darkened her eyes as she surveyed the abandoned chamber. Perhaps the dark lord had already fled his handiwork, leaving her at the mercy of the next randy group of knights to stumble upon Midgard. Her brow folded with consternation. She could almost hear their bawdy ditties like the echo of ghost songs far away.

The bawdy ditty grew louder. Her bleak musings consumed her so neatly that when the door flew open, she blinked at Gareth as if he himself were a ghost. The smile that curved her lips was like the sun breaking through a bank of thunderheads. She held out her arms to him. Gareth stopped, his song dying on an indrawn breath. A look crossed his face that Rowena could not interpret. She had the eerie feeling she was seeing the ghost of a younger Gareth, shy and almost uncertain of his welcome.

When he did not move to accept her embrace, a wave of kindred shyness washed over her. She pretended to stretch, surveying him from beneath her lashes.

"The color suits you, milord," she said lightly, referring to the length of fine wool draped over one brawny shoulder. "The shade complements your hair."

"Conduct yourself well," he replied, "and I might let you borrow it."

Gareth shoved the log into the waning fire and dumped his other burdens on the table. He crossed to the bed and dangled a kirtle of the most exquisite shade of rose in front of Rowena's freckled nose. She reached for it, but he jerked it back with a smirk, his gaze sharpening as the coverlet slipped off her creamy shoulders.

Rowena drew the coverlet up over her nose, her eyes mischievous slits of blue. "Conduct yourself well and I might let you borrow it," she said, her voice muffled.

The kirtle slipped to the floor as Gareth dove on her. Feathers flew as he rolled over, pulling her on top of him. As they settled into the soft tick, the coverlet enveloped them both. Gareth's hands were warm against her bare waist.

His eyes sparkled. "Such insolence. Little do you know what dangers I braved to procure these treasures for my lady. Three dragons I faced, breathing fire and retribution down my neck."

Rowena lifted her hips in a halfhearted attempt at escape. "Might the dragons have been christened Irwin and Freddie and Freddie once again?"

"They might." Gareth took advantage of her struggles to slide himself into a position that would have been worse than compromising were it not for his woolen hose.

Rowena grew very still. "You did slay these said dragons with your mighty sword?"

"Alas! I was unarmed. I was forced to bear the brunt of their surly looks and dastardly mutterings with the most sheepish surrender. My mighty sword was spent, sorely taxed by a winsome damsel who mocks my meager gifts with the cruelest of jests."

Rowena flattened her palms against his chest with a tantalizing wiggle. "Your mighty sword shows signs of life."

Gareth's eyes narrowed into lazy slits of passion. "You, winsome damsel, could stir a dead man to life."

He cupped her head in his hand and drew her face down to his. When she finally straightened, her hands were trembling and her breathing unsteady. "Is that the only gift you brought me? Or are there others?"

Gareth smiled wryly. "Ever the pragmatist."

He shoved her off of him, sending her tumbling to her rear with a squeal. She crouched in the folds of the coverlet as he crossed to the table to fetch his offerings.

Bowing, he set the iron pot beside the bed, pretending to struggle beneath its weight. "Your bath, milady."

Rowena frowned. "A trifle small, is it not?"

"Whine not or I will stuff you in it myself."

Rowena studied the ten-inch pot and wisely shut her mouth.

He presented the trencher to her with a flourish. A spark of interest lit her eyes.

"These gems were wrested from a ravenous dragon, indeed, with flapping ears and a most indignant stare."

"Indignant no doubt because you pilfered his cheese."

Gareth sat down on the edge of the bed, caressing her hair. "And his betrothed."

"No doubt you were paralyzed with shame." Rowena shuffled through the succulent slabs of fish and cheese.

"Only when the smallest dragon pierced me with his stare. Had it been a blade, 'twould have severed my lecherous head."

"As you were wont to sever his own last night." Rowena's fingers squeezed a grape until it squished out of its skin onto the bed.

"Hardly. I find myself growing quite fond of the lad. He is a foe to be reckoned with when armed with kettle or knife."

Her mouth fell open. "You had no intention of killing him?"

Gareth popped a grape in her mouth. "None whatsoever."

Her mouth snapped shut. "You tricked me."

He sighed. His fingers toyed with the silky flesh of her cheek. "Must we flog this point to death? How many times must I win you to convince you that you belong to me?"

Rowena swallowed the grape whole. "You did not win me last night." She calmly pushed his hand away. "You turned the dice in your mantle. You cheated."

Gareth stood, his features hardening. "The last man who said that to me got a lance in the throat."

"For what? Telling the truth?"

Gareth's foot lashed out, overturning the pot. "So I cheated! Would you have preferred I let that nasty wretch Percival carry you abovestairs? Or killed him for even daring to look at you?"

"But how do I know you did not cheat Papa out of me to begin with?"

Her serenity only infuriated him more. "Contrary to your exalted opinion of me, I am not given to cheating idiots. Or murdering boys."

"Are you given to murdering women?" The words slipped out before Rowena could bite them back.

A strange smile quirked Gareth's lips. Rowena shivered as he ran his forefinger down the length of her nose, then kissed its tip. "Only time will tell, my love. Only time will tell."

He left her then, still steeped in the echo of his careless endearment. She sat with her cheek against her knees, pondering his words and aching for his touch until Irwin banged on the door and gruffly announced that the horses were ready for their return to Caerleon.

# Chapter 16

❦

Marlys swung from bough to bough like a graceless ape. At the top of the ancient oak, the branches grew more fragile and farther apart until she was forced to scuttle up the trunk. The rough bark tore a chunk of flesh from her knee, but she hardly felt it. The last slender branch she reached for came away in her hand. A few years ago she could have scaled the top branches with no more than a creak to betray her. With a mutter of disgust, she hunched into the thin lacing of branches, hating the weight of her womanhood.

The tree cradled her like a nest, its naked branches shielding her black-garbed figure. Marlys rested her cheek against the damp bark, loving winter because it made no promises it could not keep.

The morning rain had melted the snow to muddy patches. Land and sky curved into a bowl of unremitting gray broken only by the faraway towers of Ardendonne. Blaine's scarlet pennons rippled in defiant splendor against the meek sky. If her father had lived, Marlys knew she would have been mistress there. Even now, it was only Gareth's grace that saved her from such a fate.

As a child she had fled often to this tree, escaping the rebukes of a nurse who would chasten her to "act more like a lady and less like a wild thing," escaping the mild disappointment in the eyes of a father who had wanted only sons, escaping the inescapable allure of a brother who could displease no one. In its branches she found a grace unbound by the fetters of childish clumsiness. When the hawks skimmed past on invisible sheets of air, she would dream of going with them, soaring away from Caerleon, gliding over the meadows to a place where no one chided or yelled or tweaked her nose to tenderly bait her as her brother was wont to do.

The sky was empty on this day. The hawks had sailed to that better place without her. A cramp tightened her ankle. She rubbed it absently, and lifted her head to find black dots creeping across the meadow in the distance. Her pulse quickened as she counted under her breath. Five horses. Four riders. Nay. As incongruous as Folio's prancing gait against a quilt of dun came a splash of yellow hair against a field of black. The black was her brother's chest. The yellow hair, Rowena's. Marlys dug her nails into the tree bark, driving cold black silt beneath them.

She could not see Rowena's smile, only the adoring tilt of her head toward the man who held her. Marlys wanted to throw back her head and howl. She watched them cross the meadows, her eyes hot and dry, until they disappeared into the shadows of the forest.

She shimmied down the tree trunk. Near the bottom, her heel caught on a branch. The sharp crack warned her too late. She fell backward as the branch gave, hardly recognizing the frightened cry as her own.

She lay in the leaves for a long time, feeling their wetness seep into the back of her tunic. When her breath returned, the sobs came with it, deep and shuddering with an edge that sliced her gut. When they were spent, she sat up and scrubbed the tearstains from her face with her hair. The rain beat over her in windy sheets as she sprinted toward Caerleon to welcome her brother and his lady home.

Rowena sank into the linen-lined tub with a sigh. Warm water lapped at her chin. A faint smile curved her lips as she remembered her first bath at Caerleon. This night there would be no Dunnla to scrub her skin raw. The beaming old woman had tactfully disappeared after filling the tub and booming something that sounded like "bacon home" in Rowena's ear. This time she bathed not in the kitchen but in the privacy of Gareth's chamber.

A fire roared on the hearth, its warmth ballooning through the chamber. Rowena dragged her fingertips lazily through the water. Her eyes fixed on the great bed, remembering the nights she and Gareth had lain like statues, afraid to touch one another for fear they could not stop. Only when exhaustion had claimed them had their bodies sought out the warmth of one another. They had awakened most often with their limbs entwined, the sweet smell of sleep an intimate bond between them. Tonight would be different. When Gareth returned from his tour of Caerleon, he would find her tucked between his furs, damp and clean and hungry for his touch.

The nights since they had left Midgard had been passed beneath the watchful eyes of her brothers and cousin. Little besides their hands and gazes had touched. Only once had Gareth drawn her away while the others were taking down the tent, pulling her into a copse and pinning her against a pine with his kiss until she thought he would take her then and there, quickly and secretly. But he had pulled away, driving his fingers through his hair with a groan. They had returned to mount with the others, her silly grin matching the one on Gareth's lips. Beneath the fur mantle he had wrested from a reluctant Irwin, his hands had roamed shamelessly until her giggles melted to small moans and she begged him in a tight whisper to end his exquisite tortures. Tonight she would beg him to continue them.

Rowena held her breath as she ducked beneath the water to rinse away the soap. She emerged to find Marlys standing at the top of the tub, arms crossed and one booted foot propped on its rim.

Marlys's hair hung in damp hanks. Her tunic was beaded with moisture and she smelled like a damp hound. Rowena crossed her arms over her chest, remembering their last meeting—Marlys's kindness in helping them flee. After too many sleepless nights on frozen earth, Rowena had to wonder if it was kindness or malice that had prompted Gareth's sister.

"Welcome home, pup."

"Hullo, Marlys. 'Twas hardly a homecoming without you leaping out of a tree at us." Rowena reached for the soap, keeping her face carefully expressionless.

Marlys scooped up the slippery ball and tossed it in the air. "I was around."

"You always are, are you not?"

"Only when you need me." Marlys circled the tub.

Tears stung Rowena's eyes as Marlys grabbed a handful of hair and jerked her fingers through a tangled strand. Rowena bit her lip to stifle a shriek.

"How many weeks has it been since you combed this mop?"

"I could ask you the same thing," Rowena retorted.

"It wants untangling badly."

Rowena snatched her hair out of Marlys's implacable grip. "I have no desire to be bald by the time Gareth returns."

Marlys tossed the soap in the water and took an ivory comb from the table. Her smile was a flash of startling white behind her fall of dark hair. "Trust me."

Marlys knelt behind the tub and gathered a handful of hair. With surprising gentleness, she began to work the comb through its length. Rowena's scalp tingled as the languid strokes drew her head back. She closed her eyes, sighing with satisfaction.

Marlys's voice was as soft and soothing as her hands in Rowena's hair. "Where did you spend your nights on your return to Caerleon?"

Rowena did not open her eyes. "Fields. Copses. Once the snow began to melt, 'twas pleasant enough."

Marlys abandoned the comb and curled the damp tendrils around her fingers. " 'Tis a pity he could not lodge at the keeps of his friends. I suppose his reputation is black enough without carting a bright-eyed whore all over England."

Rowena's shoulders heaved in a weary sigh. The last time she had thought herself a whore in this tub she had dissolved in tears. But then it had not been the truth. She could hardly lash out at Marlys for putting her new status into words, however cruel their intent.

Marlys gathered her hair into a knot. "You were a fool to let Gareth catch you."

"Do you see any scars marring my flesh? Your brother did not flog me. He did naught but warm and feed me."

Marlys's laugh was low. "I daresay he did. The way his hands lingered when he pulled you off Folio, I thought he was going to warm you right there in the bailey."

Rowena's eyes were as opaque as the cloudy water. "Why did you send me away?"

"You were losing your heart to him, were you not? Like all those others before you." Marlys's hands tightened into fists, tugging the tender hairs at the nape of Rowena's neck. "Is that how you would choose to spend your life? Simpering over a man who can never return your love?"

" 'Tis how you have chosen to spend your life, is it not?"

Without warning, Marlys slammed Rowena's head under the water. Rowena came up, sputtering and spitting, only to be shoved under again. The next time she came up swinging, and Marlys caught a soapy fist in the mouth.

Water flew as Rowena shook her hair out of her eyes and leaped to her feet. "Shall you drown me?"

" 'Tis more compassion than Gareth will show when he tires of your mewling." Marlys jammed her hands into her sleeves and paced to the window. She threw open the shutter and turned her face to the rain.

Rowena sat down abruptly. "The truth about your jealousy stings, does it not? I've heard the things you say to Gareth. As long as you keep him obsessed with the past and make him feel unworthy of another's love, he belongs to you. You can keep him at Caerleon, cut off from society, in virtual isolation. He will venture out to fight his tournaments, to bed his women, but he will always return to you because you will insure he believes you are the only one who loves him, despite the past."

Marlys slammed the shutter. "Of course I love him. Everyone loves Gareth. I heard it as a child until I thought it would make me ill. My mother loved him. I tore open her womb fighting to be born, but 'twas Gareth's name she whispered with her dying breath. My father loved him. He was every hope my father had. And we both know how very well Elayne loved him."

Rowena stood, pride stiffening her spine. Refusing to betray a trace of shyness, she climbed out of the tub and crossed to the linen towel draped in front of the fire.

She bent to dry herself with the stiff, warm folds.

Marlys's arms hung loose at her sides. "Not one mark did he leave on you. Unless he put a babe in your belly." Rowena straightened, paralyzed by the venom in Marlys's voice. "You'd best hope he failed at that, lest it meet the same fate as Elayne's babe."

Rowena's towel hung forgotten from her fingertips. The door swung open. She was unaware of the portrait the flames painted of her in shades of peach and gold and stricken blue.

"Begone, Marlys." Gareth stood in the doorway, a steaming cup cradled in his hand. "Now."

His expression did not invite argument. Rowena shielded herself with the towel, suddenly shy. Marlys gave her a mocking bow before sweeping from the chamber. Gareth slammed the door behind her.

Rowena turned all of her attention to drying between her toes. She could not meet Gareth's gaze with Marlys's words still spinning through her head. Elayne's cursed babe again. She kept her head inclined, praying her hair would hide her confusion.

The cup clinked as he laid it on the hearth. His hand brushed the naked curve of her spine. "Was she taunting you?"

"Sometimes I think she must hate me as much as she hated your stepmother."

Gareth's eyes darkened. "On the contrary. Marlys worshiped Elayne. Followed her everywhere like a puppy. I suppose she tired of following me."

Rowena shivered, more from Marlys's lingering miasma of doom than from cold. Gareth wrested two pelts from the bed. One he spread at Rowena's feet. The other he held like a cloak in front of him.

She arched an eyebrow. "My bed, milord? I had hoped I was done sleeping at your feet."

"Impudent wench. One bath and you fancy yourself fit for my bed." He threw the fur over her head before dragging her into his lap. The soft fur tickled her nose, making her sneeze. He poked around in the top of the fur until a golden head emerged. "Look what I found! A stray beastie among my pelts." He ruffled her damp hair. "What a lovely pair of gloves these locks would make! Or mayhaps a muff for my lady."

"Your lady would be cursed indeed at such a perverse muff. She might stuff her hands in and never retrieve them."

Gareth brought her palm to his lips. "We must avert such disaster, for her hands are precious to me indeed."

Rowena's hand lingered at his face, her fingertips tracing his warm lips. When enfolded in his arms, the doubts stirred by Marlys's words seemed a world away. The cozy scent of cloves and cinnamon wafted to her nostrils as Gareth pressed the cup to her lips.

"I almost forgot," he said. "Drink this."

Rowena recoiled from the cup. "What is it?"

"Poison, of course. What else would you expect of me?"

Rowena giggled, not sure if she should. She took a

sip and spiced cider flavored with ale slid down her throat.

"How sweetly you would drink poison for me." At his pensive tone, Rowena twisted to see his expression, but he dug his chin into the top of her head to prevent it. " 'Tis a sobering thought."

" 'Tis a pleasant poison."

He gently boxed her ears. " 'Tis only a posset Dunnla brewed for you. I bade her go heavy on the ale in the hopes you would lose your wits and I could make merry on your body all the night long."

Setting the cup aside, Rowena wiggled in a circle and threw herself against him, driving him to his back. The fur slid off her shoulders. She leaned forward, dragging her bare breasts across his tunic in a tantalizing motion.

"I've already lost my wits. I need no posset to prove it."

Gareth murmured an agreement as he cupped her head and pulled her mouth to his. Their lips lingered in a touch of flame, bound by the inextricable sweetness of warmth and cinnamon.

After several breathless kisses, Gareth wrapped her hair around his fist and pulled her head up. "Rowena, these stones are rather lumpy."

Her smile was crooked. "Suffer, sir. You've had no bath. You are not fit for my bed."

She pressed her sweet-smelling body to his. Rain pattered against the shutters as Rowena proceeded to make him forget about the lumpy stones and every other thought that had ever entered his mind. She shuddered as his velvety hardness deepened the ache within her. She squeezed her eyes shut against the tears that would come, and for a timeless moment cared naught if he had murdered a hundred treacherous women and their mewling babes.

Marlys stood with her back pressed to Gareth's door. A groan so deep it was almost a growl was followed by a tinkling bell of laughter.

"Aye, my sweet puppy," Marlys said softly, burying her face in her hands. "Jealous."

A soft moan, throaty with the exquisite agony of pleasure, drifted through the door. Marlys clapped her hands over her ears and fled down the corridor, trying to escape the bright edge of light the lovers cast. It left her in a shadow so deep she was afraid she might disappear forever. She threw herself on her own bed and stuffed the coverlet in her mouth to muffle her sobs.

# PART THREE

*Silly boy, 'tis full moon yet, thy night*
*as day shines clearly;*
*Had thy youth but wit to fear,*
*thou couldest not love so dearly.*
*Shortly wilt thou mourn when all thy*
*pleasures are bereaved;*
*Little knows he how to love that never*
*was deceived.*

—THOMAS CAMPION

# Chapter 17

❧❦❧

An early spring blew in on the winds of March. Rowena's shrieks filled the great hall one lazy afternoon as she skipped down the stairs with Gareth in pursuit. Her hair swung out in a golden arc as she danced across the hall, putting a wooden table between them. Gareth stumbled after her like a rumpled ogre, his tunic wrinkled and hair uncombed.

"Milord," she cried, resting her hands on the table as she fought to catch her breath. "I swear to you. I thought them flowers. Did you not see the tiny blooms?"

Gareth's brow furrowed in a thunderous frown, yet his eyes sparkled with amusement. "The blooms were not visible when I was plucking them out of my rump."

Rowena grinned impishly. "I offered to help you . . ."

Gareth growled and lunged across the table. Rowena squealed and darted away. Her hair drifted across his palm, an elusive softness, then was gone. She scampered toward the open door, the dove-blue wool of her skirt caught in her fists.

"Thistles!" Gareth bellowed. "The wench puts thistles in my bed!"

Rowena vanished into the halo of sunshine. Her words floated back to him on the wind. "But Little Freddie swore . . ."

"How many times have I warned you not to listen to Little Freddie? The lad despises—"

Gareth burst into the empty courtyard. The sun winked mockingly at him. He scanned gray walls covered with dead lichen, but heard only the rustle of the wind until a haunting giggle drifted back to him. He scaled the wall and sat perched on its ledge with chin in hand. At the bottom of the hill, Rowena's pert rump was all that was visible as she rolled onto a low stone wall. With a graceful kick, she propelled herself over and went skipping into the orchard.

Her laughter floated back to him as she twirled among the apple trees like a drunken pixie. Gareth shook his head, wishing he could preserve forever her childlike abandon. His smile faded. He had wanted to preserve her once before but had failed miserably. Her skirts billowed around her ankles in a cloud of blue. Gareth lifted his eyes to a sky of the same color. White-puffed cotton clouds drifted across its crisp canvas. The sun bathed his face in warmth.

But he knew that, too, would fade, bringing a night marred by darkness and doubt. Rowena spun on one foot until she collapsed in a dizzy heap. Gareth would not have been surprised had she vanished before his eyes, taking with her the boyish joy born anew in him. The only time he truly felt he possessed her was when she lay beneath him, her supple body spread to accept whatever tenderness he dared to offer. Then he reveled in the wondrous feel of her, the hair tangled in his fingers, the salty-sweet taste of her skin against his tongue. He slept each night with one arm locked around her waist, his other hand gently resting over her heart.

He was a fool to think he could hold her forever. If she knew the truth, she would hate him. And as long as Lindsey Fordyce was alive, the truth might bumble into his hall at any moment. It shook him to realize he hadn't even thought of the wretch in the last month. All of his dreams of justice had faltered before the tender light in Rowena's eyes. He dreaded seeing her trust turn to loathing when she discovered his deception.

Perhaps God had not put Fordyce in his path for revenge. Perhaps instead God had laid Rowena in his arms, giving him one last chance to make amends for his mistakes. To be the kind of man his father had bred him to be. But his own carnal desires threatened to defeat him just as they had with Elayne. 'Twould be better to begin cutting the ties that bound them before he and Ro grew even more deeply entwined. He should find her a husband and send her far away before summer's end. But how would he ever sleep when she was gone?

An apple, long dead and shriveled by winter, sailed past his ear. Rowena peeped at him from behind a weathered trunk. Pushing his dark thoughts aside, he slid from the wall and loped down the hillside. Rowena started for the shelter of another tree, but his arm shot out to circle her waist before she could take two steps. He swung her in a wide circle, ignoring the spirited scissoring of her feet.

"Thistles. A woman who would mistake thistles for roses would surely find beauty in such fruit." He waved an apple dotted with wormholes dangerously close to her nose and sang in a loud and lusty baritone, "My apple is rare and beyond compare." He dropped the apple so that his fingers could find the delicate ridge between her ribs where he knew she was most ticklish.

Her body went limp, and she collapsed over his arm, her mop of hair sweeping the fruit-littered ground.

"Mercy, milord. I beg of you." She blinked up at him prettily.

He eyed her charming rump. "From this position, I would petition King Edward for England itself if you asked for it."

"Hmmmm. A tempting prospect."

He swept her up and into his arms. He plucked a twig from her hair and gazed down at her, the laughter fading from his eyes. "Not nearly so tempting as this one." His mouth brushed the succulent fullness of her lower lip.

Gareth kissed her gently, coaxingly, until her slender arms circled his waist and her sigh of surrender grazed his lips. The musky scent of decaying apples wafted around them. His eyes opened against his will. Tiny green buds of spring unfurled against the blue sky. He slammed his eyes shut at the sight and dragged Rowena against him as if he could somehow stop the passing of the seasons with the onslaught of his body. Was he protecting her or deceiving her? His mind dismissed the question callously as demands that required no answers flooded his body in a molten stream of want.

The sun slid slowly into a pocket of rose as Gareth lifted Rowena over the orchard wall. They ambled toward the castle, his arm draped over her shoulder, her arms hugging his waist. He pushed open the iron gate to the courtyard with his free hand. Rowena turned her face to Gareth's for a lingering kiss while the shadows of twilight still sheltered them.

A majestic burst of trumpets shattered the peace.

Rowena clung to Gareth's forearms, her eyes misty. " 'Tis the first time *that* has happened when you've kissed me."

Gareth grinned. "You do my ego well, but I fear 'twas not my doing." He kissed the tip of her nose. "Wait until tonight," he whispered. "I shall give you trumpets and lutes and tabors enough to make your heart sing."

The trumpets sounded again. Gareth and Rowena ran through the great hall and out the main door, still holding hands like children. Marlys straddled the courtyard wall, grinning like a feral cat. Irwin was gaping at the men ringing the courtyard as if they were angels. The steely eye of a falcon was emblazoned on their surcoats.

Gareth snorted. "I should have known. Only Blaine would send three trumpeters with a single herald."

The grim-faced men lifted their trumpets again.

Irwin's face fell as Gareth snatched the creamy parchment from the herald's hand before they could blow. He slit the waxen seal with his dagger.

"Blaine wants us to come for Easter. To break the Lenten fast with him. What say you, Rowena, shall we . . . ?"

Gareth's question went unfinished. Rowena was gone. Without her golden head, the courtyard seemed darker somehow, more fraught with shadows. He offered the herald a puzzled smile.

"Come, all of you. Sup with us. You may carry my answer to your lord at the dawn."

The men's stern faces relaxed as Gareth ushered them into the hall. Marlys sat in the deepening darkness until a single candle flared to life in Rowena's chamber.

Well after midnight, Irwin tapped on Rowena's door. "Sir Gareth wishes to see you in the solar."

Summoned. To a chamber Gareth used to discuss with his seneschal the fate of pregnant heifers and blighted wheat crops. And thieves. Only last week the seneschal had recommended an old beldame who had stolen a wheel of cheese have her hand cut off. Rowena had not lingered to hear Gareth's verdict.

She crept downstairs. Blaine's heralds lay wrapped in their cloaks before the fire in the great hall. She pushed open the door of the solar without knocking. Gareth sat on a stool before a table examining a carved box. His scarred knuckles caressed its contents with immeasurable tenderness. Rowena caught a glimpse of ivory silk.

At the creak of the door, he slammed the box and shoved it into a cubbyhole, his dark-fringed eyes shooting her a look as guilty as if he'd just shoved a woman under the table.

"No need to look so distressed, milord. If there is naught you can do to remedy my fate, I understand."

He arched a perplexed eyebrow. "You do?"

"Aye. I expected it sooner. I can only thank God that Sir Blaine gave us this brief time together before sending his writ of arrest." She shrugged. "I seem destined for the hangman's noose. I suppose there is more dignity in being hanged for horse thievery than for bad comedy."

Gareth came around the desk to caress her slumped shoulders. "Silly goose. Do you think I'd let Blaine hang you? Those horses you took were bought and paid for with my own gold."

"The men did not come for me? I am to stay with you?" Rowena could not disguise the hope that leaped in her eyes.

Gareth gently set her aside and returned to the table, avoiding her gaze. He toyed with a feather quill. "The men came for both of us. My household has been invited to Ardendonne for Easter."

Something in his tone made Rowena wish it had been a writ of arrest instead of an invitation. "Must we go?" She clutched the edge of the table. "We could celebrate here at Caerleon. I could gather eggs and bring them to you." She would lay eggs if it would preserve the fragile happiness they had found.

"We should not insult him by refusing his invitation."

"How courteous you've become," Rowena murmured. "Why did you not wait to speak of this when you came to bed?"

He gave a feeble laugh. "I fear you and a bed are not conducive to the clear thought necessary for what must be said."

A queer pit opened up in Rowena's stomach. She sat down on an oaken bench.

"I have decided 'twould be best if you and I did not share a chamber at Ardendonne. I see no need to tarnish your reputation further."

"What reputation? No one had ever heard of me until you carried me away from Revelwood."

"I am speaking of your future reputation. You have a life to think of when this summer's done."

There would be no life without him. Rowena bit back the words with a hollow laugh. "A life of running on the moors and digging turnips requires no reputation. Rabbits are not snobs."

He met her gaze across the desk. "I owe you more than that."

"You owe me nothing."

He shuffled a sheaf of parchments with methodical hands. "A woman alone is at the mercy of any man. And don't give me that reproachful look. One word of how your papa will take care of you and I shall box your ears. If I send you back to Revelwood, how long do you think it will take him to sell you to another man? A year? A month? A week?"

Rowena sighed, knowing he was right.

Gareth took a deep breath before continuing. "I wish to find you a husband this spring, Rowena. Not some boyish lech like Sir Blaine but a real man. A good man who would treat you well and not leave you at home while he is out lifting another's skirts."

Rowena inclined her head. "I fear I have little to offer a good man."

Gareth pressed the quill into the table, splintering its tip. "Nonsense. I have a castle in southern Scotland that came into our family with my father's second marriage. 'Tis not a large holding but 'twould make a fine dower."

Rowena's voice was musing. "Marlys once told me you'd send me on my way with a brotherly kiss and a sack of gold. And you offer me a castle and a husband." She stood. "Was I that good, Gareth? If I pleased you so well, why have you tired of me so quickly?"

Gareth looked as if she had struck him. He had steeled his heart against Rowena's meek acceptance of his will, the gentle reproach he knew he would find in her eyes. But Rowena in rebellion stirred something deep within him. With anger etched on her features, she looked half-child and half-faerie, caught but not tamed.

Furious tears sparkled in her eyes. "At least Papa would make a profit from me. You would give me away. Tell me, milord, is a castle payment enough for a good man to welcome another man's whore to his marriage bed?"

Gareth stood. Rowena broke into a sob and fled for

the door. Before she could reach it, Gareth reached around her and slammed it in her face. His broad hands splayed on the door; his muscled arms on each side of her held her fast.

"What would you prefer, Rowena? Would you have me offer you my marriage bed? Is that what you wish for? To be the bride of the Lord of Caerleon. To languish beneath the sidelong glances of those who would watch your every move? To know each time you smiled at a squire or offered Blaine your kerchief as a favor, they would be wondering if that night would be the one when I would murder you in your bed?"

She braced her aching brow against the door as if she could stop his words from penetrating her mind.

Gareth's fingers dug into her shoulders. "Is that what you want, Rowena? To start from slumber each night, never knowing when the shadow of my blade might fall over you. To share your life with a murd—"

Rowena turned. She tangled her hands in his hair and dragged his lips down to hers, damming up his dark torrent of words before they could sweep her away. He groaned more in agony than pleasure as her kiss forced him to abandon his ruse of cruelty. His lips darted from her mouth to her throat to the ethereal softness of one earlobe. He dragged her against him, his gesture robbed of violence by her tender capitulation. He pressed himself to her, finding a plush hollow to match every straining angle of his body.

His mouth took hers again, finding within a wet, honeyed promise that tightened his groin until he thought it would splinter if he did not find release.

Rowena stared deep into his eyes, her gaze as fierce as his own. "Gareth, I love—"

He laid his hand over her lips. "Nay, Rowena. 'Tis a word for other men, not for me. Don't say it. Never."

She buried her lips against his palm, kissing him everywhere her mouth could reach as he carried her to the rug laid before the warm stones of the hearth. He was ready to do away with words and take their battle to a place where he was secure in the potency of his weapons. He laid his mouth over hers, muffling a cry even Dunnla would have heard through three feet of stone as his body told her what words could never say.

The white mist of dawn seeped through the arrow slits. Rowena nestled against Gareth as he carried her up the stairs. She was awake but not yet ready to surrender the night. Gareth's hair brushed her nose, its clean scent addling her until she was not sure if she was awake or asleep. She lay limp and pliant, her body a separate entity, enjoying sensations that required no thought or response. He slipped her beneath the downy softness of a pelt, fluffing the pillow behind her head, then he brought her wrist to bear against the softness of his beard.

She watched him dress from beneath her lashes, marveling at his animal grace as he stood naked, silhouetted against the hazy light. He cleaned his teeth with a cloth rubbed in soap and trimmed his beard with the razor edge of his misericord. He cast a last smoldering glance at her before slipping from the chamber.

After he was gone, Rowena rose and padded to the window. A cool breeze stirred her hair.

The Gareth that entered the courtyard might have been a different man from the one who had cradled her across his lap in the orchard yesterday and slathered her nose with kisses. His dark beard was clipped close to his chin. A belt of braided chain encircled the black linen of his surcoat. With each step, the scabbard of his broadsword clanked against muscular calves sheathed in hose as tight and immaculate as a second layer of skin.

There was a hesitancy to his movements as he slipped a parchment from his sleeve and handed it to the waiting herald. As the man and his companions mounted and rode through the bailey gate, Gareth lifted his hand. For a moment, Rowena thought he would call them back, but he did not. She took a step back as he lifted his haunted gaze to the window.

Rowena crept out of Gareth's chamber, a small trunk cradled under her arm. She closed her eyes and touched the splintered surface of Elayne's door. Creaking a protest, it yielded to the gentle pressure of her fingertips.

Sunlight drifted through the shrouded windows. A faint demarcation in the dust marked where the mysterious coffer had rested. The chamber felt as empty and barren of life as a tomb. It had been a tomb for one woman, Rowena reminded herself. And whoever had made it so had left Gareth's name drawn in blood as a damning indictment. Her features hardened as she pulled the door shut.

She slipped down a back stairwell. The solar was empty, the fire's embers burned to ash.

She knelt before the table, finding the coffer exactly where Gareth had tucked it. Her finger traced the delicate rose etched in the pale pine. Gareth's hands had carved it. A Gareth whose eyes were bright and clear, unshadowed by the past. A Gareth whose smile was genuine, whose lips had never known a sneer. Rowena would have given ten years of her life to know that boy.

She lifted the lid, half prepared to find a nest of tiny bones resting in its satin-lined confines. A scrap of ivory lay against the worn satin, forlorn and harmless. Rowena picked it up, fearful of finding a kerchief smothered in the delicate scent of rosemary. Her curious fingers plucked at the fragile silk as her hand smoothed the garment against her lap. It curled of its own volition around her fist and she saw it was not a kerchief at all but a tiny coif like a baby would wear, yellowed and stained with age.

Her hands tenderly folded the garment. She started to drop it back in the box, but after a moment's hesitation opened her own trunk and tucked it within, letting the lid fall shut before going to join the others on their journey to Ardendonne.

# Chapter 18

❧❦❧

Deciding a meager horse would not be sufficient to carry all his trunks, Irwin had wheedled a rickety field cart out of Gridmore and heaped six trunks upon it. He straddled the topmost trunk, looking more like a rotund jester than a squire in alternating squares of plum and yellow. Unlike Little Freddie, Irwin's affections had been bought with several tunics, a silver buckler, and a fur cloak that was an exact replica of Gareth's. For a gold medallion and a signet ring, he would have traded Rowena and six more betrotheds had he possessed them. Little Freddie appeared to pluck Rowena's trunk out of her hand. She shaded her eyes against the morning sun, but saw no dark-garbed knight amongst the chaos.

Dunnla waddled past with a tray full of buttery rolls, the hem of her skirt caught in the mouth of a gray-blue hound. Rowena grabbed a roll. Steam poured from the crisp crust as she sank her teeth into it. She tore it in two and tossed the other half to Little Freddie.

"Thanks," he mumbled, averting his eyes.

The sun burnished his cap of hair to silver. His

braies and tunic were a silvery green that suited his willowy figure to perfection. The hollow caves had disappeared from his cheeks.

Rowena's lips quirked at the sight of the jeweled hilt of a dagger protruding from his neat scabbard. She knew it had been a gift from Gareth. "Why are you not about your duties?"

"What duties?"

She took him by the shoulders, thinking how soon it would be that she would have to reach upward to do so. "You are a squire now. You should be seeing to your lord. Suppose he cannot gauntlet himself without your assistance?"

Little Freddie's jaw stuck out at a dangerous angle. "For all I care, he can hang himself. Did I ask for this bloody education?"

"Nay. But you'll have it anyway, won't you? Because I paid for it."

A shadow fell over them. Little Freddie lifted his gaze over her shoulder, his eyes narrowing to silver slits. "Mayhaps the price was too high."

Jerking out of her grasp, he stalked toward the stables. Rowena felt the possessive heat of Gareth's gauntleted hands before he laid them on her. He massaged her shoulders, his fingers bands of sun-warmed leather against her soft flesh.

"Do not rebuke the lad." His breath stirred the gossamer silk of her peach-colored veil. "He may be right."

Rowena did not resist as he eased her back against the muscled length of his body. Her rounded curves fit his hardness as well as his fingers fit the soft interior of his gauntlets. He rubbed his beard along her cheek, its teasing prick a caress that sent blood rushing to the nether reaches of her body. She was a breath away from feeling his lips graze the corner of her mouth when Folio's head appeared over his shoulder. The stallion butted his head against Gareth's cheek and Rowena shook herself as if awakening from a dream.

Her cheeks flamed as she saw Irwin gaping at them from the cart. Big Freddie drew a brush down a sorrel's coat, his face hidden by the horse's flank. A rush of shyness flooded Rowena at the memory of her uninhibited response to Gareth's lovemaking in the night.

She hid her discomfort by stretching out a hand to caress Folio's neck. Black and silver ribbons had been lovingly entwined in the horse's flowing white mane.

" 'Twas your brother's doing," Gareth said.

The stallion nuzzled her palm, searching for a carrot. "Does it please you?" she asked.

"Not as well as you do."

Marlys cantered into the bailey, a moldy knapsack thrown over one shoulder.

"At this rate, Blaine will die of old age before we reach his keep, brother." Marlys nudged her mount forward. Rowena had to make a quick hop backward to keep from having her toes broken. "What's it to be, Gareth? Will you mount your bitch or mount your stallion?"

Before Gareth could reply, Marlys wheeled the mare around and shoved it between Dunnla and the hound.

Dunnla shook her fist at the air. "Keep that hairy beast away from me!" It was impossible to tell if she meant Marlys or the horse.

Rowena stared after Marlys, feeling a pang of regret. It seemed their stilted camaraderie was now a thing of the past.

Gareth mounted and stretched out his gauntleted arm to her. "Shall we ride?" His eyes sparkled in the sunshine like wind-polished diamonds.

Rowena peered around the bailey to find Big Freddie and Little Freddie mounting their horses. "I had thought to have a mount of my own."

"No need for it. Folio can bear us both."

Rowena slanted a look at him from beneath her lashes. She could not resist his challenge without looking a prim fool.

She took his hand and found herself astride Folio, her back pressed to Gareth's chest. He slapped the reins on Folio's neck, sending the bells on the stallion's bridle into a jingling carol. Irwin's cart trundled behind as they trotted through the gates, leaving Dunnla beating the hound with a spoon and Gridmore blissfully waving at the moat.

The world had awakened while they slept. A mist of green crept over the ancient forest, coaxing a tiny linnet into trilling song. Buds hung like beads in quicksilver branches. Unable to resist the yellow bells, Rowena caught a spray of wild forsythia as they passed. She rubbed the velvety petals beneath her nose, then sniffed back a sneeze.

Her pulse tattooed a warning as Gareth allowed Folio to fall behind the others. He plucked the blossom from her hand and gently trailed it from her temple to her throat, leaving a trail of glittering fairy dust.

Her voice dripped innocence. "Tell me, milord. Do your plans include marrying me to a man jovial enough to tolerate your continued visits to my bedchamber?"

Gareth stiffened. He crumpled the flowers and let them fall beneath the horse's hooves before kicking the stallion into a gallop. Rowena would have been unseated were it not for Gareth's unrelenting arm around her waist. They cantered past the others and were the first to burst into a sun-soaked meadow purple with a dusting of wildflowers. Rowena leaned her head against Gareth's shoulder, her relief colored by bewildering disappointment.

Unable to resist the seduction of the sun-warmed wind, Rowena slipped the gilt circlet over her head and removed her veil. Before she could get a grip on it, the wisp of silk went fluttering upward, sailing on the air currents like an elusive feather. Her cry of dismay was drowned out by Gareth's guttural command as he spurred Folio faster, flattening the greening grasses. Her breath caught in her throat as he hauled back the reins. The blue sky tilted. Folio's hooves flailed at the air. Gareth shot out a hand and caught the veil in his fist.

Folio's hooves crashed down. At a cluck from Gareth, the stallion folded his knees and sank into a bow, tossing his silky mane.

Rowena clung to the knob of the saddle to keep

from sliding down his sleek neck. "Methinks the horse has prettier manners than his master, milord."

"Only when he has a comely lady to impress."

A shift of his knees brought the horse to a standing position. His gauntleted fingers smoothed the veil over the back of his hand with infinite tenderness. The scrape of leather against silk sent a shiver down Rowena's spine. She reached for the veil.

He dangled it just out of her reach. "Nay, milady. I have captured your favor. Contrary to what you believe, I do not surrender what is mine with such ease."

With those cryptic words, he folded the veil into a pretty packet and slipped it into the wrist of his gauntlet.

As the day wore on, Folio rocked like a cradle between Rowena's thighs. When they stopped for water, Rowena chose to mount behind Gareth upon their return to the horse. Except for a mocking smile, he had no comment. The sun bathed her face in warmth. She flattened her cheek against his broad back and let her eyes drift shut. Gareth brought one of her hands to his lips before gently fastening it under his arm.

Rowena opened her eyes to a vision of arches and towers shimmering beneath a veil of water. She blinked, half expecting a dark-eyed merman to swim out one of the windows, trident in hand. As a giant white hoof shod in polished iron came down on the keep, obliterating the battlements, Rowena realized it had been only a reflection.

She lifted her head. Ardendonne itself loomed over the lake, its delicate parapets and graceful arcades drawn like a mirage on the horizon. The afternoon sun slanted across the tiled roofs, etching shadows beneath the arrow slits and conical towers. Rowena rubbed her eyes.

Gareth felt her slight movement. He reached behind him, cupping her back with a powerful hand.

She yawned and twisted around, puzzled to find

them at the edge of the lake with Folio standing knee-deep in water. "Why did you go around? Are there trolls beneath the bridge?"

"In a manner of speaking."

A stone bridge bisected the pristine blue of the lake. Drifting toward it was a gilded boat, its bow carved into the graceful neck of a swan. With the sun in her eyes, Rowena could not make out its passengers. As the boat drifted aimlessly toward the bridge, a woman ducked into the bottom of the boat to keep her elaborate headdress from being swept off. Rowena watched for nearly a minute, but the woman's head did not reappear.

"Trolls on the bridge, too." Rowena followed Gareth's finger to find Irwin's cart parked dead center on the bridge.

He was flanked by Rowena's brothers. They leaned hopefully over the other side of the bridge, waiting for the swan-boat to reappear.

Rowena swallowed. "Curious trolls. It seems Little Freddie's education is advancing faster than I'd hoped."

"Indeed. We'd best reach him before Blaine does if we hope to salvage any remnant of his innocence. Hold on."

His golden spurs touched Folio's sides. Rowena wrapped her arms around Gareth's waist as the horse broke into a canter. Beads of water hung like dewdrops in the sun's rays before splintering to mist her skin with their ebullient spray.

She caught a blurred glimpse of other boats skimming the lake, a circle of squires slamming each other to the ground at the water's edge in a game of football, bursts of brilliant saffron and cherry as ladies strolled like roses along the green swath of lawn.

They galloped out of the lake and across the sloping shore, reaching the small dock as the boat rocked gently into its mooring.

Gareth reined up Folio. Rowena peeped out from behind his shoulder. Blaine reclined in the bottom of the boat, the back of his head resting on folded arms.

His knees shamelessly straddled the bow. A glow that had little to do with the sinking sun softened the sharp planes of his face. A slightly askew headdress popped up, perched upon a throat as graceful but infinitely more flexible than the wooden swan's. As her neck swiveled to include Gareth in her sultry stare, Rowena thought unkindly that a lizard might make a more apt comparison for the lady Alise.

Blaine shaded his eyes against the sun. "Hullo, Gareth. I thought you another peasant bearing eggs for Easter."

"I shudder to think of your uses for them. You give new meaning to the religious feast days."

Blaine flicked one of Alise's long, blond hairs off his clinging hose. "Is rapture not considered a religious experience?"

Gareth scowled at the sky. "No thunderheads, thank God. I hate to be near any body of water when you blaspheme so."

Tiny waves lapped at Folio's hooves as Blaine climbed out of the boat. "Lady Alise gives the best . . . ah, rapture . . . that I know." Alise ducked her head demurely as Blaine helped her out of the boat. "But I don't have to tell you that, do I, Gareth?"

As Rowena met Alise's haughty almond gaze, she felt the bright armor of sophistication she had polished at Caerleon fall away like scales. How Gareth must have laughed at her own feeble attempts to please him! 'Twas no wonder he no longer wanted her in his chamber. Her grip loosened until her hands laced only in the links of his hauberk.

Blaine's smile etched becoming crinkles around his eyes as his gaze lit on her. "It seems you've brought me a gift far more precious than eggs."

Without awaiting Gareth's permission, Rowena slid off Folio and into Blaine's waiting arms. One of her braids had come unlooped and the cheek she had pressed to Gareth's back while she slept was as pale as cream while the other cheek had pinkened beneath the rays of the sun. She had no way of knowing she looked like a harlequin, half-woman, half-child, no less beguiling in her bedraggled state.

Blaine ran his hands over her sides, stopping wisely when his thumb was a hair's breadth from the curve of her breast. "And as fragile as eggs, I do believe."

Rowena wiggled out of his grasp. "Your memory serves you poorly, Sir Blaine."

He stroked his smooth chin with a grimace. "Not as poorly as you might think. My jaw still aches when a storm brews." Gareth dropped between them on the balls of his feet, and Blaine fingered his chin, eyeing the taller man warily. " 'Tis aching as we speak."

"Not as much as it will be if you don't keep your hands to yourself," Gareth retorted. He looped an arm around Blaine's neck and pulled him toward the castle. "Who knows where those hands have been?"

"Ask Alise." The mocking cry came from the bridge. Marlys sat on the stone wall, dangling her booted feet over the edge.

Blaine's eyes narrowed at the sight of Gareth's sister perched on his bridge like a vulture. "You said there were no thunderheads. Or did you say dunderheads?"

Irwin waved happily from the bridge. Gareth rolled his eyes skyward. "Neither."

Little Freddie appeared like a wraith at his side. Gareth slapped Folio's reins into his hands. They ambled up the gentle slope with Blaine and Gareth in the lead, finishing each other's sentences with the easy familiarity of old friends. Rowena kept a polite distance from Lady Alise and tried in vain to tuck her braid back into its neat loop. After it unrolled for the third time, she tugged irritably until the other braid came tumbling down. She was beginning to feel as invisible as she had on her first visit to Ardendonne. Part of her wanted to join Marlys on the bridge. At least Marlys's hatred was an acknowledgment of her existence.

They passed beneath a line of budding oaks. "When are you going to build those flanking towers your father planned? Ardendonne would crumble like a confection in a siege," Gareth was saying.

"Edward has bought us peace," Blaine replied. "Why waste gold on blocks and mortar when there are so many other pleasant ways to spend it?"

Rowena lifted her gaze to the airy towers and flapping pennons fixed on silver spires. There *was* something ethereal and impermanent about the castle. Unlike the sturdy ramparts of Caerleon, Ardendonne looked as if a good rain might melt it to sugary syrup.

She bit back a grin. "If I'd have thought the castle edible on my last visit, I would have devoured the barbican without a qualm of conscience."

Blaine and Gareth both turned around. Rowena blinked, hardly aware she had spoken aloud.

"A delightful prospect." Blaine's gaze dropped to her lips. Gareth's face was impassive, but Rowena sensed something less than pleasure in his eyes.

Blaine threw out an arm in a grand gesture. "Try to think of my castle as one gigantic sweetmeat concocted solely for your pleasure."

Rowena started at a trill of music from the tree above them. A willowy figure swung down from a low-hanging branch and landed at her feet. "Beware. Blaine applies that philosophy to everything in life. Including his guests." The minstrel Mortimer thrust a long, slender pipe down the front of his hose. His gaze caressed Little Freddie. With a casual motion, he flipped a strand of hair out of the boy's eyes. "Charming. Who brought the hors d'oeuvres?"

Gareth fingered the hilt of his sword. "Keep your hands to yourself, Mortimer. Your fingers have probably been in more ungodly places than Blaine's."

The minstrel swept his own fall of hair out of his eyes. "Jealous, Gareth?"

Little Freddie colored, understanding the exchange better than Rowena would have hoped. She gave him a shove in what she hoped was the direction of the stables. He reluctantly obeyed her unspoken command, craning his neck all the way. She half-expected Gareth to draw his sword and lop off the minstrel's head.

Instead he plucked the hautboy from the band of

Mortimer's hose and lay its tip against the minstrel's thin lips. "If you would use your venomous tongue for the purpose it was intended, I might not be forced to cut it out of your head."

Spittle flew as Mortimer blew a hasty note. He skipped backward, disappearing behind a glossy hedge of hawthorn. Pink flowers bobbed in a dance of their own as his head popped up.

"Why, Sir Gareth, if I used my tongue for the purpose it was intended, you might not want to cut it out of my head." With a sly wink, Mortimer went sliding down the hillside, piping bell-sweet notes into the crystalline air.

Gareth's eyes narrowed. "He should thank God I am not armed with bow and arrow."

Blaine clasped his hands, shooting a penitent look at the sky. "I add my prayers to his. Mortimer would look passingly stupid with an apple in his mouth."

Before Gareth could threaten to dismember a third person on their jaunt to the castle, Rowena danced forward and grabbed his hand. She swung it back and forth like an overexcited child. "Did Sir Gareth tell you why we've come to Ardendonne, Sir Blaine?" She ignored the warning pressure of Gareth's fingers. "Sir Gareth is seeking a husband for me."

Blaine's eyes widened. "Benevolent, is he not? 'Tis hard to picture him in the role of doting uncle. You mustn't duck your head, Gareth. Humility does not suit you."

Gareth dropped Rowena's hand, shooting her a veiled look that clearly promised revenge. Blaine linked his arm in hers and inclined his head. "What sort of husband would please you, Lady Rowena?"

Out of the corner of her eye, she saw Gareth fall behind, his hands clasped behind his back. Alise trotted forward to put herself beside him as they reached the drawbridge.

Rowena pursed her lips thoughtfully. "Someone gentle and well-favored. Pleasant of speech and manners. Sweet of temper. Not given to brooding or crotchety behavior."

Blaine cast a maddening grin over his shoulder.

"Kind to kittens?" Gareth growled. "Respectful of virgins?"

"That leaves Blaine out," Alise purred.

"How would you know?" Blaine retorted. He lifted one of Rowena's braids to his lips. "If you will throw in well-endowed with gold and generous of hospitality, I know just the fellow for you."

Rowena blinked innocently at him. "Did I mention faithful?"

"Damn." Sir Blaine dropped the braid. "If a man did not meet one of your qualifications . . ." He stroked his chin thoughtfully, ". . . say, for instance, he bore no fondness for kittens, would you cast him out and break his heart?"

Rowena danced up the drawbridge. "Is he handsome?"

"Very."

"Sweet-tempered?"

"The sweetest."

"Young?"

Blaine shrugged. "Thirty-three."

"Thirty-three?" Rowena cried in a horrified tone. "Why his muscles would be as soft as porridge and his faculties fading to dust! I want a man for a husband, not a doddering mummy."

She spun around to test the effect of her words. Gareth gave her a look hot enough to sizzle her braids off.

"Careful, milady." Blaine stretched out a warning hand as her train caught on a splintered plank.

She tugged the cotte with both hands, forgetting the satin was not as sturdy as her usual garments. The train ripped, the force of her tug sending her reeling toward the moat. Her arms cartwheeled madly. Her toes curled on the edge of the drawbridge in a last vain attempt to stop her descent into the murky blue water.

Leather-clad arms circled her waist. She hung suspended over the water for a breathless moment, caught in the haven of those arms before Gareth pulled her back. It was a long moment before she realized that

Gareth's face was buried in her throat and Blaine was as pale as parchment.

Alise's small, pink tongue darted out to moisten her lips. "The warm snap allowed Blaine to stock the moat earlier than usual. Another step and you would have been the one gracing the table with the apple in your mouth. If we could have found more than your bones, that is."

Rowena's legs folded, and Gareth sank to his knees with her. She closed her eyes and rubbed her cheek against the beaten softness of his gauntlet. He caught her shoulders and pushed her away with an effort that would have been visible to a blind man.

" 'Tis a miracle my doddering steps reached you in time. My faculties are not as sharp as they used to be."

With that virulent reproach, he left her sitting on the edge of the drawbridge. She shrugged away the comforting hand Blaine laid on her shoulder. He and Alise disappeared into the castle, murmuring behind their hands. Rowena rested her head on her knee, content to watch the sun shimmer across the rippling lake.

A familiar hand cupped the back of her neck. "C'mon, pup. Unless you want to sleep in the stables with Big Freddie, we'd best find a chamber."

"Why are you only nice to me when no one else is?"

Marlys caught both of Rowena's braids in her hand and pulled her head back. "I'm a fool for a stray."

"Mayhaps you are only a fool."

Marlys let that comment pass and helped Rowena to her feet. By the time they reached the castle door, she had Rowena smiling with a ribald and very exacting description of what had happened in Blaine's boat using Latin terms Rowena could only pretend to understand.

# Chapter 19

Although Rowena had expected her flirtation with Blaine to goad Gareth into some sort of response, she had not expected it to be total disdain. They might have been guests in separate castles for all the attention he paid her that night. Gone was the seductive charm he had wielded so well during their journey from Caerleon. Gone the tender consideration for her comfort. Gone the growling ogre with the jealous eye. His features had hardened like a diamond hewn from some exotic rock, arresting in its attraction but devoid of all human emotion. Rowena would have preferred surly condemnation to his apathy.

Every hour seemed to transform him back to the dark lord of Caerleon who had stolen her away from Revelwood. His mood had steadily worsened since arriving at Ardendonne. The more genteel the crowd around him, the more savage he became. He answered every polite attempt at conversation with a curt reply or a sarcastic sally that left the other person bleeding before he even knew he had been cut. If offended feelings could kill, Blaine's great hall would have been littered with bodies.

At table he was seated near Blaine, above the salt cellar with the lords of the highest rank. Rowena sat at the end of the table, stuffed between a rotund lady and her leering son. She noticed miserably that Gareth was the only knight without a lady to share his trencher. The lady Alise divided her time between drinking out of Blaine's chalice and plucking sugared raisins from Gareth's manchet. When Gareth's gaze did chance to graze Rowena, his eyes would linger for a moment as if he were trying to place her. Then they would move on as if not pleased with the memory.

Rowena toyed with her honeyed pear, mashing it until the buttered honey ran into a lake in its center. When Alise rose to join the dance, Rowena was only too ready to slip into her seat.

"Good evening, Sir Gareth. I hope the partridge was to your satisfaction."

His voice was cool. "At my age, I do well to gum the wafers. I haven't found you a husband yet, if that's what you're plaguing me about. Mayhaps that pimpled lad at your side would suffice. He is probably not out of napkins yet."

Rowena's charming smile was belied by the words she hissed under her breath. "Stop being cruel. 'Twas your idea to pawn me off on another."

Gareth reclined on his elbow as if he hadn't heard her, his grace as lethal as that of a snake. Rowena felt like a dowdy mouse waiting to be swallowed. The curious glances of the others at the table pricked her skin like invisible fingers. She had approached him. They both knew it would be a crass insult if he did not offer her something from his manchet. He bit off half a sausage and held the other half out to her.

"May I tempt you?"

Rowena bit back the obvious reply as she reached for it. He pulled it back. "Allow me. A lady should not soil her dainty fingers."

He leaned forward, the sausage cradled between thumb and forefinger. The succulent scent of the meat wafted to her nostrils. Gareth was rewarded with a teasing rumble from the beast she had thought tamed in the pit of her stomach. Rowena cringed inwardly.

The beast awakened another emotion—anger. If Gareth wanted to play, then play she would.

Her lips parted in an artless smile. "How could I resist your kindness, sir?"

She took the tempting morsel between her teeth. Her lips closed around Gareth's fingers and lingered. She lapped away the juices of the meat like a lazy cat, taking his finger into her mouth all the way up to the second knuckle, tasting the tang of leather in the tiny hairs that dusted his fingers.

His own lips parted, but no words came forth. Rowena's sultry gaze was wasted. Gareth's gaze was locked on her lips, bewitched by the slaking spell of their coral softness against his flesh. A vicious triumph sang within her. Let him be caught in his own trap.

She drew back and inclined her head, granting him the flash of a dimple.

"Delicious," she murmured. "Have you any cheese, Uncle Gar—"

He lay his moist fingers on her lips. "Don't."

The trap snapped closed with a sigh of its velvety jaws. Too late, Rowena realized her head was still inside. Curious onlookers forgotten, Gareth tugged her lower lip between thumb and forefinger and lay his mouth against hers. Her resistance melted like spun sugar beneath the exquisite pressure of his lips. His victory was brief but fierce.

He freed her. Rowena dazedly put her elbow in his manchet. The wheat bread crumbled, sending honey dribbling into her lap.

Gareth rose with an impeccable bow. "Sleep well, milady." As he started for the stairs, Alise excused herself from the dance and followed him. It was impossible to miss the triumphant look she cast back at Rowena.

Well after midnight, Rowena lay on her feather mattress, listening to Marlys's broken snores. A silvery orb of a moon peeped in the narrow slit of a window.

She ached for Gareth with a physical pain that frightened her. Worse than the ache was the terrible fear that if she went to him now, she would not find him alone.

She threw back her thin coverlet. What would be worse? To lay alone in an agony of indecision? Or to pad her way to Gareth's chamber and push open his door to find him locked in a swirl of pale, blond hair? Rowena could not decide so she lay there until the ragged rhythm of Marlys's snores lulled her to an uneasy sleep. She awoke only once to find that the coverlet had been drawn over her and tucked neatly under her chin. She rolled to her side in the cocoon of warmth, believing she had dreamed the soothing touch of lips against her brow. Marlys's bed was empty.

Blaine draped one of his long legs over the arm of his chair and pasted on a benevolent smile as his villeins shuffled past, bearing the traditional offering of eggs to mark the end of the Lenten fast and the beginning of the feast that would be Easter at Ardendonne.

He hooked a woven basket on one finger and peered within. "Gads, eggs! What an original thought! Did you come up with it yourself?"

The peasant gave a toothless grin and wagged his head in assent. Blaine reached into the leather pouch dangling from his belt. His slender fingers flicked a silver penny that went spinning through the air, catching the afternoon sunlight as it clinked to the floor and went rolling under a table. The peasant dropped to hands and knees and scrambled after it.

Blaine waited until the man had gummed the coin a few times and backed out, bowing all the way, before tossing the basket behind him to a smirking page.

"What smells worse? The peasants or the eggs?" he whispered to Gareth.

"The peasants," Gareth replied without hesitation, only half listening.

Gareth propped his foot on his chair as a bevy of giggling maidservants shoved a long table against the wall.

Their giggles grew shriller as they peered over their shoulders at him, then buried pinkened faces in their linen aprons. During his idyllic weeks with Rowena at Caerleon, he had forgotten what it was like to be feared and mocked. His fingers tightened on the carved arm of the chair.

Blaine's lips curved in a noble smile. Only the slight flaring of his nostrils betrayed him as a wizened old woman with feet wrapped in cowhide limped forward. The instant she turned away, Blaine flipped her bag of eggs over his shoulder to another page, who would doubtlessly use them to pelt the first unsuspecting squire who dared to make merry at his lower status.

A low whistle escaped Blaine's lips as a shy figure drifted toward them. Gareth sat up. The girl could not have been more than thirteen. Blond hair that had yet to lose its baby fineness hung over her face. Dirt smudged her nose. But there was still a promise of beauty in her slanted eyes and full bottom lip.

She curtsied awkwardly. Her tongue toyed with an empty tooth socket in her bottom jaw. "Eggth, Thir Blaine. Me mum thent them for the Eathter featht."

Blaine caressed the girl's cheek. "God bleth her thweet thoul." From the corner of his mouth, he said, "What do you say, Gareth? Would you care to join me in taking this one abovestairs and introducing her to a real feast?"

At one time Blaine's suggestion would have only annoyed Gareth. Now he felt a knot of disgust tighten in his gut. "However debauched your guests might think me, raping children bearing Easter eggs is not among my many vices."

Blaine gave an offended sniff. "Hypocrite. The girl is not much younger than what you've been dipping into. Besides, I've never resorted to rape. I've never had to." The girl looked from one of them to the other, not understanding a word of their rapid French. Blaine licked his finger and gently wiped away the smudge of dirt on the girl's nose. "Would you like a bath, child?"

"Nay. She would not." Gareth snatched three silver

coins from his own purse and thrust them into the girl's grubby paw. He gave her a gentle shove toward the door. "Go," he commanded. "And keep your silly self away next year. And the year after that," he added as an afterthought. The girl obeyed, grinning sweetly over her shoulder at Gareth with a look that said she had forgotten Blaine's existence.

Blaine flung the tiny basket behind him with enough force to crack the speckled eggs against the page's temple. "What ails you, Gareth? Picturing your own little charity child at the mercy of some lecherous liege lord? How do you expect to find a husband for her when the only wedding gift he can expect from you is a dagger across his throat?"

Gareth leaned back in the chair and closed his eyes. "You've been around Mortimer too long. You are turning into a genuine bitch."

" 'Tis a fine accusation from a man in the devil's own temper. Did you only come to Ardendonne to terrorize my guests and cast your shadow of gloom over our joy? Your brooding visage may be attractive to the ladies, but I find its dubious charms beginning to pale."

Gareth opened his eyes. The shadow of a smile touched his lips. "You are only fussy because Alise came to my chamber last night before she came to yours."

"For all the good it did her. I am not a fool, Gareth. She did not bear your scent when she crawled into my bed."

"You would not have refused her if she had."

Before the words were out, Gareth wished he had bitten them back. Blaine stood. His mouth had a pale, pinched look about it that Gareth recognized from boyhood. Blaine's eyes narrowed as Rowena came drifting down the stairs in a cloud of purple velvet. His lips thinned in a smile of ferocious joviality.

"Blaine, I——" Gareth started.

"Don't bother with an apology. I'd be cranky, too, if my leman was sleeping in my sister's chamber. Especially if my sister were Marlys."

With that parting stab, Blaine crossed the hall and offered his arm to Rowena. Gareth's knuckles whitened as he pushed himself out of his chair. His path was blocked as a ragged form came lurching into the hall, sending the page in the doorway sprawling.

The page climbed to his knees only to be knocked flat again as a bellowing figure came stumbling after the first. "Thief! Bring back me eggs, ya bloody thief!"

An ominous patch covered one eye of the pursuer. His other eye gleamed murder as he raised a hewn cudgel in a hand with only an ugly scab where his smallest two fingers should have been. Rowena took a step backward as the first man flung himself facedown at Blaine's feet, landing on the sack he was carrying with a sickening splat.

His fingers clutched at Blaine's boots. "Mercy, milord! I beg you. I sought only to honor you with gifts when this murdering miscreant fell on me outside your doors."

The second man skidded to a halt. Gareth grabbed his hairy wrist before he could bring the cudgel down and stain Rowena's skirts with the man's hapless brains.

The peasant squirmed, but after glancing over his shoulder to find a knight restraining him, he lowered the cudgel with a respectful bob. "He's a lyin' wretch, milord," he said to Blaine. "I was standin' outside awaitin' me turn to be presented when the scurvy dog snatched me sack from me hand and darted past. I've known ye since ye were a lad, Sir Blaine. I'm given to wenchin' and robbin' meself, but I'm not no liar." He raised the cudgel. "Give me leave and I'll bash his skull in."

Blaine put out a restraining hand. "Nay, Jack. Leave this to me." He deepened his voice deliberately. " 'Tis a duty of your lord to mete out justice where it is due."

Gareth rolled his eyes. The man sprawled at Blaine's feet smeared kisses all over his boots.

"Begone, Jack," Blaine said soothingly. "Before we condemn any man to hanging, 'tis best to examine the motives that drove him to such desperation. Especially on Easter," he added with a benevolent smile at Rowena.

At the threat of hanging, the man began to grovel anew. Eggshells cracked beneath him as he crawled toward Rowena and began to kiss the damask hem of her skirts. Gareth was beginning to wonder if Blaine had paid the man for this stomach-turning performance.

"I beseech you, milady," the stranger whined. "Intercede for me with your noble husband. I throw myself upon your kind and gentle mercy." He clawed his way up Rowena's skirts and raised his head.

The change in Rowena's expression should have warned Gareth. His eyes widened as she jerked her skirt out of the man's hands. Her foot came down on his fingers with enough force to elicit a strangled yelp. The man scuttled backward. Blaine's mouth fell open as Rowena stalked him, stamping on whatever appendage she could reach as if the man were a spider that had crawled out of the wainscoting.

"I will give you gentleness," Rowena hissed. "I will give you kindness. I will show you the same mercy that you showed me when I crawled to you, half-starved and begging for sanctuary."

Gareth caught the man by the scruff of his tunic collar and lifted him out of Rowena's reach. The man slowly twirled until he faced the knight. Gareth gave a chilling smile, all of his noble ideas forgotten.

As Lindsey Fordyce dangled between Gareth's smile and Rowena's flashing eyes, he choked out to Blaine, "Hang me, sir. Please."

# Chapter 20

"Now, Rowena, are you not being a trifle bit hard on Uncle Lindsey?"

Rowena burrowed her face deeper in the pillow, her hands clenched into fists. Whose idea had it been to send Irwin in to cajole her? Either Marlys or Gareth was capable of such perversity.

"Leave me alone," she said, her voice thick from crying. "I hope Blaine hangs him."

Irwin lifted a strand of her hair and peered with concern at her reddened nose. "Not much chance of that with such a staunch champion as Sir Gareth. Why he has done everything but give him the clothes off his back! You should see your papa right now, garbed like a king, entertaining Sir Gareth with woeful tales of his misfortune."

"Then I hope Blaine hangs Gareth."

Irwin sighed and his hand stroked the nape of her neck. "Odd to think, if things had been different, you and I might have shared a bed like this."

That got Rowena's attention. She dove out of the bed and slid down the wall to a sitting position, crossing her arms over her scanty chemise.

Irwin shrugged. " 'Tis just as well. Since we are cousins, our children might have been cursed with four arms or been addle-witted."

"Or fat," Rowena added maliciously.

Irwin just smiled. "Listen, Ro. Listen to what you're missing."

He cocked his head. The rumble of distant laughter rolled up through the floor. A steady drumbeat swelled, intertwined with the piping of the hautboys and the siren song of a lute.

Rowena rubbed her swollen eyes. They felt as though she had salt beneath her lids. "I won't do it. I refuse to come down until Easter is over or Papa is gone, whichever comes first. I cannot bear to see him and Gareth with their heads together. 'Twas humiliating enough to have Gareth welcome him as if he was his own prodigal papa. Poor Papa. He won't know Gareth has severed his head until he's walking around with it in his hands."

Irwin laid across the bed and propped his chin on the heels of his hands. "Gareth was asking Uncle Lindsey a lot of questions. They were discussing your betrothal."

"Have they found me a suitably decrepit knight?"

"Several names were bandied about."

She stared at the floor. Emotions sifted like sand across her face. When she raised her eyes, there was more of slate in them than blue. "Perhaps I should go down and find out how sincere Gareth is about being rid of me."

Irwin gave her arm a friendly cuff. "That's my girl." He rolled off the bed. "If you decide to tell them all to go to hell in a handcart, I'll still marry you."

After he had gone, Rowena went to the basin and splashed cold water in her stinging eyes. Her face was still dripping when she knelt to unlatch the leather straps of her trunk. As she pawed through its contents, the silken coif fell to the floor. She stared at it for a long moment before tucking it into the bodice of her chemise.

If Gareth wanted to welcome her papa to Ardendonne for some inscrutable reason, then welcome him she would, but he had best be prepared to answer as many questions as he asked.

Gareth swirled his wine in the bottom of his chalice, catching a glimpse of his own bored countenance in its depths. He quirked his lips, experimenting with a new expression as Lindsey Fordyce regaled him for the fifth time with the tale of woeful luck that had brought him crawling to Rowena's feet. *Slithering*, Gareth amended under his breath. The forced smile only made him look sick. He abandoned it and drained the chalice, savoring the last tart drop on his tongue. As Fordyce polished off his sixth chalice of burgundy wine, a sympathetic murmur or nod was all it took to keep him talking.

The round, blue eyes that had once reminded him of Rowena's were laced with red. Drops of spittle hung on his heavy lips. If the man was stupid enough to be taken in by Gareth's pretense of genteel concern, it was a miracle Rowena hadn't been born a drooling idiot.

And Rowena was no idiot. He could still feel the sting of the look she had given him when he had taken her papa under his wing.

Fordyce droned on, sputtering something about a rabid bear who had robbed him in the forest. He had only stopped at Ardendonne for a little food for his journey to Caerleon. Word of his daughter's good fortune had reached him, and he had hastened to rush to her side to share in her joy. Gareth's blunt fingers pounded out a rhythm on the scarred table as Mortimer's lutestrings soared into throbbing melody. He should have known it was Rowena's good fortune that would lure Fordyce into his trap, not her ill treatment. He had been a fool to believe otherwise.

Dancers clasped hands, sweeping past Gareth in a dizzying funnel of color. Marlys galloped through their lines, gleefully hurling both ladies and men out of her path. Irwin stumbled helplessly after her, vanishing into the twirling arms of the carol, a twitching tail to Marlys's kite. Blaine spun Lady Alise in their midst, his

slender hands leaving hers only long enough to clap out
a crisp cadence to match the drums.

Fordyce slapped the table with his pudgy hands like
a great overgrown baby. Fearful of losing his attention
to the seductive swirl of color and music, Gareth
grabbed the flagon and poured a fresh stream of wine
into the man's chalice.

The wine swelled over the goblet's rim as Rowena
appeared on the stairs. The deep red velvet of her high-
waisted kirtle was gathered below her breasts and
secured with a gold chain. Her hair fell away from her
face in soft wheaten wings to be caught in a filigree
crespine at her nape. In contrast to the delicate lemons
and dusty blues flitting about in the dance, Rowena
glowed like a pale ruby lit by a fire from within.

Gareth jumped to his feet, biting off a curse as the
wine found a crack in the table and dribbled onto his
knee. He swiped at his hose. Rowena was a distraction
he could ill afford if he hoped to wring any truth from
her loquacious father.

"Rowena, my angel!"

Fordyce lurched forward, then recoiled as his aching
knuckles reminded him that her earlier greeting had
held more violence than warmth. Gareth took the
opportunity to shove him back in his chair.

"Papa!"

Everyone gaped as the charming minion of the dark
lord flung herself down the stairs and toward the long
table, trailing belled sleeves that rippled between the
feet of the dancers like velvet snakes. She sidestepped
Gareth with tidy grace and threw herself into her
father's lap.

Lindsey Fordyce cringed, but when she began to
smother his fuzzy pate with the tenderest of kisses, he
realized this was not some new attack and clutched her
to his breast. Drunken tears spilled down his red-veined
cheeks. Gareth realized with a jolt that whatever his
many faults, a part of Lindsey Fordyce truly loved his
only daughter. His hands clenched into fists. He could
not help but feel betrayed at the sight of them cheek to

cheek, their blond heads blended in a single mist of gold. He half-expected Elayne's specter to appear behind them, jeering at his arrogance for believing he could ever break the bonds of their charmed circle.

The crowd demonstrated its approval of the tender sight with a smattering of applause. Mortimer launched into a gentle ballad. As the minstrel's eyes met Gareth's, a dark message passed between them. Mortimer's blond head lowered in imperceptible acknowledgment.

Blaine appeared behind Gareth like a mischievous gamin. " 'Tis not every day our jaded spirits are witness to such a tender reunion. Touching, is it not?"

"Dazzling," Gareth replied.

"Dear, dear, Papa," Rowena crooned. "I pray you will forgive me for my earlier tantrum. I was overwrought and quite beside myself." She smoothed his tunic and reached in her chemise for a scrap of silk to dry his tears with. "Once I had some time to examine my actions, I was appalled by their unfairness. I am your child. 'Tis not mine to judge you. Say you will forgive me. I shall surely die for want of it."

Fordyce burped happily and patted her rump. "There now, lass, you know I've never been able to stay angry at my girl. There'll be no more talk of dying now. Life's a peach. We've each other and a full flagon of wine." He frowned into the flagon, mystified to find it nearly empty. He mopped his forehead with the kerchief Rowena had given him. "Best of all, child, your kind knight has offered me consolation and companionship this Easter feast."

Fordyce beamed up at Gareth. Ignoring Gareth's scowl, Rowena looped an arm around her father's neck. "Beware, Papa. His consolation is a rose with venom-tipped thorns, worthy of more caution than another man's enmity."

Fordyce waved the kerchief at Gareth. "Always was fond of the lad. Taught him how to dice, I did."

"I should have known," Rowena said smoothly.

Gareth frowned, his gaze fixed on the scrap of silk bouncing beneath his nose. He reached for it, hypnotized by the tantalizing motion. The sheen of the torchlight reflecting off the silk caught Fordyce's attention at the same moment. He pulled it back, smoothing it with reverent fingers.

With a lopsided smile, Fordyce dropped the scrap on Rowena's head. "There. It looks as lovely on your little curls as it did the day Dunnla stitched it for you." Before Gareth could stop him, he held up his goblet for her to use as a mirror.

Gareth watched over her shoulder as Rowena's gaze slowly shifted to her reflection. She reached out a finger and touched the polished silver. Blond hair. Blue eyes swollen to sultry fullness from crying. A ridiculous scrap of fabric on her head. The goblet threw back her reflection in painful clarity as she came face to face with Elayne de Crecy's daughter. Gareth held his breath, waiting for her to toss the contents of the goblet into his face.

Rowena hiccuped with the echo of a giggle, addressing her reflection. "Oh, God. At least he didn't bury me in the orchard."

Gareth wanted to take her in his arms, but knew he didn't dare leave Fordyce tripping along the dark paths of his memory alone. He might not be given another chance. If he could clear the de Crecy name enough to give it to Rowena as his bride, there would be years and years to plead for her forgiveness.

Blaine stamped his feet impatiently as Mortimer's fingers flew over the strings in rollicking rhythm. "Come, milady. If it suits your papa, we shall celebrate this reconciliation with a dance."

Gareth snatched Rowena up and thrust her into Blaine's arms. She was as limp as a rag doll. "Her papa and I have not finished our dealings. Take her."

Blaine smiled wickedly. "With pleasure."

As Blaine swung Rowena into the dance, her face broke into a fiercely radiant smile. Gareth sank into his chair, stroking his beard and wondering what she was up to now.

Lindsey Fordyce patted his thighs absently as if

surprised to find them empty. His gaze followed Rowena through the dancers with wistful hunger. Gareth watched the man's face with something akin to pity, praying his own need for the girl did not show so blatantly.

There was a primitive grace to Rowena's dance, a tantalizing hint of the moor creature she had been. Gareth's hands fisted as Blaine pressed his lips to her nape. His tension was not relieved by the coy glance Rowena gave Blaine when they once again came face to face.

Fordyce lifted the brimming chalice to his lips, his hands trembling as if palsied. "She puts one in mind of her mother, does she not?"

Gareth drew in a breath, not daring to move. At first, he believed that treacherous thought had fallen from his own lips. Fordyce was blithely nodding in time to the music.

"Does she now?" Gareth said lightly, the cost of the casual question betrayed by the rhythmic tic in his jaw.

Rowena and Blaine threaded through the dancers, hand in hand, moving toward the arch of the stairway.

Fordyce thumped the chalice down. Wine sloshed over its rim and Gareth thought about communion for the first time in years.

"My Althea didn't have Rowena's spunk though. Her infernal delicacy prevented me from cherishing her as I might have."

"Althea?" Gareth echoed stupidly as his precious plans cartwheeled and came crashing down before his eyes.

Blaine drew Rowena into the shadows below the stairs. They seemed to be arguing. Rowena glanced back at the table, an unreadable plea in her eyes.

Fordyce rambled on. "Aye, my darling wife was sickly from the beginning. There were sacrifices to make. I kept her out of drafts and encouraged her to always pull her washtub into the sunlight. I gave her a few months respite between sons and resolved to seek out others to relieve those baser needs a man is prey to."

Gareth felt as if he were going to be sick.

"Now my Rowena has never had a sickly day in her life. I daresay she could bear the attentions of even the randiest knight." He nudged Gareth with a leering wink.

Rowena's slender wrists crossed behind Blaine's neck as she pulled him down to her kiss. Gareth stood, shoving his chair back with enough force to topple it.

Seeing Gareth start forward, Mortimer brought his tune to a crashing end. The drummers lapsed into silence. The dancers stumbled to an awkward halt.

The minstrel inclined his head, his limp hair gleaming in the torchlight. With delicacy and grace, his long fingers stroked the taut strings, coaxing forth the first haunting notes of a ballad they had heard only once before.

Gareth froze in his tracks. Tossing back his long hair, Mortimer sent his voice soaring in a sweet tenor unblemished by dissipation, plaintive with an innocence he had lost when only a boy at the hands of his father's most trusted knight:

> *The fair Elayne*
> *Unfairly slain . . .*

Even the flames dancing on the hearth seemed to quail before the melody. Shadows flickered on the walls, tightening throats with their sudden proximity. Mortimer had lost his audience. All eyes were riveted on the tall, dark man in their midst.

> *Her faithless hand*
> *Stilled by a name . . .*

Gareth heard a metallic thump behind him. Wine splashed around his ankles like blood. He turned. Lindsey Fordyce's face had gone deathly pale as the lies he had told so often and so well that he had come to believe them fell away like scales. His throat worked, but only a meaningless moan came out.

A vicious song of triumph strummed through Gareth's

blood. He met Rowena's stricken gaze across the hall and felt a brief moment of regret. But even that could not dim a burst of elation so intense it nearly blinded him.

He turned away from Lindsey Fordyce. There would be time enough for truth between them. He hid his smile behind a sneer and put a hand on his sword hilt. He had one more performance to make as the Dark Lord of Caerleon. After tonight, he would leave them to find a new player for their petty dramas.

With a snarl that would have struck terror in the staunchest of men, he shouldered his way through the dancers, coldly shoving them out of the way. Mortimer continued singing as if oblivious to the thundering cloud about to descend on his head. A dark-thatched squire threw himself in front of Mortimer, but Gareth pushed past him as heedlessly as if he had been a flea.

His fist closed around the strings of the lute. A last discordant note trembled in the air before the minstrel's song died to a silence so palpable that Gareth's harsh breathing was audible to everyone in the hall. Gareth snatched the lute. He lifted it above his head as if to smash it, saw Mortimer's imperceptible wince and hurled it to the squire behind him. One fist caught in Mortimer's tunic, driving the slender man back until he slammed against the wall. His legs twitched helplessly.

"You fool! Did you not heed my warning the last time I heard that obscenity of a ballad pass your lips?"

Mortimer's attempt to shrug looked as if it were breaking his bony neck. " 'Twas a pretty tune, milord. My memory failed me," he rasped.

"I warned you that your life would fail you if that melody ever fell from the strings of your lute again."

"The people, sir. They hunger for new tunes. 'Tis my duty to satisfy them."

The crowd gasped and took a step backward as Gareth dropped Mortimer and spun around. He hefted his sword. "I shall satisfy with my blade any man who requested such a song. Does any man dare to step forward?"

The broad blade shimmered in the torchlight. No one

even dared to scratch their nose. Gareth turned back to find Mortimer crawling quietly toward the door.

He kicked him in the rump. "Flee, you knave and sing no more in my presence or any other this night. Another note from you will be your last."

Gareth fought an insane desire to burst into laughter as Mortimer dropped his head between his legs and winked at him. The minstrel's silk purse bulged with Gareth's gold as reward for his performance.

Gareth sheathed his sword and dusted off his hands as if contact with Mortimer's quivering flesh had dirtied them.

A magical path opened before him as he made his way back toward the table. For once, the sly looks of mingled excitement and condemnation amused instead of angered him. He would be free of them soon enough, leaving them with the shame of their lifelong mistake. Perhaps Mortimer would even compose a charming ballad about it. He smiled without realizing it.

The smile faded as the path before his table cleared. The table was empty. The coif lay trampled among the rushes. Lindsey Fordyce was gone.

# Chapter 21

Dragging Papa was like dragging a water-logged walrus. His squat body seemed to have gone boneless. It had taken all of Rowena's strength to tug him out of his chair, to make him understand it was imperative that they flee while Gareth was diverted. He still did not seem to comprehend her hissed pleas or the frantic desperation that drove her.

She had believed she could cast her father upon Gareth's mercy without a qualm of conscience. But when his arms had encircled her with such pathetic eagerness, she had realized that despite his failings, he was still her papa. She could no more bear to see harm come to him than she could bear knowing it was the man she loved who had inflicted that harm.

She had thought to distract Gareth by goading him to jealousy and turning his wrath toward her. But her plan had failed miserably. When Mortimer had started to sing that accursed ballad, Gareth's thoughts had turned toward the past instead of toward a future they might now never share.

They staggered through the courtyard past a circle of kneeling squires. Dice rattled like bones on the cobblestones. Her father went sprawling.

"If he can't stay up now, I daresay you'll not get him up later," called a pock-marked squire.

"Take me instead," cried a weasel-faced boy who couldn't have been much older than Little Freddie. "I am always up."

They cackled, their faces twisted into goblin masks by the flickering torchlight. Rowena caught the back of her father's tunic and pulled, feeling every muscle in her back stretch like lute wires ready to snap. The squires shrugged and went back to their game. She wished for the comforting sight of Marlys in the group. How her sturdy strength would help! She shoved Papa forward. A narrow thread of spittle trailed from his lips as he gibbered in a ceaseless stream. Rowena had to fight the urge to box his ears.

Mumbling something about "sweet hospitality," he reeled to his feet. Their momentum carried them off the flagstones and into the dew-slick grass. The cozy lights of the stable winked below.

Rowena hooked her hands under his arms. "Come, Papa. We haven't far to go."

"But I have come too far already," he mumbled.

Using her knees to support his weight, she steered him toward the stable. The stable door had been thrown wide to usher in the warm spring wind. Big Freddie and Little Freddie looked up from their own dice in surprise as Rowena and Papa burst inside. The horses nickered a welcome. The comforting smells of fresh, sweet hay and musty horses brought tears to Rowena's eyes. She swayed. Big Freddie stepped forward and caught her in his arms. She buried her face in the burlap of his tunic, his honest sweat as sweet a fragrance as any perfume. Papa cursed as he stumbled into a pile of manure.

She clutched at Big Freddie's tunic. "A horse. We must have a horse. I cannot take time to explain, but Papa must have a horse."

Big Freddie scratched his head. "He came on no horse."

Rowena shook him, helpless to stem her rising hysteria. " 'Tis of no import if he came on an elephant. I need a horse now."

Little Freddie caught her elbow. "Gareth?"

She nodded mutely and blessed the shining  beacon of his mind as he ran from stall to stall, throwing open doors.

"There is no stallion here that Folio could not catch with Gareth astride him," he finally pronounced.

Rowena paused for a moment. "Then give me Folio."

Big Freddie blanched. "I cannot be giving away my master's horse."

"Would you rather see your father struck dead before your eyes?" she asked. A hard glaze descended over Little Freddie's face. "I know he is no prize. But he is our father. I cannot watch Gareth kill him in cold blood. It would kill me—" She stumbled to a halt.

Little Freddie flung open the last door. Powerful white forelegs pawed at the hay. The other horses milled nervously in their stalls. Throwing an exasperated look between the two of them, Big Freddie slipped a bridle studded with emeralds and onyx off a peg and tightened it over Folio's graceful neck.

Little Freddie lay a saddle across the horse's back with a tight smile. "There is a practical consideration, you know. Gareth will be spared killing Papa. Folio will probably throw and trample him before he can get down the drawbridge. The stallion does not know Papa."

Rowena's jaw tightened. "He knows me."

Little Freddie's hand froze on the saddle's pommel. "You are going with him?"

"Only until I can get him to a place where he will be safe. Then I shall bring Folio and return."

"To what? Boiling oil? The gibbet?"

Rowena lowered her eyes. "I shan't be afraid of Gareth. I have to believe he will not hurt me."

"I pray your faith is not misplaced."

"As do I." Rowena took the bridle with a firm hand.

Folio pranced out of the stall, casting a shadow on the wall that dwarfed them. Rowena peered around, perplexed. Papa had disappeared. Big Freddie found him curled in an empty grain bin, snoring happily. He threw Papa over his shoulder while Rowena prepared to mount Folio.

Bracing one hand on Little Freddie's bony shoulder, Rowena hefted herself astride the stallion. She smiled weakly and tangled her hands in Folio's silky mane, struggling to hide from her brothers a fear bordering on terror. Free of Gareth's mastery Folio was a wild-eyed and quivering creature, like some monstrous unicorn out of a maiden's nightmare. She did not need the horse to remind her she was maiden no more.

Folio danced sideways as Rowena's brothers lifted her groaning papa behind her. His sudden burst of drunken energy was nearly their undoing.

"That-a-way, girlie!" Papa jerked Rowena's hair out of its net and slapped it on her back like silky reins. He bounced up and down, driving his heels into the beast's sides. Folio surged forward, ready to make a new door in the planked walls of the stable. Big Freddie stepped in front of the horse with a grunted command that brought the horse to a trembling halt.

Rowena eyed her brother with newfound admiration. He grinned sheepishly.

As he steered the horse in a circle, Little Freddie caught her ankle. "Godspeed, love. I will detain Gareth for as long as I can."

Then the pressure of his fingers was gone and Folio was pointed toward the windy night. Without awaiting a command from Rowena, the stallion shot forward. The small remnant of sanity Papa still possessed drove his arms around her waist with desperate strength. The courtyard passed by in a blur of tattered images—the excited shouts of the squires as the phantom horse thundered past, a peasant stirring from his drunken stupor long enough to glance up, a knight clutching the silken shoulders of the lady on her knees in front of him, his eyes round with surprise. The courtyard wall loomed. Rowena pressed her eyes shut, dreading the terrible sensation of weightlessness that would be theirs when Folio leaped, the timeless moments before his forelegs caught on the top of the wall and sent them crashing down in a tangle of shattered bones.

The horse veered. She opened her eyes. They were through the first gate and heading for the drawbridge. Sparks flew as iron-shod hooves struck the drawbridge. Papa lost his grip and slid sideways. They went careening toward the oily black arms of the moat. Rowena threw herself to the opposite side until she clung by little more than the muscles of her thighs.

The stallion shot across the lake's bridge toward the beckoning meadows. With every hoofbeat, Rowena expected to slide beneath the horse's belly and have her skull split by his flailing hooves. Her hair whipped around Folio's legs, spooking the horse further. As his hooves struck the soft turf at the top of the hill, he reared. Rowena screamed as the horse slipped out from under them. She and her father went rolling down the steep slope in a tangled ball.

She ended up flat on her back, staring up at a creamy belt of stars scattered across a royal blue sky. She remembered a night long ago, when she had lain cradled in the arms of the moor, canopied by just such a sky and blissfully innocent of the lethal charms of knights and their intrigues.

She remembered toddling after the woman she had believed to be her mother. Tugging at her sun-warmed skirts as she bent her slender back over a washtub. A back bred for the comforts of nobility. A back her papa had finally broken spewing out his sons in a desecrated castle while he dabbled with whores like Elayne de Crecy. She closed her eyes briefly.

Suddenly, she wanted nothing more out of life than to lay in the wet grass forever and watch the clouds scuttle across the moon. Folio was doubtlessly gone now, and there was really nothing left to do but lay there until Gareth came and killed them. Papa chuckled.

"There now, Elayne, I'll have none of that teasing and nuzzling. You always were a lusty wench when you caught a man down."

A chill that had nothing to do with the damp grass beneath her shivered through Rowena. She looked over at Papa, expecting to find a half-rotted specter poised over him.

Folio nuzzled his throat, shimmering like mist in the moonlight. Papa shoved his head away with a giggle. The horse looked at her with such a placid expression that Rowena wanted to laugh.

She rolled over on her stomach and crawled on her elbows to her father's side. Folio nuzzled the back of her neck with his velvety muzzle.

"Papa?" she whispered.

"Aye, child?"

"Did you kill my mother?"

"Of course not. Little Freddie killed Althea. 'Twas not his fault. She just wasn't strong enough to bear another birth."

"Not Althea, Papa. *My* mother—Elayne."

His eyes cut to her in a moment of stark sobriety. He gave a defeated sigh. "I should have wrung her comely neck. But I could not. All I could do was shout and mewl and almost break my blasted neck fleeing that fool boy. Who could blame me, though? Lad or not, there was death in those eyes of his."

Rowena rolled to her back. They lay there like long-time companions watching clouds shift across the stars. She felt little surprise. He had only confirmed what she had suspected all along: Lindsey Fordyce hadn't the guts to kill a cockroach.

"What did you expect, Papa? He was in love with her. To walk in on such a tryst . . ."

Papa sighed. "No tryst. We were quarreling. She refused to come away with me. She saw no reason she could not stay and play lady of Caerleon twice over by marrying her husband's son. So I wanted you. I wanted to take you to Althea. She had longed for a girl child for so long. We were tugging on you like a pair of foul-mouthed harpies when the lad burst in." A long forgotten shame quickened in his eyes. "I dropped you."

"On my head, no doubt."

Her father gave her a reproachful look. "I dove out the window. I thought your cries would haunt me forever."

An idea split the darkness of her thoughts like the moon breaking through the clouds. "Papa, how did you get me? Who brought me to you?"

A slurred murmur was her only answer. Papa had lapsed into semiconsciousness and was softly singing. A cry from the turret over the drawbridge shattered the serenity of the countryside.

Rowena straddled her papa's chest. "Papa, listen to me, I must know. After Elayne was murdered, who brought me to you? Think!"

He winced in remembered pain. "Damned boy broke my leg. Cut my rope while I was still fifteen feet off the ground. I had to crawl to my horse. The farrier broke it again before he set it. The butcher."

She shook him by his tunic. His head bounced on the rich turf. "Papa, please! How did you come to bring me to Revelwood? Who gave me to you?"

The bright clarion note of a trumpet brought Folio's neck up. The stallion tossed his head, his mane rippling like a cascade of satin.

Papa's belly heaved beneath her. Rowena realized with horror that he was crying. "I could not believe my lovely Elayne was dead. Hadn't the strength to get off my pallet. Thrust the child into my arms." His trembling hand sought one of her loose curls to dry his tears with. "I wanted my little Rowena so. Had to take her away before the sins of the mother were visited on the child."

Rowena lifted her head. "Who, Papa? Who told you such a terrible thing?"

She leaned forward, straining to hear his sibilant answer.

The clatter of hoofbeats on wood split the darkness. Folio whinnied shrilly as a dark shape separated itself from the castle above and came hurtling into the night.

# Chapter 22

For years Rowena would remember the nightmarish contortions it took to get herself and Papa remounted. Sweat streamed down her face to be joined by tears when, after they were seated at last, Folio balked at her command. His ears pricked toward the approaching rider. His tail twitched. Rowena cursed in frustration and pounded on his back with her fists. The rider came at them, laid low over a charger's back, hell-bent and in no mood for conversation. Rowena knew the life of the limp, pathetic man draped behind her hung in the balance.

The dig of her heels finally set Folio into motion. Some long forgotten memory of a coltish game flickered through his equine brain. He wheeled around and dashed away from his approaching master, swishing his tail in a teasing flash of white. Rowena clung to the reins with one hand, her other arm struggling with her father's dead weight.

Folio's long legs stretched in a gallop. Wind stung Rowena's eyes. She dared a look behind her and saw in amazement that the distance between them and their pursuer was actually growing. Even with the weight of two riders, Folio possessed the speed and strength to fly through the thin spring grasses. As they swept over a rolling knoll, Rowena thought the horse would surely soar up and into the sky toward the siren purity of the moon.

A seamless edge of black bordered the meadow. Rowena swung Folio toward the forest, unable to differentiate between the pounding of her heart in her throat and the pounding of hoofbeats on the turf. They plunged into the shadows. Rowena drew rein and Folio slid to a reluctant halt.

From far behind them came the parting of the crackling grasses before a tide as inevitable as the wind. They had very little time. Rowena flung herself off the horse and stayed her father's leg when he would have followed.

"Papa, can you hear me?"

He slumped over the stallion's neck and opened one bleary eye. "Hmmmmm?"

Rowena grabbed his ears and pushed her face into his. "You must hold on! You must ride! Ride until you reach a castle or a village. Halt for nothing and no one. Do you understand?"

She released him. His head struck the pommel of the saddle. He groaned. "Break my neck," he mumbled.

"You may. But Gareth will sever your head if he catches you."

He made a supreme effort to straighten. Rowena gave his thigh an approving pat. "There now. Make haste, Papa. Ride like the wind."

Lindsey Fordyce's lips curled in an echo of the sunny smile that must have once charmed Elayne. "I shall be back for you, lass. As soon as I make my fortune. I will bring you ribbons and gold as much as your little paws can carry."

His wispy hair and faded blue eyes swam before Rowena's gaze. "Aye, Papa, I shall be waiting."

Folio was as much in thrall to his master as she was. Rowena knew she must take drastic measures to stop the stallion from simply running in a circle. She fished beneath the tatters of her skirt until she came up with a headless pin, shiny and dangerous in the dappled moonlight. She lay her cheek against Folio's silky hide, snuffled an apology, then jabbed the tapered point in the tender haunch.

The stallion plunged into a rear. Rowena stumbled away from the drumming hooves. Papa clung to the saddle with tenacious strength, caught in the wine-soaked haze of a drama more real than he would ever realize.

"Away, destrier!" he bellowed. "We shall slay those Arab heathens yet and return the Holy Cross to Jerusalem!"

A flash of white and they were gone. The thunder of approaching hoofbeats shook the earth. They slowed as Gareth guided his mount into the forest. Without giving herself time to think, Rowena scrambled up the widely spaced branches of a sturdy elm, wishing wildly for Marlys's helm.

She caught a slender branch in her sweaty palms as a nightmare in black and silver came plunging through the underbrush. She squeezed her eyes shut and dropped, using the force of her swing to slam into the rider. She wrapped her legs around his shoulders as they fell what seemed a hundred feet from the back of a gigantic midnight charger. She kicked at the beast's hooves as they rolled, spooking it into terrified flight back toward the way it had come.

A gauntleted hand caught her by the throat and slammed her to her back. A muscled arm drew back a sword. For one terrible moment, Rowena thought Gareth would not recognize her before that gleaming blade descended. For an even more terrible moment, she saw the cold light of recognition dawn in his eyes without stilling the descent of the blade. Ten inches of steel whistled past her ear as Gareth drove the sword into the mulch beside her cheek with a cry of rage and anguish that threw the night noises of the forest into dead silence.

She lay there in his lethal grip, her fragile pulse cradled by leather-encased fingers stripped of any semblance of mercy. A tear slipped out of the corner of her eye and traced a path down her dirt-streaked cheek.

Gareth grabbed her by the bodice of her kirtle and jerked her up. "How could you?" He shook her like a doll, then lowered her back to the ground.

He stood abruptly, his head cocked, listening for any sign of horse and rider. The lonely cry of a nightjar mocked him.

"Gareth?" she whispered to his heaving back.

He silenced her with a ragged gesture of one hand. "For twenty years, I've sought the man who dishonored my name. The man who cast his shadow over my father's every hope, dream, and ambition for me. The man who turned every countenance away from me, slammed every door in my face. I've spent half my life searching for that sniveling coward."

"And his golden-haired babe?"

He whirled around. "Aye. The babe Elayne brought to Caerleon, passing it off to my father as the legitimate offspring of her dead husband. Her lover followed shortly thereafter, offering his services to Caerleon." He took a step toward her. Rowena refused to flinch from the bitter blackness of his gaze. "Marlys thought it would be revenge enough to send that golden-haired babe home to Papa raped and bloated with a bastard of her own."

The wind blew cool against Rowena's heated cheeks. "Too merciful for you, eh? You preferred something far more diabolical," she said.

"All I wanted was the truth. I've lied my whole life to find it."

"Don't speak to me of truth. The word is a mockery on your lips. Nay, Gareth. 'Tis not the truth you seek." She climbed to her feet. "You want your name cleared. You want someone to blame for the murder they condemn you for. You want to punish someone for the pain you've endured."

"I suppose your jovial Papa convinced you he was innocent," he hissed.

"Papa broke his leg when you cut his rope. He could barely crawl to his horse much less return up those stairs to plunge a sword in Elayne's breast."

Gareth snorted. "Another Fordyce family fable. You lie almost as well as your mother." Rowena wouldn't have thought it possible, but his brow darkened further. "Tell me, then, my dear." He took a menacing step toward her. "If your precious Papa did not kill Elayne, then who did?"

A shaft of moonlight penetrated the clouds. Rowena had not prepared herself for that question. Gareth must not see her eyes. With the cunning of a trapped animal, she spun around to flee, but his arms circled her before she could take two steps. She made no struggle. Gareth's heart pounded a mad rhythm against her spine.

The silky heat of his voice poured into her ear. "So he has convinced you that I am a murderer."

She leaned her head back against his shoulder, choosing silence for her shield. A hot tear squeezed out from between her eyelids.

His hands slid slowly up her shoulders, gliding beneath the tangled weight of her hair to cup her throat. He curled his leather-clad knuckles inward, trailing them over her smooth skin with unbearable tenderness. Rowena flinched as if he had struck her.

His low chuckle sent fingers of fear skittering down her spine. "Fickle creature. Now you shrink from my touch. Was it so long ago that you received it with eagerness? Was it only two nights ago that you lay beneath me, begging me to—"

"Gareth, don't . . ."

"Don't what? Don't continue? Or don't stop? Why don't you let me show you what an adoring stepbrother I can be?" His fingers grazed the swell of her breast, then dipped into her kirtle to caress her tender nipple with practiced eroticism. Fear and desire tightened her throat.

"Cease your torment!" she cried, shoving his hand away. "I cannot bear you making sport of me." She twisted out of his grasp and backed away from him.

He followed her step for step, holding his hands out in front of him. "Why do you shy away now, little sister? These murderer's hands pleasured you well enough when it suited you. You cared not if they were dripping blood."

Rowena tossed her hair back. Harsh bark cut into her shoulder as she came up against a tree. She forced herself to laugh, blinding herself to the pain she was causing him, biting back the truth about who murdered Elayne because she knew it would utterly destroy him.

"Shall you have me now, Gareth? Shall you bed me as you bedded all those other women who dared to look at you askance? Will you use your body as a weapon to silence me? Or will you close your eyes and pretend I am my mother? Have you been doing that from the beginning?"

He continued to advance on her. His lip curled in a snarl meant to be a smile. "I've already had you. And I must say you tumbled into my bed easier than most. I suppose you cannot help it with the blood of a whore flowing through your veins."

Rowena forgot she had been deliberately goading him. She forgot everything but the haze of red that drifted over her eyes. Her fist came around, slamming into his jaw in a blow that staggered him and would have fallen a lesser man.

Her every knuckle ached as if it had been shattered, but that could not silence the perverse triumph singing through her veins. The melody was sweet but brief. As Gareth caught her shoulders and pinned her against the tree, she began to ponder the consequences of her actions. To her surprise, he was grinning like a naughty demon spurned from the gates of hell. His face, stripped of light, was not the face of a loving man she had known once in another lifetime, but the face of a young man little more than a boy—wild with infatuation, sick with jealousy.

"You golden-haired little bastard. I always knew you'd be more trouble than you were worth."

His lips closed on hers. He pushed his fingers through her hair, drawing her head back until her mouth was helpless beneath the merciless assault of his kiss. The taste of his blood stung her tongue where her blow had driven his cheek against his teeth. Rowena felt herself drawn into the maelstrom of his dark desire as if every moment of her life had brought her to this place to be held captive by her love for this man.

She moaned as his tongue feverishly stroked the deepest recesses of her mouth. His knee slipped between her legs, nudging upward with crass finesse until her own fingers crept up to tangle in his hair. He drew back. There was no darkness on earth black enough to dim the luminous emotion in Rowena's eyes.

His breathing was harsh. "You are a fool, milady. You should have fled with your father." He caught her face roughly between his palms. "If I murdered your mother, do you not believe me capable of murdering you? Your fickle heart has cut me far deeper than Elayne's ever could." He stroked her trembling bottom lip with his thumb.

Rowena laced her fingers in his and drew his hands downward. She pressed his palms to the thundering pulse in her throat and held them fast, even when they jerked convulsively.

"Go on," she said. "Murder me if 'tis what you desire. You hated me when I was a babe. You hate me now. You can tell them I fled with Papa. There are leaves enough to cover my body. No one will ever know. I shall try not to struggle. There. Would it be easier if I closed my eyes?"

Gareth's fingers tightened slightly.

Rowena kept her eyes closed, steeling her body against the trembling that threatened to seize it. "Why do you hesitate? You were going to kill Papa, were you not? Can you deny it? You were going to condemn him without benefit of questioning or trial, just as you were condemned. I set him free. So should I not take his place in the executioner's hands?" Her arms crept down to her sides. She stood there, achingly passive in the power of a man who could snap her neck with a single flex of his broad thumbs.

Gareth's grip softened. Rowena's eyes fluttered open.

"Nay, sweet ladylove. The freedom of death will be denied you." His lips brushed her earlobe in a mocking caress. "These executioner's hands can think of a thousand pleasant things to do to you that they could not do to your papa. You will serve me well enough alive. I will see to that." His eyes sparkled with an odd light as he knelt at her feet and tore the hem from her skirt. "Give me your hands."

Rowena felt as if they were reliving a scene that had happened centuries ago. "There is no need."

"You've been running from me ever since you promised that the first time."

Rowena held out her wrists, and he twined the length of brocade around them.

"If I try to run, you could just hit me over the head with something," she mumbled.

"I prefer my women conscious," he said in clipped tones. "I hate for them to wake up tender and sated and not remember why."

Rowena felt a flare of genuine hatred. "An honorable nobleman, are you not?"

He jerked the bond, making her crash into his chest. He pulled her up until they were nose to nose. "You stole any hope of honor for me when you freed your father. 'Tis time I started living up to my reputation. If you give me another of your speeches on chivalry, I swear I shall gag you."

Rowena wisely bit back a retort.

They emerged from the forest to find Gareth's mount grazing in the meadow. The destrier lifted his massive head. Despite his jarring size, he lacked the prancing nervousness of Folio and stood docile as Gareth secured a rope around Rowena's snug bonds and mounted. Without so much as a glance at her, Gareth nudged the horse into a sedate walk. Rowena supposed it was of no import to him whether she stumbled behind or lay down and was dragged back to Ardendonne on her belly. She prodded her feet into motion.

Ardendonne winked like a misty diamond studding a dusky crown, the parapets and towers silhouetted against the pitching clouds. She was shocked to find it so near. Folio's speed and her fear had led her to believe they had left it far behind. How could its glow remain so welcoming when her whole life had been shattered? The winds gusted, carrying over the rustling grasses a clarion's song, distorted by time and distance. She swiped a tear from her cheek with bound hands. When Gareth pivoted in his saddle, she was plodding behind him, her eyes locked on the ground.

He snorted. "Such a charming picture of persecution. I daresay you would look lovely gracing a cathedral window. Your demure stance and blameless eyes would melt the heart of the staunchest sinner."

"If he had a heart."

Gareth's tone was deliberately light. "If such a sinner had any dealings with women, no doubt his heart was cut out and fed to his lady for supper."

"Then God take pity on her, for she would have starved on such meager fare."

Gareth doubled the horse's pace. Rowena stumbled after him, too angry to regret her impertinence. She gave a start of surprise as his voice rang out in a lusty baritone.

Mortimer would have never dared sing of these amorous adventures of a wench named Rosaleen in mixed company. Rowena did not understand half of the lewd verses, but from the dark glances Gareth hurled over his shoulder after the most perverse lyrics, she had the discomfitting sensation that she would before this night was over. When she could no longer bear his gloating smirk, she joined in and bellowed out the next chorus with such enthusiasm that Gareth lapsed into brooding silence.

Her satisfaction was short-lived. The graceful arch

of Blaine's bridge clattered under the horse's hooves.
Wind and moon raked the lake into silvered peaks.
The drawbridge loomed before them like a black
tongue poised to draw them inside the yawning
maw of the castle. Rowena shivered as they passed
beneath the arch, all that was grace in Ardendonne's
construction dying in the first stale breath of its
debauchery.

The bailey reeked of stale wine, sweat and a pot-
pourri of earthy smells Rowena did not dare to name.
As Gareth dismounted, her gaze went of its own volition to the stable at the bottom of the hill. He tossed the
reins to a squire she did not recognize. The boy's eyes
widened as they fell on the rope which bound her to
Gareth.

Gareth jerked on Rowena's bonds, paying her no
more heed than if she were a recalcitrant terrier on the
end of a leash.

"Have you . . . ? Where . . . ?" Rowena started, but
could not find the words to finish.

"Did you expect to find your brothers' heads piked
on the gate? Sorry to disappoint you. I've decided to
stop holding them responsible for the willful acts of
their relations."

Rowena choked out a sigh of relief. It was not nearly
as late as she had imagined. The squires still rattled
their dice on the cobblestones. The stuporous peasant
had been replaced by a snoring herald.

The squires slyly nudged each other and muttered
among themselves as those who were not blind drunk
spotted Rowena and Gareth.

A knight stumbled out of the door, dragging a
plainly garbed maid. He thrust her to her knees in front
of him, his hands fumbling with the points of his hose.

Rowena hastily looked away.

"Before this night is over, I shall remedy your shyness," Gareth murmured.

Rowena's feet froze. She did not even feel Gareth's
eyes on her as he turned to gauge the effect of his
cruel words. She paled as her fragile illusions came

crashing down around her. Somehow she had convinced herself that there was nothing he could do to her that she could not forgive. Somewhere in the back of her mind, she had even harbored the childish hope that he might forgive her, that he would laugh away her folly and draw her under his arm with a tender kiss. She swayed as a pain more piercing than grief speared her heart.

Wrapping the rope around his fist, Gareth reeled her in like a fish.

He steeled himself against the lost eyes she raised to his face. "Come, Rowena," he growled. "I am in no mood for dillydallying."

Her gaze darted wildly around the courtyard. "I cannot bear them staring at me."

"You will learn to bear it soon enough. I did."

He jerked the rope, but her feet stayed rooted to the cobblestones. He jerked harder, and she dragged her feet, her lips set in a mutinous line.

Gareth's entire countenance dissolved in a sweetness so profound that Rowena was terrified. He caught her shoulders and drove her straight back into the shadows until the stone wall dug into her shoulder blades. His hand cupped her head as he bent her over his arm in a kiss so darkly passionate that even the most astute observer would have sworn they were lovers too long torn apart. A snicker from the squires was followed by a bray of laughter.

Gareth drew back. His arms stilled her frantic struggle with no visible effort. "I swear to you, my ladylove," he said between clenched teeth, "if you are so eager for my touch that you can go no further, then we will take our pleasure here like those others."

In counterpoint to his threat came a rustle in the ivy behind them, a man's groan thick with the muted agony of pleasure. Rowena's fingers tugged on his sleeves, and she pressed her forehead to his breastbone in a wordless plea.

Gareth shoved her roughly into motion, the cost of

his cruelty betrayed by his harsh breathing and the stiff jut of his jaw.

His stride was sure and steady as he marched them into the hall. He ducked beneath the linked hands of the dancers in an unswerving path for the stairs. When Rowena faltered, he jerked the rope, ignoring the horrified gasps and offended glares from those not draped insensibly over the tables or each other. Rowena knew she must look like a hoyden. She had lost her slippers. Her hair hung in tangled disarray down her back. From the corner of her eye, she caught a glimpse of something smudged with dirt, which she could only assume was her nose. The ruby kirtle hung in lank tatters around her ankles.

She shrank into herself, believing their disapproval was of her. The last plucked note of the psaltery wavered in the air. A dwarf stopped pounding his tabor, and a steady murmur swelled to a hum.

"How dare he!"

"The poor child."

"Heartless wretch!"

"He may treat her like an animal on his own lands, but surely Sir Blaine will not allow it in the sanctity of his castle."

Gareth stared straight ahead, as if he had been struck blind as well as deaf.

They had reached the stairs when Blaine broke from the crowd and stepped in front of them. His expression held such kind concern that Rowena felt tears sting her eyes. Alise hovered at Blaine's elbow like a nervous wren.

The crowd held their breath, straining to hear Blaine's soft words. "For once, they are right, Gareth. I cannot allow this."

No one had to strain to hear Gareth's reply. "She stole my steed and gave it to another man."

Even Blaine winced and recoiled from those words. A horrified murmur went up from the crowd. Alise smiled.

Blaine went down on one knee at Rowena's feet and

caught her bound hands in his own. "Sweet lady, say it is not so! Did you not know what a mount means to his knight? What the stallion was worth?"

Rowena forced a wry smile. "More than me, it seems."

Gareth interrupted. "If you will cease groveling at the thief's feet, we will proceed."

Blaine stood, his slender form possessing more dignity than Rowena would have thought possible. "Gareth, I beg you. Surely for the sake of our friendship, you could show mercy to this sweet—"

Gareth's words fell like thunderclaps in the hushed silence. "Felon. She stole my horse. Do I take her upstairs or would you care to hang her?" He thrust the end of the rope at Blaine as if it were of no concern to him which course was taken.

Alise tugged at Blaine's sleeve. "Hang her, Blaine. Do let's hang her."

Gareth's nostrils flared as he shot Alise a look of pure contempt. She slipped behind Blaine, who stepped back from the swaying rope as if it might bite him.

Gareth pushed past them, and Rowena felt Blaine's sympathetic hand brush her shoulder as they passed. At the top of the narrow staircase, Gareth came to a halt with a bemused curse. Rowena stumbled into his back.

He drew her in front of him. "I've never had to face so many obstacles to get a woman to my bedchamber. Have you the pope crouching under my bed?"

Marlys squatted at the end of the corridor like a nesting gargoyle. Between lank strands of hair, her face was stark white.

Her voice had lost its confident cadence. "I must speak to you, Gareth."

His fingers lightly traced Rowena's collarbone. "Later."

"Now."

Rowena's eyes blazed a brilliant blue, narrowing in both a warning and a plea. She laughed lightly. "If you've come to plead for me, save your breath. Blaine did a much prettier job and his pleas fell on ears of stone. I fear it will take more than pleasantries to soothe your brother's wounded vanity."

"Like a human sacrifice?" Marlys bit off.

"A charming one, at that," Gareth said pleasantly.

With a choked cry, Marlys leaped to her feet and fled past them down the stairs.

Gareth soon had them secured behind a chamber door with the bolt dropped home.

Rowena stood lost at the door while Gareth went to the window. The moon cast his silhouette in wax.

"The remonstrances of your friends are touching, are they not?"

"But ineffectual," she murmured.

Her heart plummeted as she saw the linen sheets humped and tangled on the bed. She would rather he kill her outright than lay her beneath him on a feather mattress that only last night may have held the mold of Alise's body beneath his. She spun around, a cry catching in her throat, and pressed her forehead to the door.

Gareth's head flew up as the piteous sound arrowed straight to his heart. He crossed to her. His rough hands cradled her shoulders as his husky voice rocked her with shivers.

"Your shyness would be more convincing if my body were not incensed with memories of your wanton surrender to me. I cannot sleep. I cannot eat. I cannot think without your image rising unbidden before me. Your poison is sweet, but fatal. I can find no antidote except to partake of it again and again until I've purged it from my soul or died trying."

Rowena leaned her head back. Tears slipped down her cheeks, wetting his beard. "What do you want from me, Gareth? Shall I scream so the others can hear me? Shall I drop to my knees and plead for your mercy?"

"Your knees would be as fine a place as any to begin."

He pulled her around and pinned her against the door. His lips harshly took hers. His tongue stoked the embers of desire deep within her to hungry flames with a violence that warned her his own need was tinged with madness. His knee flexed between her legs, opening her to the brutal caress of fingers sheathed in leather. His palm rubbed the tatters of her dress against her, using leather against velvet as a fiery conductor of his will until her struggles deepened to tortured writhing. He scooped her up, one arm cradling her hips, his other palm still cupping the hot, damp fabric between her legs.

He lay her back on the bed, pulling her hips to its edge. Her legs dangled on each side of his thighs. He pulled his tunic over his head, revealing a dark mat of crisp hair.

"You are as spineless as your father," he snarled. "You'd give yourself to a man who hates you before you would fight for yourself."

His words were like ice water tossed on the flames of her love. She lay stunned before their virulence and injustice. Gareth reached for the points of his hose. If his hands had not been poised there, he would have received the full force of her convulsive kick to his groin. As it was, his hand shot down in a reflex born of knighthood, catching her slender foot in his grasp.

He gave a low, taunting laugh. "There now, girl. I knew you had your mother in you somewhere. 'Twas only a matter of baiting her to life."

Rowena sat up, jerking her foot out of his hand. "The two of you deserved each other."

She scooted back on the bed, and Gareth crawled after her. "You've inherited her deceit, treachery, and fickle heart. Perhaps 'tis time I taught you some of her other tricks."

"As she taught you?" Rowena shot back.

She rolled over, planning to launch herself off the bed and flee this vicious demon she had thought to be her lover. Gareth's arm snaked around her waist. He slid her facedown beneath his weight. She sucked in a sharp breath to scream, but before she could cry out, his hand clapped over her mouth. She tasted leather against her teeth.

"If you scream, you shall summon Blaine and his minions," he hissed in her ear. "And if you think his chivalry possesses no price, you are mistaken. Do you want to be the whore of one man, or two?"

Rowena slumped against the feather mattress, defeat etched in the slender curve of her spine. When Gareth turned her over, her eyes were as dark with bitterness as his own.

His knuckles brushed her cheek in a caress that was achingly tender. His lips grazed her temple, tasting tiny hairs like spun sugar against his tongue.

"How will I ever forgive you for this?" she asked.

His lips nestled into the hollow of her throat. "If I am a murderer, why should I care?"

Rowena ached to speak, but held her tongue, painfully aware of the price she must pay for her silence.

As he undid the hooks at her bodice, Rowena lay malleable beneath his hands, holding back a shudder even when he exposed her nakedness to his burning gaze.

She flinched at the unfamiliar feel of leather against her nipples. The sensitive nubs tightened and contracted with a will of their own. Gareth lowered his heated lips to first one and then the other, taking them into his mouth and gently suckling until her hands caught in his hair. He lifted his shaggy head and met the ferocity of her gaze over twin peaks silvered with moonlight and frosted with the wetness of his tongue.

He pulled off his gauntlets.

She caught her breath as his blunt fingers slid between her legs, weaving an erotic spell with a delicacy that should have been impossible. Gareth watched her face, captivated by the fleeting glimpses of a pleasure she could no longer hide. Her body tensed and shuddered as he dipped one finger into her with paralyzing gentleness, soothing the swelling membranes he found there with her own silken nectar. His finger ravished her with agonizing slowness, preparing her for the deeper filling soon to come. Her lashes fluttered against her flushed cheeks. Her head rolled from side to side, the coral softness of her lips forming soundless words against the pillow of her hair. Gareth's fingers worked their magic in maddening rhythm until a shudder harder and deeper than all the others rocked Rowena and held her fast.

Her throat arched and she fell back against the mattress, biting back a cry. Gareth felt the muscles of his abdomen tighten convulsively. Rowena opened eyes dark and misty with passion and bitterness as he withdrew his fingers from her and gently teased their dew over her taut nipples. He slipped his finger into her one last time. The pungent scent of leather assailed her nostrils as he gently drew it across her lips, pearling their softness with a glistening honey more potent than nectar. His mouth closed on hers, the taste and scent of her surrender fusing them together in a bond stronger than blood.

His knee nudged her thighs apart. He barely had his hose untied and down over his hips when Rowena felt the tip of a blade more lethal than any sword press against her softness, following the throbbing course his fingers had charted. She buried her face against his throat as he teased her, rubbing against her but holding back. Her teeth nipped his collarbone. Her moan reverberated against his ear. His fingers laced around hers, pinning her palms in a prison of deceptive softness underlaid with a hardness as fine as steel. She clutched his hands as a matching hardness knifed deep within her.

Gareth took her, making her his own with tantalizing strokes, each longer and deeper than the last until Rowena shuddered, filled so deeply that she no longer knew where her body ended and his began. His breathing quickened as he rocked between her hips until the tenuous thread of his own control snapped and a guttural groan escaped his throat. Rowena arched against him as he poured his seed into her, impaling her against the bed with the force of his need.

The moon sank like a pale pearl into a black sea, casting its exhausted beams over a floor strewn with gauntlets, hose, and velvet.

Gareth drew Rowena up in the center of the bed to face him. His fingers pushed through her tangled hair, his nails coming to rest against her scalp like tender blades. "I once swore an oath to you—on my knees." His hand tangled in her hair. She slid irrevocably down the merciless contours of his body until her cheek lay against the satiny heat of his thigh. Her hair sheltered her burning cheeks from him. He reached down and gently tilted her chin until she was forced to meet his gaze. "Now, sweet lady, you may swear your oath to me."

Rowena's eyes widened, but the honeyed languor of their lovemaking still held her in its thrall. She was beguiled by the strength of his will. His hands and body guided her through this tender initiation until the sweet acquiescence of her lips and mouth wrung a groan of mortal pleasure from deep in his throat. He threw back his head, teeth clenched in a primitive portrait of ecstasy. Exultation rolled through Rowena's veins like thunder as Gareth cried out a need for her that required no words.

The moon fled before the clouds that gathered on the far horizon. Rowena lay with her face buried in the crook of Gareth's arm. His hand absently traced half-words and pictures on the flat planes of her sweat-sheened stomach.

"You will find me no husband, will you?" she murmured against his skin.

Gareth's fingertips paused in their gentle motion. He shook his head.

"And you will not let me go come summer, will you?"

She lifted her gaze. Gareth's arm tightened around her neck. "I will never let you go."

Despair darkened her own eyes at the tenor of those words. Once she had prayed to hear them, but not spoken like that, not thrown out like a black-edged threat laced with more hatred than love. She blinked back tears as he rolled her to her stomach and mated her with a savage intensity that left her incoherent and mercifully incapable of further thought.

Rowena stared blindly at the gray dawn creeping through the narrow window. The distant, lonely crow of a cock warbled to a pensive halt. She gazed at the man beside her as if he were a stranger. A lock of tousled hair fell over his brow. Sleep had soothed the lines etched around his mouth, but as she watched, a shadow of a grimace tightened his lips as if even the peace of sleep eluded him. Rowena did not care to witness his pain. She had enough of her own to deal with. She nudged away the knee thrown over her thigh and scooted out from under his weight.

She slipped Gareth's tunic over her head. The heavy camlet felt rough against her nakedness. The garment covered her to the knees. She paused at the door before returning to the bed to draw a linen sheet over Gareth's sprawling form. He rolled to his side, pulling her pillow under his chin with a slurred murmur.

Sleeping bodies littered the great hall like the victims of some merciless plague of pleasure. Rowena stepped over the stained skirts of a spread-eagled maid whose cheek was pillowed on the rump of a pock-marked page.

As she passed through the bailey, Rowena filled her lungs with damp morning air untainted by the stench of sour wine and unwashed flesh. At the top of the draw-bridge, she stopped. Her bare toes curled against the splintered wood as she gazed wistfully at the stables. She had come to seek the solace of her brothers' company only to discover that far more than the rich dirt of the list separated them.

A chasm had opened between them, a chasm deepened during the long night when Gareth had used her love as a weapon to tame her, used his dark skills to wring cries from her she did not even recognize as her own. The courage that had driven her to defy him deserted her at the thought of facing Little Freddie half-dressed with swollen lips and tangled hair. She knew the evidence of Gareth's possession was as fresh as the lingering tenderness between her legs.

She hugged herself, wishing she had thought to bring a shawl into a morning that still held a breath of winter. Clouds smothered the horizon, and the scent of rain drifted to her nostrils.

Bracing herself against the castle stones, she crept out along the narrow ledge overhanging the moat and sat down, dangling her feet over the dark mirror of water. Mist drifted across the lake in veils of white, obscuring the bridge. If she started walking now, how long would it take her to get to Revelwood? she wondered. And how long would it take Gareth to come after her and drag her back?

*I will never let you go.*

His icy words echoed in her head. Gareth de Crecy was a powerful man. He could lock her away, keep her prisoner at Caerleon forever if he so desired. She imagined herself sitting in a lonely tower, watching from the window as he brought a wife to Caerleon, growing withered and gray while he fathered sons and slowly forgot the blinding passion that had once bound them.

She pressed her wrists to her eyes, praying the clean ache might erase her tortured visions. When she opened her eyes, something milky white was bobbing on the surface of the moat. She blinked, wondering if her eyes had deceived her.

Climbing up on her knees, she leaned over as far as she dared. A tantalizing edge of white drifted toward her. She hesitated before stretching out her fingers, having no idea if Blaine's vicious fish were an inch long or as big as whales. Drawing in a deep breath, she snatched at the object.

Her hand closed around a smooth cylinder and pulled it streaming from the water. It was a bone, the long, slender web of fingers still tangled in the strings of a wooden lute. A shrill scream ripped from her throat, shattering the morning silence. Her scream went on and on until Blaine pried the thing from her hand and enfolded her in his arms, pressing her face into his shoulder.

# Chapter 23

The seneschal's keys jingled wildly as he loped into the donjon. He cast the hearth a curious glance. Rowena returned it unblinkingly until he looked away. "Milord, milord, they set up a cry outside the doors! Whatever shall I do?" He trotted at Blaine's pacing heels, wringing his plump hands.

"Tell them to go to hell," Blaine gritted out.

The seneschal trotted faster. "They do not understand, Sir Blaine. First they were snatched from their sleep and tossed out of the castle like yesterday's cabbage. Half of them are still drunk. The mood is ugly and the rumors are getting uglier. The doors of Ardendonne have never been bolted against any man—knight or villein." He lowered his voice ominously. " 'Tis beginning to rain. I heard cries for a battering ram."

Blaine turned on the man, his patience frazzled to an end. He snatched him up by his tunic. "You are the seneschal, are you not? Pull up the drawbridge. Lower the cursed portcullis."

The man blinked. "The portcullis. Of course. I

forgot we had one. I shall be at it right away. Mayhaps 'tis not rusted."

Blaine released the man, and he scampered off, happy to have a concrete task. Blaine blew out a long breath and ruffled his hair, looking more a perplexed thirteen than a self-assured thirty-three. Freckles dusted his pale cheeks.

A maidservant with eyes still swollen from the night's debauchery stumbled in from the kitchens. She cleared a scrap-littered table with one arm and dropped her tray. She managed a sloe-eyed wink at Blaine before turning to run into the door frame with a thump that made Rowena wince.

Blaine squatted in front of where Rowena huddled on the hearth and pressed a warm mug into her icy palms.

"Ale would serve you better. I shall have it mulled with cinnamon if 'tis the taste that plagues you."

Rowena cupped the mug gratefully, breathing in the steam. "Nay. 'Tis milk I wanted," she said through chattering teeth.

She blew the skin off the surface and took a deep draught. The creamy warmth spread like courage down her throat. Blaine pulled the edges of the blanket around her, patting her shoulder awkwardly.

Outside the chamber, a tremendous clanking of chains was followed by the throbbing groan of an iron pulley that had fallen into disuse before ever being used. The massive portcullis slid out of its mooring with a screech that set Rowena's teeth on edge.

"Careful with that crank now, Owen," came a wavery cry.

"I got it, mate. Oh, dear!"

"Stand clear!"

"Watch your feet!"

The muffled thump of bodies diving was followed by the crash of spiked bars striking stone. The echoing clang went on and on, dying with a finality that left Blaine's face as bereft as a child's.

" 'Tis not rusted," Rowena said in a vain attempt to cheer him.

Safe behind the iron bars of the portcullis, Blaine's seneschal and his hapless cohorts flung open the main doors. Rain pelted the cobblestones. Thunder cracked like a whip. Rowena's face flushed as a roar of disapproval rocked the castle. She huddled deeper in the blanket as individual threads unwove themselves from the bellowing tapestry of fury.

"Send out the murderer!"

"Justice for Mortimer!"

"Hang the dark lord!"

Blaine was across the chamber before she realized he had moved. "Close that door," he shouted. "And bolt it. If you open it again, the mob can have what is left of you after I've shoved you through the portcullis."

His men obeyed with a fawning chorus of, "As you wish, sir."

"Good God, Sir Boris, get in here." Blaine reappeared with a gray-haired knight in tow.

The man rubbed his red-rimmed eyes, finally bringing them to focus on Rowena. He was less disheveled than most of the occupants of Ardendonne, though he wore only one gauntlet and his tunic was on backward. Rowena curled her bare feet under the blanket, realizing she had no right to pass judgement while garbed only in Gareth's tunic and Blaine's blanket.

"Is this the girl?" the man asked Blaine.

"It is," Blaine replied.

Sir Boris gave her a courtly bow Rowena hardly felt she deserved while dressed like some bawd escaped from the wharfs of Londontown.

Blaine did not stand on the ceremony of introduction. "I am at a loss, Sir Boris. What am I to do?"

"Being the oldest and wisest lech here, I suppose the burden of counsel falls on me. Can you summon your father?"

"I fear not. He is dead."

"Oh, dear, I'd forgotten. Hmmm." Sir Boris smoothed back gray hair peppered with black. "Unfortunate situation. Sir Bryan would know just what to do.

He took care of it the last time Gareth got himself into such a pickle."

Resentment flared in Rowena. "Why does everyone have to assume Gareth got himself into anything? Mayhaps someone else got him there."

Sir Boris squinted at her as if seeing her for the first time. "Now, child, you must understand what the people believe, what they've believed for years. Everyone heard Gareth threaten Mortimer. 'Twas not the first time. His temper is as black as his reputation."

The knight's kind gray eyes and utter calm frightened her more than the rantings of the mob. She stood. The blanket slid from her shoulders. "Your temper might be black, too, if you'd lived your whole life under the shadow of gossip and innuendo."

"A minstrel's bones carry this beyond gossip, Rowena," Blaine said. "A man died last night."

Rowena turned on him. "And you believe Gareth killed him?"

Blaine's eyes clouded briefly. "I don't care if he did," he finally said. "I'll not turn him over to that clamoring mob."

"Good lad. My sentiments exactly." Sir Boris clapped him on the shoulder. "We shall have a trial before the rabble can hang him. We will send for some of the king's best knights."

"So *they* can hang me?" Gareth leaned against the door frame, his arms crossed in a study of casual arrogance. Rowena wondered how long he had been standing there.

Their gazes met. His eyes swept her in a velvet caress, uncertainty stamped on his features. The night loomed between them, as dark and impenetrable as his eyes. Rowena had to look away. She forced herself to remember how he had used his body and her need as weapons to weave a punishing net of pleasure. Steel threads garroted her heart as she fought the urge to run to him. She sat down and drew the blanket around her shoulders like a mantle.

Gareth's mouth twisted in a bitter travesty of a

smile. "What good knights would you summon to my defense, Sir Boris? From my window, I believe I caught a glimpse of Sir Damien and Sir Leitchfield leaping about in a charming demand for my blood. Shall they head my tribunal?"

Blaine sank down in a chair as Gareth sauntered into the chamber and propped his hip on the edge of a table.

Sir Boris cleared his throat. "Gareth, you must try to understand their position. Mortimer was an extremely popular minstrel. A treasure of the court since he was little more than a lad. A pampered favorite of the king."

"And more of his barons than I'd care to recount." Gareth smiled pleasantly.

"The man had his weaknesses. As we all do. But his follies were more than outweighed by his talents."

"As multifaceted as they were."

"Dammit, Gareth," Blaine erupted. "Stifle your flippant tongue. Sir Boris is trying to help you."

Sir Boris's hands trembled as he plucked the flagon off the tray and filled a goblet. For an instant, Rowena wanted to shake Gareth as badly as Blaine did.

Sir Boris grimaced at the warm goat's milk and set the goblet down without drinking from it. "The people feel Mortimer belonged to them. With his ballads and the spell he wove with words and music, he became the voice of their lives. They were willing to overlook his dalliances, his childish sulks—"

"His drunkenness?" Rowena added softly.

Sir Boris swiveled around to look at her. "The thought occurred to me, too, child. He may have simply stumbled into the moat." He shook his head as if to clear it. "But a hundred witnesses heard Mortimer sing his last ballad, heard Sir Gareth threaten him and saw the bard leave the hall never to be seen alive again."

Gareth applauded dryly. "Now that has the ring of a fine ballad. Such dramatic flair wasted in a knight!"

It was more to still Gareth's flagellating tongue than to defend him that spurred Rowena to speak. "Sir Gareth could not have killed Mortimer. He was with me all night."

Sir Boris looked so pitying that she might have made the admission she had bedded a troll.

Her cheeks flamed as Gareth gave a short, ugly laugh. "Your loyalty is touching, milady, but there is no need to lie for me. Everyone saw me leave the hall alone. Just as everyone saw us return together."

Sir Boris chose his next words with care. "The less the young lady's name is bandied about, the better. There have already been some very—to put this delicately—distasteful rumors. Bringing them to mind will only blight your reputation further and fan the flames of outrage."

Gareth snorted. "What do those paragons of moral virtue dare whisper about Rowena?"

Sir Boris's gaze was uncompromising. "That you carried her off to Caerleon against her will. That you keep her chained to your bed, a slave to your unnatural desires."

Gareth's mask slipped as he realized the cost of the rumors he had spread himself to torment Lindsey Fordyce. Like a blind man he groped for a steadying corner of the table. The eyes he raised to Rowena were stricken with the knowledge that his anger of the night had turned rumor into prophecy.

It was he who had to look away first. "None of this is your concern. If they want me that badly, let them come lay siege to Caerleon."

Blaine sat up in his chair. "And if they bring Edward's armies with them? What then, Gareth? Civil war? You cannot fight everybody in England."

"Why not? I've been doing it all my life."

Boris laid a steadying hand on Blaine's shoulder and faced Gareth. " 'Tis with great regret, my son, that I suggest you be confined until the knights arrive. 'Twill satisfy even the most bloodthirsty of the lot outside."

Gareth swung around. The threat of barely checked violence was written in every powerful inch of his body, making it seem even larger than it was. The suggestion of confining such a presence seemed as ludicrous as trying to harness the deep swell of thunder that rolled across the roof of the donjon.

He slid off the table, his swagger as deliberate as a taunt, and held out his wrists to Blaine. "Cart me off to the dungeon, friend. Have you no chains in this palace of pleasure?"

Blaine slapped Gareth's hands away, and even Sir Boris had the good grace to look embarrassed. "Your chamber will be sufficient. I shall entrust my son with your safekeeping. He is young and not so easily swayed by the opinions of others."

As Gareth's gaze fell on Rowena's inclined head, his lips softened in a smile more wry than mocking. "A marvelous and dangerous trait. Guard it well."

By the time Rowena had lifted her head, he had thrown a cheerful arm over Sir Boris's shoulders and was guiding the man from the chamber, leading him in a discussion of the latest tournament rules.

Blaine covered his face with one hand, casting Rowena a despairing glance between his fingers. Outside the hall, a cry of warning was followed by the thud of a heavy body striking the floor. The blanket fell away as Rowena sprinted for the door. She gave a cry of dismay at the sight of Gareth's form crumpled on the stones.

She flung herself to her knees and cradled his head in her lap. "What have you done to him?"

A bewildered looking young knight stood over him. He gave the broadsword in his hand a sheepish glance. "I saw his arm tighten around Papa's throat. So I hit him over the head."

"You knave. You might have killed him!" The young man quailed before the contempt in Rowena's voice.

She soothed the hair from Gareth's brow, crooning words of comfort he could not hear. His chest rose and fell evenly. His dark lashes rested against his cheeks. He looked so peaceful, he might have been sleeping.

Sir Boris rubbed his throat, swallowing convulsively. "It was as the boy said. The lad did right."

"I suppose he was trying to kill you, too. Mayhaps he is in the throes of a murdering frenzy and is going to massacre us all." Rowena laid a lopsided kiss on Gareth's ear, daring the men to tear him away from her.

Blaine knelt in front of her. "Of course he wasn't going to kill Sir Boris. I know Gareth. He was going to escape and take his battle away from Ardendonne. I promise you, Rowena, if Gareth gets outside those gates, someone will die. And it very well might be him." The harshness of his words was tempered by the palm that gently cupped her cheek. "Let me protect him. From himself."

Rowena's arms fell to her sides. None of the three men met her eyes as they gently took Gareth from her and carried him down the dimly lit corridor.

A swish of Rowena's kirtle and a tremulous smile was all it took to convince Sir Boris's son that she must see Gareth immediately. The young knight watched her traverse the dim hall, admiration for her courage in the face of such trials written plainly in his besotted eyes. Perhaps he should examine his feelings about Sir Gareth. Any man who could inspire such devotion in so enchanting a creature could surely not be as wicked as they said. The memory of her eyes blazing brightly up at him over Gareth's prostrate form lent itself to day-dreams where it was his own head cradled in her soft lap. He slipped around the corner to give her the privacy he had promised.

The best Ardendonne could offer for a dungeon was an isolated cell off the corridor from the kitchen wing. It was one of the few chambers in the castle with an iron lock placed to protect the salt and other precious spices. A grate of iron bars was set in the thick oaken door.

Rowena stood on tiptoe and peered through the bars. A tallow candle burned within the cell. It took a long moment for her eyes to adjust enough to make out the shadow of a man sitting on a barrel.

"Gareth?"

"Could you not wait to gloat at my hanging?" Gareth swung his long legs around. The candle threw his features into sharp relief as the shadow of a wince crossed his face. He rubbed the back of his neck. "Damned pup nearly killed me."

Rowena stuck her nose through the bars. Hulking crates and kegs were stacked along the walls. The pungent scent of ginger and cloves tickled her nostrils. "Folio came back."

"Was your papa's corpse draped across his saddle?"

"I fear not. He came back quite alone, stepping in high spirits and tossing his head in shameless pride at his independent jaunt." She peered around the shadowy cell. "Is it terribly unpleasant in there?"

"Not terribly. I've yet to find any skulls of former occupants, and Blaine has spared me the rack. You must find that a pity."

Rowena's fingers curled around the cold iron. "And you must think me a vindictive wench."

Gareth slipped off the barrel and laced his fingers around the chill bars, laying them lightly against her own. The soft heat of her skin seamed to be the only thing of substance in a world gone awry. He waited for her to recoil from his touch. She did not.

"Why shouldn't you be vindictive? I earned my reputation last night, did I not?"

Rowena knew he wasn't speaking of the murder so she couldn't offer him the comfort of denial. "Will you answer a question for me?"

"I owe you that much."

"When my moth—" Rowena could not bring herself to say the word. "When Elayne died, why did you defend yourself to no one? There had to be those who would have believed you. Sir Blaine's father? The priest?"

He bowed his head until they stood forehead to forehead. His nose gently brushed hers. "My father raised me to be the best. I was to be the strongest, the wisest, the kindest knight England had ever known. All of his dreams of honor died in the breath of Elayne's kiss. The same night I lay with her, my father died choking in his own blood. I felt as guilty of murder as they claimed me."

She gave his fingers a quick, hard squeeze, then stepped away from the door. "All will be well, Gareth."

Gareth straightened. "Of course it will be. They are going to hang me and you are going to be free."

She shook her head, shooting a wild glance at the end of the corridor. Her voice dropped to a whisper. "They won't hang you. When I prove you did not kill Elayne, everyone will know Mortimer knocked his own silly self off the drawbridge."

Gareth went white in the sickly light. "Have you gone mad?"

She smiled happily. "Nay. I am quite sane."

Gareth lifted his head. The full import of her words penetrated the blackness of his heart in a ray of light that cut as mercilessly as it warmed. "You mean last night you did not belive me a murderer? You let me believe . . . why I could have . . ."

"What? Murdered me? Pshaw! You'd be hard pressed to give me a sound spanking!"

Gareth tried to thrust his hands through the bars but got no farther than his fingers. They flexed threateningly. "Don't count on it. If I could reach you right now, I would wring your pretty little neck."

Rowena wagged a finger at him. "Temper, temper."

He rattled the bars with a growl, then spun around to pace the narrow confines of the cell. "Who, Rowena? Who do you believe killed her?"

"Not now. There will be time enough for that later."

Gareth flung himself at the door, realizing her voice was a mere echo of what it had been. She was already fading like a wraith down the shadowy corridor.

"Rowena!" he bellowed. "Get me out of here. You little idiot. Don't you dare put yourself in danger."

Her voice floated back to him, its notes as melodic as a song. "No danger, milord. Only truth."

The pitter-patter of her slippers died away. Gareth threw himself at the door, kicking and beating until the stubborn oak gouged craters in his knuckles. His curses swelled to a roar. He battered himself against the door until his throat closed. His voice died to a hoarse croak. It was not until he lapsed into complete silence that his hapless young guard went to fetch Sir Blaine, fearing his prisoner had driven himself into an apoplexy.

# Chapter 24

The sun broke through the clouds as Rowena strode across the bailey, paying no heed to the muddy goop sucking at her pattens. The clouds split asunder, revealing snatches of cerulean so brilliant they put a spring into Rowena's step, despite her grim mission. The sun painted streaks of silver and gold on the clouds' black underbellies.

Upon hearing of Gareth's imprisonment, the mob had dispersed, murmuring their satisfaction. The gates of Ardendonne had been thrown open. A swath of lush green lawn rolled down to the lake. Raindrops sparkled like diamonds on every blade of grass and minty bud. Rowena was still blinded by their brilliance when she ducked into the tiny chapel and closed the door behind her.

A cobweb trailed its gauzy fingers across her face. She swiped it away, fearful of a bloated, vengeful occupant dropping on her head. The stone chapel clung stubbornly to the winter chill. Her eyes adjusted slowly to a darkness broken only by fragile sunbeams pushing their way through the dusty stained-glass window set

high above the altar. Her nostrils twitched at the rank
smell of mold and disuse.

Mahogany kneeling benches were heaped carelessly
against the wall. Rowena fought an irreverent desire
to giggle, wondering if Blaine had shoved them aside
for dancing. The archangel Michael, flaming sword
raised high, scowled down at her from the window.
A low growl came out of the shadows in front of
the altar.

Rowena froze at the unholy sound, the hair on her
nape bristling. She had heard a sound like that only
once before, when rising out of a stream, she had come
face to face with a rabid badger, spewing bloody foam
from his nostrils and wounded beyond recognition. Pity
had swallowed her terror as, with a deft flip of her
wrist, she had dispatched it with her hunting knife. She
cursed the soft kirtle she wore for having no pocket in
which to hide knives.

The growl came again, followed by a terrible,
heaving groan.

"God be damned!" A hoarse voice exploded into
venom.

Rowena wiped her sweaty palms on her skirt and
walked slowly toward the altar.

"God's nightgown!" A dark garbed figure sprang up
from the floor. The dark shape writhed and heaved,
sucking in a breath to let out an agonizing moan.
Rowena ducked behind a pew. Another curse was followed by a ringing crash.

She peeped over the back of the bench. In the arc of
sunbeams crossing the dust-sparkled air, an avenging
harridan in black and silver railed at God and ravaged
the dusty chapel. The creature shuddered, shielded by a
mat of tangled hair. It emanated a musky scent deeper
than that of fear. Rowena crept nearer. She flinched as
the figure tossed the altar cloth on the stones and
stomped it with both feet. A gauntleted hand shredded
the thick webs that draped the altar.

Clawlike hands reached for the golden cross.

Rowena straightened as her clear voice rang from

the rafters. "You may surrender the relic. The undead do not walk at Ardendonne."

Marlys spun around, cross in hand, her eyes as wide as if she expected to find God himself, waiting thunderbolt in hand to rebuke her for her blasphemy. The defiant set of her chin did not relax.

" 'Tis what you think," she snarled.

Rowena slowly moved forward. "If you were expecting the Almighty, I fear to disappoint you."

Marlys's shoulders slumped as Rowena gently plucked the cross from her hands and returned it to its burnished base. What she had mistook for growls were only sobs, sobs so deep and wracking it was as if Marlys's heart was being torn out by each one of them.

Rowena reached for one bucking shoulder, half afraid Marlys might turn on her like the wild creature she seemed and snap her hand off. Marlys froze at the touch, then flung her head back. Between dark strands of hair, Rowena caught a glimpse of eyes swollen to slits from weeping. She had to grit her teeth to keep from flinching before the malice within those eyes.

"What in the hell do you want? Have you come to tell me they've hanged him?"

Rowena took a slow, measured breath. "I should hate to think you were here cowering in the chapel if they had."

Marlys brushed dust off her tunic in a crisp motion that reminded Rowena painfully of Gareth. "Would you prefer I don a white kirtle and weep prettily on Blaine's shoulder while my brother swings from the gallows?"

"Impossible. You do not own a white kirtle. And you do not weep prettily."

"I haven't had as much practice as you have." Marlys leaned one hip against the altar as a mantle of insolence seemed to fall across her shoulders. "What do you want?"

"I want to help Gareth."

Marlys snorted. "Want to help get him hanged most likely. Were it not for your pathetic little performance in the hall last night, the wrath of the people might not be stirred against him." Marlys bit a crescent of dirt from beneath her fingernail.

Rowena toyed with the dust on the altar, absently tracing circles with her finger. "I know who killed Elayne."

A muscle in Marlys's cheek twitched. She shrugged. "According to the mob out there this morning, so does everyone else."

Rowena gave Marlys a maddening smile. "But we know they're wrong, do we not?" She locked her hands behind her back and paced a few steps away.

Marlys's low-pitched laugh sent a chill down Rowena's spine. "So who do you think slew the bitch?"

Rowena arched an eyebrow in mild curiosity. "Why do you call her 'bitch'? Gareth told me you worshiped her."

"Gareth was wrong." Rowena was silent until Marlys grudgingly continued. "When there was no one else around to toy with, the pretty lady would call me into her chambers. She would braid my hair with her long, beautiful fingers until she got bored with it, then send me away when some new diversion presented itself."

"Like Gareth?"

"Like Gareth." Marlys smiled slowly. "But sometimes I did not go away. She thought I did, but I did not."

Rowena bowed her head. "The hiding place in the cupboard."

Marlys nodded. "I would watch them. I watched her weave her web of pretty poison around him, teaching him courtly manners and music. He struggled at first, like any fly caught in the sticky syrup of a spider's trap. But he stopped struggling soon enough. Who could resist such sweetness?" Rowena closed her eyes briefly, not wanting to hear more but unable to stop listening. "As a student of lovemaking, my brother was an apt pupil, quick to learn and attentive to a fault. But I do not have to tell you that, do I?" Marlys turned her back on Rowena. Her hands clutched at the edge of the altar in some hidden emotion.

Rowena crept nearer. "Were you in the cupboard the night Elayne was murdered? Did you see Gareth come?"

Marlys's shoulders hunched. She gave a bitter laugh. "I saw everybody come. I saw your father sneak through the window and fly back out as if winged when Gareth stormed in. I saw Gareth raise his sword to Elayne only to drop it at her feet. I saw Elayne throw herself on the bed, weeping as if her black heart were broken."

Rowena caught Marlys's elbows in a tight grip. "And then?"

Marlys jerked out of Rowena's grasp. Her gaze fell on the tracings in the dust which had somehow twisted themselves into an awkward and misspelled scrawl of her own name. She wiped them away.

"You know, don't you?" she asked. Rowena would have sworn there was a note of wry tenderness in her voice. "I was the last to come. I killed her, then I pried you out of her stiff and bloody lap and took you to your father."

Marlys spun around. The abrupt motion flung the dark mop of hair out of her face. Rowena flinched, struck anew by the magnetic force of a beauty Marlys could never completely hide. Their gazes locked. Marlys offered her a smile of sweet and terrifying proportions.

Rowena held her ground. "You have to tell him. He has been punished enough. Last night, I was punished for my own silence. How long can it go on? You were only nine years old. You were a hurt little girl. He will forgive you."

Marlys sneered. "You're as bad as Mortimer. Always bringing back the old story, making it all new again."

"Mortimer?" Rowena breathed. She took a smooth step backward.

"Ro," Marlys said warningly.

Anther step. Rowena's heel came up against an over-turned kneeling bench. Rowena whirled and broke into a run. Before she could reach the door, Marlys's weight crashed into her, slamming her to the flagstones. Tears stung her eyes as Marlys wrapped a fist in her hair and jerked her head back with vicious strength.

"Chin up, pup. Your first whimper will be your last."

Rowena's muscles went limp as she felt the icy blade bite into her throat.

# Chapter 25

Marlys and Rowena strolled arm-in-arm through the bailey, chattering cheerfully.

"What shall it be, Marlys?" Rowena ground out between teeth clenched in a smile. "Will you stab me like Elayne or throw me into the moat like poor Mortimer?"

Marlys gave the chief porter a friendly wave as they passed beneath the arch of the main door. The sharp tip of her dagger poked beneath Rowena's ribs. "Mortimer never knew when to bridle his flapping tongue."

Rowena threw the stable a longing glance. There was no sign of a hulking figure or a cap of silver-blond hair. "You shan't get far without a mount."

She yelped as the blade pierced the thin linen of her kirtle and dug into her bare skin.

"It seems you and Mortimer share many traits."

They started across the drawbridge. Rowena kept her eyes fixed straight ahead, refusing to look at the oily sheen of the moat waters. She heaved a sigh of relief when they stepped off the drawbridge into the damp grass. Her relief was short-lived. Marlys doubled her pace down the slope, and Rowena realized all of her hopes lay in the castle behind them. With each jog of Marlys's gait, the dagger blade jabbed beneath her arm.

Red and yellow pavilions were scattered along the lawn. Marlys gave a group of squires a careless salute, tugging Rowena toward the gentle arch of the bridge. The bloated lake shimmered beneath the caress of the afternoon sun. Rowena's flesh stung as the blade nicked her side.

"Sweet Christ!" she exploded. "Could you not grant me a quick death like the others? Must you torture me?"

Glancing nervously behind her, Marlys abandoned her ruse of kindness and gave Rowena a hard shove. The slick grass slipped out from under Rowena's feet. She careened down the slope to land on her rear. From where she lay, there was nothing visible but an endless vista of rolling meadows and the crenellated edge of one tower peeping over Marlys's forbidding shoulder. Marlys sheathed the dagger. She stumbled down the hill, jerked Rowena up, and pushed her toward the open meadows. Her hands held the strength of a man's, all calluses and sinew.

Rowena whirled around, her back stiffened with rage. Marlys drew a length of rope from her jacket.

The anger seeped from Rowena's body as a darker memory touched her. "You good folk of Caerleon are always prepared, are you not?" she said ruefully.

She stood stiffly while Marlys bound her wrists, noting the sweat that beaded Marlys's upper lip. They started across the fields with Rowena trudging behind, bound to Marlys by the rope twisted around her captor's fist. As they slid through a ditch, Marlys gave the rope a vicious jerk. Rowena stumbled, but straightened before Marlys could cast a mocking glance over her shoulder. The rope chafed her wrists, increasing Rowena's irritation with each step.

"Why, Marlys? Whatever do you hope to accomplish?"

"Gareth cannot know," Marlys replied without

turning around. "He would never, ever forgive me if he knew I let him take the blame all these years."

"Do you think he will forgive you for killing the woman he loves?"

Marlys whipped around and strode back to Rowena. She slapped Rowena hard. The hand she raised to mop her own brow trembled violently.

Rowena did not speak after that. They traversed the long miles in silence. Marlys led and Rowena slogged behind until her feet felt as if they were mired in iron. She lost one of her pattens in the muck of a stream bank but refused to ask Marlys to halt so she could retrieve it. She limped along for several miles in one shoe, then kicked the other away. The soles of her feet had once been as tough as leather, but after her sheltered life at Caerleon, she felt the bite of stones and the keen sting of the thistles with each step. The worsening slump of Marlys's shoulders revealed her own exhaustion. With a meanspiritedness that surprised her, Rowena hoped she would fall. Some gleeful sprite within her imagined pouncing on Marlys and choking her with her own rope.

She had been watching her feet for so long, entrenched in her pleasant fantasies, that she stumbled into Marlys's back without even realizing she had halted. The tangy fragrance of pine wafted to her nose. She lifted her head, surprised to find they had reached the top of a steep hill.

The sun splintered the clouds in a burst of lavender and pink. A twilight wind dried the sweat on her brow.

They stood side by side like old friends, the rope hanging slack between them.

Marlys's voice was husky and musing. "I found this place when I was a child. We spent each summer at Ardendonne. Blaine and Gareth were always play jousting or riding their new ponies. I was left to my own devices. I would lay at the top of this hill with my chin on my arms and imagine what it would be like to be a knight, to come thundering across that plain on a powerful charger."

"It must have been lonely."

Marlys shrugged. "I had the hawks and the wind for my companions. Some days those were enough."

"And other days?"

Marlys turned her face away. The impending night cast a shadow over her profile. Branches rustled as she ducked into the trees. Rowena followed before she could be jerked along. A ring of low-lying pines made an almost impenetrable shelter. A perfect circle opened at the top. A handful of brave stars scattered their feeble light against the dusky sky.

Rowena peered beneath the shadowy branches. "Have you a privy pot tucked away somewhere?"

Marlys unsheathed her knife.

"Never mind. I can wait."

Marlys swaggered toward her.

Rowena backed away until she reached the end of the rope. "If you are going to sacrifice me, couldn't you at least find a rock to do it on? I am deserving of the same courtesy Moses showed to Joshua, am I not?"

" 'Twas Abraham and Isaac, idiot. How my brother fell in love with such a lackwit, I will never understand." The blade traveled down Rowena's throat in a tender caress. "Or maybe I do."

Rowena flinched as the dagger slid downward, leaving her hands bound but slicing the rope that lashed her to Marlys.

Marlys flicked a wheaten strand of hair out of her eyes with the gleaming blade. "Go find the privy pot, puppy, while I find supper."

After a few moments, Marlys returned, tossing a limp squirrel and an armful of brush in the center of the clearing. Rowena sank down cross-legged while Marlys built a fire, skinned the squirrel, and roasted it on a clumsy spit.

Marlys tore the meat into hunks and squatted in front of her. Rowena glared at her, but her stomach betrayed her with an angry whine. She opened her mouth reluctantly. Marlys poked a bit of meat inside.

The meat was tough but tasty. She had eaten much worse in her days at Revelwood.

"Why bother to feed me if you are going to kill me?"

Marlys grinned. "Have you not heard of the fatted calf?"

Marlys fed her until she would eat no more, then wiped the grease from Rowena's chin with a tender swipe of her own sleeve. She settled on the other side of the fire and tore into the meat with relish.

"Will you let them hang Gareth?" Rowena asked.

Marlys sucked grease from her fingers. "He will find a way out of it. He always does."

"But at what price, Marlys?"

"Why should you care?"

Rowena lowered her eyes to the fire.

Marlys set the meat aside. "I would have never treated you as he did last night."

Rowena met her dark gaze, realizing that Marlys had not bothered to veil her face since fleeing the castle. "How do you know how he treated me? Have you a hiding place in the cupboard at Ardendonne?"

"Nay. But I had a chamber next to his. And I had ears."

Mortification warmed Rowena's face. "I am surprised we did not hear your shrieks of laughter."

"How could you? You were making enough noise of your own."

Rowena trembled with impotent anger. Marlys lifted a mocking eyebrow. "You are a fool, Rowena Fordyce. When will you come to understand that you are no more to my brother than any woman is to a man? You are a piece of property to be possessed, traded, won, stolen or sold to the highest bidder to make a desirable alliance."

"Is that what you were to your father?"

"I was nothing to my father. Only Gareth existed for my father. I couldn't even be bad enough to goad him into beating me. Lying, stealing, cheating, fighting. I tried them all but Gareth got more attention for one carved bird or a well-done turn at the quintain."

"So you tried murder?"

Marlys's smile was chilling. "Father was stiff in the ground by then. But no less loving toward me than he was in life."

A branch shifted on the fire, sending up a shower of yellow sparks. Marlys yawned and cracked her knuckles. She stretched out on the bed of pine needles and closed her eyes. Rowena flopped to her side, devouring Marlys's unveiled features with unabashed curiosity, searching for traces of Gareth in the curve of a stubborn jaw, the mocking slant of heavy brows against an ivory forehead. Marlys's beauty was a dark and palpable thing, pulsing with substance and allure. Rowena understood why Blaine had pursued her so heatedly in his younger days and had learned to hate her with a passion equal to his lust when she spurned his suit. What might have bloomed between them had Marlys not sought to retreat within the ugly shell she had fashioned for herself?

"I could have been your friend," Rowena said softly, hardly aware she had spoken aloud.

Marlys opened her eyes. They stared at each other through the shimmering firelight. "Not enough, Lady Precious. Never enough."

Rowena rolled over. She lay staring into the darkness long after Marlys had lapsed into careless snores.

Rowena burrowed her nose into the nest of softness beneath her head, believing she was back at Caerleon, tucked beneath the pelts of Gareth's bed. She rooted in the soft linen, finding somewhere within a hint of Gareth's clean, musky scent. Snow drifted down in her dreams, burnishing her world with a fresh, sweet frosting of white.

"Wake up, you silly bitch. I haven't all day to coddle your precious ass."

Rowena bolted upright as a booted foot slammed into her rear. She knuckled her eyes with her bound hands. Marlys stood over her, snarling like a rabid harpy. The sky behind her head was a startling blue, as if God had dipped his brush in a fresh vat and painted the world anew. The wrens chirped a cheerful morning song.

Marlys drew back her foot again, and Rowena scrambled to her feet. Before Marlys could snatch it up, Rowena saw that Marlys's overtunic had been folded and tucked under her head sometime in the night.

Marlys shoved her hard. "If you have any needs to take care of, do it now. We won't be stopping again until nightfall."

Rowena stumbled into the shelter of branches, her back to Marlys. She met her needs in an agony of embarrassment, hearing Marlys's short laugh as she struggled with her tattered skirts, her bound hands tingling to life. She straightened. Pine needles caressed her cheek. She lifted the curtain of branches, lured by the gentle wind stirring their limbs into creaking song.

Dawn was long past. The sun had started its arc through the morning sky. In the meadows below, the last tendrils of mist drifted into oblivion in the warmth of its slanting rays. Her breath caught in her throat.

"God's blood, Ro!" Marlys exploded behind her. "It should not take you half the morning. Am I going to have to—"

The voice died abruptly as Marlys burst through the foliage and saw what Rowena saw. "Sweet Jesu," she breathed. Her nails dug into Rowena's arm.

Far below them, a knight and stallion came charging across the meadows, melded into one like some mythical creature out of Marlys's fantasies. Gareth bent low over Folio's back, shifting the horse's path with the slightest tightening of his thighs. Rowena knew the power of those thighs. A shaft of sunlight struck the steed's golden bridle. Folio's mane streamed behind him just as Gareth's own dark mane whipped at the air, gilded to blue by the sun. Five horses poured over the horizon behind Gareth, but neither Rowena nor Marlys paid any heed. They only had eyes for Gareth and his irrevocable drive toward their hill.

Marlys's grip changed, and Rowena saw that tears

streamed down her cheeks. Her hand fell limply away from Rowena's arm.

Gareth plunged toward them. Folio's hooves blurred to white, showing no signs of slowing. Rowena thought Gareth would drive him straight up the steep hill, but at the last possible second he sawed back on the reins, bringing Folio to a rearing halt. The stallion's whinny rang in the air.

Rowena's eyes drank in Gareth's features, watching relief soften and then exasperation tighten the tiny lines around his mouth.

"You foolish little girls! What do you mean going off on such a harebrained quest? You almost got me killed."

The glance Gareth threw over his shoulder reminded them of the horses behind him, black shadows rolling across the meadows. Gareth slid off Folio and started up the hill.

"Gareth."

He stopped, frowning at the sharp note in his sister's voice. His gaze passed between the two women.

Rowena slowly raised her bound hands.

The puzzled expression in his eyes deepened. "What the devil? I thought you went off to find a murderer."

"I did," Rowena said gently.

When Gareth started up the hill again without comprehending, Marlys's arm snaked around Rowena's waist. Sunlight glinted off the blade she pressed to Rowena's throat. Gareth froze, his hands on his knees.

His gaze lit on Marlys and stayed. Her chest heaved against Rowena's back.

"You," he said. It was not a question.

Marlys tossed her head back, her sneer answer enough.

"All those years you let them believe it was me."

"I had no choice," Marlys cried hoarsely. Her hand jerked. The blade bit into Rowena's tender flesh. "They could not touch you. You were Lord of Caerleon. I would have spent the rest of my life chained up in a madhouse or cloistered in a nunnery."

Gareth's mind was quicker than Rowena's. "And Mortimer?"

"He was bent over fluffing up his hose. It only took a tiny bump. He didn't live long enough to hear me beg his pardon."

Gareth's eyes locked on Rowena's face. A thin line of blood trickled into the hollow of her throat. She pressed her eyes shut.

"Free her, Marlys."

Marlys's arm tightened around Rowena's waist. "Why? Your sword bites deeper than mine. You've spilled more of her heart's blood than I ever will."

Gareth took a step up the hill. Marlys dragged Rowena back until the pine branches quivered around their shoulders.

He took another step. "How you must have hated me."

Marlys's face crumpled. "You fool! Elayne hurt you. I could not bear to see you hurt. Don't you know? Don't you understand? You were the only one who was kind to me. Even when I left your life in ruins, not once did you lose your grace, your courage. You are everything I ever wished to be."

Hoofbeats bore down on them. Marlys cast a wild glance at the meadows.

Tears sparkled in Gareth's eyes as he stretched out his hand. "Marlys. Love. Come to me. I shall take care of you. I won't let them hurt you."

Marlys's voice hardened. "Nay. Back down the hill, Gareth. Away from Folio."

The blade touched Rowena's throat again. Gareth obeyed without hesitation. He spread his arms in surrender as Marlys shoved Rowena down the hill in front of her.

Recognizing both women's scents, Folio twitched but did not flee when they stumbled against him.

"Your sword, brother," Marlys snapped.

Gareth unbuckled his sword and tossed it to the ground at her feet. Marlys clutched a handful of Rowena's hair in her fist as she draped the buckler over

Folio's saddle and mounted. The sod trembled with the approach of Gareth's pursuers. Marlys leaned over Folio's slender neck.

For a fleeting instant, she buried her face in Rowena's tangled curls. Rowena felt the breath of her whisper against her ear. "I could have never hurt you. Never."

A careless shove. Gareth's waiting arms enfolded her.

Marlys straightened with a jaunty grin that cut straight to Rowena's heart. "Take care of her, brother. If I hear you did not, you will answer to me."

With those words, Marlys wheeled the stallion in a circle. She unsheathed the sword and lifted it in the air as she galloped away from the approaching riders. Her battle cry floated back to them on the wings of the wind as she thundered toward the distant horizon, as free as the knight she had always dreamed of being.

"Marlys!" Gareth's hoarse cry was caught by the wind.

Rowena gripped his arm. "Let her go, Gareth."

Gareth's legs crumpled. Rowena's hands reached for his tunic. He dropped to his knees in the soft turf as a hawk flew in front of the sun and went soaring in Marlys's path until both of them were only shadows against the swaying grasses.

# Chapter 26

❧✦❧

Rowena sank to her knees beside Gareth, nuzzling his shoulder with a wordless murmur of comfort. He cupped her cheek with his hand, his thumb brushing the thin scarlet scratch marring her throat.

"Did she hurt you?" he said gruffly.

Rowena shook her head with a tremulous smile, remembering Marlys's last words to her—words that Gareth could not have heard. Gareth gave the scratch a tender kiss. His lips traveled upward, at first gently, then devouring hungrily her chin, her cheeks, her nose. She answered his kisses with her own, savoring the rough caress of his beard against her skin. His lips found hers. The tangy grit of their sweat bound them together in a taste more precious and infinitely more lasting than goblets of nectar. Gareth rested his forearms heavily on her shoulder.

His head dropped. "Whatever shall I do without her?"

Rowena pressed her brow to his with fierce strength. "You will go on. As she would want you to."

His lips quirked in a half-smile. "When you say it with such conviction, I almost believe it possible."

"All is possible, milord—"

The rest of Rowena's reply was drowned out by the thunder of hoofbeats. She threw herself at Gareth's chest, fearing they were to be trampled. The thunder rolled to a halt. For a long moment, nothing was heard but the stamp and shuffle of hooves and winded snorts. Rowena opened her eyes to find a circle of disapproving faces glaring down at them. The most disapproving was Irwin's moon of a face glowering down from a dun palfrey. Little Freddie and Big Freddie rode nondescript chestnuts. Sir Boris shifted his bulk on his mount, a length of rope dangling conspicuously from his saddle.

Blaine gave a disgusted snort that would have done any of the horses proud and bounced off his black stallion. Gareth's arm circled Rowena protectively.

A pretty black ring around one of Blaine's eyes matched his horse perfectly. He flung out both arms. "Is this what you escaped for? To make merry in a meadow with this beleaguered child? Was it worth all the bodies you left littered across my hall?"

Rowena stiffened.

"Courage, child," Gareth whispered. "Unconscious, not dead." To Blaine, he replied, "You are only testy because yours was one of them."

"You're damned right I'm testy. 'Tis extremely bad form to render your host unconscious. 'Tis against all the rules of hospitality. The Prince of Wales would shudder."

" 'Tis extremely bad form to lock your guests in the spice cellar."

Blaine conceded that point by turning around and kicking a rock. He frowned at the horizon. "Where the hell did Marlys go?"

Rowena opened her mouth. Gareth gave her arm a warning squeeze. "My sister is no concern of yours. She made that clear at an early age."

"Painfully clear." Blaine rubbed his side at the

remembrance. "Mayhaps she did not choose to see you strung over the nearest tree."

Little Freddie and Big Freddie exchanged a worried glance. Rowena pulled out of Gareth's arms, ignoring his warning glance. "Marlys did not flee to exile so you could go on bravely bearing the burden of her guilt."

Blaine whirled around. "Guilt?" He fixed Gareth with a hard stare. Gareth climbed to his feet, dusting off his hose.

Blaine's eyes surveyed the horizon. He let out a slow breath, more of admiration than surprise. "So the cantankerous little bitch killed Mortimer."

"And Elayne," Rowena added. Gareth gave her a dark look.

Blaine started for his horse.

Gareth was there with his hand on the bridle. "Going somewhere?"

"To fetch a murderess."

"For hanging?"

Blaine arched an eyebrow. "I had a more private incarceration in mind. With myself as caretaker, of course."

"You had your chance at taming Marlys. There won't be another one."

Gareth's bulk was immovable. Blaine cast a hopeful glance at Sir Boris. The elderly knight studied his fingernails. Rowena gave Gareth's arm a supportive squeeze.

Blaine bit off a curse. "I ought to hang you in her place if only for your treatment of this sweet lady. And not necessarily by the neck."

Rowena paled. Gareth neatly tucked her behind him. "As I told you once before, Blaine, if you have any complaints about my care of this sweet lady, you may challenge me to a joust."

"I have a passel of complaints," Blaine hissed.

Gareth rolled his eyes.

Blaine shook a finger in his face. "You kept her at Caerleon against her will. You brought her to Ardendonne on the end of a rope. Then you allowed her to be abducted by a murdering madwoman. Your care, sir, leaves much to be desired."

Gareth yawned. "So what is it to be? Shall you hang me or challenge me?"

In one smooth motion, Blaine jerked off his gauntlet and whipped it across Gareth's face. Gareth did not flinch, although the leather left a reddened welt on his cheekbone.

"So be it," he said stiffly. "What are the rules of this joust."

Blaine paced away, his hands locked behind him, then paced back. "The prize," he said, "is to be the Lady Rowena."

Rowena waited for Gareth's snort of laughter, his refusal of such a ludicrous wager. "Allow me to clarify that," Gareth said. "The prize is to be the *hand* of the Lady Rowena—in marriage."

"Why my hand?" Rowena mumbled. "Why not my head or my leg?" She tugged on Gareth's sleeve.

Gareth felt the fluttering motion and said out of the corner of his mouth, "Do not fret, my love. 'Tis not a bride Blaine seeks. He will withdraw his challenge."

Blaine shoved his fingers into his gauntlet. "Very well. A bride the lady shall be."

Another gauntlet came sailing through the air, striking Gareth on the temple. "Count me in." Irwin's face had gone as pale as snow, but his voice did not quiver. "She was mine to begin with."

Rowena peered around the circle of men with her mouth hanging open, wondering if they had all gone mad.

" 'Tis settled then," Blaine said. "A tournament tomorrow afternoon with Rowena sitting in the seat of the Queen of Love and Beauty. He who is unseated is lost."

Irwin swayed in his saddle. Big Freddie righted him with a punch to his shoulder.

They all turned to stare as Rowena backed away from Gareth.

Gareth's brow furrowed. "What is it, love?"

"Have you lost your senses? Did you learn nothing from Marlys? A woman is not a possession to be sold or won. Mayhaps if you could have ever convinced her of that, you would not have lost her."

They gaped at her as if she had sprouted horns and a tail. Big Freddie scratched his head.

Blaine looked genuinely puzzled. "You should be thrilled, Rowena. Most women would find it the highest honor to have a joust fought in their name." He looked to Sir Boris for help.

The knight nodded, a distant look in his eyes. "The Queen of Love and Beauty holds the seat coveted by every lady in the land."

Gareth stretched out a tentative hand, as if afraid she might flee. His voice was low, meant only for her ears. "A knight cannot refuse a challenge and keep his honor."

She turned toward the open meadows, pushing her way past Irwin's horse.

Gareth strode after her. He caught her arm in a grip that was less than courtly. "I've lost everything, Rowena. I cannot afford to lose you."

"Nonsense, milord," she said softly. "You've gained that most precious thing you've sought your whole life—your honor. I hope it warms you at night."

With those words, she gathered her tattered skirts in her hands and marched away through the crackling grasses. Clutching a handful of mane, Little Freddie steered his mount in a circle.

He twisted around with an insulting dip meant to be a bow. An impish grin curved his lips. "With your leave, milord?"

Gareth shooed him away with a growl. Little Freddie trotted after his sister. Gareth did not take his eyes off Rowena until she mounted behind Little Freddie without relaxing the proud curve of her spine. Then he rubbed his pounding temples.

Blaine dug a sharp chin into his shoulder. "Women! Grand and mysterious creatures, are they not?"

"How would you like another black eye?"

Blaine backed away hastily. At Sir Boris's tactful suggestion, they started back toward Ardendonne in a bedraggled parade. Blaine and Gareth shared the black stallion, struggling not to touch each other. Irwin trailed behind, praying and crossing himself in a sudden fit of piety.

# Chapter 27

❧❧❧

The slick waxed leather slipped from Irwin's hands. After the fourth try, he managed to buckle the cuirass only to discover he had the leather armor on backwards. Perhaps if he wore his helm backwards and walked backwards, no one would notice. He mopped his dripping brow, wondering what madness had possessed him to challenge Sir Gareth to a tournament. Damn Rowena's prettiness, anyway.

She had looked so soft and appealing clinging to Sir Gareth, her nose smudged with dirt, her skirt stained with grass. It had reminded him of the times they had wrestled as children. He had conveniently forgotten that it was always she who ended up on top and he who ended up squealing for mercy like a gutted pig. He had also forgotten the sharp lash of her tongue until she had flung Sir Gareth's pledge of honor back in his face with the force of a whip.

He stripped off the cuirass and wrestled with it until he got it turned around. He plopped down on the floor in a crackling heap. As his fingers fumbled with the laces on the chausses, he regretted chasing Big Freddie

from the chamber. He could not bear for his cousin to
see his shaking hands. And he could not bear to see the
tears Big Freddie kept dashing out of his eyes when he
thought Irwin was not watching.

The leather thong snapped in Irwin's hand. He
hurled it away with an ineffectual oath. He hobbled
over to the bench and lifted the coif-de-maille. The links
of braided chain curled around his hand. He lowered it
over his head, staggering under its weight, and silently
cursed the fat-headed knight generous enough to loan it
to him.

His neck craned forward like a turtle's as he groped
for the silver helm, struggling not to lose his balance. As
he dropped the helm over his head, a cudgel came down
against the side of his neck.

He straightened for an instant, then dropped like a
stone. The helm struck the floor with an echoing clang.

He lay blissfully insensible as a pair of hands jerked
off his helm and lowered his head gently to the floor.
His coif-de-maille was stripped off, followed by
chausses, cuirass, and short tunic until his pale mound
of a belly rose and fell over nothing more than his linen
slops. After a thoughtful pause, the narrow scrap of
linen was unwound and added to the pile.

He rolled to his side, mumbling something about
strawberries steeped in jam, and never hearing a bolt
drop outside the door with a final thump.

"Come forth, knights, come forth!"

A shrill burst of trumpets poured into the air like
liquid gold. Without rising from his stool, Gareth lifted
a corner of the tent flap. A triangle of sunlight penetrated the hazy interior of the tent. The herald's invitation was not directed at him. In a testament to his
prowess as master host, virtually overnight Blaine had
managed to arrange a series of minor jousts and melees
to entertain his guests.

"Had Richard had such organized commanders, Saladin's hordes would have fallen in a single combat," he
muttered.

"From laughter, no doubt," came a muffled reply.

Gareth grunted an agreement as jesters and tumblers garbed as knights streamed out of a striped tent, flipping and tripping over one another in gay abandon. He let the tent flap fall, content to sit in the scarlet gloom. A boy's slender form, apparently headless, was stretched out on his stomach at his feet.

Gareth yanked the boy's ankles, and Little Freddie's head appeared inside the tent with a disgruntled expression.

"No need to wallow about on your belly, lad. You may go outside and watch the proceedings in a civilized manner."

Little Freddie brushed himself off, the jut of his lip stopping just short of a pout. "I am to attend to you as your squire. 'Twas Rowena's command."

"Why? You dislike me nearly as much as she does."

"Not quite."

Gareth could find no answer for that. He stood and paced the tent, his chain mail hauberk clinking with each weighted step. He had been up and armored since dawn. Rollicking laughter filled the air outside the tent. He turned to pace the other way. Little Freddie placed the stool Gareth had vacated just inside the tent flap where he could peek out at the festivities. A snort of boyish laughter escaped him. Gareth stopped his hand short of patting the boy's cap of blond hair. His gauntleted fingers curled at the memory of gossamer blond strands cupped in his palm, and a frustrated despair flowered deep in his belly.

"What else did your sister have to say this morn?" His words came out more harshly than he intended.

Freddie shrugged. "She refused your request for a scrap of cloth or trinket to gird your lance with."

The screams of laughter died. An expectant murmur arose from the list. Gareth drew himself up straight. Little Freddie scrambled through the pile of Gareth's belongings in the corner. Gareth had left nothing in the castle. After this ridiculous tournament, he planned to claim his lady and go. He inclined his head. Little

Freddie stood on tiptoe and slipped a black surcoat trimmed in silver over the knight's hauberk. Gareth stood motionless as the boy cinched a silver chain around his waist. He wore no sword. His only weapon would be the lance propped outside, its sharp tip blunted with a rounded coronal.

A trumpet sang out, casting a reverent hush over the crowd. Little Freddie hefted Gareth's helm, but even on tiptoe, his height was not sufficient. With an apologetic grimace, he clambered atop the stool and placed the helm on Gareth's head. Gareth flipped the visor up.

His pulse quickened of its own volition as the trumpets trilled a mighty flourish.

Once again, the heralds cried in unison, "Come forth, brave knights, come forth!"

This time their cry was not followed by a rush of grinning jesters. Two men stepped out of tents set at opposite ends of the list. After the hot, still air of the tent, the rush of fresh wind ruffled Gareth's brain, making him giddy. The sun blinded him. For a long moment, he could make out nothing but dark shapes on a tapestry of velvet green. He mounted the black destrier Blaine had provided him, wishing for Folio.

The world slowly came into focus. The hillside below the tilting ground was dotted with colorful tents. Canopied pavilions lined the grassy list, gaudy with scarlet and emerald hangings, undulating with the tense movements of those seated within. For a long moment, the only sound was the pennants fixed atop the pavilions flapping in the wind.

Then a mighty roar burst from the farthest pavilion and traveled like a wave down the list. Feet stamped in unison until it seemed the pavilions themselves might collapse in protest. The thunder of applause rocked the air. Little Freddie tossed the lance. Gareth caught it in a gauntleted hand. It was then that he realized every face was turned toward him. Every cry of approval was being sent to his ears. The crowd climbed to their feet, ignoring their slender host mounting his caramel destrier at the end of the field. They lifted their voices with one accord to cheer Sir Gareth de Crecy, the Dark Lord of Caerleon.

Word of his innocence had spread through this curious crowd like wildfire. With one voice, they sought to rectify the misdeeds of twenty years. At Gareth's command, the destrier trotted forward until the center gallery came into view. Brightly garbed ladies thronged the wooden rail. Kerchiefs and ribbons fluttered from their delicate fingers.

Gareth had waited for this moment for twenty years. But now his peers' salutes were as hollow to him as the vacant seat on the gallery, the throne of honor—the traditional place of the Queen of Love and Beauty. The crowd's colors seemed garish, their voices shrill. Gareth's head pounded as he wheeled the horse back to his end of the list, hearing beneath his helm a vitriolic whisper. *You've gained that most precious thing you've sought your whole life—your honor.*

He longed to see the golden flash of Rowena's hair in the sunlight. To find her slender figure leaning over the gallery rail to cheer him to victory. He had fought many jousts in his life—some to the death. In each, he had counted on his pride to carry him through, knowing within himself that right could make might whether they believed him or not. Knowing that beneath his grim facade lay the boy his father had born and bred to be a man of honor. Today, in the most important tournament of his life, he felt hollow and silly. He had nothing left to prove, except to Rowena, and he had the cross sensation that he was going about it in completely the wrong way.

Blaine drew his finger across his throat. Sir Boris, the appointed marshal of the tournament, trotted to the center of the list to a new burst of cheers. Sunlight glinted off gold as a row of trumpeters lifted the bells of their horns in the air. A melodious flourish sounded. Gareth's knees tightened on the satin blanket draped over his steed.

Sir Boris boomed out, "In the name of God and St. Michael, do—"

He stopped as Gareth raised his palm. The knight leaned down and whispered something in his squire's ear. Little Freddie ducked into the tent.

Blaine made a disparaging comment that Gareth could not hear but which drew a handful of snickers from the crowd. Little Freddie reappeared and handed him something. Gareth affixed it to the pole of his lance. A sigh of approval arose from the ladies as a veil of peach silk rippled in the wind. They could not know the veil had been captured from Rowena, not given freely. Rowena had never surrendered anything to him freely, except herself. He did not dare delve into the memories that thought evoked. He signaled to Sir Boris that he was ready to proceed.

Sir Boris cleared his throat and began again. "In the name of God and St. Michael, do your battle!"

The heralds chanted in response, "Do your duty, valiant knights!"

They scattered, clearing the list for battle. Gareth slammed his helm shut. The world narrowed to a swath of green with his opponent at the end of it. He lowered his lance and raised his shield. His heart pounded in his ears.

Golden spurs touched destriers' flanks. The horses leaped forward in a rush of hooves. Chunks of turf flew as they thundered toward each other from opposite ends of the list. Gareth bent low over the charger's back, bracing himself for the blow to come.

For a fleeting instant before his lance struck Blaine's shield, he caught a glimpse of narrowed brown eyes through the slits of Blaine's visor. Lance struck shield with a mighty crack. Both lances held. The impact vibrated up the length of Gareth's arm and down his spine. He swayed but held his seat. The crowd roared its approval.

Gareth could not help glancing at the gallery as he galloped past. The lady Alise blew him a kiss. The seat of honor was still empty. His horse reeled around. A throng of peasants shoved against the ropes enclosing the far end of the field. Men shouted coarse suggestions on how to defeat their lord. A woman with a broad, sun-wrinkled face thrust a little girl in the air. She tossed a bouquet of heather on the field.

Gareth's mount trampled the blooms heedlessly as he drove toward Blaine once again. He bent over his pommel. The horse's mane whipped at his helm. Wind whistled through his visor. The crowd disappeared. All that lay before him was the long, straight stretch and the falcon carved on the shield of the knight hurtling toward him. Gareth fixed his gaze on the falcon's eye. He lowered his lance a fraction of an inch. He refused to think of the lance driven at his own shield. He refused to think of the weeks his muscles would ache from the impact. All he thought of was the brightly blinking eye of the falcon.

He closed his eyes on impact, knowing before Blaine's lance struck that he had won. Blaine's lance splintered with a terrible crack, folding in the knight's hand like a broken twig. The crowd gasped. Gareth pushed on. Blaine's stallion sank back on his haunches. The unrelenting force of Gareth's lance sent Blaine tumbling head over heels to the turf.

Blaine's horse wandered off to munch grass at the foot of the ladies' gallery. A laughing young maiden crowned his ears with a chaplet of gillyflowers. Blaine's squire trotted out to his master, but Blaine waved him away.

Without dismounting, Gareth leaned over and stretched out a gauntleted hand. "Come, my friend, arise. Be thankful you did not wager your castle."

Blaine sat up and pulled off his helm. He glared at Gareth and rubbed his ringing ears. "What is a castle with no lady to crown it?"

Gareth grinned. "I've recently begun to ask myself that same question."

The crowd whooped as Blaine took the hand Gareth proffered. Gareth hauled him to his feet. Applause filled the air. Blaine spread his arms and made a bow that would have done any jester proud. He staggered slightly as he straightened.

"The next time my friend and I will take our spats to the chessboard or the hazard dice," he called out to good-natured jeers and catcalls.

"Not hazard." Gareth shook his head emphatically. "Never hazard."

Blaine slapped his knee. "I hate to leave you like this, but I see a gallery of sympathetic ladies waving me forward. There is nothing like a wounded little boy to bring out their maternal instincts. I see several laps I'd love to recover on. Besides, you've another challenge to meet."

Gareth snorted. "I think not. If I know Irwin, he is halfway to Revelwood by now."

Sir Boris stepped forward again, followed by a line of beaming heralds. "As tradition demands, I must ask if there is any other knight who cares to challenge Sir Gareth in tourney today?"

Several knights found this an opportune moment to pick their teeth or kiss their favorite ladies.

"If any man cares to step forward," Sir Boris intoned, "let him do so now or forever—"

A horse appeared high on the hill.

"—hold his silence," he finished weakly.

Gareth pushed his visor back farther on his brow, squinting at the dark shape silhouetted against the afternoon sun. A balmy wind dried the sweat on his face. The list sank into silence.

The helmed figure lifted his lance. The crowd murmured at the obvious challenge, entranced by the mysterious figure. Gareth frowned, trying to determine if the rider possessed Irwin's bulk. His challenger gave him little time to ponder.

Raising shield and lowering lance, the rider charged down the hill. Gareth slammed his visor down. The crowd caught its breath in a collective gasp as the white stallion's hooves left the ground, clearing the ropes strung at the end of the list with a mighty leap. Sweaty palms grasped the rails as the watchers wondered if the challenger was going to run Gareth down, casting aside all rules of the tilt.

Gauntleted hands sawed on the reins, bringing the stallion to a rearing halt. Gareth blinked. An icy tendril of sweat trickled down the back of his neck. The stallion was not Folio. Tufts of black starred its forelock and mane.

The stranger made a cutting gesture toward the marshal, and Sir Boris's words came tumbling out as if he cared very little for the thought of standing between two such unpredictable opponents. "In the name of God and St. Michael, do your battle!"

The heralds' response was gibberish. They shoved each other out of the way, heedless of the trumpeters they trampled.

As Gareth faced the rider, an unfamiliar sensation tightened his gut. He was afraid. The fear infuriated him. If this was Irwin's idea of a prank, he would turn the lad over his knee after he bested him. He raised his lance with a growl that sent the ladies in the gallery swooning into each other's arms. The hair on Blaine's nape stood on end.

The stranger raised his shield. Two sets of booted feet slammed into their mounts' flanks. One set wore spurs. The other did not. The horses lunged forward, beating a cloud of dust out of land still damp from the spring rain. The stranger's shield was unmarked. Gareth could find no target to aim for. The ground rolled out from beneath his destrier's hooves and before he was ready, lance struck shield with a jarring blow. Both riders swayed but kept their balance. The crowd's cheer was muted, as if they were still held in the stranger's thrall.

There was barely time to wheel around before the rider charged again. Gareth cursed under his breath, still reeling from the last blow. He searched for any hint of humanity beneath that unmarked helm. Sunlight glinted off the narrow slits, mocking him with its deceptive brightness. The visor held its secrets, sealed tight by shadows. He was only halfway toward the center of the field when his opponent's lance slammed into his own. His horse reared, hooves flailing at the air. Anger tightened his jaw.

He knew by now that he was not fighting Irwin. Irwin possessed neither the skill nor the grace to maneuver stallion, lance, and shield simultaneously. The rider came at him again, relentlessly driving his mount down the emerald swath of green that separated them.

In the flash of time before their lances clashed, Gareth straightened and held his lance high. The rider lunged forward, shield and body braced for the blow from Gareth's lance. When that blow did not come, the momentum of the stranger's lunge carried him into Gareth's shield, following the pass of his own lance through shield, then air. The force of the blow shuddered Gareth. He gripped the stiff saddle with his knees. His mount lurched in an awkward circle. The tip of his lance caught on the roof of the gallery, and the wooden stake ripped the peach veil in two. The coronal blunting the tip of his lance fell into Alise's lap.

Spurred by the rending of the veil and unaware of what had happened to his lance, Gareth swung the long pole around, hoping to catch his opponent off guard. Struggling to control his own stallion, the rider lifted his shield an instant too late. Sunlight reflected off steel. A woman screamed as the silver tip of Gareth's lance pierced the rider's armor.

The crowd came to its feet. All was silence.

Gareth stared in disbelief as blood poured over leather, staining silver to red. His lance thudded to the ground. The white stallion pranced sideways, away from Gareth. The rider slumped, clutching his pommel with rigid arms. One of the heralds began to mumble in Latin.

Time passed in a haze that knew no moments. No squire took the field to aid his wounded master. Gareth shoved his visor back, his blood freezing to ice in his veins as a horrible suspicion was spawned in his mind. The rider doubled over. With a determination that daunted Gareth, gauntleted fingers curled around the helm. He wanted to close his eyes, unable to watch the fall of long, dark hair he knew would follow.

The rider lowered his head and wrenched the helm away. Wheaten curls spilled over ashen skin.

The list exploded into movement. Blaine screamed for a physician. The physician screamed for a priest. Alise fainted. A small, silver-haired figure detached itself from the farthest tent and came sprinting down the long stretch.

But it was Gareth who reached Rowena first. He plunged off his destrier, forfeiting his victory, and caught her in his arms as she fell. He eased her to the ground. The slickness of blood stained the stallion's pristine coat.

He cradled her across his lap. Golden curls poured over his surcoat. Her blue eyes were dimmed with a haze of pain. She ran a gauntleted finger along the curve of his jaw.

Her lips curled in a small smile. "I am free, milord. I have won myself."

Her sandy lashes fluttered against her cheeks as she lapsed into a merciful faint. An errant spurt of wind tore the veil from the gallery post and sent it soaring upward until it was only a splash of peach against a sea-blue sky.

# Chapter 28

Big Freddie guided Rowena's head over the edge of the bed with swift, competent hands. His broad palm cradled her forehead as the meager contents of her stomach came forth. Her eyes did not even flicker. Her damp lashes lay against her cheeks like drowned spiders. Blaine reached out a hand, but Gareth lurched past him and out the door. Big Freddie gently lowered Rowena's still form back to the pillows as Blaine followed Gareth with Little Freddie trailing behind.

They found Gareth on the battlement, clutching the parapet and taking ragged gulps of air. He wiped his mouth with the back of his hand and turned to go back inside. Blaine stopped him.

"You need rest. You've had no sleep in three days. Give yourself some time."

Gareth shrugged his hand away. "She may not have any time. She needs me. I cannot abandon her."

"Big Freddie is tending her."

Gareth pushed Blaine's hand away a second time, but stumbled as he started for the door. He turned abruptly back to the parapet, gripping the stone. He raised his face to the cool rain misting over the balcony and closed his eyes briefly. Shadows lay like bruises beneath his eyes.

They stood in silence, listening to the drowsy patter of rain tripping from a distant gutter.

"The sickness is good for her," Blaine gently said. "The physician says that the more of the wound's poison she purges from her body, the more chance she has to live."

"Are the fits good for her? I had to throw myself on her with all my strength last night just to keep her from flying off the bed. Are the fevers good? Or the chills? Or the nightmares?" Gareth's voice broke. His head dropped. Rain drifted across the balcony in misty sheets until his hair hung in limp strands around his face.

When Blaine could give him no answer, Gareth lurched back into the castle. Blaine followed. Little Freddie stood staring over the gray bowls of fog that hung over the distant hills. Blaine had stayed faithfully at Gareth's side since Rowena had taken ill. No one knew what dark secrets the two men had shared the first night they spent bolted in Rowena's chamber. Voices raised in heated argument and the echo of a hoarse sob were the only clues. Once there was even a loud crash like that of a body being slammed against the door.

But when morning came, Rowena was still alive. Gareth had refused to allow the priest to administer the words that might grant her soul an unfettered passage into Purgatory. The Lord of Caerleon had willed that she would live. And she had. Little Freddie felt his own lips form the words of a prayer, stiff and half-forgotten from disuse. When words failed him, his eyes scanned the grim sky, pleading that God might recognize enough of His own arrogance and passion in Gareth's love to have mercy on them all.

Little Freddie sat in the doorway, stroking the yellow hound that lay across his lap. Gareth dipped a cloth in water and dabbed at Rowena's parched lips. A waxy coolness had claimed her skin in the wake of the fever that had wracked her body through the long night.

Her skin was stretched tight over the bones of her face, giving her once rosy cheeks a sunken pallor. He lifted her to a sitting position and bent her slight weight over his arm. The bandage on her side was clean and dry. He plumped up the pillows and laid her back down.

Blue eyes stared up at him. Gareth's breath froze in his throat. Then one corner of her mouth lifted in a weak smile.

"Thank you, milord." Her voice cracked. Clearing her throat sent her into a shuddering cough that ravaged her body with its force.

She closed her eyes. Gareth leaned forward and peered into her face. Her eyes flew open again, huge and bright.

"Gareth?"

Her bright gaze was uncompromising. To escape it, Gareth picked up a comb and gently drew it through the limp strands of hair spread across the pillow.

"Aye, my love?"

"Are you terribly angry with me?"

His smile softened his answer. "Furious."

"Forgive me."

The comb froze in mid-motion as her head fell to the side. Her lips touched his wrist.

He twisted a strand of hair around his fingers, letting the smooth skein cut into his hardened flesh. She yawned and nestled her cheek into the pillow, her breath coming evenly for the first time in days.

The curl he had made slipped out of his fingers. Gareth stood and strode from the tower, stepping over boy and dog without breaking stride. He sank down on the narrow staircase, dropped his face in his arms, and quietly cried.

Blaine's head flew up as the door to the donjon crashed open. He dismissed the seneschal at his side with a careless flick of his hand. The man dropped the parchments he had been gathering with a grateful squeak and sidled past the hollow-eyed knight in the doorway. Gareth was garbed in mail and surcoat. A broadsword hung at his side. Blaine steepled his fingers under his chin, fearing the worst.

A pouch of gold sailed through the air, thumping to a halt on the oak table.

Blaine frowned at it. "I charge you no rent. You are my guest."

" 'Tis not for you. 'Tis for Rowena."

Blaine relaxed. He tossed the pouch back. "Give it to her yourself."

Gareth plunked the pouch down and leaned over Blaine, supporting his weight on his hands. "I won't be here."

Blaine's brow puckered. He loosened the pouch's drawstrings and peered inside. His eyes widened. " 'Tis a substantial sum."

"Enough."

Blaine snorted. "Enough to purchase an earldom."

"If she so desires."

Blaine leaned back in his chair and propped his heels on the table. "Is that what you wish?"

"She has won her freedom. That dower should give her the freedom to choose any man she wants." He added deliberately, "Or no man at all."

Blaine grinned sheepishly, picking a thread off his knee. "You trust me with her gold, but not with her."

"I'd be a fool if I did. I do, however, trust you with her brother. There is enough gold in there to ensure Little Freddie a proper education."

Blaine lifted a mocking brow. "You wish me to mold him in my image?"

"Heaven forbid. I wish you to mold him in your father's image."

Blaine's fingers tenderly smoothed the worn parchment beneath his hand.

Gareth studied it. "Flanking towers?"

Blaine shrugged. "Some old sketches of my father's. I was considering some additions to Ardendonne."

"Your halls were deserted."

"I sent the guests packing. With invitations for May Day, of course."

A smile touched Gareth's eyes. "Of course." He gave Blaine's shoulder a hard clasp and started for the door.

"Gareth?"

Gareth turned, reluctantly.

"What shall I tell her when she awakens calling your name as she is wont to do?"

Gareth raised eyes as dark as midnight. "Tell her I am not worthy of her. I had no right to believe I was."

He was halfway through the door when Blaine's mutter reached his ears. "Damn your pride."

He whirled around. "Aye. Damn my pride. My pride almost killed her." His voice softened. "I'll not give it another chance."

With those words, Gareth left his friend staring blankly at the parchments in front of him. He strode past the alcove where Little Freddie crouched. The boy slipped out of the shadows as Gareth disappeared into the sunbeams streaming through the main door.

Little Freddie stood for a moment, fists clenched, then started for the stairs. His sure feet pounded up the curved staircase. He sped along a narrow hall, then up a set of steeper stairs. His breath came in quick gasps as he darted down a sloping corridor. His hands fumbled with a latch. He burst onto the battlements into a rush of sun and wind that whipped tears from his smarting eyes. His hands curled over the sun-warmed parapet.

Far below, a stallion emerged from the stables. The dark-garbed knight took the reins, leaving Big Freddie to slump against the stable wall.

As Gareth swung a long leg over the stallion's back, Little Freddie's nails dug into the stone. It was nearly impossible to tell where the black sheen of the stallion ended and the surcoat of the knight began. Gareth urged the horse into a gentle lope down the road that bypassed the lake, the long, winding road that led away from Caerleon.

Little Freddie held his breath as Gareth reached the

first curve in the road. The horse slowed, and Gareth guided it in a prancing circle. Even through the distance that separated them, Freddie felt Gareth's eyes find the sheen of his blond hair on the tower. The knight raised a gauntleted hand in salute.

Little Freddie waved both arms wildly, leaning over the wall until the deepening green of the world below tilted. Gareth lowered his arm. He slapped the reins on the stallion's back. The faint tinkling of bells reached Freddie's ears. The stallion turned, breaking into a gallop, carrying its solitary rider around the bend of the curve and out of Freddie's sight. He came back into sight on the next curve—a lonely black speck on a never-ending ribbon of tan. Little Freddie was still waving when he felt the faint pressure of Sir Blaine's hands on his shoulders.

Tasting the salt of tears on his tongue, he swiped at his nose with his sleeve. "How will I tell her he isn't coming back?"

Blaine squeezed his shoulders. "He'll be back, lad. Don't worry. He'll be back."

Even as he said it, Blaine wasn't sure if he was trying to convince the boy or himself.

# Chapter 29

❧❧

A burst of wind and rain tore the leaves from the branches. They danced and whirled in a chaotic frenzy, taunting Gareth with their crackling refrain. The cold, damp breath of autumn blew down his neck. Beads of rain clung to his beard. He huddled deeper in his cloak, trying to conjure up the vision of his own warm hearth and Dunnla's face wreathed in a welcoming smile. The long, lonely months away from Caerleon, skirmishing with the Scots at Edward's side, had dimmed that vision, blurring it with other memories: a flash of white teeth beneath tangled, black hair; wheaten curls, heavy and damp from a bath, catching every scrap of light the fire tossed away; a bloodstained lance lying in the dirt. The horse jolted into a hole, and Gareth bit his lip, thankful for the cleansing pain. Memories were dangerous and best left alone.

A bundle of wet leaves slapped his neck. He peered upward. Between the black net of branches, the gray sky deepened to the charcoal of twilight. There was no sun to mourn the day's passing. Rain had fallen with leaden weight from dawn to dusk.

Ancient trees lined the wide road, massive and knowing. Unblinking eyes watched him from sockets of bark and moss. Had they always been so menacing? He could feel their weight like the heaviness of his spirit, bearing down on his chest, constricting it until every breath was a burden. Tendrils of mist drifted between them, uncurling their gnarled fingers to beckon the weary traveler. Gareth shivered, cursing his own fancies. He clucked at the horse, hastening its walk to a gentle trot. A crackling fire and a flagon of ale would ease his imagination. One more bend and he would be home.

The tree above his head exploded in a flurry of leaves. A giant bat flung itself from the lowest limb with a bloodcurdling screech. There was only time to half raise an arm to protect his face before the creature was upon him. His yell of dismay blended with the beast's rabid squeal as they both went toppling from the stallion's back into the wet leaves. Gareth's head struck a dead branch. His ears rang and suddenly there were two beasts bouncing gleefully on his chest.

"Surrender," the creature growled, raising a menacing stick.

Gareth blinked. The two beasts blended into one. The bat wore a black helm with a dent where the nose should have been.

Gareth shook his head, silencing the irksome bells. His fingers slowly uncurled. He lifted his palms to each side of his head in a gesture of surrender.

"Ha!" came the triumphant cry.

The head bowed. Hands sheathed in leather gauntlets cracked with age reached for the battered helm.

A new set of bells took wing in Gareth's head—a mad carillon that would have put the bells of any cathedral to shame.

The helm tumbled to the leaves. Gareth was choked in a fall of long, blond hair. Rowena flung it behind her with a wicked grin.

Her eyes sparkled. "An easy victory, milord."

"I always was when it came to you." Gareth's hands reached for her. His thumbs encircled her wrists, probing and rubbing to insure she was bone and flesh, not just a tantalizing illusion spawned from his weary mind. "If you are a robber baron, I have no gold. A beautiful wench broke my heart and won my gold."

"Did she give you these?" Rowena neatly plucked a gray hair from the new sprinkling at his temple.

Gareth's hand slipped beneath her hair, cupping her beautiful sturdy neck. "Losing her gave me those."

" 'Tis just as well you are a pauper. I possess a mighty castle and all the gold I need." She leered at him. " 'Tis not gold I seek."

"Then why have you accosted me, wench?"

At her slight wiggle and coy sidelong glance, Gareth forgot his exhaustion. "I've been waiting many long days and nights for a knight to capture," she whispered.

"So you could carry him away to your enchanted castle and make merry on his body all the night long?"

She sniffed. "You malign me. My intentions are honorable. I have a priest waiting to hear our vows."

"And has he married you to every knight who traversed this road? Mayhaps you have a chest of headless knights awaiting me to take my place among them."

" 'Tis a chance you'll have to take."

She made his choice easier by leaning forward and gently pressing her lips to his. Gareth drew her down to a kiss that left them both breathless. He pulled her face to his shoulder with a reverent sigh.

Rowena laughed huskily against his throat. "Bested by a girl. Methinks you've grown soft in your travels."

"Carry me off to your priest and I shall spend my lifetime proving you wrong."

With a devilish slant of one eyebrow, he wrapped his arms tightly around her, molding their bodies together. His lips found hers again, drinking of the grail of sweetness he had found at the end of his lonely quest.

She pushed against his chest. "For shame, sir. You seek to do your proving without benefit of a priest." She drew a strand of her hair across the tip of his nose.

His nose twitched. He frowned solemnly.

Rowena clutched his hauberk. "Why do you glower so? What ails you, milord?"

He gestured at the branch above their heads. "Before I make my oath, milady, tell me, is this what I have to look forward to every time I return to my bride?"

"Nay, milord. This is what you have to look forward to."

She threw both arms around his neck. They rolled over, oblivious to the sodden leaves clinging to them. Gareth stared down into eyes as blue as the skies of his childhood.

Rowena squealed as he stood and scooped her up in his arms.

He strode toward the castle, ignoring Rowena's half-hearted struggles. "Gridmore!" he bellowed. "Get out here and fetch some rope. I've captured a robber baroness."

He rubbed the tip of his nose to hers. Rowena froze, mesmerized by the desire in his eyes, the paralyzing tenderness of his smile. "And I believe I shall keep her."

She pressed her cheek to his beard, her voice muffled. "For the winter, milord?"

"Nay, milady. Forever."

Rowena lifted her head as they rounded the bend. Torchlight blazed from every window of Caerleon. The rain fell harder. Rowena's arm curled trustingly around Gareth's neck as Little Freddie pelted out the main door to welcome them. The sight of Irwin wrapped in a fur cloak and waving cheerfully from the battlements only deepened Gareth's smile. The Dark Lord of Caerleon had come home.

## About the Author

*USA Today* bestseller Teresa Medeiros has well over two million copies of her books in print. She was recently chosen one of the Top Ten Favorite Romance Authors by *Affaire de Coeur* magazine. A former Army brat and registered nurse, Teresa wrote her first novel at the age of twenty-one and has since gone on to win the hearts of both critics and readers alike. Teresa currently lives in a log home in Kentucky with her husband Michael and four lovable neurotic cats.

If you loved

## Shadows and Lace,

and were spellbound by the tremendous national bestseller

### Breath of Magic

let the delightfully irresistible voice of

## TERESA MEDEIROS

bewitch you with her newest novel

of desire aflame and magic unleashed.


### Touch of Enchantment


Coming from Bantam Books in summer 1997

*Turn the page for a sneak peek into this exciting new release....*

*Tabitha Lennox* hated being a witch. The only thing she hated more than being a witch was being a rich witch. But she had little or no say in the matter, having been born the sole heir of both her father's mutibillion-dollar empire and her mother's rather unpredictable paranormal talents.

Her mama had named her Tabitha, pronouncing it a good solid Puritan name. Her daddy had smoothly agreed, but the reason for his wry chuckle had not become readily apparent until the eight-hundred-mil-lionth rerun of *Bewitched* on Nick at Nite choked a scandalized gasp from her mother.

"Did you know that cheeky little brat was named Tabitha?" she asked, referring to Darrin and Samantha Stevenses' precocious progeny.

Her daddy lowered his *Wall Street Journal* and blinked behind his reading glasses, his gray eyes disarmingly innocent. "Sorry, darling. It must have slipped my mind."

But a hint of a smirk betrayed him. Tabitha's mama launched herself across the cozy great room, pummeling him with one of the fluffy couch pillows until they both collapsed over the ottoman in a giggling heap.

"You really can't blame me," her daddy gasped, tickling her mama into submission. "Your second choice was *Chastity*!"

As their playful tussle dissolved into a tender kiss,

four-year-old Tabitha rolled her eyes at the plump black cat lazing on the hearth and returned her attention to her laptop computer, wondering why her parents couldn't just communicate through E-mail or their lawyers like the parents of all the other children in her Montessori preschool.

From an early age Tabitha craved the soothing boredom of routine the way other children craved toys and candy. Although her parents made a convincing show of normalcy with their faux-Victorian house nestled in the Connecticut countryside, she knew instinctively that far more than her father's wealth set her apart from her playmates.

Several of her peers rode to school behind the smoked-glass windows of stretch limousines or hosted birthday parties at The Four Seasons, but none of them ever came home from school to find the family cat quoting Shakespeare to a shelf of engrossed plants or a trio of elves peering at them from beneath the shrubbery. Tabitha's mama didn't just bake cookies. She baked dancing cookies that had the unnerving habit of popping themselves into Tabitha's mouth every time she opened it to complain. Tabitha would proudly display her completed homework only to have it vanish into thin air the night before it was due.

Her father would frantically help her duplicate her fractions while her mother conjugated French verbs and apologized profusely, explaining that she'd never had a great deal of control over her magic. But even though her dismay at causing her daughter distress was genuine, her mama could never quite hide the pride she took in her unusual gift.

Tabitha didn't consider it a gift. She considered it a curse. Which explained why on her thirteenth birthday, when her casual wish for purple icing on her birthday cake sent sugary globs of it coursing over her stunned head, she experienced no wonder but only frigid horror.

Trailing purple goo, she fled up the stairs and threw herself on her ruffled bed, weeping as if her little heart would break.

Her parents followed, sinking down on each side of her to exchange a helpless glance over her sobbing form. Her daddy patted her heaving shoulder while her mama stroked her sticky hair.

"Don't cry, *ma petite,*" her mama murmured. "It's not so bad. You'll soon get used to the idea of being special."

When she could finally catch her breath, Tabitha blurted out, "You don't understand! I don't want to be special! I want to be normal." She snuffled into the *Beauty and the Beast* comforter that she had always detested. "I want you two to yell at each other instead of kissing all the time. I want my toys to stop talking and the forks to stop running away with all the dishes. I want to live in a trailer park and wear clothes off the rack and"—her voice broke before rising to a wail— "eat my birthday dinner at Shoney's!"

This startling declaration provoked an even more puzzled glance and a shudder of distaste from her father.

Despite her frequent and often disastrous brushes with the supernatural since that day, Tabitha continued to turn up her rather plain little nose at Disney movies with their talking teapots and singing mice, much preferring the stolid gloom of Ingmar Bergman festivals to those silly princesses always yearning for Prince Charming to swoop down off his white stallion and carry them away.

Tabitha Lennox had no choice but to believe in magic.

But she didn't believe in fairy tales.

Or happy endings.

Or Prince Charming.

Yet.

It was at moments like this that Michael Copperfield keenly missed his pony tail. Since he could no longer tug on it when faced with an insurmountable frustration, he was forced to snap a pencil in two to relieve his tension. "You don't seem to understand the gravity of the situation. Your parents have disappeared."

The young woman slumped in the leather chair opposite his desk didn't even bother to look up from the reports she was studying. "That's hardly an unusual occurrence, Uncle Cop. My parents disappear all the time. At parties. From taxicabs. During stockholder meetings. They once vanished into thin air for the entire second act of my senior play." She spared him a brief, mocking glance before flipping a page of the report. "You should try explaining *that* to your high school drama teacher."

Her lackadaisical acceptance of his news only increased Copperfield's sense of urgency. He rose and came around the desk, forcing her to shift her attention from the software configurations she was studying to his troubled face. "It's different this time, Tabitha. They didn't just wink out of focus for a few minutes or wish themselves to Paris for lunch. This time their entire plane disappeared. Over the Bermuda Triangle."

Tabitha blinked owlishly at him from behind her glasses.

Copperfield pressed his advantage. "The plane vanished over a week ago without so much as a blip on the radar. The navy's sent out search planes and ships to comb the site, but they haven't found even a trace of wreckage. Of course, that's not unusual in that area. I'm trying to hold the press at bay for a few more days, at least until the navy has completed its search, but I can assure you the disappearance of one of the richest men in the world isn't going to go unnoticed for long."

Tabitha's skeptical chuckle sounded forced. "So

what's your theory, Uncle Cop? Have they been seized by a foreign government? Kidnapped by a terrorist organization?" She hummed a few notes of the *Twilight Zone* theme. "Abducted by a UFO?"

He retreated to his chair and sank into it, feeling far older than his fifty-five years. "I'm afraid their plane may have gone down."

Silence permeated the office for an entire sweep of the second hand on the brass desk clock before Tabitha burst out laughing. "Don't be ridiculous! This is just another one of Mama's little paranormal hiccups. The plane will probably reappear exactly where it vanished or pop into the landing pattern at La Guardia just in time to give one of their air traffic controllers another nervous breakdown." As if to escape his pitying scrutiny, Tabitha rose and went to the window, shoving a listless strand of blond hair out of her eyes. "You forget that Tristan and Arian Lennox have an uncanny way of wiggling out of trouble. Remember when the Lamborghini crashed? They walked away without a scratch. And wasn't it you who told me how they once traveled back in time to 1689 to defeat my evil grandfather, proving once again that true love conquers all?"

The note of cynicism in her voice disturbed him. "A theory you don't concur with?"

"It's a charming hypothesis, Uncle Cop, but you have to remember that this is the twenty-first century. True love is no longer in vogue. Romance has been replaced by cybersex with nameless, faceless strangers or holographs of your favorite video stars."

Cop snorted quizzically. "And you find that preferable?"

Tabitha shrugged. "The advantages are obvious." The window reflected her pensive expression, making her appear less convinced than she sounded. "No connection, no commitment . . . no risk."

Copperfield shuddered but reminded himself that his

rebuttal would have to wait. He had more immediate business at hand. "Your parents may have been lucky enough to find true love, sweetheart," he said gently. "But that doesn't make them immortal."

Tabitha swung around to face him, thrusting her hands deep into the pockets of her baggy tweed trousers. "Have you forgotten that my mother was born in 1669? She may not be immortal, but she looks damn good for a woman approaching her three hundred and fifty-first birthday."

He sighed, having learned from long and bitter experience that arguing with a Lennox usually produced nothing more satisfying than a pounding headache.

Recognizing that more drastic measures would be necessary, Copperfield withdrew a manila envelope from his desk drawer and held it out to her. "Your mother asked me to give this to you in the event of her . . ." His fingers tightened on the file, paralyzed by a spasm of doubt. It was almost as if handing it over would give his unspoken words the irrevocable ring of truth.

Tabitha stared at the envelope for a long moment before blithely snatching it from his hand. "You're going to be embarrassed by your melodramatics when my parents come popping out of an air conditioning duct at the next Lennox Enterprises board meeting." She started to flip open the metal clasp, but Copperfield closed his hand over hers.

"Arian said you might want to wait until you were alone to open it."

Tabitha frowned down at the envelope. Although she kept her voice light, her bravado appeared to be wearing thin. "What is it? Their last will and testament? My adoption records? I always told Mama and Daddy that I was too imagination-impaired to possibly be their natural child."

Copperfield cupped Tabitha's chin and gently drew off her glasses. Her somber gray eyes surveyed him uncertainly. Her thick mop of blond hair had been cut in an efficient bob, yet the feathery bangs persisted in drifting over her eyes whenever she relaxed her guard. At twenty-three, Tabitha was nearly as tall as he and twice as awkward, her gracelessness itself oddly endearing. Her even features revealed the keen intelligence that had allowed her to enter MIT at the tender age of fifteen, earn her doctorate in virtual technology before she turned twenty, and achieve the status of department head in the Lennox Enterprises Virtual Reality Division in less than three years. But beneath her layer of cool competence lurked a disarming hint of wistfulness, of dreams unfulfilled and wishes unvoiced.

As Copperfield gazed into the face of the child he loved nearly as well as his own daughters, he was seized by a pang of nostalgia. Tristan Lennox had become far more than just his blood brother since two lonely little boys had exchanged a solemn oath in that Boston orphanage all those years ago. He had become his friend.

"Oh, you're your parents' child all right," he murmured. "Have I ever told you how very much you remind me of your father?"

Dodging his affectionate caress, Tabitha retrieved her glasses and slid them on, her tight smile revealing more than a trace of bitterness. "You shouldn't tease me so, Uncle Cop. My mother used to say the same thing and I always thought it was a little cruel." She swept her shapeless lab coat from the back of the chair before he could protest. "You knew—" She faltered, betrayed by her hesitation. "You *know* Daddy better than anyone. He's always smiling and laughing, finding pleasure in the simplest things. He's graceful and still drop-dead gorgeous, even at fifty-six. He's loved and respected by everyone who's had the pleasure of working with him. He's *nothing* like me."

Tucking the envelope beneath her arm, she flashed him a brittle smile before throwing open the door to reveal the brass plaque that read MICHAEL

COPPERFIELD, EXECUTIVE VICE PRESIDENT. "Give Aunt Cherie my love. I'll call you if . . ." The look she shot him was openly defiant. "*When* I hear from my parents."

After the door had slammed in his face, Cop went around the desk and sank into his chair, torn between laughter and tears. "You didn't let me finish, Tabitha," he muttered, rubbing his burning eyes. "You remind me of your father . . . *before* he met your mother."

As she stepped from the shower, a dripping Tabitha Lennox groped for her glasses before she even reached for the towel. She knew most of her co-workers poked fun at her behind her back for clinging to the archaic devices when corneal molding had been perfected nearly a decade ago, but she preferred the cool solidity of wire frames to having her eyeballs manipulated by a stranger. Her eyesight wasn't really that bad and sometimes she suspected she wore them more out of habit than need.

She towel-dried her thick hair and slathered cold cream on her face before wiggling into a pair of cotton panties and the sturdy L.L. Bean pajamas she'd draped over the towel warmer before entering the shower. The heated flannel enfolded her like an invisible hug. She could not resist a contented sigh as she slid her feet into a pair of plush slippers designed to resemble giant chipmunks—her one concession to whimsy.

Tabitha padded through the penthouse living room to the efficiency kitchen, pointedly ignoring the manila envelope she'd tossed on the couch after returning from her meeting with Uncle Cop.

She dragged open the freezer to peer inside. Her hand wavered between a Lean Tureen frozen dinner that promised zero calories due to the addition of *Phat!*—the dramatic new fat substitute—and a frosty tub of Häagen-Dazs. After several seconds of agonizing, she defiantly chose the ice cream.

So what if she had a few extra pounds clinging to her midriff? Her baggy slacks and lab coat would hide a multitude of sins and it certainly wasn't as if anyone was going to be seeing her without them.

As she fished a tablespoon from the silverware drawer, a furry head butted into her ankle.

"Well, hello, little Lucy," Tabitha crooned, squatting to spoon a dab of ice cream into the kitten's bowl. "Did you miss Mommy while she was at work?"

The tiny black cat had been a twenty-third-birthday gift from her parents. Rightly suspecting that Tabitha would be inconsolable after family cat Lucifer expired at the crotchety old age of twenty-two, her father had arranged for Lucifer's sperm to be frozen until it was needed. With the animal overpopulation crisis finally resolved, test-tube kittens were becoming all the rage.

Still skirting the couch, Tabitha paused at the wall keypad to choose a musical selection from the digitalized menu. Nina Simone's throaty warbling filled the room, coaxing a wry smile from Tabitha's lips. She already had a little sugar in her bowl.

Lacy flakes of snow drifted past the glass expanse that formed the north wall of the living room. As the ice cream slid down her throat, Tabitha watched them fall, thinking how pleasant it was to be warm and cozy with a winter storm raging right outside the window. In the past few months the penthouse had become her haven—the only place where she truly felt safe.

She knew it had wounded her parents when she retreated there right after her graduation from MIT. They had rejected the spacious suite located at the pinnacle of Lennox Tower years before in favor of a sprawling Victorian mansion with no climate control system and windows that swung open to beckon in both sunshine and rain.

Tabitha had always felt like an intruder there. Although they made every effort to draw her into their charmed circle, she chose to remain standing outside, too shy to accept their invitation. She would never break her parents' hearts by telling them that she felt more at home with the anonymous strangers battling their way through the snow-clogged streets far below.

Tabitha set the empty bowl on the carpet and Lucy materialized to lick it clean. Hugging back a chill, Tabitha frowned into the deepening darkness. It was easy enough to reject her parents' idyllic lifestyle when she knew they were out there somewhere, arms always poised to embrace her. But the very thought of a world without their laughter, their tenderness toward one another and toward her, added a bleak edge to her loneliness. An edge dangerously near panic.

Determined to confront her fears, Tabitha swung around to face the couch. The envelope lay where she had left it, utterly innocent of the turmoil it was causing.

As Tabitha gingerly picked it up, a tiny thrill of dread coursed through her. For the first time she understood Uncle Cop's reluctance to hand it over. His words still haunted her.

*Your mother asked me to give this to you in the event of her . . .*

"Stop being a superstitious doofus," Tabitha muttered. "It's an envelope, for heaven's sake, not Pandora's box." Refusing to delay the inevitable any longer, she tore open the clasp and dumped the contents.

A silvery disk skittered across the coffee table. Tabitha's practiced eye quickly identified it as a videodisk. She took it to her modular workstation and popped it into the appropriate drive, praying it wouldn't be one of those maudlin presentations favored by funeral directors in which the dearly departed's last words were nearly drowned out by sobbing violins.

The forty-five-inch screen that had replaced the crude monitor when the television, computer, stereo, and home-security systems were consolidated winked to life.

Tabitha found herself gazing up at an image of her mother seated on a stool with the impish grace of an elf perched on a mushroom. She wore a vintage Chanel suit, red to match her lipstick.

Before she was forced to so ruthlessly curb her imagination, Tabitha had fancied her mama a fairy princess. Delicate, ethereal, and petite, Arian Lennox possessed an otherworldly quality that even the ravages of time hadn't been able to erase. The wiry threads of silver she stubbornly refused to color only enhanced the lustrous beauty of her dark hair. Shallow laugh lines bracketed her lush mouth and sparkling eyes.

It wasn't her mother's fault that Tabitha had always felt like an ungainly elephant next to her. Or that she secretly wished she'd inherited her mama's looks and her daddy's talents, instead of the other way around.

Suppressing a wistful sigh, Tabitha stabbed the button that would activate the video.

*"Hello, my darling Tabby Cat."*

Her mother's husky voice actually seemed to warm the room, its Gallic lilt provoking a rush of nostalgia. Her mama hadn't called her by that particular endearment in years—not since Tabitha had pronounced it too undignified for a mature young lady of her advanced seven years. Tabitha's eyes stung. Too many hours spent gazing at a video screen, she told herself, blinking hard. Lucy hopped into her lap and Tabitha absently began to stroke the kitten.

Her mother cast a guilty glance over her shoulder before placating the camera with a mischievous smile. *"Your father would never forgive me if he knew I was doing this."*

"That's where you're wrong, Mama," Tabitha murmured. "Daddy would forgive you anything."

But as her mother's dazzling smile faltered to an expression that was pensive, almost somber, even Tabitha felt a chill of doubt.

The invisible camera seemed to disappear as her

mother fixed her with a penetrating gaze. *"Parents have very little control over which traits they pass on to their children, my dear. Sometimes it's gray eyes, or big feet, or an insatiable fondness for ice cream."*

Tabitha gave the empty bowl a rueful glance.

*"Or, as your father would say"*—Tabitha smiled as Arian sat up straighter and adjusted a pair of imaginary reading glasses in a dead-on imitation of Tristan Lennox—*"the ability to manipulate the space-time continuum and convert thought energy into matter."* A conspiratorial wink. *"I prefer to simply call it magic."*

Tabitha's smile faded along with her mother's.

*"I'd be lying if I told you it didn't distress me that you've always considered that particular trait more a nuisance than a gift. But I suppose I can't really blame you. You always tried to be such a good little girl. I'll never forget how hard you cried the day the principal sent you home from school because he believed you'd set off all the sprinklers out of spite. I thought my own heart would break."*

Tabitha's cheeks burned with remembered mortification from that incident and a hundred more like it. Like the time she'd innocently admired a dress displayed in a store window only to find herself standing stark naked in the middle of the mall, surrounded by laughing classmates. Or the time the boy she adored had finally asked her out only to be turned into a frog during their very first kiss. He'd taken Viveca Winslow to the senior prom and Tabitha hadn't dared kiss a boy since.

Almost as if anticipating Tabitha's thoughts, her mother leaned toward the camera. *"Your father and I are deeply concerned about the way you've withdrawn from the world. Neither one of us can stand to see you lock yourself away in that penthouse like a princess in a tower."*

Tabitha snorted and wiggled her feet, discomfited by the guilt in her mother's big brown eyes. "Yeah, Mom.

A princess wearing chipmunk slippers and cold cream. You always were an incurable romantic."

*"After much soul-searching, I've concluded that you might not view your talent as such a curse if you could only achieve some small measure of control over it."*

It was Tabitha's turn to lean forward in her chair, riveted by that single seductive word.

Control.

*"That's why I've decided to share with you the only secret I ever kept from your father."*

Tabitha's mouth fell open. Good grief! Was she about to learn she'd been sired by the mailman?

But the story that followed was even more incredible. Lapsing into occasional French, Arian rambled on about magic charms, warlocks, corrupt ministers, microprocessors, and wicked magicians until Tabitha's head began to reel with the effort it took to follow her dizzying flights of logic. Her mama's talent for circumventing a point had always been one of her less endearing traits. By the time Arian paused for breath, Tabitha had decided her mother was either poking fun at her or in desperate need of psychotherapy.

But the look Arian gave her was so tender, Tabitha could not help but be transfixed by it. *"So now you understand why I let your father believe I destroyed the amulet all those years ago."*

Tabitha frowned, more clueless than before.

*"I trust you will use it wisely, my dear, to focus and restrain your remarkable powers."* Before Tabitha could prepare herself, her mother touched two fingers to her lips and blew the camera a kiss, the bittersweet longing in her eyes unmistakable. *"No matter what your future may hold, you have already made me very proud. Au revoir, ma petite."*

Her image froze.

Tabitha sank back in her chair, clutching the kitten's downy fur. Lucy squirmed in protest.

*"Until we meet again, my darling,"* her mother had said. Not farewell. Not good-bye. *"Until we meet again."*

Tabitha found scant comfort in the words. Her parents had begged her to accompany them on their tropical vacation, but as always, she'd insisted she was too busy, her presence too vital to her department. Had she agreed, she might have been on that plane with them.

Dear God, what if they were really gone? she thought, allowing herself to consider the possibility for the first time. Her sweet, charming mama? Her beloved daddy—the man she had always regarded with a wistful mix of love and hero worship?

Blinded by tears she could no longer blame on eyestrain and choked by all the loving words she'd never spoken, Tabitha stretched out a hand toward her mother's image. "Oh, Mama," she whispered. "I wish . . ." The word died in her throat, smothered by bitterness. She must never wish. It was the one thing denied her, because neither money nor magic could protect her from the disastrous consequences of her longing.

Tabitha reached down and tapped the escape key. She had forgotten to cancel her audio selection, so as her mother's image faded to blackness, the first haunting strains of Nina Simone's "Wild Is the Wind" drifted through the room.

# DON'T MISS THESE FABULOUS
# BANTAM WOMEN'S FICTION TITLES

*On Sale in November*

## AFTER CAROLINE  *by Kay Hooper*
*"Kay Hooper is a master storyteller."* —Tami Hoag
The doctors told Joanna Flynn that she shouldn't suffer any ill effects from her near-fatal accidents, but then the dreams began. Now she must find an explanation, or she'll lose her mind—perhaps even her life.
___09948-5  $21.95/$26.95

## BREAKFAST IN BED
*by sizzling New York Times bestseller Sandra Brown*
Sandra Brown captures the wrenching dilemma of a woman tempted by an unexpected—and forbidden—love in this classic novel, now available in paperback.
___57158-3  $5.50/$7.50

## DON'T TALK TO STRANGERS
*by national bestseller Bethany Campbell*
*"A master storyteller of stunning intensity."* —Romantic Times
Young women are disappearing after meeting a mysterious stranger on the Internet, and it's Carrie Blue's job to lure the killer . . . without falling prey to his cunningly seductive mind.
___56973-2  $5.50/$7.50

## LORD SAVAGE  *by the acclaimed Patricia Coughlin*
Ariel Halliday has eight weeks to turn a darkly handsome savage into a proper gentleman. It will take a miracle . . . or maybe just falling in love.
___57520-1  $5.50/$7.50

## LOVE'S A STAGE  *by Sharon and Tom Curtis*
*"Sharon and Tom's talent is immense."* —LaVyrle Spencer
Frances Atherton dares to expose the plot that sent her father to prison, but soon she, too, is held captive—by the charms of London's most scandalous playwright and fascinating rake.
___56811-6  $4.99/$6.99

---

**Ask for these books at your local bookstore or use this page to order.**

Please send me the books I have checked above. I am enclosing $____ (add $2.50 to cover postage and handling). Send check or money order, no cash or C.O.D.'s, please.

Name _____

Address _____

City/State/Zip _____

Send order to: Bantam Books, Dept. FN159, 2451 S. Wolf Rd., Des Plaines, IL 60018
Allow four to six weeks for delivery.
Prices and availability subject to change without notice.        FN 159 11/96